BETH KERY

BEHIND THE CURTAIN

HEADLINE
ETERNAL

First published in Great Britain in 2017
by HEADLINE ETERNAL
An imprint of HEADLINE PUBLISHING GROUP

Published by arrangement with Berkley Publishing Group,
A member of Penguin Group (USA) LLC,
A Penguin Random House Company

1

Cataloguing in Publication Data is available from the British Library

ISBN 978 1 4722 4069 9

Offset in 10.4/15.11 pt Sabon LT Std by Jouve (UK), Milton Keynes

Printed and bound in Great Britain by CPI Group (UK) Ltd, Croydon, CR0 4YY

Headline's policy is to use papers that are natural, renewable and recyclable
products and made from wood grown in well-managed forests and other
controlled sources. The logging and manufacturing processes are expected
to conform to the environmental regulations of the country of origin.

HEADLINE PUBLISHING GROUP
An Hachette UK Company
Carmelite House
50 Victoria Embankment
London EC4Y 0DZ

www.headlineeternal.com
www.headline.co.uk
www.hachette.co.uk

ACKNOWLEDGMENTS

My deepest gratitude to Hasna for giving me such invaluable insight into Moroccan culture. And thank you, wonderful reader, for taking these romantic trips with me throughout the years.

PART ONE

Chapter One

Asher's longtime friend Jimmy Rothschild wore an amused expression as he watched the waitress walk away.

"That look might rock it in Aleppo or Cairo, my friend, but you're scaring the locals in the good old U.S. of A.," Jimmy joked quietly, nodding at the back of the retreating waitress, and then Asher's face. Asher knew Jimmy referred to his full beard and rough appearance. Or possibly he'd been frowning as he ordered from the blonde, thinking more about the meeting with his parents tomorrow morning than being civil and pleasant in front of a pretty woman.

Or maybe everyone really *did* notice how out of place he felt in the city he'd once called home.

Rudy Fattore, his other friend, snorted. "The waitress wasn't afraid of him," Rudy told Jimmy with a wise air. "She was thinking about where to start in on him. With that beard and tan, Ash reeks of the desert and intrigue. Trust me, women love the smell of danger. He's giving off that most-interesting-man-alive cachet.

It's concentrated testosterone, I'm telling you." He ran his fingers across his own clean-shaven jaw. "I may not be up for a Pulitzer Prize or a job as the *Gazette*'s new European bureau chief, but I'm still an award-winning photojournalist, aren't I? Maybe I'll give a beard a spin."

"You'd only be overcompensating for the lack of hair on your head," Jimmy said. He smiled calmly at Rudy's glare.

"You tried to grow a beard in college and it sprouted in patches," Asher reminded Rudy.

"Things are different now," Rudy insisted. "I've got eleven years on that patchy kid."

Asher grinned despite his bad mood. Rudy was always good for a laugh. Well, most of the time, anyway.

He slumped in the uncomfortable, sleek chair, searching the upscale Lincoln Park French bistro. It took him a moment to realize he was scanning for a potential threat among the loud, carefree crowd of diners. He halted the instinctive reaction with effort. He, along with a lot of other Western reporters, had been banned from entering Syria several years ago. It was his time spent in Syria that had given him an edginess he couldn't seem to shake. It was weird being back in the States after spending most of the last eight years in various parts of the Middle East.

Not a lot had changed in the old Lincoln Park neighborhood. Even Petit Poulet, the French bistro, looked unchanged. Yet everything looked strangely gray and muted to him, like he was a sleepwalker in a dreamworld of the past that had remained strangely congealed in time while he—Asher—had transformed into something alien that didn't fit into the scene anymore. Of course he'd been back in the States several times since becoming a foreign correspondent years ago. Maybe it was being in the familiar restaurant with his childhood friends that made things especially surreal. He hadn't been out with both of them in years.

Jimmy still lived and worked here in Chicago, but Rudy had moved to L.A.

In fact, the three of them hadn't been together in eight years. Not since those bittersweet days in Crescent Bay that had been, in many ways, the last, elusive hours of his youth.

"Are you *actually* going to meet Madeline in the morning wearing that beard?" Asher forced his mind out of his nostalgic musings at his friend's question.

Jimmy was right to question his grooming choice. Jimmy Rothschild had known Asher's mother, Madeline Gaites-Granville, almost as long as Asher had. Their mothers had been friends forever, hobnobbing in their exclusive social circles and either bragging or complaining about their sons. His mom would probably have a stroke, seeing her only son's swarthy skin and thick beard.

Maybe he'd shave before showing up for the dreaded brunch in Winnetka tomorrow. His full beard and one of his mom's silver-and-crystal-gilded brunches definitely wouldn't mix. Asher resented that it mattered, but what else was new?

"If what you told me is true," Asher said to Jimmy as he lifted his glass of Chivas, "Mom's going to have more to worry about than my beard."

"What's that mean?" Rudy demanded. When Asher remained brooding and silent, Rudy turned to Jimmy. "What's going on?"

Jimmy exhaled slowly. "I told Asher earlier that according to my mother, Asher's parents are under the impression that the prodigal son has returned home to Chicago to do his filial duty and *finally* take over the helm of the Gaites-Granville media empire," Jimmy replied with attempted levity. Still, his dark eyes looked worried as he examined Asher. Asher frowned, trying unsuccessfully to tamp down his ever-present mixture of annoyance and guilt when it came to the topic of his parents.

"I didn't have a clue that's why they thought I was coming to Chicago. I have some rare time off between jobs, and I owe them a visit after being away for over two years. That's all. It was purely coincidental, me being here close to my birthday," Asher said.

"It's not surprising that Clark and Madeline jumped to that conclusion, though. You know it's the moment they've waited for now for thirty years," Jimmy pointed out fairly.

Asher slouched his large body further down in the uncomfortable chair. *Of course* his mom and dad thought that was why he'd come to Chicago this autumn: to lay claim to the principal of his trust fund. How could he have been so stupid as to blunder into a hornet's nest?

If he accepted their money, he'd have to follow their plan for his life, wouldn't he? Maybe that was never explicitly said, but it had certainly been the depressing implication Asher had gotten since he was nine years old.

His parents couldn't fathom that Asher had rarely thought about his inheritance for the past ten years. He willfully repressed the idea of that money, along with all the invisible strings attached to it. Strings? Try titanium chains. Those hundreds of millions of dollars had come to symbolize his parents' hold on him. No, it better represented Asher's refusal . . . *no*, his *inability* to give them what they wanted. What they *needed*: a suitable, polished, *biddable* Gaites-Granville heir.

That inheritance, along with all the other privileges his parents offered, was the crown Asher cringed at the thought of accepting. But according to his parents, that symbolic crown was his privilege. His birthright.

His duty.

Bullshit.

He grimaced at the snarling voice in his head. Asher had done whatever he wanted with his life, despite his parents' rampant disapproval. Publicly, his mother and father had broadcast their disapproval of him with every glance and gesture. In private, they'd threatened dire consequences in regard to his choices. When he'd remained steadfast in his plans, they'd stiffened their backbones and pursed their lips against their anger with such silent forcefulness that sometimes Asher feared they'd shatter into a million pieces just from disappointment. And all the while, Grant and Madeline just *waited* for the day when Asher would return to toe the line.

They believed that day had finally come.

"*Right*, the big day is finally around the corner," Rudy drawled presently, snapping his fingers in remembrance. "I've been waiting for you to turn thirty since we were at Stanford. I mean, you haven't exactly been a pauper up until now, seeing as how your grandfather left you a nice little nest egg, and that's more money than most of us will ever see in a lifetime. But that's all petty cash compared to the big enchilada. It's finally here: your thirtieth birthday and *total* control over your trust fund. *Freedom*, man. What are you going to buy first? Please say a racecar. You'll have to get me one too, to have someone to practice against. Wait, no . . . a yacht. Hey, the three of us should plan a trip to climb Mt. Everest! Or what about a beach house like that one your parents have in Crescent Bay? The chicks love that. Damn, you're going to get *laid* morning, noon and night—"

"He's not accepting it." Jimmy interrupted Rudy's fantasizing bluntly.

Rudy blinked. "Not accepting *what*?" He studied first Jimmy's, then Asher's stony faces. His blank expression turned incredulous. "You're not accepting control of your trust fund? Are you *crazy*?"

"How can he accept Madeline and Clark's money when he's planning on leaving the country again? He's going to London to become the *New York Gazette*'s European bureau chief. You know that," Jimmy reminded Rudy.

Rudy set down his highball glass with a loud clunk. He looked floored. Asher was thankful to Jimmy for backing him up. Jimmy knew what it was like better than Rudy to have that gilded cage hovering over you for most of your life, ready to crash down at any moment. Jimmy had finessed his parents a lot more gracefully than Asher ever had, though. He'd remained in Chicago after getting his law degree, and he'd quickly earned a reputation for being a brilliant criminal prosecutor. Rudy and Asher were two of the few people on the planet allowed to call him Jimmy. Most people in his professional and social circles knew him as James Rothschild, Esq. Elite local power brokers had already tagged him as a promising candidate for the state house of representatives. But despite all his career success, Jimmy had quietly but steadfastly defied his parents' designs for his life and determinedly carved out his own path. He routinely ignored or denied his parents' little fantasy scenarios among their social circle about him being the most desirable stud in Chicago.

"Last I heard, money travels just fine overseas," Rudy insisted heatedly. "There's no stipulation on that trust fund that says Asher has to live in Chicago or Winnetka if he accepts his inheritance."

"There're stipulations, all right," Asher replied grimly.

"But not legal ones," Rudy protested, glancing over at Jimmy for assistance. "Clark can't stop him from taking what's his legally, can he, Jimmy? He can't *force* Asher to become an executive at GGM and become a WASP clone of himself, for Christ's sake. Take the money and run, Ash."

"I don't want the money, Rudy," Asher snarled.

"But they'll probably just give it to that traitor, pretty boy cousin of yours, *Eric*." Rudy hissed the name as if he'd just said a dirty word. He referred to Eric Gaites-Granville, who hailed from the New York faction of the family. Rudy had disliked Eric ever since they'd met eight years ago, in Crescent Bay. Because of

Eric's actions that summer, his dislike had quickly morphed to hate. Asher wasn't in disagreement with Rudy's assessment. Not in the slightest. He'd hated his cousin from the cradle.

"They gave Eric the position you were supposed to have at GGM a couple years ago when you went to Cairo, after the Syrian government kicked all the Western reporters out. Your parents thought for sure you'd be returning home to Chicago after that, but you stayed in the Middle East. Why wouldn't they give Eric your trust fund too, if you won't take it now?" Rudy demanded.

Asher shut his eyes and grasped for patience. Jimmy groaned and shifted in his seat.

"Give it a rest, Rudy. It's not up to you. If Ash doesn't want to take his parents' money, it's his choice. Don't you get it? That money may mean freedom to you, but it means the opposite to him."

"But—"

"Can we please change the subject? I asked you guys out tonight for a little R and R before this meeting with my parents tomorrow. You didn't come all the way from L.A. just to lecture me, did you?" he asked Rudy.

Rudy opened his mouth to protest but then noticed Asher's expression. Air puffed out of his mouth. He shook his head resignedly.

"If only I could have your problems, Ash."

"I'd give them to you in a second if I could."

"Meaning you'd give me your parents?" Rudy asked wryly. "I doubt Clark and Madeline would ever claim *me* as a surrogate son. They've barely put up with me being your wild Italian friend from the East Bronx. They thought I was going to jump 'em the first time we met. The nerve of me, to get a scholarship to Stanford and be picked as their precious son's roommate. But no worries, I've charmed my way into their shriveled little blue-blood hearts since then."

Asher laughed. Yeah, Rudy could be annoying at times, but

there was no one truer. He hadn't hesitated to say he'd fly into Chicago immediately when Asher told him he'd be in town, even though they hadn't done anything but converse through e-mail for the last two years.

The waitress returned, serving them their appetizer of *moules à la biere*. This time, Asher did take notice of her warm smile and cautious but engrossed glances at him from beneath heavily mascaraed eyelashes. He tried to work up some returned interest but failed. Maybe he'd lost the talent for casual flirting. He'd been seeing Claire Moines, a German television correspondent based out of Istanbul, for over three years before their long-distance romance had finally fizzled out. Between a grueling work schedule and Claire as a placeholder girlfriend, he'd grown pitifully backward in the skills of wooing a woman. Rudy took over, smooth-talking the pretty waitress. His charming grin and rapid-fire one-liners were stale as old beer to Jimmy and Asher but apparently fresh and appealing to the waitress.

"Hey, you know what might get your mind off your doomsday meeting with Clark and Madeline tomorrow?" Rudy asked. He pulled his gaze off the retreating waitress's swaying ass with apparent effort. "Yesenia."

"What's a Yesenia?" Asher wondered, digging into the mussels they'd just been served.

"Oh, yeah. *Yesenia*," Jimmy said, his usually somber expression growing animated. "The singer. She performs over at the State Room. They converted the old State Theatre into a nightclub, and Yesenia headlines there."

"What's so great about her?" Asher asked.

"She's supposed to be incredibly talented, for one. I read about her in *Inside Chicago* recently. She writes her own music: jazz, blues, pop, R&B. She just got a recording contract too, from an indie studio."

"Forget all that. All you need to know is she's supposed to be hotter than Hades," Rudy interrupted. "I read a small article about her in the entertainment section of the *Times*. She's starting to bust out of the local scene and is getting some national interest. I'm dying to see her show. You'll get what I'm saying when you see her, Asher. Or more accurately, when you *don't* see her."

Asher paused with his fork in midair and gave his friend a half-amused, half-exhausted glance. Rudy grinned slyly.

"See, that's the whole thing that Jimmy failed to mention—"

"I thought her *music* was the most crucial thing," Jimmy interrupted.

"Yesenia performs behind a curtain," Rudy continued as if Jimmy hadn't spoken. "It's a sheer curtain, so you can make out her smoking body and the way she moves and everything. But you can't really see the details of her face. Her performances and lyrics are supposed to be off-the-charts sexy, but in an understated, unique way. The press has taken to calling her the Veiled Siren."

"Why does she sing behind a curtain?" Asher asked, thinking the whole idea sounded ridiculous.

Rudy waggled his eyebrows. "No one really knows that, do they? That's part of her mystique. Her allure. She makes people wild to tear down the curtain and get a good, *hard* look at her, if you know what I mean." Asher rolled his eyes. Rudy's grin widened. "There are rumors about why she does it. Supposedly, she has some pretty bad scarring. She doesn't want anyone to see her face. *But*—" Rudy nodded down to the chair where he'd set his camera case. As a talented freelance photographer specializing in celebrity photos, Rudy was rarely without the primary tool of his trade. "The Veiled Siren can't stay under wraps for long, as popular as she's becoming. What do you say we try to get a glimpse behind the curtain tonight? She's right on the cusp of becoming famous, it sounds like. I'll probably get a good buck for an unmasked photo of her."

"What's your plan? Have Asher and me jump on the stage and jerk down the curtain while you snap photos?" Jimmy asked sarcastically. "We're thirty, Fattore, not eighteen. You're not putting me at risk of getting arrested. *Again.*"

"What are you complaining about? Tiger Woods never prosecuted, did he? Don't *worry* about it. Let's just go to Yesenia's performance and we'll see if any opportunities arise for a photo," Rudy suggested with fake innocent casualness. He noticed Asher's doubtful look. "I'm not gonna do anything illegal," he said. "Come on. Are you guys in?"

Asher shrugged. The woman's performance sounded distracting. It might keep his mind off the dreaded morning meeting. For a few minutes, anyway.

"I'll go for the show, but I'm with Jimmy. You're not roping me into any of your stupid schemes. I still haven't forgiven you for that extremely *personal* case of poison oak you gave me when you insisted I hide with you in the woods to get that picture of Jennifer Lopez leaving that vacation house in Big Sur. I swear I feel a rash coming on every time I hear her name."

"At least you weren't arrested," Jimmy muttered in a beleaguered fashion under his breath.

"Yeah, and it's not my fault you exposed the general because you had to pee," Rudy told Asher.

"What was the logical outcome of that scenario? There was nothing else to *do* but drink that Jim Beam you brought while we were sitting there like idiots in the woods. I'm just saying: No. Stupid. Stunts," Asher repeated succinctly.

"You better believe it," Jimmy said sternly.

Asher smirked at Rudy's wounded-puppy-dog expression.

Chapter Two

Asher was fondly familiar with the State Theatre. His grandfather—Grandpop—had taken him there for several plays when Asher was a kid, and once for a behind-the-stage tour of the historic building. Grandpop was the only person who had ever really made him feel connected to—and even a little proud of—the Gaites-Granville family history. Christian Ambrose Gaites-Granville may have been one of the shrewdest CEOs of the GGM empire, but he was also an amateur historian. Asher always suspected that he enjoyed and identified much more with his weekend hobby of research and explorations into Chicago history and his family tree than he ever had his role as ruthless executor of GGM. His hobbies had certainly been the means by which he'd bonded with his only grandson. Asher had adored Grandpop. Walking through the ornate front doors of the old theatre caused a sharp pain of loss to go through him.

The old theatre had stood empty for years until, according to Jimmy, a slick European entrepreneur nightclub owner and musician manager had reopened a portion of it as a club. As he and his friends entered the showroom of the posh venue, Asher recognized the remaining Art Deco panels and crown moldings intermingling with the modern finishes. A gorgeous, sophisticated-looking hostess showed them to a four-top at the back of the showroom. The show hadn't begun yet, but the place was going to be packed. He gave his drink order to a waitress and examined the well-heeled crowd. Apparently, Rudy and Jimmy hadn't been exaggerating about the woman's popularity. As they waited for their drinks, a man with a microphone introduced Yesenia.

The opening notes of an evocative bluesy number resounded throughout the club. Everyone grew hushed with anticipation. Despite his preoccupation, Asher found himself catching the mood of the crowd. The heavy indigo curtain parted.

Another curtain was revealed, a sheer crimson one that was hung to the center and to the right of the dimly lit stage. A four-piece band was situated to the left of the curtain, the musicians' faces fully revealed to the crowd. Manufactured wind gently blew across the red veil, making it ripple in a liquid, sinuous movement. He squinted to see behind it. Was there an outline of a woman emerging from the matrix of light and shadow, or was his imagination playing tricks on him?

Suddenly, her voice filled the club in a low, velvet seduction. The hairs on the back of his neck stood on end. He sat forward in his chair, straining to see behind the undulating veil. The prickling on the surface of his skin amplified, as if his nerves had jumped to life at the sound of her smooth, resonant voice. The vague shadow of her grew clearer, the outline of a woman's body as she subtly moved to the beat of the music.

The outline of a *beautiful* woman's body.

"I told you," Rudy muttered smugly to the left of him, but Asher was too focused to respond. He searched for details obsessively while her clear, soulful voice echoed in his head and throbbed in his veins. The lyrics were poetic, fraught with longing and *very* sexy. The music was bluesy and unique, involving a combination of notes he'd never quite heard before. She wore some kind of pale, clinging dress. The material flowed over her body almost lovingly, caressing every lithe curve. She glided closer to the veil, her hips swaying and pulsing gracefully in time to the music. He realized that like the curtain, the dress she wore was partially translucent. Beneath the two sheer boundaries, he could make out long, shapely legs and the outline of her shifting pelvis and hips as she moved to the beat. The uncommon prickling of his nerves transferred to his sex. He hardened with amazing speed.

"Jesus," he muttered under his breath, a little floored.

"She's incredible, isn't she?" Jimmy breathed out.

"There's an Arab influence," Asher whispered to himself at the same moment he made the realization. Of course. Yesenia was an Arab name, wasn't it? That was what made her music so unique. Among the jazz, blues and R&B influence in her song, he recognized the rhythmic intervals he'd often heard in Arabic music during his years in the Middle East and North Africa. For some reason, the realization added an element of uneasiness to his enthrallment.

"What did you say?" Jimmy whispered as the band played the final lingering notes of the ballad, and Yesenia stilled. Asher didn't respond. Every nerve in his body tingled. His cock throbbed sharply, as though her voice itself had been caressing that sensitive flesh, and it now protested at her silence. He craned forward in his seat, increasingly irritated by the veil and space that separated him from the singer.

What the hell is wrong with you?

Then the music began again—this song having a more pop feel

to it—and her liquid, velvety voice flowed over him, both agitating and soothing his nerves. Admittedly, it was sexual, what he experienced in that moment. But something else had awakened inside him at the sound of her strong, fluid voice and the vision of her beautiful body and pulsing hips . . .

. . . Something Asher had thought had died in him that summer eight years ago.

They stood huddled in the dark alley outside the State Room.

Idiots, all three of us, Asher thought darkly.

No, just two fools were present: Jimmy and him, for letting Rudy talk them into this. Rudy was just being himself.

Rudy had herded them out of the club following Yesenia's third encore. She'd held the audience completely under her spell for the entire performance. Perhaps Asher most of all, a fact over which he was increasingly confused and irritated. He'd finally allowed Rudy to push him out of the theatre when it became clear Yesenia wasn't returning to the stage.

Outside in the alley, the setting was worthy of a horror film: a chilly, damp, foggy autumn night. The nightclub served food, Asher realized. His nose crinkled in distaste when he inhaled the smell of rotting garbage from a distant Dumpster.

Sure, he'd told Rudy he wouldn't be roped into anything stupid. But when Yesenia's electric performance had ended, he'd chosen to forget his protest. He'd agreed to join Rudy at the backstage exit. Maybe Rudy had known all along that the Veiled Siren would make him curious. If so, he'd been right.

Rudy reasoned that since no one could get a photo of Yesenia leaving the theatre by traditional means, then she must exit night after night secretly through the back entrance. And even though part of Asher thought the plan was imbecilic, he'd gone along with it.

Why?

Because by the end of her performance, his desire to see that singer was ridiculously sharp and strong.

Yet another part of him was increasingly uncomfortable, though. Not just because of how stupid he felt hovering in a deserted alley, ready to pounce on an unsuspecting woman. Yesenia clearly didn't want to be seen. And with every second that passed, Asher found himself growing pricklier.

He didn't want Rudy to photograph her. He didn't want Jimmy—or *anyone*—seeing her, for that matter.

Himself? Well, that was a different matter altogether.

Suddenly, all he wanted was to get his friends out of that alley. The sluggish rain that started to fall was the final straw.

"She's not coming out this way. Let's go," Asher said, his tone not inviting argument.

Rudy shifted his readied camera and peered at his watch. "Just a few more minutes—"

"I'm going," Jimmy interrupted bluntly. "So is Asher. Come on, Fattore, it's late and I've got a court date early in the morning. I can't believe I let you talk me into this." He turned and stalked toward the distant lit street. Rudy lingered, casting an undecided look at the back doors of the theatre.

"She's not coming out this way," Asher said. "Trust me. This is a waste of time."

Rudy wavered but then relented. He walked up next to Asher, putting his camera away in its case. He looked a little downcast but then rallied with his typical Rudy optimism.

"At least the show was worth it, right?" he asked Asher as they exited the alley.

"Yeah," Asher said, looking straight ahead at Jimmy's tall, retreating figure. "I'll give you that."

The next morning, Asher noticed the sun breaking through gray clouds and streaming onto the Chicago skyline as he headed back into the city. The image penetrated his furious, agitated state. He glanced dazedly at the dashboard clock. It was just now eleven a.m.

He hadn't even made it a full hour in Winnetka with his parents before all hell had broken loose.

A sharp pain sliced through his volatile state, making him grip the steering wheel hard and clench his teeth. Asher had *tried* to be gentle with them. He loved his parents. Didn't he? They were the only family he had.

If you care so much about them, how come you couldn't bring yourself to even shave your beard before you showed up at their house? In the end, you couldn't even make the smallest concession for their comfort, could you?

He'd been kidding himself in thinking that the meeting would be difficult and unpleasant, but bearable. Only seconds after they sat down at the table and he stated his plans, everything had exploded. Or more concisely given the stiff, WASP restraint of his parents, it had imploded.

For seemingly the hundredth time, he recalled his father's pale face and hurt, bitter blue eyes.

"How is it possible that every time I imagine you couldn't disappoint me more, you find a way to do it, Asher?" his father asked him, each word a quiet, piercing bullet. "This childish scheme you're imagining will not *occur."*

"How does being offered the New York Gazette's *European bureau chief position in London before my thirtieth birthday equate to* childish*?" Asher wondered, floored by his father's im-*

mediate, total rejection, and mad at himself for being caught off guard. Why did he continually believe there was a chance that one day things would get better between himself and his parents? "It's a highly respected job, one that plenty of men and women twice my age want. You know that, Dad."

"I could have given you the equivalent of that job at any one of our papers years ago."

"I didn't want to be given it. I wanted to earn it."

"You're a Gaites-Granville. You were born with newspapers and news in your blood. You don't need to earn anything."

"That's bullshit," Asher stated as calmly as possible. His mother hissed his name repressively for cursing.

His father was ignoring both of them, already thinking up obstacles to Asher's plan. "The Mandor Media Group may be our biggest rival, but—

"I'll never understand how you could have taken a job with them when you knew perfectly well how much it would hurt your father. It was like you willfully stabbed him in the back and left him here to bleed while you gallivanted across the globe, only thinking about yourself . . . even changing your name merely to Gaites. What would your grandfather think of you lopping off half of your family history, all for the ease of a byline?" his mother asked in a quivering voice.

"Mom—" Asher began, wincing at her choice of words.

"Dick Brannigan still owes me a favor or two," his father continued ruthlessly as though Asher and his mom weren't even there. His dad referred to the CEO of Mandor Media, the New York Gazette's parent company. "I'll be contacting him later today. That position in London isn't going to be available any longer. Not to you, it's not." His father rose from the elaborately set dining table and stalked away several feet, mumbling under his breath the whole time. "Of all the nerve, trying to undermine *me by bribing my own flesh and blood to continue working with them. And* you—*" He'd spun suddenly and glared at Asher. "To go along with it all. Don't you know Mandor Media and the* Gazette *just want you as a war trophy, stealing away the heir of their rival? They're doing this to spite me, and as usual, you're giving them exactly what they want."*

Asher flew out of his chair at that, rattling the silver on the table and startling his mother.

"That's right, Dad. It's all about you, isn't it? Isn't *it?"*

"Asher, please don't shout," his mother murmured, glancing in the direction of the kitchen, where the cook and the maid were. Asher had been spoon-fed the idea that only the most common, coarse people ever showed emotion in public. But he continued, undaunted.

"The Gazette *only wants me because I'm your son, not because I've worked my ass off reporting about complicated truths and convoluted class, religious and socioeconomic realities in war-torn regions, or that I found a way to tell those truths, despite heavy censorship; not because I've won a Medill Medal for my writing, or because I've built up one of the finest networks of informants and contacts in the Middle East for a Westerner. Not because one of my pieces has been nominated for a Pulitzer Prize.* No. *They only want me because I'm* your *fucking son!" he bellowed.*

His father looked like he'd just been stabbed, but stood proud and tall. Of course.

"If you think that you're gaining control of your trust fund and then moving off to London to work for my rival, you're sadly mistaken. That trust represents generations of hard work by Gaites-Granvilles. It's meant for a man who appreciates all the blood, sweat and tears that went before him. It's meant for a man *who will add to it for future generations. A* man, *Asher. Not a spoiled brat who only thinks about himself."*

"Someone like Eric?" Asher asked bitterly, referring to his cousin.

His father merely stared at him, his mouth clamped tight.

"I'm glad you brought up the trust," Asher said, matching his father's mood and donning the well-used cloak of cool indifference he often wore in his parents' presence. It was the only manner of communicating that they acknowledged. And to think, his parents always claimed he'd never internalized anything *they'd taught him. "Because I meant to tell you: I don't want it. I never wanted it. Keep your money, and all the strings attached to it. Eric is the perfect person to get the trust. Personally, I'm surprised you haven't transferred it to him before now. It's your prerogative. But me?" He tossed the napkin he'd been fisting onto the table. "I'm done with that damn trust and everything it represents. I'll be in the city for another week or so, if you ever decide you'd like to see me for reasons besides arguing over money."*

He walked out of the dining room, feeling like his brain was boiling inside his skull.

Unfortunately, his fury hadn't been enough to cancel out the heart-piercing sound of his mother's single choked sob behind him as he cleared the doorway.

God, he was a heel.

No, his father had been the royal jerk, threatening Asher's job. Would he really call in some marker with Brannigan over at Mandor, and have Asher fired from his position at the *Gazette* even before he reported for his first day? It was a possibility, Asher acknowledged grimly as he took the ramp into the city. He knew and respected Dick Brannigan a lot, and thought the feeling was mutual. Brannigan was a fierce individualist who came from a long line of tough, in-the-trenches reporters. A dying breed.

Brannigan wouldn't be intimidated by his father easily. But

who knew what bit of knowledge his father might hold over the Mandor CEO's head?

Why was it such a complete impossibility to be civil to them? He didn't *want* to disrespect his parents, but it was as if the die had been cast. They would never see eye to eye and he would forever disappoint them.

He would always play the role of the ungrateful, insensitive son.

By the time he entered his condo, he was exhausted all the way to his bones. He still hadn't acclimated to the time zone. But his intense fatigue was far more than jet lag, he acknowledged as he stripped off all his clothes and fell into bed. He felt pummeled by that meeting. He was asleep within a minute, craving the blank numbness of unconsciousness.

His brain seemed to have other plans for him, though. Because his dreams were far from detached . . .

He walked along a familiar wooded path, his steps fast and eager. He listened with strained expectation . . . but for what?

For her.

She was nearby. So close. Every time he approached the secret lake and the minutes slowly ticked away to their meeting, his body grew tight with anticipation. It was as if being away from her, even for a night, made him doubt the miracle of her existence, question the very reality of something so amazing. He resented anything that kept her from him.

His hands itched to touch her. She was just ahead in the clearing, near their silent, secret inland lake. He escalated to a jog on the wooded trail, muscles straining, his teeth clenched in mounting arousal and need.

Then he heard it, the sound of her voice . . . her sweet, addictive siren song.

Yesenia? That singer from the club who held him fast in her spell? What was she doing here? *In Crescent Bay?*

Just as he had the confusing thoughts, the setting of his dream faded and altered. But his target somehow remained the same: that beautiful, soulful woman, that elusive creature he needed to touch. To possess.

He now rushed down a shadowed tunnel with closed doors to the right and left, his target somewhere ahead of him. Where was she? The same target—the same pull—he'd experienced in the woods, he felt again. But this time, he couldn't hear her voice. Only a thick silence—the unbearable absence of her—pulsed in his ears.

But she was *here. Somehow, he knew it, despite the fact that he couldn't see or hear the proof of her.*

His nerves prickled with anxious arousal. Something was about to happen. Something explosive.

Amazing.

There. Through that door.

He pushed the partially opened door wider and entered the room behind it. It was like an electric lash stung him, momentarily freezing his heart and stinging the blood in his veins.

She stood with her back to him in the corner of the dimly lit, featureless room, her graceful spine slightly bowed, her head lowered in a poignant pose. He couldn't see her face. Her body was draped in a thin, transparent veil. He could see her naked, feminine curves beneath the thin boundary. Her name burned his lips, but for some reason, he couldn't voice it.

He came up behind her, grasping her hips, the sensation of her curves and softness, of her lush body rushing him. She remained nameless in his mind, but he'd never known a woman more completely. He dipped his knees and pushed her bottom against his cock, and God it felt good: round and firm. Sweet.

Her head fell back, her long, dark, fragrant hair a decadent, sensual blessing spilling across his cheek and lips. She sighed his name, her smooth, resonant voice amplifying his lust. His hands moved across her taut belly, ribs and full, thrusting breasts. Her magnificence overwhelmed him.

He found her throat with his mouth and pulled her against him rhythmically, absorbing her soft moans. He felt his senses opening like a thousand floodgates. His lips traced a graceful shoulder. The thin veil chafed his sensitive skin and hungry mouth, but it didn't matter. Beneath it, he felt the heat of the woman, the lissome arch of her back and the firm, soft globes of her ass. He raged for her, the sensation of her naked body covered by the veil striking him as painfully erotic. He had to fuse with this woman, to know what it was to burn at the core of her.

The wave that joined them as they pulsed together rhythmically swelled, and his need became reality. His clothing and the veil disappeared, evaporated by pure lust. He sank into her snug, warm flesh—the sensation almost excruciating, it was so sweet. She quaked around him. He grasped a high, firm breast. His world pulsed in a red haze for a desperate moment. He thrust deeper into her, grinding his teeth together in agonized bliss.

"I know your name," he seethed next to her ear before he bit at the delicate shell and felt her exquisite shudder. "And it isn't Yesenia."

He awoke with a start. Sweat slicked his naked body. His cock felt like a huge, heavy ache. For panicked seconds, he didn't know where he was. The luxurious, mussed bedclothes and the dim room were completely unfamiliar to him, so different from the seven-story walk-up apartment where he'd been living for his last assignment in Cairo. His sex throbbed in agony. He fisted himself, wincing. The tugging sensation of his pumping hand brought back the dream. Even before he understood where he was fully, she took over his brain.

He groaned, thick and harsh, and began to jack himself rigorously. The memory of her had attacked his brain, a forbiddingly sweet, unbearable remembrance. Because with memory of her had come the cruel knowledge that his arms were empty.

He climaxed in a desperate frenzy.

He lay on his side on the bed panting, his large, rigid body releasing the tension packed into his muscles only gradually.

What *was* this? Why the dream? Why the desperation? Was it some kind of bizarre reaction to returning to Chicago? Not only soldiers had trouble assimilating when they returned home to the States. Reporters were known to struggle too.

Or perhaps his odd emotional state related solely to that ugly meeting across the splendidly laid dining room table?

To the fact that he'd disappointed and hurt his parents yet again?

No. It was all about *her*, plain and simple.

How could that be?

I know your name.

His sweat-slicked skin roughened at the evocative memory from his dream.

He realized he was staring at the bedside clock but hadn't been really taking in the time. He blinked, propping himself up on his elbow. The clock read five minutes past eight. No light filtered in around the drawn curtains. It was dark out. Amazingly, he'd slept solid for over eight hours.

A feeling of urgency tore through him. He rolled over and picked up his phone off the bedside table. He was supposed to meet Rudy tonight for dinner. He texted a quick excuse, saying he was jet-lagged and not feeling that well. Could they get together for lunch tomorrow, instead?

He lunged off the bed. Until that very moment, he hadn't been conscious that he'd planned to do it all along.

If he showered quickly and hurried, he could still make her performance at the State Room.

No, he didn't really believe in his vague, increasingly uneasy suspicion that he knew that singer. But he was irrevocably drawn to her as if he really *did* recognize her.

Laila.

The forbidden name rolled through him, making his lungs freeze.

Just hearing the word echo in his head made him ache all over again.

It was Friday, and the club was even more packed than it had been last night. The pretty, model-thin hostess had just walked away with four patrons. A dark, sleek-looking guy approached him, smiling. Asher shook his hand and asked for a prime table. He included two one-hundred-dollar bills inside his palm with the handshake. The tall man's smile widened, even though he never once glanced at the denomination of the bills he'd just nonchalantly slid into his pocket. Asher found himself seated at a reserved table, just feet away from the stage. How well would she be disguised, from this vantage point? Would he be able to recognize her?

There's nothing *to recognize.*

You're losing it. Do you honestly believe that that beautiful, shy girl would put on such a sexy, compelling show for a roomful of strangers?

Then the curtain parted. Soulful, plaintive piano and saxophone notes filled the small theatre. The drums joined in, and he saw her shadow appear as if out of a mist, her hips pulsing to the beat. All his ruminations and doubts faded in the face of fascination. She glided toward the veil. She began to sing.

Her pure, yet powerful voice poured into all the empty voids inside him.

And Asher knew it didn't matter if she was a stranger or a girl who had haunted his dreams for years.

He *had* to look upon the naked face of the woman behind the curtain.

After Yesenia's performance that night, Asher didn't wait in the dark alley. Instead, he stood behind a two-foot-thick, peeling, white-painted cement column in Chicago's vast underground subway network, counting the seconds by the throb of his pulse at his throat.

Even though he hadn't allowed himself to dwell on it, he'd first had the suspicion last night while standing in that alley. The idea originated from Grandpop's stories and their tour of the State Theatre when he was eight years old. The State was hooked into Chicago's subterranean world, a network of tunnels, many of which were still in use today, that incorporated dozens of newer and older buildings, multilevel underground streets and of course, the subway and train stations. Many of them had been established during Prohibition to lead to speakeasies or for illegal alcohol transport. It had occurred to him as he watched Yesenia hypnotize the audience so completely that *this* was how she was making her escape night after night from rabid fans, hungry reporters and determined entertainment photographers, like Rudy.

She was accessing the old tunnels.

He recalled from his times with Grandpop that a stretch of tunnel led from the old State Theatre to an underground delivery road for some of the older Chicago skyscrapers. Rumor had it that Al Capone had even used it. Nowadays, the stretch of tunnel led to the Red Line of the subway.

He felt even more stupid than he had last night, slinking around in the alley. Clearly, Yesenia didn't want to be seen. If it was true she was scarred, wasn't this beyond intrusive of him? Wasn't it cruel? Plus, he'd probably frighten her, a man stalking a woman in this dim, mostly unused portion of the tunnel . . .

. . . A woman who nightly made a bold statement that she didn't want to be seen up close.

He knew his behavior was odd and obsessive, but he also knew one thing: he wasn't going to rest until he gazed directly on her face, until he could silence this weird suspicion that it was her.

It *couldn't* be her. She'd walked away from him so long ago because her family found him appallingly ill-suited. Everything he stood for was a threat, and in direct contrast to what they'd hoped for their beautiful young daughter. They believed he'd sullied her, that he'd come *this* close to shaming the entire family.

He'd come more than close, though. Her parents would have gone apoplectic on the spot if they'd ever known what had transpired between him and their precious girl in the private world they'd made together.

But her parents had never fully learned that secret, thank God. She and Asher had successfully created their own world—or so they'd thought—a place of mystery and wonder, intense desire and vibrant beauty. A place they'd both belonged.

Until she'd made her choice, forsaken it all and walked away, that is. Until she'd smashed their private little paradise to smithereens one day. Yes, it had been his asshole cousin Eric who had first betrayed them; her furious father, uncles and cousin who had separated them; and her hurt and shamed mother who had solidified that rift.

But in the end, it had been her choice, hadn't it? A choice that she'd continued to make for eight years.

Laila.

This time the forbidden name brought a wave of distilled fury and hurt along with the longing. He wouldn't have guessed that so much anger still existed inside him.

He shifted his booted feet restlessly. Only the sound of water trickling sluggishly from a metal pipe and the muted voices on the distant train platform entered his hearing. No one seemed aware of this portion of the tunnel.

Just when he was about to give up on his irrational—no, ludicrous—mission of pouncing upon an unsuspecting, extremely private stranger, he heard it: a light, rapid tread approaching his location. He eased around the column and started back abruptly, holding his breath.

A hooded figure walked rapidly in his direction, the closeness of it surprising him. He stayed concealed, watching as the figure passed. Only the lights from the platform ahead and an old, dust-encrusted exit light permeated the gloom. It was enough for him to make out that the person wore loose-fitting cargo pants, running shoes, a backpack and sweatshirt with the hood up. Her form was slight and graceful. Despite the baggy clothing, he made out the curve of feminine hips and the hint of a round bottom.

It's her.

He never told himself to do it, but suddenly, he was following her. She clearly didn't want to be noticed. Everything about her slightly hunched posture, her haste and her hands in her pockets shouted unapproachability. But there was something else about her, the gliding gait and the delicate, graceful arch of her spine. She called out to some nameless thing rushing in his blood.

What the hell are you going to say? She was going to be scared, being accosted here by a stranger.

Why didn't you shave your damn beard?

At six foot three and a hundred eighty-five pounds, he was intimidating enough to a solitary female without the dark, thick facial hair adding to the scenario.

Her pace suddenly increased. He kept up. Had she heard him behind her? The sound of an approaching train in the distance reached his ears. No, she'd heard her train and was hurrying to catch it.

The name burned on his tongue, but he couldn't bring himself to shout it. Anger and shame and disbelief at his unexpected need prevented it. What if it *was* her? What if she *was* scarred, and the last thing she wanted was to be seen?

What if she didn't even remember him?

The anxious questions hammered in his head, blending with the inevitable roar of the approaching train. Suddenly she started to jog. So did he. They entered the station at the same moment as the thundering train.

"*Wait*. Stop."

The train screeched to a halt, the racket obliterating his call. The doors jerked open, and she was getting on. For a split second, he paused in his pursuit, uncertain. Was he wrong? Was he crazy, chasing after a stranger because of a vague suspicion, an intensely erotic dream . . . an unexpected, bittersweet memory of an infatuation that he would have sworn he'd abandoned years ago?

A slender hand grasped at the metal rail just inside the doors. His heart slammed against his breastbone in recognition.

"Laila."

Her head snapped around at his call.

He stared into a pair of startled-looking, almond-shaped green eyes. He lunged toward the entrance, shock vibrating in his flesh. The train doors slammed shut between them.

"No," he bit out, furious. Desperate. She stepped closer, her eyes wide. For a charged moment, they stared at one another through the glass. Asher soaked in every detail like a parched sponge would water. He saw shocked recognition on her face, and that made desperation redouble inside him. He slammed his palm against the glass.

"*Laila*," he repeated, his fingers clawing at the rubber-lined seal between the doors. The train began to move. He saw her mouth form his name, and she was sliding away from him.

Again.

He jogged down the platform, keeping pace with her, not knowing what the hell he was doing for a frenzied moment. He only knew he couldn't take his eyes off her rigid, disbelieving face.

The face of his dreams. The face at the center of a stupid young man's anguish. *Her* face. Unscarred. Unchanged.

Perfect.

"*Laila.*"

His shout mingled with the metallic rumble of the train exiting the station. He stood there panting as the sound faded; his brain tried to catch up with his heart, shaken by the impact of his past slamming so jarringly into his present.

Did he understand why Laila Barek had decided never to see him again, never correspond with him, to deny everything that had happened that summer in Crescent Bay eight years ago? Rationally, he did. With the benefit of maturity, and after spending time in various Arab countries, that logic had become clearer. She'd been nineteen years old. She'd been in college, yes, but she was still dependent on her parents' wishes, expectations and demands. A Moroccan-American female might seem a lot like any typical American girl much of the time, but the ties to tradition and family were strong.

Those ties of love and loyalty had been enough for her to walk away when she'd been nineteen and he'd been nearly twenty-two, despite what they'd shared . . . despite the fact that she'd told him she loved him and always would.

He shook his head like a wet dog, trying to diminish the immensity of the moment. He hadn't been prepared. Yes, the thought had been there, but it had been vague, the tiniest suspicion . . . too incredible to be real. Of course, she had the talent. There had never been any doubt of that. Still, he couldn't believe it was really *her*: her staring at him through the glass, *her* putting on that evocative, sexy performance in that club . . .

All behind a veil.

He blinked and started, the veil suddenly taking on a whole new meaning for him. The barrier hadn't been there to hide any scars. The veil had been set to protect something else. And Laila had been the one to erect it.

Maybe she hadn't changed that much, after all.

He turned and walked alone down the empty platform.

You're not a naïve, idealistic kid anymore. Some people just aren't made to be together. Your worlds are way *too different.*

He didn't think he could survive watching Laila move away from him another time. That first time had hurt more than he'd allow himself to admit.

And everything that had come *before* Laila walking away? Well, that had been something so rare and beautiful, the loss of it had changed him forever.

Chapter Three

Eight years ago
Crescent Bay, Michigan

Her mother, Amira Barek, had left the patio doors and windows open wide to the beach as she cooked. Laila inhaled the divine scent of fresh lake air mixing with the date cake cooling on the counter. Her *khal-ti* Nora had brought the cake over minutes ago along with a fresh batch of almond cookies and taknetta—Moroccan butter cookies. The family would gather on the terrace this evening for supper.

Her mom watched her soap opera on the little television on the counter while she sealed a dish with tin foil. A pot of tagine steamed on the stove.

Laila lifted a corner of the aluminum foil to see what they would grill out on the deck tonight. Despite her uncommon restless mood and desire to flee the cottage—she didn't know where, just *some*where—her stomach rumbled with hunger. She'd spent nine summers now with her extended family in the charming beach town of Crescent Bay and knew that fantastic food was one of the many highlights of the traditional vacation. Her mom and aunties became inspired during their weeks spent on the lakeshore dunes, scheming daily to outdo each other's cooking.

"What time will we eat?" Laila asked.

Her mother pulled her attention off her soap opera—one of many on a list of favorite American and Arab soaps, and even recently, a Telemundo sizzler. She patted the back of Laila's hand fondly before finishing sealing the foil on the dish.

"We'll eat when your father and uncles get here, of course," she said, handing the dish to Laila. Laila carried the dish over to the refrigerator. During their extended summer vacation in Crescent Bay every year, only the aunties and the kids stayed on full time. Laila's dad, Anass Barek, and her two uncles commuted back and forth from Detroit for their jobs. They would stay in Crescent Bay for the weekend before returning late Sunday night, Laila's dad to his collision and glass repair shop, and her uncles to their jobs as line supervisors at Ford Motors.

"The girls and I were hoping to check out that music festival going on over in Crescent Bay tonight," Laila said as she shut the fridge door, testing the waters of her mother's response. If her mother agreed that she could go out with her cousins tonight, then her father would agree when he arrived, as well. Her father was typically more tolerant than her mother. Zara and Tahi's parents tended to be more permissive in what they allowed their twenty-year-old daughters to do, as well, a fact that could work either in Laila's favor or against it. Sometimes her mother was more agreeable to a venture if Zara and Tahi accompanied her. At other times, Zara and Tahi might be deemed a tad wild, at least where Laila was concerned. Even though Laila's birthday was only eight months after Zara's, and six months after Tahi's, she'd somehow been labeled early on as the "young" one that everyone had to look out for. It galled Laila to no end. The fact that her mother had had some health issues after she'd given birth to Laila, and afterward could no longer have children, didn't help in taking the obsessive, protective focus off Laila. Zara and Tahi had older and younger brothers and sisters, while Laila was an only child. The cousins' parents were more "broken in" than Laila's, at least in Laila's opinion.

From experience, Laila knew that her mother tended to be a little more carefree and tolerant in Crescent Bay, however. She had her fingers crossed she'd get no argument for tonight's plan. Her mom's attention was already caught again by her soap opera.

"It's Friday night. Your father is getting here for the first time this summer. Why do you have to start running around already? You'll stay in."

"But Zara and Tahi—"

"Those girls run wild every night. Just because they do something doesn't mean you have to," her mother murmured distractedly, her pretty, large brown eyes fixed on the television screen. "Crescent Bay is about relaxing and celebrating your good fortune and family, not running around to rock-and-roll parties."

Laila started to correct her mother—the festival really did offer a diverse collection of local and regional artists: jazz, rock, R&B, pop, Irish folk music, and yes—one traditional Arab female singer. Instead, she paused to tactically regroup. For a moment, she watched the drama unfolding on the television with her mom.

"You'll miss the last episodes of the season on your favorite Arab shows here in Crescent Bay," she murmured. The cable here in tiny Crescent Bay didn't pick up the Arabic-language stations they were able to get in Detroit, where Laila's family lived. There were large, established Arab and Moroccan communities in the Detroit area. Like many of her friends, Laila straddled two cultures, existing in both. At times, she found that navigation seamless and as easy as breathing.

At other times, it could be a considerable challenge. Now that she'd turned nineteen and completed her first year of college at

Wayne State University, she was finding the negotiation for her independence from her parents and close-knit family increasingly difficult. And at times, tiresome. Even though her parents had insisted she live at home while she attended college, Laila had still gotten her first taste of a wider world out there. It had lit a fire in her. She usually loved their idyllic family vacations in Crescent Bay. This year, she was uncharacteristically restless and claustrophobic.

Her mother gave her a mischievous glance. "Your cousin Zarif taught Nora and me how to TiVo all our shows. The girls and I are going to have a marathon when we get home," she said, referring to her sister Nora and sister-in-law Nadine.

Laila grinned. It tickled her, how Laila herself, Zara and Tahi were referred to collectively as "the girls," and so were her mother and aunties. "You're turning so modern, Mom. First your iPod, and now TiVo."

"Don't be silly. Your father only got me that iPod so that I could listen to my music while I work."

Laila saw her "in." Her mother loved her music even more than she loved her shows. Moroccans in general were crazy about music, and Laila and her mother were no exception.

"There's going to be some Arab music performed at the music festival in town," Laila said with seeming casualness as she lifted the lid on the pot on the stove and stirred the fragrant contents.

Her mother cast her an interested but wary glance. "Some shameful pop version of it, I suppose? Something like that pollution you listen to?"

"*No*, Mamma," Laila assured her. "You know there are a lot of Arabs that have settled here on the shoreline. This is a traditional singer, honest."

She held her breath while her mother studied her closely. Her mother, her *khal-ti* Nora, and her grandmother had always been, and still were, considered fine singers and musicians in their community. Laila had inherited their talent, although she preferred to write music and poetry versus sing.

"Well, I suppose since we have nothing special planned for tonight . . ."

"Thank you, Mamma," Laila enthused, planting a kiss on her mother's cheek. Her mom patted the side of her head in a warm gesture.

"We'll be home by eleven," Laila assured her.

"Ten o'clock," her mother corrected, her loving, maternal gaze going instantly sharp. "And don't you let that wild Zara keep you out a minute later. I tell you, that girl will be the death of her mother," Amira Barek insisted. She closed her eyes and mouthed a silent, fervent prayer as to that not being the case.

"I think I'm going to go for a swim before dinner," Laila said, easing out of the kitchen.

"Be sure to tell Zara I said ten o'clock," her mom said distractedly, her gaze already drawn back to her soap opera.

"I will," Laila assured her. She didn't mention she wasn't planning on seeing Zara until tonight at dinner. Her cousins were at the local beach, undoubtedly stirring up every male on the shoreline with their tiny bikinis, practiced flirtations and lush beauty.

Laila would swim alone at the hidden beach she'd discovered four years ago, a place she cherished as her own private secret.

With a heavy feeling of inevitability, Asher swung his roadster down the gravel drive. In the distance, he saw the sprawling, white-shingled home on the bluff and the pale blue expanse of Lake Michigan taking up the entire horizon. A sharp feeling of nostalgia went through him. A pang for the loss of his childhood? He hadn't been to the Gaites-Granville summer mansion since the July before he'd left for college.

He'd used to love coming here when he was a kid. An assortment of his relatives and his parents' friends might be there on the weekend, which could be a miserable experience. During the summer weekdays, however, Asher was often left there just with his nanny, Berta, and occasionally with Jimmy Rothschild as an additional companion.

It was Berta and Asher's well-kept secret that his nanny often left him to his own devices during those golden days and sultry nights. He'd swim, skimboard, and make friends at the local public beaches. He'd captain his little Sunfish, exploring the coastline to his heart's content. When he got older, he'd had the speedboat at his disposal. He'd relished being alone at the house or hanging out just with Jimmy, thriving without the feeling of someone standing at his shoulder constantly monitoring him . . .

. . . Ready to disapprove and correct him at any moment.

Now he was here again for one last idyllic summer.

He had to admit: it had felt good, seeing how proud his parents were of him as he'd received his degrees, with distinction, in both journalism and international affairs. His father had been smiling broadly—a rare sight—when he handed Asher a Scotch on the rocks at his graduation party at the Union Club five weeks ago.

"Take some time off before you start work. Spend a couple weeks at Crescent Bay with your friends. The car and all the other stuff were gifts from your mother and me. But this is my personal gift to you, from father to son: one last carefree summer vacation. Goof off a little, have a few summer flings, do some things you'll never tell your mom and me. Because I'm here to tell you, once you start the grind of work, there's no going back. After that, you're a man, son."

Asher's fate seemed to press down on him as he drove nearer to the house and the Lake Michigan landscape. He'd wanted to tell his dad the truth as they'd shared that drink together at his party. In the end, he hadn't, though. His father had looked so happy and proud of his gift of a last carefree summer vacation . . . so proud of *him*—

Asher. Asher could count on one hand, with a couple fingers to spare, the number of times he'd made his father look that way. He hadn't had the heart to tell him that his gift had felt like he was throwing Asher a bachelor party before a marriage he'd never agreed to.

Because the fact of the matter was, he *was* going to have to do something adult and serious at the end of this vacation. It just wasn't what his mom and dad believed it was. His parents thought that he was going to take a managerial position at Gaines-Granville Media in August. Asher had never really agreed to that. But his parents operated on assumptions when it came to their only son, not Asher's actual choices.

The truth was, he'd already accepted a position as a reporter at the international affairs desk at the *L.A. Times*. He hoped to eventually get moved to a foreign post. Just this morning, he'd flown back to Chicago from Los Angeles after meeting with his new managing editor at the paper, signing an apartment lease and making other arrangements for his August move.

His parents had thought he'd been visiting a girlfriend in Bel Air, which was kind of true. He had met up with Anna, a girl he'd been seeing casually during his final two months at Stanford. He'd been so preoccupied with making arrangements for his new life that he'd apparently insulted Anna with his lack of attention, however. She'd been fairly pissed at him by the time she'd dropped him off at the airport this morning. On the flight to Chicago, Asher realized he wasn't all that worried about it, a fact that had him feeling sort of guilty. Anna and he weren't serious or exclusive, but clearly, he'd been insensitive.

What's new?

According to his mother, he'd been born with a singular knack for insensitivity.

Anna Johansson aside, the die had been cast. At the end of this supposedly idyllic, carefree vacation, he was going to have to be an adult, all right. He was going to have to look his parents in the eye and tell them point-blank he had no plans whatsoever to take a job at Gaites-Granville Media. He was used to disappointing them, but this seemed especially harsh on his part.

Feeling weighed down by his thoughts, he pulled into the turnabout at the back of the mansion. He immediately recognized Jimmy's dark blue BMW—sophisticated and sedate, just like Jimmy—already parked there. One of the other two cars must be a rental. Rudy Fattore had flown in at Asher's mother's request and rented a car at O'Hare. It was a sign of how much his parents wanted to please Asher that his mother had arranged the trip for his questionably respectable college roommate. Formerly, Rudy had barely been tolerated.

Rudy and Jimmy were the only friends he'd mentioned to his mother that he wanted for companionship on this "last holiday." Who did the ivory-colored Aston Martin belong to, though? Asher wondered uneasily. *It* certainly wasn't a rental.

"It took you long enough to get here!" someone called from behind him. Asher twisted in the seat to see Rudy Fattore coming out the front doors. The tension broke in him in an instant. He laughed. Hard.

"I see you've already found the beach," Asher said dryly as he stepped out of his car. Rudy wore a pink child's flotation device with a swan's head stretched tightly around his waist, wet swim trunks and flip-flops. He carried a glass of Scotch in one hand and a soggy cigar in the other.

"First place I headed after I got here. But we're out at the pool right now. This place is fucking amazing. I knew I lucked out, getting you in the roommate lottery. And guess what? Your mom got me a first-class ticket on the flight." Rudy shoved the cigar in his mouth and grinned around it. "Imagine it, a Fattore in first class. Come on, Jimmy's at the pool. We just broke open a bottle.

Your cousin is kind of a dick, but he brought a box filled with unbelievable Scotch, not to mention these kick-ass Cubans."

Asher froze in the process of lifting his suitcase from the backseat.

"My cousin?" He blanched and glanced over at the jaunty Aston Martin. *"Eric?"* he asked, referring to his twenty-three-year-old distant cousin. Eric had been a pain in his ass ever since they'd first been thrown together in the playpen at family functions.

"Yeah," Rudy said, frowning around his cigar. "Didn't you know he was going to be here?"

Ice shot through Asher's veins, despite the sunny day and eighty-degree temperature. He couldn't believe it. *Of course.* His parents' gift hadn't been completely innocent, had it? They just hadn't been able to resist subjecting him to their version of a lesson. Eric the Perfect, their concept of an ideal Gaites-Granville male from the New York side of the family, had been sent to set an example for Asher.

And knowing Eric, he knew *exactly* why his presence had been requested and was all too ready to gloat about it in front of Asher.

"No," he muttered, lifting his suitcase and unclenching his teeth. "I had no idea Eric was going to be here. If I had, I'd have stayed in California."

And he'd worried this supposed carefree, idyllic vacation was going to be tough, considering his guilt factor. Now he had Eric to deal with on top of it all. He saw movement out of the corner of his eye and turned to see Jimmy coming out of the house along with the source of his mounting annoyance. Eric grinned broadly, coming toward him with his hand outstretched. Jimmy followed, looking worried. He knew what Asher thought of Eric.

"All hail the graduate," Eric boomed, pumping Asher's unwilling hand. He waved his glass of Scotch, the gesture every bit that of the prince of the castle. "Hope you don't mind us getting started without you. The beach and the pool beckoned."

His mom was always commenting how much Eric and Asher looked alike—both of them well over six foot, dark hair, blue eyes, skin that tanned easily. Every time she said it, Asher ground his teeth together and disagreed furiously in the privacy of his mind. His father was an avid Eric fan in general, but Asher had heard him disagree with his mom on this topic. "*Asher doesn't look like he spends hours in front of the mirror every day like that boy does.*" Or, once: "*Good-looking? Sure? Eric's as good-looking as the prettiest girl in the country.*"

Asher had always appreciated his father's infrequent disagreement with his mother on that topic.

"We were just discussing which local beach we should hit first this afternoon," Eric continued, seemingly blind to Asher's furious frown. "If I remember correctly from when we were teenagers, Crescent Bay South had the hottest tail." His cousin flashed his million-dollar smile and waved back at the house. "We've got the whole place to ourselves this time, Ash. No sneaking girls into the guesthouse this summer, eh? I have to admit, though. The sneaking was part of the fun, wasn't it?"

Jimmy's sympathetic, concerned gaze helped Asher restrain himself from spewing a stream of vicious curses.

Two hours, a dip in the pool, the hot sun and a generous amount of premium Scotch later, Asher was feeling a little less rough around the edges.

"He's not that bad," Jimmy said quietly when he noticed Asher's dark glance at Eric's back as he went to take a call inside the house.

"He's not that good," Asher said, turning his face up to the intense sun and closing his eyes behind his sunglasses.

"How bad can he be? He's even better-looking than you, Ash," Rudy said brightly from Asher's other side.

"You thinking of asking him out?" Jimmy wondered sarcastically.

"I know you saw him first," Rudy countered quickly. "Seriously, I just meant that Ash usually draws the chicks in our direction like a magnet. With douchebag along, it'll be like some kind of Gaites-Granville super magnet." He made a sucking sound and zoomed his hand in the direction of his chest.

"Shut up, Rudy," Asher mumbled without any heat.

He suddenly had an urge to run. From what, he didn't know. His life, maybe. It was like he could sense more than see two giant steel doors starting to close in on him.

He stood from the lounge chair and reached for his tennis shoes.

"Where're you going?" Rudy asked.

"For a run."

"I'll go with you. It'll clear the Scotch fumes," Rudy said, standing.

Asher didn't really want a companion, but Rudy was harmless enough.

They'd made their way a half mile down a stretch of empty, white sand beach when someone called out behind them. Asher glanced back.

"Wait up. You didn't tell me you were going for a run," Eric said, his nearly naked, muscular body gleaming in the hot summer sun.

"I know it," Asher muttered.

Eric caught up. Asher gazed straight ahead and picked up his pace, pulling slightly ahead of the other two men. Eric started describing to Rudy in detail his rigorous daily workout routine at his super-exclusive Manhattan club. Asher ran faster, until distance and the sound of the waves faded his cousin's smug diatribe from his hearing.

He knew *what* he was running away from, of course. But

until he reached a rocky embankment and the end of the beach, he hadn't known what he'd been headed *toward*.

The secret lake.

He hadn't visited it in four years.

He came to a halt next to the rapidly flowing stream. Kids always thought of a place they'd discovered as their own. That was how Asher had thought of the inland lake ever since he'd accidentally come upon it while hiking in the woods when he was eight years old.

"Fuck. The beach ends here? I don't remember that," Eric said in an angry tone behind him a moment later.

"Geography can be so damn inconvenient," Asher said.

First Eric, then Rudy came to stand beside him. "Can we cross it?" Eric asked, nodding at the stream.

"I've tried it before. It's deeper than it looks, and fast. The rocks are tricky. I got my ankle caught between two of them once and nearly drowned," Asher said. He glanced over at his cousin speculatively. "*You're* welcome to try it, if you want."

Eric tensed, obviously sensing Asher's simmering irritation at his presence. He abruptly grinned.

"My cousin. Always the joker. No, I think I'll just take a dip in the lake to cool off, but thanks for the offer," he said, already untying his shoes.

"That sounds good." A sweaty-looking Rudy agreed, attacking his shoelaces. "You coming, Ash?"

"You guys go ahead," he said as Eric plowed into the surf. Rudy jogged in after him, whooping at the feeling of the cold water splashing against his overheated body.

While Eric's back was turned and Rudy took a dive into an oncoming wave, Asher jogged inland along the banks of the stream, seeking the coolness and cover of the shrouding trees ahead. As he entered the canopy of the woods, his perspiration-dampened skin roughened and prickled. The sounds of the distant waves and his companions' shouts faded. The wind rustled the leaves of the trees, creating a flickering of gold and green light all around him.

He slowed.

It had been years since he'd been here, but he was able to make out the path, overgrown as it was by weeds and brush. For some reason, his heart raced faster now than it had when he'd been running on the beach. He strode rapidly along the trail, his muted footsteps the only thing interrupting the thick hush that had descended.

A strange prescience overcame him. The surface of his skin tingled as if from electricity. It felt like the atmosphere before a storm, but there wasn't a cloud in the clear blue sky. Was he really looking forward *that* much to seeing the place of his childhood? Or was it just his longing to escape his life and disappear for even a few seconds into a place no one else knew about that had him so tense with anticipation?

The stream flowed from the inland lake just ahead.

Abruptly, he paused on the path. He strained to listen, thinking his ears had fooled him for a moment.

Then he heard it for certain: the sound of a woman's clear, melodic singing.

His feet moved without him telling them to. Between the branches of overhanging oak, sycamore and maple trees, he spied the still, green waters of the small but deep lake. Her singing continued in the distance, each note flickering along his sensitive skin and amplifying his sense of the otherworldly.

He left the side of the swift stream and began to circle toward the south side of the lake. Without any conscious intent, he moved on the forest floor silently. He wasn't trying to be stealthy. It was just that he didn't want to take the chance of interrupting her song. The soothing sound of trickling water intermingled with the sweet notes. His gait quickened, his muscles straining tight.

Finally, he paused in the shadow of a bowed sycamore at the edge of the familiar rocky, rough sand beach, peering through the foliage to find her.

He stilled. His already roughened skin grew even tighter.

She stood knee-deep in the shallows, water running in streams down graceful arms, high breasts and a smooth, taut belly. As she tossed her head to the side, a spray of water flew from waist-length dark hair like a shower of sparkling diamonds. She fisted the wet mane at her nape and pulled, causing a rivulet of water to cascade along a breast and down her ribs and belly. He watched, enthralled, as her full, dark pink lips moved.

"I may be blind, but you I can see," she sang.

Her eyes flickered and suddenly she was staring right at him. He was sure he hadn't moved and given himself away. One second, she'd been utterly lost in her own private world; the next, she'd sensed him. For an electric few seconds, neither of them moved. He didn't breathe and was sure she didn't either.

Asher considered himself a good writer. He despised hyperbole and strived for lean, matter-of-fact prose. But how could you *tell* a truth like the one he experienced at that moment as he stared in wonder at this naked, glorious woman? It was something *felt*, not told. It was like unexpectedly sighting a mythical creature or something. His senses overflowed with the reality of her. His lungs forgot how to work. Even his blood seemed to come to a screeching halt in his veins.

She was the most beautiful thing he'd ever seen, let alone imagined. The inland lake had long been his secret, special place.

But somehow, she'd just made it sacred.

She suddenly started. Fear leapt into large, almond-shaped green eyes. The spell was shattered. He staggered onto the beach, his hands up.

"I'm sorry. I didn't mean to scare you. Don't be afraid," he begged. "*Please*," he added desperately when he saw her glazed expression of shock and fear. The thought of her being afraid of him made him sick.

"Ash? Where are you?" Rudy called in the distance, his voice muffled by the trees. Asher's eyes widened. Hers did too. She lunged toward the beach, her lithe arms covering her bare breasts and dark pubic hair. She pulled back, her desperate gaze jumping from the pile of clothing and what looked like several notebooks on the beach over to him.

He shook his head, a horrible feeling swooping through him when he realized she was looking at him like a wild, trapped animal would at its captor. She was wondering about her chances of escape with him standing so close. He stepped backward quickly away from the shoreline, giving her space.

He heard a sound like a branch snapping. "What the fuck, man? Where'd you go?" Eric yelled, irritation ripe in his tone. He heard the sound of Eric and Rudy tramping on the distant path, their tread much louder than his had been. More aggressive sounding too, he realized as he took in the girl's panicked expression.

"I'm going," he said very quietly. "I'll lead them away from you. Don't worry. You're safe."

She stared at him mutely, a strange, blank expression of shock on her beautiful face.

"I won't let them see this place either. It was my secret place too. Once."

He took one last look at her, absorbing her like a man inhales his last breath before he submerges underwater for a long dive.

Then he turned and hurried into the forest, intent on intercepting his friends and preventing their intrusive gazes.

Chapter Four

"What are you, half asleep or something?"

Laila focused with effort on her cousin's beautiful, artfully made-up face. Twilight was falling, and the wrought iron streetlamps had just switched on along Main Street in charming downtown Crescent Bay. Zara stared at her, half in puzzlement and half in exasperation as she held out an ice cream cone in Laila's direction.

"Sorry," Laila mumbled, accepting the cone. She swiped her tongue across the chocolate chip cookie dough ice cream with determined enthusiasm.

"You've been weird ever since dinner," Tahi declared bluntly. They stood in front of the outdoor-indoor ice cream parlor. Music filtered across the street from the crowded downtown park. A jazz band currently had center stage at the music festival. "Did something happen to you this afternoon?"

An image of the dark-haired guy standing on the beach, wearing nothing but a pair of blue swim trunks and tennis shoes, popped into her mind's eye against her will. His body had been long and hard and intimidatingly virile. So *male*. His chest wasn't super hairy, but there had been some fine, dark hair in the middle of a powerful chest, trailing off into a thin line between his ribs and down a taut abdomen. At first, her brain had been shocked into stupidity, as if she'd never seen a man before and didn't know what he was.

Which made sense, Laila thought as she rapidly ate her ice cream. Because even though she'd seen men wearing swimsuits at the beach and in movies and television, she'd never seen one like *him* before. Seeing him standing there had struck her as intensely intimate, for some reason.

Maybe because you were naked, stupid.

And maybe because you could see his erection through the trunks when he'd lunged onto that beach.

Both thoughts caused her cheeks to burn. Why couldn't she stop picturing it? His obvious arousal had panicked her in the moment. But now, she couldn't seem to stop thinking about it. Or his eyes. Or the concerned, almost panicked expression on his handsome face as he'd backed away from her.

Someone snapped their fingers in her face. She blinked and saw Tahi giving her a puzzled look. "*Hello*."

"Hi," Laila mumbled, licking her ice cream more determinedly. In the periphery of her vision, she noticed Zara and Tahi sharing an incredulous glance.

"What is *up* with you?" Zara demanded loudly. She grasped Laila's upper arm and started to pull her toward the curb—in order to interrogate her away from the crowd milling around the ice cream parlor, no doubt. In midmaneuver, however, she glanced toward the street and immediately froze. A change came over her cousin in a split second. Laila recognized the temptress smile that spread over Zara's face.

Her secret was safe for now. More interesting prey must be approaching.

"Hello," a man said smoothly behind Laila. "Something tells me you're not from around here."

Laila turned slightly and saw a tall, dark-haired young man. A swooping sensation went through her stomach until she focused in on his face and saw the blatant, heavy-lidded glance of appreciation he was giving every inch of Zara's tanned, knockout figure. Laila was used to seeing similar lewd stares at her cousins. Zara and Tahi were both beautiful and dressed a lot sexier than Laila did. At least when they were out, they did. The buttoned-up, modest clothing Zara and Tahi wore when they left the house usually ended up flung all over the seats of Zara's Ford Focus within minutes of them leaving their parents' field of vision. Her cousins had perfected the art of the fifteen-second vehicular wardrobe change.

"What makes you think we're not from around here?" Zara purred, her big hazel eyes and curving smile a blatant invitation.

"Because this little backwoods town could never have produced something so exotic. So fantastic," the guy said huskily, stepping closer.

Laila mentally rolled her eyes at the guy's reference to them as *exotic*. It rubbed her the wrong way, as though they were outsiders in the idyllic small town. Besides, coupled with the almost indecent sexual hunger in the guy's gaze as he checked out Zara, the word took on an additional offensive charge. She didn't *always* think people meant to be racist when they called her or a family member exotic.

But she *definitely* got that bad taste in her mouth when this guy said it.

Still, Laila had to admit, he *was* very good-looking. Zara was an accomplished manhunter. Knowing her cousin the way she did,

Laila could tell that Zara was feeling like she just hit the jackpot. Although his dark hair and tall, lean, muscular body had initially made Laila's heart jump because she'd thought of the man on the beach, he was completely different. His face was almost too perfect, like the guys on her mom's Telemundo soap. And if the man on the beach had been giving her that lean, ravenous look this guy was giving Zara, Laila's panic would have gone full-blown.

"So where *are* you from?" the good-looking guy asked Zara.

"From her accent, I'd guess Chicago or Detroit," another guy said to Tahi, nodding in Zara's direction. "Rudy Fattore," he said, bold as brass. He held out his hand to Tahi.

"You're right. Detroit, born and bred. And from your accent, I'd guess New York," Tahi said without hesitation. She shook Rudy's proffered hand and matched his brash grin. Oh, what Laila would give to have her cousins' poise around guys. Rudy was shorter and nowhere near as good-looking as Mr. Perfect Face, technically speaking, but he was cute. He seemed to exude warmth, charm and the promise of a good time.

"East Bronx, to be exact. You've got a good ear on you. Among other things," Rudy said, wagging his eyebrows suggestively. Tahi laughed and rolled her eyes. "So what are three gorgeous ladies like yourselves doing in Crescent Bay?"

"We're here on vacation," Tahi said.

"Looking for a good time. Just like everyone else," Zara murmured, never breaking her steamy stare with Perfect Face.

Laila shifted awkwardly on her feet. She was pretty used to this scenario: Zara and Tahi always managed to attract a horde of men, but Laila was rarely included in those first few rounds of flirtation. The bold attracted the bold, apparently. A third man lingered on the curb. He was good-looking, with nice, serious, dark brown eyes. Maybe, like Laila, he was the shy one of the group. He smiled and stepped toward her, nodding in greeting.

"Hi. I'm Jim Rothschild," he said politely.

"I'm Laila," she replied, shaking his hand. "And these are my cousins, Zara and Tahira."

"You can call me Tahi," Tahi told Rudy with a smile.

"Lucky me. Oh, and that's Eric, but you can just call him Pretty Boy," Rudy said with a dismissive wave at the tall guy. Eric was too involved in a quiet conversation with Zara to notice. "And this is—" Rudy turned around in a complete circle and gave Jim a dubious look. "Where'd Asher go?"

"Still listening to the music, I think. He didn't want ice cream. Oh . . . here he comes."

Laila glanced in the direction where Jim looked at the same time she licked her ice cream cone. She froze with the ice cream on her tongue. The guy who had seen her naked today strode across the empty street toward them.

He looked beachy casual in a pair of khaki shorts and an untucked blue-checked button-down that skimmed his lean, muscular torso appealingly. He moved with the kind of bone-deep, easy, athletic confidence that Laila always noticed and admired, probably because she knew she didn't possess it herself.

I can't believe this. He's walking over here.

She suddenly didn't know what to do with her arms or legs . . . or how to breathe. All she could do was stare stupidly. His expression was preoccupied and serious, seemingly in direct contrast to his informal dress and lazy saunter as he approached his friends. Garnering her will, she forced muscle movement, moving the ice cream cone away from her mouth and rapidly licking her lips clean. It felt like she swallowed gravel instead of cream.

His face wasn't just handsome, it was strong. The nose was a little large, but well-shaped, the eyebrows dark and thick, the granite jaw slightly square and whiskered. Laila had found it an interesting face even when panicked there on the beach . . . full of character. So *male.*

She couldn't unglue her gaze from it now.

Those electric blue eyes that she recalled so vividly from this afternoon suddenly zoomed in directly on her. His confident stride faltered a few feet from the curb. So did her heart.

"Ash, my man. Come and meet these beautiful fellow vacationers," Rudy called smoothly.

Ash, of course. Short for Asher. That was what one of the guys had called him earlier in the woods. He recovered his composure and approached them. Laila's heart started an escalating drumroll in her ears.

"This is Tahi and Zara," Rudy began. Zara glanced distractedly around Eric's broad shoulders and grinned appreciatively at the newcomer. But Asher wasn't looking at Zara. "And this is—I'm sorry, it was Lisa, right?"

"Laila," she said, her voice barely above a whisper. She couldn't squeeze anything else out of her throat, because *his* stare hadn't left hers since it first landed on her.

"Laila," Asher repeated, as if he'd heard her perfectly, even though she'd been mumbling. He stepped toward her and took her hand in his. She swallowed thickly, unable to think of anything logical to say, but unable to look away from his stare either. His bronzed skin and dark hair emphasized his light eyes. He stood so close, she could see the black pinpoints in the blue and green of his irises. She had the impression he could see straight down to the heart of her. *Oh God.* He'd probably tell them all any minute now that this was the naked girl he'd caught at the inland lake.

Please don't give away my secret. No one's ever seen me like that.

It was a crazy, stupid, silent plea. He squeezed her hand warmly. Had her panic shown on her face?

"Asher Gaites-Granville," he said, but it was like he was trying to tell her something other than merely stating his name. His gaze flickered downward. "Uh . . . your ice cream. It's melting." She watched in rising confusion as he walked toward the counter of the ice cream parlor. He returned with several napkins. He nodded at the sticky liquid on her wrist and thumb and handed her the napkins.

"Do you think I could talk to you for a minute?"

She looked up in the process of dabbing the ice cream off her skin, her mouth hanging open in surprise.

Asher pointed behind her. "Just over there, under that tree would work."

She glanced uneasily behind him, but Tahi, Jim and Rudy were all talking casually. Eric was leaning over Zara's upturned face. Her cousin's expression looked hungry. Sultry. Laila recalled her mother saying dramatically for the hundredth time that Zara would be the death of her mother. In that moment, it seemed like a definite possibility.

"Yeah, sure," she told Asher, walking into the cooler air under a leafy oak tree thirty or so feet away from the others. She halted and turned, her heart in her throat, and looked up at Asher Gaites-Granville. He started to speak, then exhaled uneasily.

"You looked like you were going to be sick when you saw me back there," he said.

"Which time?"

He blinked. He had the most amazing eyes. They looked darker and bluer in the dimmer lighting. "Both times, to be honest. It's not the most complimentary thing for a guy to see."

Laughter bubbled out of her throat unexpectedly. He smiled at the sound. *God, he's gorgeous.* Her laughter faded. So did his.

"I'm sorry, for . . . for interrupting you like that this afternoon," he said rapidly. "I wasn't spying on you. I mean . . . I was for a little bit—to be honest—but it was only because you took me by surprise. And because . . . you know."

Her cheeks burned. She stared down at her melting ice cream blindly.

"You didn't tell your friends about it, did you?" she asked in a hushed tone.

"Of course not. Laila?"

Her chin jerked up at the sound of his deep voice saying her name so quietly . . . so tenderly.

"I wouldn't. Not about that."

She blinked uncertainly, confused by the intensity of his tone. She saw him swallow thickly, and thought maybe he was a little knocked off-guard too.

"I'd never even let my friends know about that lake, not even Jimmy. I'd never blab about seeing you there. That's what I wanted to tell you. You don't need to look so afraid."

She just examined him for a moment, tethered by his stare. She nodded once, believing him completely for some reason. Something like relief broke over his face. Shyness swelled in her. Even though she believed her secret was safe with him, he'd *still* seen her stark naked.

Why today, of all days, did I have to be a little rebellious, and skinny-dip?

What did he think, seeing me naked?

The memory of his obvious arousal rushed into her brain. She viciously damned her hot cheeks.

"You said it was your secret place too. Once," she said awkwardly, keeping her face lowered to disguise her blush.

"Yeah," he said, shoving his hands into his pockets and shifting on his feet. His legs were tanned and long and very strong looking. She glanced up at him cautiously when he didn't immediately continue. "I haven't been back there for four years, since I went to college in California. My parents have a house down a ways on the beach. I used to go to that lake regularly."

A smile flickered across her mouth.

"What?" he asked.

"My family's been coming to Crescent Bay for summer vacation since I was little, but I just discovered that lake four years ago. I've been going there ever since."

"One guardian of the secret lake leaves, another one takes over," he said quietly. Her smile widened. She liked that idea, fanciful as it seemed.

His eyebrows arched. He leaned toward her slightly. "And you've never taken anyone there?"

She shook her head. Her skin tingled in heightened awareness from their hushed conversation. From his nearness . . .

"Not even your friends back there?"

"They're my cousins. And no. It's my special place."

"Now it's ours, then."

A dull roar sounded in her ears.

"It's a good place to be alone, isn't it?" he asked after a pause.

"Yeah. A good place to escape." His gaze sharpened on her. She looked down at the soggy cone she was holding. "I'm just going to . . ." She waved at a garbage can a few feet away. When she returned from throwing away her ice cream, he hadn't moved.

"Where did you go to school in California?" she asked.

"Stanford. I just graduated."

"Congratulations. I wish I were close."

"To graduating?"

"Yeah. I just finished my freshman year at Wayne State."

"I thought you looked young."

"I'm nineteen." She became aware of her defensiveness when

she saw his small smile. "You can't be much older, if you just graduated."

"I'll be twenty-two this fall."

"Oh," she said, feeling self-conscious. She'd felt more on equal footing talking about the secret lake, a place they both considered special. At the moment, he seemed so much more mature than her. Not only was she younger than him, she was well aware she'd lived a somewhat isolated existence, compared to most American girls, given her family's relative conservativeness and overprotective nature. She still had ten or eleven o'clock curfews, for goodness' sake. She'd never lived away from home, even for a few days. Maybe he was thinking the same thing about how immature she seemed, because he seemed to hesitate as he looked down at her.

"What are you studying at Wayne State?" he asked, but she had the impression he'd been about to say something else and edited himself at the last second.

"I'm still technically undecided as far as a major. But I'm going to declare business this fall."

"Business, huh?" he asked, grinning.

Her backbone straightened. "What's so funny about that?"

"Not funny. Just unexpected."

"How would you know what to expect of me one way or another?" she asked incredulously.

He put up his hands in a surrender gesture. "It was just an impression, that's all."

"Based on what?"

"Your singing. Your love of privacy in a picturesque spot." He dipped his head and spoke more quietly. "Your tendency to do something romantic, like swim naked there alone. The notebooks. I thought maybe you were a writer or something."

Her skin roughened. "Notebooks?" she asked in an unnatural, high-pitched voice. *He'd noticed her music notebooks?*

"Yeah. They were on the beach this afternoon, along with your clothes." She blanched and stepped back, feeling even more naked than she had when he'd seen her without her clothes on.

"Jesus. I'm sorry, why is that such a big deal?" Asher wondered, clearly at a loss as to how to respond to her reaction to him seeing a few bundles of paper and some pencils.

"Nothing. It's nothing," she said hollowly, mentally scurrying to hide her sudden discomfort. She was glad night had fallen. She crossed her arms over her chest, feeling overexposed. No one knew about those notebooks, not even her mother. They were the source of her greatest pride.

Her greatest shame.

"I used to go there to write sometimes," he said.

She started and glanced up at him. "You did?"

"I just thought maybe you did too," he added.

She swallowed thickly, overly aware of her pulse leaping at her throat. God, she was acting so jumpy around him. He probably thought she was an idiot.

"Wha . . . what kinds of things did you write there?"

"Just stories." She met his stare, curious despite her discomfort. "Observations I've made. News stories, mostly. I'm a reporter." He shrugged. "Or I will be, in a few weeks. Officially, anyway. I've had plenty of internships before now. But I start at the *L.A. Times* this August. International desk."

"That's great."

"Thanks," he said. He gave her a questioning glance. He expected her to say what she'd been writing in those notebooks, but it was a too deeply buried secret to rise easily to the surface.

"It's not financial equations, is it?" he asked her with gentle amusement. "Or a detailed plan to start your own company." Her pulse leapt higher at her throat when she saw how closely he studied her reaction to his questions. There was warmth in his eyes. Somehow, miraculously, he'd seen that her heart wasn't in the idea of studying business. That was her parents' dream, not hers. She wanted to shout out that *of course* it wasn't financial equations or business plans. Who would escape to such a private, beautiful place to think about *business*? Instead, she pursed her lips uncertainly.

"That's okay. You don't have to say anything. I can see the truth."

"You can?" she breathed out in uneasy amazement.

"I imagine you're a poet or an author or something. Or maybe a songwriter? I've never heard that song you were singing before."

She blinked, the hairs on her forearms standing on end.

How in the world—

"Why would you think that?" she asked numbly.

He leaned forward. The flesh of her right ear and neck prickled with heightened awareness at his nearness.

"Even if you weren't writing poetry, specifically, in your secret place, I'm not far off. Am I? You've got the eyes of a poet. You're an artist, not a businesswoman, Laila," he said very quietly.

She just stared up at him, struck dumb by the accuracy of a stranger.

Asher felt a little guilty for setting her off balance. But mostly, all he could think about as he leaned down close to her was the fresh peachy scent from her long, unbound hair. He inhaled deeply, his entire body going on full alert. Her neck looked too slender and delicate to hold up such a thick, glorious mass of hair. The brown, gleaming waves fell all the way to the small of her back. *All* of her looked slender and delicate, except her huge, expressive, light green eyes. And those high, firm breasts, of course, which he knew firsthand were far from small. While the curves of her hips were compact, she was so feminine. She looked like she'd fit perfectly in the palms of his hands . . .

She made a soft, sexy, gasping sound and his trance fractured slightly. He realized he was leaning down over her, his mouth only inches away from her neck, staring down the length of her at the tight, curving hips he'd been imagining—vividly—cupping in his hands. He noticed her startled expression but thought she seemed a little entranced, as well.

She's way too young, and I'm only going to be in Crescent Bay for a few weeks.

But she's so *blessed beautiful.*

He'd never seen anything like her. He wasn't sure how to operate in her presence. All the rules he'd learned about the sexual dance somehow didn't seem to apply anymore.

Swallowing thickly, he stepped back.

"Hey, Laila," one of the girls behind him shouted. Asher looked over his shoulder. He saw it was the knockout Eric had been hovering over like a vulture that had called out. "We're all going over to Chauncy's Place to dance."

Asher knew the local bar and dance club. He hoped Laila would go. He wasn't finished talking to her.

Not by a long shot.

Laila pulled her cell phone out of her back pocket and tapped the screen. "We can't," she called. "We have to be home by . . ." She halted herself, giving Asher a nervous, apologetic glance. "We have to get home," she amended, pointing significantly at her cell phone.

The cousin's laugh sounded snide. "No, *you* have to be home. *We* don't have a ten o'clock curfew."

A flash of dislike went through Asher toward this particular cousin. Maybe she and Eric deserved each other.

"We can drop you off on our way over to Chauncy's," Laila's other cousin said, her tone kinder.

Laila ducked her head. His heart went out to her. He knew she was embarrassed. Still . . . he was a little concerned at the conversation.

"You *are* nineteen, aren't you?" he asked her quietly. Her cousins did look older than her, but that might have just been the trick of their sexier clothes and makeup. In contrast, Laila looked fresh. Untouched.

"Yes," she hissed, giving him a sideways glare. She bit her full lower lip. "It's just . . . my parents . . . It's a long story. I really should be going." She started to walk away, but he caught her arm at the elbow. She turned back, her long hair brushing softly against his hand. The streetlights made her green eyes shine as she looked up at him.

"Meet me. Tomorrow at the secret lake. One o'clock?" For a moment, she didn't respond. "Please," he added, growing desperate at the idea of not knowing when he'd see her face again.

"I'll try, but I can't guarantee it. I might have to help my mom—"

"Then the next day at one. Or the next." His hand tightened slightly on her bare arm, absorbing her heat . . . the incredible softness of her skin. Her eyes widened. "I'll be there, every day at one. Okay?"

She just nodded. He let go—very reluctantly—and watched her walk away.

Chapter Five

Asher's mouth was starting to hurt from blowing up the rafts. It didn't help his discomfort any that he sat at the edge of the lake alone doing his task.

She's not coming.

He took one last inhale and puffed the last bit of air into the raft before he capped it. He felt dizzy from the effort. *And for what?* he wondered impatiently. It had to be going on two o'clock, and there was no sign of Laila. Yes, he'd told her last night that he'd continue to wait there every afternoon until she came, but it was hard to tamp down his sharp disappointment at not seeing her.

He was in the process of getting his phone out of his backpack to check the time when he suddenly froze. He listened extra hard but couldn't identify what had caught his attention. The forest surrounding the calm lake was almost preternaturally quiet.

He glanced to his left. His hands dropped to his sides as he watched her walk onto the beach, her face alight with the afternoon sun and something else . . .

Anxiety? Restrained excitement?

Her thick hair was pulled into a high ponytail. The hairstyle emphasized the pretty tilt of her large green eyes. She wore a plain white T-shirt that showed off her smooth skin and golden-brown tan and a pair of snug jean shorts that distracted him hugely. Her legs were long and toned.

He unglued his stare from them as she approached him, a shy smile on her lips. Her eyes seemed alight with warmth.

"I'm sorry I'm late. My mother and aunts needed help with dinner. My oldest cousin decided to come unexpectedly from the city for the night. It's like preparing for the prince's arrival whenever he comes," she said, rolling her eyes.

He held out his hand to relieve her of the load she carried over one shoulder. She'd brought a backpack too. "How many people from your family vacation here in Crescent Bay?"

"My mom and dad. My dad's brother and his wife—they're my cousin Zara's parents—and Zara's younger sister and brother, Sophia and Noor. Zara has an older brother who is a captain in the Navy, Driss. But he's stationed in San Diego, so he doesn't come anymore. Then there's my mom's sister and her husband—Tahi's parents. Tahi has a little brother, Jamal, and an older brother, Zarif. He's the one I was just talking about. Zarif is doing a surgical residency at Henry Ford Hospital, plus he's engaged, so we hardly ever get to see him. So when he does come around, we have to roll out the red carpet." She paused and they shared a smile. "He's actually pretty cool. I'm just kidding about the prince thing. Then there's my Mamma Sophia. She's my mom's and aunt Nora's mother. She lives with us."

"That's quite a list."

She laughed. "I know, it's crazy."

"Tahi told me last night that your last name was Barek."

She nodded. He'd never known anyone's eyes could shine like hers did. "It's a Moroccan name," she murmured.

"But you were born in the States?"

"Yeah. Actually, my mom was too. But my grandma and grandpa had just recently immigrated to New York when she was born. My dad was born near Tangier, but he came to the States with his parents when he was seven."

"Have you ever been? To Morocco?"

She shook her head. "Not yet. Zara and her family have gone a couple times. My dad is really busy with his shop, and my mom and I look out for Mamma Sophia, so we haven't had a chance yet. I still have a lot of family there. I'd like to go."

"I'd like to go too."

She blinked. "Really?"

"Why do you look so surprised?"

She shrugged and gave him a dubious glance. "I dated a guy in high school who thought Fez was just a hat. Morocco isn't a destination at the top of most Americans' list, that's all."

"Yeah. I love traveling, seeing other cultures firsthand. The closest I've ever gotten to Morocco is Cairo, but I'll get there someday. One of my majors was international relations."

"So that's why you got a job being an international reporter?"

"Yeah. I'd like to be a foreign correspondent. Do you speak Darija? What?" he asked, noticing her surprised glance.

"Not many white guys know the name of the dialect of Morocco." He shrugged, and she laughed softly. "If you're trying to impress me, you're succeeding."

"I had a few classes in Arabic in college. And if you're impressed, then my work here is done."

Color stained her cheeks, making her even more beautiful, if that was possible. She laughed to hide her embarrassment at his comment, but he thought she looked pleased, as well. "Yeah, I speak Darija. But mostly only with my family, and that's really a kind of Arabish, a mixture of Darija and English. What about your family?"

"What languages do they speak?"

"No. Who are they? How many are there? Where do they all live?"

"Oh." He shrugged. His family seemed minuscule in comparison to hers. "My folks live in a northern Chicago suburb. I'm an only child."

"So am I. But Zara told me this morning that Eric was your cousin . . ."

"He is. But I don't consider him family."

She looked confused, and he realized he'd been a little sharp. He attempted a smile to smooth things over. "Sorry. Eric belongs to the East Coast Gaites-Granvilles. Our great-great-grandfathers were two of four brothers. My ancestor was kind of a lone wolf. He brought his share of the newspaper business to Chicago and created this kind of family schism. At least back then, it did. These days, the scar has healed. At least on the business end of things. But Eric and I aren't close. His presence here is my parents' idea of keeping me in line."

Her confusion turned to bewilderment. He shook his head. "It's a long story."

She laughed softly at that, probably because she'd told him the same thing last night about her parents.

"Family," she said.

"Family," he agreed dryly.

For a second, their stares held. He experienced an overwhelming urge to close the distance between them, to feel her mouth beneath his . . . to sink into her taste. He probably would have with another woman.

Maybe she'd read his mind, because her gaze skipped nervously away and landed on the beach.

"Oh. You brought rafts. That's great," she said, waving at the two yellow floats lying on the beach.

"Yeah. Did you wear a suit?"

She nodded. "It's hot, isn't it?" Her gaze skittered down over his body to his swim trunks. He wore a T-shirt, but even through the fabric, he felt her stare on his skin. Arousal tickled at the base of his spine and tingled his sex. He felt himself getting hard. He bent to hide his reaction, acting intent on pulling a towel out of his backpack.

"I brought a towel. We can share it," he said. His uncontrollable sexual reaction when it came to her irritated him. He'd seen her fear and anxiety yesterday when he came upon her swimming naked, so lost in her private thoughts. So vulnerable. The last thing he wanted to do was to scare her off.

"I brought one too," she said breathlessly.

He tossed off his T-shirt. His sideways glance told him she was staring at his chest. There was *definitely* more than just anxiety in her gaze. He hoped he wasn't kidding himself. He took several steps toward the shoreline.

"You coming in?"

"Yeah," she assured him, but she made no move to follow him. He realized she was self-conscious about the idea of peeling off her clothes in front of him. As interested as he was in watching her strip—the image of her wet, naked body gleaming in the sun had been plaguing his every waking and sleeping moment—he plowed into the water, keeping his back to her and giving her space.

You could use a dunk in the cold water anyway, lecher.

Neither his self-condemning thoughts nor the sudden plunge into the lake did anything to cool the rising fever in him, though.

She hurried out of her clothing, keeping an eye on Asher as he knifed through the water, his gleaming back and flexing muscles capturing almost her entire attention. The remainder of her awareness focused on her own body: on how self-conscious she felt in the black two-piece she'd borrowed from Zara this morning in preparation for her meeting with Asher. Her mother frowned on bikinis, at least in Laila's case. Laila liked to swim and paddleboard, so she usually preferred sportier swimwear anyway. But she had been known to borrow her cousins' bikinis, once they were at the public beach's changing room and away from her mother's disapproving gaze.

Why did you have to do it today, though? she wondered as she adjusted the bikini briefs anxiously while she stood on the shore, assuring herself Asher wasn't watching.

But the question was stupid. She knew why she'd done it. He was the most attractive guy she'd ever met.

Ever imagined.

She wanted to look good in front of him. Sexy.

She stood at the edge of the lake when he surfaced a moment later.

"Do you want me to bring in the rafts?" she yelled when he turned toward shore, wiping his wet bangs back. He'd swum out quite a distance.

"Yeah," he called, heading inland toward her. A whole swarm of butterflies fluttered in her stomach as she retrieved the rafts and flopped them onto the surface of the water, knowing all the while he watched her. She waded into the cold water, shivering.

"You brought a lot of stuff with you," she commented as she maneuvered the two rafts toward him and he approached. The inland lake was deep and cold. As always, she part dreaded, part relished the idea of plunging her whole body into the chilly water. "How far away is your house from here?" She shoved one of the rafts in his direction. He grabbed it.

"Just a half a mile that way," he said, waving to the south.

"Not that huge white house? The one with the pool and everything?"

He nodded.

"But that's . . . that's like a mansion, isn't it?" she asked disbelievingly. She'd jogged with Tahi down that section of the beach a few times. The sprawling *white house*, as they'd dubbed it, rarely seemed occupied. They used to speculate about the people who lived there, amazed at the idea that someone would own such a magnificent beach house and use it so rarely. After Tahi and Zara had returned home last night from Chauncy's, Laila had questioned them incessantly about any new details they'd learned about the guys, but most especially Asher. Zara had told her that she'd gotten the impression that Eric and Asher came from a really old, wealthy family.

"*They're like American royalty or something*," Zara had stated wisely, excitement shining in her eyes. She had obviously been nearly as taken with Eric as Laila was with Asher. Tahi had whispered amusedly to Laila that Zara and Eric had gotten very close last night. "*They were practically sucking each other's faces off in an empty corner of Chauncy's.*"

"It's big, I'll give you that," Asher said presently, stating the obvious with a careless shrug.

"What is the Gaites-Granville family business, exactly?"

"Gaites-Granville Media," he said in a flat tone. "It's a conglomerate of newspapers, television stations, magazines." He heaved his long body onto the raft, belly down, spraying Laila with water in the process and scattering her thoughts.

"*Hey*," she protested, laughing. Realizing she was getting soaked anyway, and that she might as well get it over with, she hefted herself onto her raft in a sitting position. She made a squeaking sound of discomfort when the raft temporarily sank below the surface and she was submerged in cold water. She noticed Asher's wide grin of amusement and splashed him in the face. He looked surprised.

"What'd I do to deserve that?"

"You laughed at me," she told him succinctly, settling herself on the raft and lying on her back. She closed her eyes as the bobbing raft stilled. The hot sun felt nice against her chilled skin. "*Never* laugh at Laila," she teased.

"You're right," she heard him say after a pause. Something in his tone made her lift her head off the raft cushion. Her grin vanished. He was staring at her body with open appreciation. He noticed her looking and met her stare. The honest male heat in his gaze made her breath catch in her lungs.

"Laughing is the last reaction that comes to mind when I look at you."

Maybe he shouldn't have said something so obvious—so sexual—but it had just popped out. He shook his head ruefully and gave her an apologetic glance. "Sorry, I didn't mean to come on so strong. It's just . . . you're the most beautiful girl I've ever seen."

Her full, damp lips parted in what appeared to be amazement. He couldn't help but smile. She was so fresh. So unexpected.

"Don't tell me no one has ever told you that before."

"They haven't," she said with a strange, dubious certainty. She propped her upper body up on her elbows. A small smile flickered across her lips. "I'm guessing my dad doesn't count?"

"He most definitely doesn't."

"Yeah. He's obligated to say I'm prettier than Zara and Tahi. He's my dad," she said, her smile widening. He'd made her uncomfortable with his compliment, so she was making light of it.

"They're like sisters to you, aren't they? Zara and Tahi?"

"Yeah. Our three families are really close. Sometimes a little *too* close," she added, rolling her eyes. "Plus, my mom and dad are friends with like . . . *everyone* in a six-block radius of our house in Detroit. In the summertime especially, I feel like I live my life in a fishbowl." He gave her a questioning glance. "Because everyone in our neighborhood sits on their porch when it's nice out. Sometimes it feels like I can't make the smallest move without someone documenting it and reporting it back to my mother or one of my aunts or something. Plus, my dad owns a collision and glass repair shop, and he's really good. I waitress at a restaurant near where I go to school, and sometimes it seems like every fourth or fifth person I wait on has had their car repaired by him after a wreck."

"That's why you said coming here to the lake is like an escape?"

She hesitated. "I don't want to give you the wrong impression. I love my family. It's just—"

"It's no fun, living under a magnifying lens," he said. He grabbed her raft with one hand and brought it alongside his, keeping his expression casual to prevent a return of her nerves. He lined them up so they lay side by side, he on his stomach and she on her back, their faces only a foot or so apart.

"You sound like you know what that's like. Living under a magnifying glass," she said after a pause.

"I do."

"But you've been living in California for the past four years, haven't you? And you said you only consider your mom and dad family. Whose eyes have been on you?"

He gave a small shrug. "Let's just say my parents are extremely farsighted."

"Tell me about it," she said softly.

"What do you mean?"

"What's it's like for *you*. Living under the magnifying glass."

She looked so somber, it gave him pause. It struck him then

that as unlikely as it seemed, as different as their worlds probably were, she might really understand. So he began to tell her—haltingly at first, because he wasn't used to talking about his relationship with his parents—how one of his first memories was of them looking down at him so expectantly . . . how another of his first memories was their expressions of frustrated disappointment.

"I can't please them," he said after talking for a while. "So I gave up trying. A long time ago, actually."

"That's so sad," Laila murmured. "I can't believe they wouldn't be proud of you, having just gotten two degrees from Stanford."

He grimaced. "My dad hated the idea of me going to Stanford, a liberal, West Coast school. He wanted me to go to Harvard, like he did. Like Eric did. Like most Gaites-Granvilles did. But, to be fair, they *were* proud of me at graduation."

"They were?" she asked, leaning toward him. She started in surprise when the bottom of her raft scraped the shore. Their rafts had bobbed inland while they talked, Asher realized, and the beach was only a few feet away.

He nodded, holding tighter to her raft while he used his other hand to paddle, pulling her off the shore and back out to deeper water. His hand slid off the slippery plastic and they started to separate. She made a surprised sound and reached for him. He caught her hand and their rafts bumped together again. She laughed breathlessly. Their gazes held.

He didn't let go, and she showed no sign of wanting to pull away from his grasp. In fact, she laid her head back on the air mattress pillow, her stare fixed on him.

"The only reason they were proud is because they think I'm going to start working at Gaites-Granville Media now that I'm done with school."

"You say that in the present tense," she said slowly, a look of concern crossing her face. He was intensely aware of the feeling of her soft, warm hand in his. He reached with his finger, feeling her pulse. Her heartbeat was strong. Fast. She was as affected by their touching skin as he was.

"That's because I haven't told them yet," he said, distracted. In all fairness, he'd been pretty preoccupied by her nearness the entire time he'd talked. It was challenging, lying side by side with the most gorgeous girl he'd ever seen, who was wearing only a bikini. But his distraction spiked high as he rubbed her wrist and absorbed the feeling of her beating heart. "Not that I'm not going to work for GGM, or that I've already taken a job at the *L.A. Times*."

Her expression was so full of compassion it made him self-conscious. Why had he spilled all his family drama like that? It wasn't like him. Thanks to his parents, he'd learned long ago to hold his feelings in . . . to give nothing away that might later be used as future ammunition against him.

"When will you tell them?" she asked.

"I'm supposed to go to Chicago to see them after this vacation. I'll tell them then. Do you think that's selfish of me?" he asked after a pause. "To take this vacation, and then to disappoint them at the end of it?" He frowned. "Of course you do. You'd do anything for your family."

"*No*. I don't think you're selfish. You said it was your father's graduation gift to you, a last opportunity for a carefree vacation before you enter the adult world. That's true, whether you work for GGM or the *L.A. Times*." He stroked her more boldly, gliding his fingertips against her inner forearm. She was so soft. So beautiful.

"I think it's really brave of you, Asher."

He watched her full lips moving with a razor-sharp focus. Her words seemed to skim across his sensitive skin, roughening it. Still, he was a little disbelieving.

"Brave?"

She nodded. "You're living your own truth. That's a really courageous thing to do." A spasm crossed her face, like she'd just experienced some small pain. He leaned closer, concerned.

"What's wrong?"

"I couldn't do it. I could never be that brave," she said. He couldn't have heard her near-whisper if he weren't just inches away from her moving mouth.

"Sure you could," he insisted.

"You don't understand," she murmured.

"Maybe not. I'd like to try, though."

She gave a shaky laugh and shook her head, as if to minimize the importance of what she'd said. There was a defined black circle around the clear, light green of her iris. The smile faded from her lips . . . ripe-looking, dusky pink lips. She parted them. He caught a glimpse of her tongue, and suddenly, it was happening.

He was taking his first taste.

Chapter Six

She saw the way he was looking at her, his bluish-green eyes gleaming from beneath heavy eyelids. She felt his stare in her lungs. It made them heavy and difficult to expand. Then he was leaning closer. His warm mouth brushed against her lips, and her lungs released. She gasped softly and moved her mouth against his.

It was the sweetest kiss: questing and sun warmed and gentle. Laila had never known there was a part of her that was frozen, deep down inside, until she felt it thaw beneath Asher's mouth.

His tongue dipped between her lips. Heat unfurled in her belly and expanded like a heavy ache to her sex. He cradled her jaw with one hand and kissed her more deeply, their rubbing, tangling tongues, his taste, all of it making her dizzy. She ran her hand along his naked shoulder, loving the sensation of dense muscle gloved in smooth, sun-kissed skin. He made a low, rough sound in his throat and leaned further into her, his kiss growing hungrier and more demanding. The ache at her core grew sharper. She twisted her hips toward him, increasingly desperate to relieve the pressure there. The air mattress slipped out from beneath her.

Suddenly, she was plunging beneath the surface of the cold water.

She felt his hand on her upper arm. He hauled her up to the surface. He struggled to stay on his raft while holding her. She found her footing at the rock-and-sand bottom of the lake. She sputtered with laughter.

"You okay?" he asked.

"Yeah," she said, wiping water and wet hair out of her face. She grinned from ear to ear. He smiled.

"It's kind of a rare talent, making out on air rafts," he said.

"One that apparently you possess, and I don't," she replied dryly.

"It must be a genetic talent, because I've never done it before," he assured her with a pointed glance. "Screw it," he said, swinging his body into the lake and shoving his air mattress toward the shore. "It's a wasted talent if I'm the only one who has it," he said before he took her into his arms.

All her amusement faded at the sensation of his long, hard body pressing against hers in the cool water. She stared up at him—he was a good eight or nine inches taller than her. His head blocked the afternoon sun. His face was cast in shadow, but she saw that he'd sobered as well. And suddenly, he was kissing her again, and she could feel his body through the thin material of his swim trunks. It was like that moment when she'd first seen him on the beach and witnessed his arousal, the sheer flagrancy of his maleness, but this was a thousandfold times that experience. It shocked her a little, the intimacy of it all. Before she'd considered male desire exciting, but also *coarse*, somehow. Crude. Often tiresome. Never beautiful.

Until now.

His arms closed tighter around her. One large hand cupped her hip and shaped it to his palm, the other wrapped around her waist. She moaned softly into their kiss, loving the way she fit into his embrace. Her fingers dug gently into the muscles of his back, and then she was delving them into his wet hair. She pressed closer to him, using her hold on him to tilt his head slightly as she twisted hers, deepening their kiss. Distantly, she was a little amazed at her sexual aggressiveness, but he'd started a fire in her. She felt it sizzling at her core, making her hunger. Ache. His hands began to slide up and down her body, as though he were learning her and pleasuring her at once, stroking and rubbing . . . building the friction in her. She felt his erection swell against her belly, and suddenly, he was lifting her.

She rose out of the water. Their kiss continued, even more wild and ravenous at the new angle. He grabbed one butt cheek and pressed her tightly to him, the long, rigid column of his cock pressing against her sex. They moaned in unison.

He broke their kiss and pressed his mouth to her throat. She opened heavy eyelids, dazed by the bright sunlight and Asher's hot mouth moving on her neck. And all the while, his arousal burned against hers.

"Tell me how to say 'I want you' in Moroccan," he said gruffly against her neck.

She smiled and pressed her lips to his cheek. He was so unexpected. "*Kan bghik*," she murmured.

"*Kan bghik*," he said, and he lifted his head. His gaze smoldered as it toured her face. His fingers moved on the bare skin of her buttock just beneath her bikini brief. She felt his erection lurch against her. "And you, Laila?"

"Yes," she whispered, swallowing thickly. "I want you too. Isn't it obvious?"

A shadow passed over his handsome face. "Ah. I sense a *but* in there." When she didn't argue, she saw his jaw muscles tighten. He set her back on her feet. Reluctantly, she moved back from the temptation of his body several inches. The barrier of the cool water did little to soothe her firing nerves. He released her slowly but grasped her hands in his beneath the surface of the water. She was thankful for that.

"I barely know you," she said, staring down at the rippling, glistening water. It was the most obvious of a whole host of concerns she had, like that her parents would never allow her to date a rich white boy who was only in Crescent Bay for a last summertime fling with his friends, or that he was moving to California soon, or that she wasn't even sure he wanted to *date* her. Possibly he just wanted to have sex.

And then there was the fact that she was a virgin . . .

Yeah. That was a pretty big worry.

He released one of her hands and touched the bottom of her chin with one fingertip. "I realize that. I do," he said seriously when she gave him a doubtful look. "I didn't ask you here to have sex, Laila."

"Really?"

He exhaled in frustration. "Okay, I do want to have sex with you. Obviously. A lot," he added dryly. He held her stare. "But I meant it when I said I didn't ask you here specifically for that. I like you. You're beautiful and sexy and sweet and . . . special. I've never wanted someone the way I want you," he said in a preoccupied fashion, as if he were having the realization for the first time. Euphoria rushed through her at his words. But then this his mouth went hard.

"I am being selfish, though. You're not the kind of girl I should be fooling around with, under the circumstances. That's what you're thinking, right?"

"I don't know what I'm thinking," she confessed. "I know what I'm feeling. And it's a little . . . overwhelming."

"Yeah," he agreed. His damp fingertip caressed her cheek. She went still beneath his touch, her nerves tingling in awareness. When he noticed her entranced expression, he dropped his hand with a rough sigh.

"You say you barely know me, but I spilled my guts out earlier to you . . . all my deep, dark, boring secrets. Maybe you need to tell me one of your secrets. In the spirit of getting to know each other, and all," he added fairly when she gave him an amused, doubtful glance.

Maybe he was right. She felt butterflies flicker in her belly. She inhaled to still the sensation.

"Okay. You guessed correctly. Yesterday." She noticed his questioning glance and swallowed down her nerves. "I do write poetry. And music. And lyrics. I'm still amazed you knew somehow." She met his stare willfully, despite her flaming cheeks. "I've never told another soul that before."

"You haven't?" he asked her slowly.

She shook her head.

"Why not?"

"Because it's a stupid, childish obsession." The words burst out of her throat. "I don't even know why I do it!"

"Yes, you do."

"I do?" she asked, stunned by his confidence.

"Yeah." He squeezed her hands under the water. "Think about it for a minute."

She did, replaying the feeling she got when she finally had a few private moments to herself and could pull her music and lyrics out of the old toy chest stored at the back of her closet. She thought of how it felt when she finished a song to her satisfaction, and the rush that went through her when she finally got the perfect lyric or caught the exact nuance of meaning she wanted with her poetry.

Joy. That was what she felt then. Pure and simple.

"It makes me happy," she whispered, a tremor of feeling going through her at the realization.

"Then it's not childish or stupid. Far from it." He leaned down and brushed his lips against her cheek. "I told you that you were an artist," he murmured. She looked up at him and smiled shakily.

"Thanks," she said.

"For what?"

"For being the first and probably only person to ever call me that."

She felt his smile in the deepest part of her. "An artist isn't something you're called. It's something you *are*."

She swallowed back the lump in her throat.

"I really have to go," she said reluctantly, noticing the position of the sun in the sky. "Tahi and Zara will be waiting for me at Crescent Bay South."

"They're covering for you?"

She nodded, avoiding his stare.

Among her cousins, she was typically the voice of moderation and reason, but that didn't mean she hadn't learned how to maneuver around her parents to function in the world. Still, she hated straight-out lying. Yes, she'd dissembled many times before in order to escape to the inland lake, but that'd been different than today. On those previous occasions, she hadn't been misleading her family to secretly meet a guy that her parents would wholly disapprove of her seeing, especially under such intimate circumstances.

"So Zara and Tahi know that—"

"I came to see you today. Yes. I just didn't tell them where we planned to meet."

They both moved at once, starting to walk toward shore. Laila shivered when they reached the beach. They toweled off in silence,

Laila glancing with furtive desire at Asher as he dried off. Now that they weren't touching anymore, she wished they were.

"You'll come back tomorrow," he said suddenly, his intensity startling her. She turned and saw the seriousness of his expression.

"I . . . I don't know if I can," she said, thinking of her cousin Zarif's visit. "The whole family will probably go to the beach, and my uncles and cousins will probably go fishing. We'll do a cookout and everything. I'm not sure when my cousin is leaving."

He nodded, but he looked strained.

"The next day? At one o'clock again?"

"Yes. I'll try."

Asher decided they should leave the air mattresses there. No one else seemed to know about the lake, anyway. She helped him store them behind some large boulders at the edge of the beach after they'd finished dressing.

"Do you have a phone?" he asked afterward.

She nodded and retrieved it from her backpack. They exchanged digits and repacked their phones. Afterward, they stood facing each other, the silence causing a heavy pressure to press down on her chest.

"Your parents wouldn't want you to see me. Would they?" he stated rather than asked.

She gave him an apologetic glance and shook her head. "I'm sorry," she confirmed softly.

"Don't apologize. I think it sucks, but I get it. *Have* you, though? Dated other white guys? Before, I mean?"

"Yeah. In high school a few times, and once for a little bit in college," she admitted. "But it never lasted for very long. I guess the guys didn't like sneaking around all the time. Or that I couldn't be with them at the drop of a hat."

"Are you arranged to marry someone?"

"*No*," she assured him. "Arranged marriages aren't that common for Moroccans. Zarif—my cousin—found his own fiancée, and my auntie and uncle really like her. But even so . . ."

"She's Moroccan?"

Laila nodded.

"You love your parents . . . your entire family a lot. Don't you?"

She opened her mouth, searching for the right words to explain.

"They're my whole world," she said tremulously after a moment.

A silence descended.

"Would it help if I came over and introduced myself to them? If I was honest about—"

"No," she interrupted, shaking her head rapidly. "Trust me, that wouldn't be helpful at all. Especially if we ever want to see each other at all while we're here."

His expression hardened. Maybe he was considering all the complications that came with her for the first time too, and was finding the whole thing unappealing. At the very least, he probably thought she was *way* too much effort for a summer fling.

"Well, I guess I should be going," she said, her heart suddenly feeling like a stone in her chest.

"I'll see you here. The day after tomorrow?"

Relief coursed through her. "Yes. Hopefully. I'll text if something comes up."

When he didn't say anything else, she turned to leave.

"Laila," he called when she got several yards away. She turned back. He hadn't moved.

"Anytime you're free, and you think you might be able to meet, text or call. Just assume I'll want to see you. No matter what time it is. No matter for how long."

She saw it then for the first time: that hard glint of determination in his light eyes, the stubborn set to his jaw, the diamond-hard focus. It suddenly struck her that Asher Gaites-Granville wasn't like anyone she'd ever met in her life. He was like a force of nature: powerful and undeniable.

What she'd said before about her family being her whole world was true. But Asher had entered the picture. And somehow, she knew her world was about to change.

Chapter Seven

By prearrangement, she met Zara and Tahi at Crescent Bay South beach after she left Asher. That way, they could all arrive at the cottages at the same time, and Laila's secret would remain safe. She was so preoccupied by her meeting with Asher, she was unsurprised to see Asher's friends Eric, Rudy and Jim on the beach with Zara and Tahi. While Tahi, Rudy and Jim sat on beach towels, talking and listening to music, Zara and Eric lay several yards away, Zara flat on her back and Eric leaning over her, his bronzed muscles gleaming in the hot summer sun.

"How's Asher?" Rudy asked Laila slyly when she approached. Laila shot Tahi a condemning glance.

"Hey, why do you assume *I* gave you away?" Tahi defended.

"I don't think Asher would," Laila said.

"You're right. He wouldn't," Jim said levelly. Laila gave Asher's friend a small smile for his loyalty.

"But Zara would," Tahi muttered.

Laila rolled her eyes and glanced over at her cousin, who was in the process of drinking from a silver flask. She giggled loudly at something Eric said.

"Has she been drinking?" Laila asked, frowning.

"Not much. I don't think, anyway. That flask isn't very big," Tahi said, standing and grabbing her beach cover-up.

"Zara, we're going," Laila called. Zara sat up partially and cast a sullen glance their way. When Eric kissed her neck seductively, she turned her attention back to him. Their mouths met and clung. Laila watched, her brow creased in worry, as Eric pushed her cousin back on the towel and kissed her deeply.

What right have you got to be worried about her, when you were doing the same with Asher a half hour ago?

Maybe she was worried about *both* Zara and herself.

"Rudy asked us to go to Asher's place tomorrow night. We're going out on Asher's boat, and then we'll cook out and swim," Tahi said as she picked up her beach towel and shoved it in her bag. "Did you know his family owns the white house?" she asked with incredulous excitement.

Laila nodded.

"Hey . . . is that where you two met this afternoon? His place?"

"No," Laila said, helping her cousin pick up her belongings from the beach. "And you know your brother is going to be here tomorrow night. We won't be able to get away."

"No, Zarif has to leave at four to take his precious Mina to some hospital benefit. We'll be free," Tahi said, giving first Laila, then Rudy a significant glance. Rudy grinned.

"We'll see," Laila said distractedly. For the moment, her only concern was unpeeling Eric from Zara so that they could get back in time for dinner.

Thankfully, her mother was over at her aunt Nadine's cottage helping to prepare the dinner when Laila got home. Her father, Zarif, Noor and her uncles had gone fishing on a rented boat. Laila rushed into the only bathroom in the cottage, desperate for some privacy, wild to be alone with her thoughts.

She felt restless and tense as she stood under the hot spray of the shower. She kept reliving the moments in Asher's arms, when their bodies were sealed tight together . . . the moment he'd lifted her so effortlessly, and his rigid erection had slid against her sex.

Her hand slid between her thighs. She touched herself, her finger coming away slick from her previous arousal.

Her present one.

She couldn't rid herself of memories of him. He remained in her blood and in her flesh, even though he was miles away. A fever had settled on her. The water suddenly felt too hot. She turned it to a cool setting, willing the water to soothe her simmering, tense body. It wasn't *working*. Her hand pressed between her thighs again. Her eyes shut, and she vividly saw Asher's fierce gaze as he looked down at her. He'd looked like he'd wanted to eat her alive—

"Laila, hurry up. Mamma has to use the bathroom!"

She jumped guiltily at the sound of her mother's loud voice just feet away on the other side of the closed door.

How could I have ever liked *staying in this tiny little house? I feel like I'm being smothered.*

"Just a *second*, Mamma," she yelled, unable to keep the irritation out of her voice. She immediately felt doubly guilty about it, because Mamma Sophia, her grandmother, whom she adored, was probably standing next to her mom in the hall and had heard her rude tone.

She hurriedly finished washing, feeling flustered and strained and guilty, her nerves still prickly from unfulfilled arousal.

That night, they sat out on her uncle Reda's and aunt Nadine's large terrace for a delicious dinner that stretched all the way through a brilliant sunset over Lake Michigan into a star-filled night. The bungalows they rented had fire pits installed on the decks, and Laila's father and Reda got a blaze going. Her mom and aunties had outdone themselves, as usual. In honor of Zarif's presence, they served Zarif's favorites: a chicken tagine, sweet onions, almond and honey raghaif, and fruit. Despite her recent prickly mood, Laila found herself enjoying the excellent food and the happy, fire-lit faces of her family. She thought her father, uncles and cousins all looked very relaxed and handsome with their deepening tans following their fishing trip. Even Mamma Sophia had felt well enough to attend. Her thin face looked alight as she talked with her eldest grandson. During tea and dessert, Tahi, who sat next to her, whispered in Laila's ear.

"Since it's so hot, we're moving over to Nadine and Reda's sleeping porch tonight."

"Really?" Laila whispered, relief sweeping through her. While they vacationed in Crescent Bay, they always rented the same three cottages on the beach. Zara's family usually got the largest one, because they had the most children. That cottage possessed a screened-in porch that faced the lake. Traditionally, the three girls—Laila, Zara and Tahi—slept there on hot nights. Laila welcomed the idea tonight. In Crescent Bay, she had to share a room with Mamma Sophia. Normally, this was no problem for her. She loved her grandmother. They shared a special bond. Mamma

Sophia had once possessed a lovely singing voice, and she'd taught Laila every Moroccan and traditional Arab song she knew. Until arthritis had crippled her fingers and her heart had grown weak, Mamma Sophia used to play the piano regularly. She'd been Laila's first and best piano teacher.

Her grandmother also used to read to her frequently when she was a little girl. Laila credited Sophia largely with her love of words and music. Now that Mamma Sophia was older, and her eyesight and her arthritis had grown worse, leaving her bedridden much of the time, their roles had been switched. Laila now often read to her, or merely visited with her while they sipped tea and Mamma Sophia lay propped up in bed.

So she felt a little guilty at not wanting to share a room with her grandmother tonight. But she found the idea of sleeping in the open air of the porch especially appealing, given her recent bouts of restlessness and claustrophobia.

Of horniness, a snide voice in her head added.

But that didn't change the fact that if she couldn't be alone, being with her cousins on the large sleeping porch in the open air was the next best thing.

At around one o'clock in the morning, Laila, Zara and Tahi were still awake. The three of them formed a triangle on the floor of the sleeping porch, each of them lying on top of an air mattress and a sleeping bag. It was a warm, humid summer night. Thanks to the rows of opened screened-in windows, the cool lake breeze, her brief sleepwear and a humming fan, Laila was comfortable, however. The interior of Zara's family's bungalow had been silent and dark for hours now. Thanks to years of experience, the girls knew that the distant sound of waves hitting the beach and the fan easily muffled their quiet conversations from the sleeping household.

"He told me I should come to visit him in New York this fall," Zara said, referring to Eric.

"Is that where he lives?" Laila asked.

Zara nodded. "He works in Manhattan. He's the East Coast manager of marketing—or something like that—for Gaites-Granville Media. I know it's something in marketing, and he's the head of it. That's just another thing Eric and I have in common: marketing."

"You mean he's taken two classes in it at the local junior college too?"

"Shut up, Tahi. You're just jealous. You know Eric got his degree in marketing from Harvard last year. He lives in Great Neck Estates, where all these really rich people live," Zara said, focusing solely on Laila.

"So he works for his daddy and lives with him too," Tahi said drolly. "Do you *really* think all those stuck-up, rich WASPs are going to welcome *you* with open arms?"

"You live with your daddy," Zara shot back, her eyes gleaming in the darkness.

"So do you," Tahi reminded her.

"Cut it out, you two," Laila said wearily in her frequent role of peacekeeper between her cousins.

"It's not the same thing at all. Their house in Great Neck is a huge mansion, even bigger than Asher's parents' house on the beach," Zara said, once again speaking solely to Laila. Laila couldn't help but notice that her cousin had avoided responding to Tahi's cynical comment about Eric's family welcoming her with open arms. Knowing Zara, her cousin was having uncertainties about that issue too, and was willfully repressing her concerns. Zara always did have the ability to focus solely on a good time. "He has a whole wing of the house to himself, and his own entrance and everything. Can you believe it? I've never even met a millionaire before. Now I'm dating one. And you are too, Laila."

"Asher and I aren't dating," Laila assured her. "And Asher isn't a millionaire. His parents are wealthy, that's all."

"Same difference. Who do you think is going to inherit all that money? Asher is an only son, and Eric only has an older sister to split things with. Tahi, you should blow off that Rudy and focus on Jim. Eric said Jim's family is loaded," Zara said.

Tahi rolled her eyes and scooted closer to Laila. "You met with Asher today. There has to be *something* to tell. Jim said that Asher is really interested in you."

"He did?" Laila asked, her skin roughening.

"Yeah. So did Rudy. You've been dodging our questions all night. Zara's told us practically everything, including the direction Eric swirls his tongue when he kisses." Zara made a disgusted sound and slapped Tahi's shoulder. Tahi rubbed the spot on her skin and ignored her. "Come on, spill it. Tell us what happened when you met with Asher."

"We just went to a beach close to the white house and swam." Laila sidestepped the question. "We talked. He's really smart. He's starting work at the *L.A. Times* later this summer as an international reporter."

"He's so gorgeous," Tahi said fervently.

Zara frowned. "Eric told me that Asher was going to work for GGM in Chicago."

Laila's heart jumped into her throat. "Oh . . . I shouldn't have said that about the *L.A. Times*. *Don't* say anything to Eric. Asher hasn't mentioned it to his parents yet. *Please*, Zara? I mean it."

Zara shrugged. "No problem, it's no sweat off my back." Laila exhaled in relief. She'd almost blown things for Asher. He'd want to be the one to break the news about his job to his parents, not have them hear it from Eric or by a rumor. "But why does he want a job as a reporter? He can't make very much money doing that compared to the kind of job he'd get at GGM, can he? Unless the *L.A. Times* is one of GGM's newspapers?"

"I don't think so," Laila said, thinking. "I don't think Asher wants to work for the family business."

"That seems kind of stupid. I'd—" Zara stopped speaking abruptly at the sound of movement just outside the porch. A slow smile curved her full lips.

"They're here," she whispered, her eyes shining in the darkness.

"*Who's* here?" Tahi hissed when Zara rolled over to the floor on all fours.

"The guys. They went to a club over in Crescent Bay tonight. Eric said they'd stop by afterward."

"But . . . how did they know you'd be out *here* on the porch?" Laila asked disbelievingly, watching in amazement as Zara stood and smoothed her long, tumbling hair, all the while peering out the windows into the darkness. Someone scratched a fingernail softly against one of the screens. Excited anxiety shivered down Laila's spine at the furtive sound.

"Because I told them," Zara whispered. "I told him we'd *all* be out here. That's the reason I asked Baba if we could sleep on the porch tonight, dummies." Zara leapt gazelle-like over Laila's reclining form and rushed over to the screen door. Laila made out several tall male shadows in the moonlight. She and Tahi shared a look of openmouthed shock. Zara was by far the most daring of them all, but she'd never been quite *this* audacious before.

"She's lost her mind," Laila whispered.

"I was wondering why she wore makeup and her jewelry to bed," Tahi muttered, before she too leapt up from her sleeping bag.

"*Tahi*," Laila hissed, but apparently Zara's madness was catching. She watched, frozen, as Tahi slipped out the screen door after

Zara, her pale T-shirt gleaming in the moonlight. She heard the very muffled sound of a male voice over the sound of the waves on the distant beach.

Was Asher out there?

Her heartbeat started to hammer in her ears in the strained silence. She wasn't sure how long she lay there in stunned amazement and mounting excitement, but suddenly, the screen door opened silently. Tahi came to kneel beside her. She whispered near her ear.

"Asher is up on the dune road. He refuses to come down to the beach."

"Why?"

"Eric said he wanted to drive Rudy's car after they left the club, and he brought them all here without telling them where they were going. Asher is furious. Rudy says he might calm down if you go up and talk to him."

"But why is—"

"We're all going to take a walk down the beach. The moonlight is really bright. You should just run up the dune and talk to Asher."

"Tahi, we can't. *Ami* Reda and Nadine are going to find out we're gone."

"Are you kidding? We'll be even quieter gone than we were while we were talking all night, and they never hear *that*. You're not going to leave Asher up there all alone, are you?"

Her cousin stood silently. Her lungs frozen, Laila watched Tahi silently slip out the screen door.

Chapter Eight

A few minutes later, she jogged up the dune, the sand feeling cool beneath her bare feet. Her heart chugged like an out-of-control locomotive in her chest. She wore only her sleeping attire: a pair of thin cotton shorts and a tank top.

She'd never done anything like this before. Sure, she, Zara and Tahi had come up with some pretty elaborate stories in order to sneak off to parties, or on a few memorable occasions, to attend concerts at the Palace in Auburn Hills to see performances by some of Laila's favorite music idols.

But she'd never snuck out of the house in the middle of the night to meet up with a guy. Laila couldn't imagine doing it for anyone other than *him*.

Why hadn't he come down with the other guys?

She squinted above her and made out the top of the dune against the moonlit sky. The road was just several yards past it.

Asher is up there, somewhere.

Just thinking his name called to mind his gleaming light eyes, the intense expression on his handsome face, his hands coasting across her bare skin, his tall, strong body . . .

A stitch pierced her side, the result of her nervousness and erratic breathing. Tahi had said Asher was furious and didn't want to come down to the cottage, like the other guys had. But *why* was he mad, precisely? Did he not want to come with the others because he'd decided he didn't want to see her, and was irritated that Eric had stopped here?

The thought made her feet falter as she crested the top of the dune. *Damn.* Why hadn't she thought of that possibility before she ran like a crazy woman through the night?

Because I would have done much more for the possibility of seeing his face again, she realized with a sinking feeling.

Fuck this.

Asher checked his watch impatiently. They'd been down there for over ten minutes. Eric had taken the keys to Rudy's rental car with him and left Asher stranded.

He couldn't believe the balls of Eric, or that Rudy and Jimmy had gone along with his dumb-ass scheme. It had been Eric who had masterminded the whole thing . . . him and Zara, Laila's cousin. Not that Asher was excusing Rudy and Jimmy for going along with the whole thing.

Didn't Eric get how much trouble Laila and her cousins could get in, if they were caught? No. All that selfish jerk cared about was his dick.

All you're worried about is that Eric will ruin your chances of seeing Laila in the future. So Eric took it a step further than you would have tonight. You were all too willing to cross the line this afternoon, a sarcastic voice in his head said.

But that'd been different. When it was just Laila and him, everything was different.

Just thinking her name made him grit his teeth furiously. What was she thinking, right this minute? He cursed under his breath and pushed himself off the parked car door, where he'd been leaning. He lunged into the road.

Fuck Eric. He'd walk home. And pray his idiot friends didn't get caught so that there was a chance he'd see Laila tomorrow or the next day—

"Asher."

The hairs rose on his arms at the breathy call. He turned and saw Laila walking toward him. She appeared luminous in the moonlight. Her long hair tumbled around her shoulders and down her back. His gaze lowered. *Jesus.* She was hardly wearing anything.

She approached him, her bare feet looking pale and somehow vulnerable on the blacktop of the road.

"You're not wearing any shoes," he said stupidly. It wasn't all she wasn't wearing, he thought, jerking his gaze off the vision of her breasts pressed against very thin, nearly translucent fabric. In the bright moonlight, he could easily make out her small, erect nipples.

"I know. I wasn't wearing any when your friends arrived," she said, an uncertain smile on her lips as she approached him.

He frowned. "They didn't . . . they didn't see you, did they?" For some reason, he hated the idea of Eric or his friends seeing her so vulnerable. So beautiful.

"*What?*" she asked shakily, coming to a stop in front of him. She glanced down at herself and crossed her arms over her chest self-consciously. "No, I don't think so. They were all walking on the beach already."

He barely stifled a curse. He shoved his hands in his jeans pockets, realizing how idiotic he'd sounded. She was wearing more now than she would at a beach in a bikini. It was just that . . . he was even more aware of her than he had been at the beach this afternoon. She'd looked like something out of a dream, walking toward him with her dark hair spilling around her shoulders and the moonlight making her smooth limbs gleam . . .

He shook his head when he realized she was staring at him worriedly.

"I'm sorry about all this. It wasn't my idea," he assured her, waving a hand toward the beach in the distance.

"I know. Tahi told me that you didn't want to come down. And that you were mad," she said softly.

"I didn't want Eric to get you in trouble," he bit out, fury building like steam in his blood all over again. "He's not my friend, by the way." He noticed her confusion. "You called him my friend earlier. He's not. He's a distant relative, and I'd be blessed if I never had to see his smug-ass, pretty boy face ever again."

She looked a little blank with shock, and he realized how blisteringly pissed he'd sounded. He opened his mouth to apologize, but suddenly, she laughed softly. He stilled at the vision of her small white teeth.

"He really is. *Pretty*, isn't he?"

"Don't tell me you've joined his fan club," he said, glancing at her darkly from beneath a lowered brow.

She put up her hands in a surrender gesture, barely hiding a grin. "I'm hardly a fan. Zara, on the other hand, is ready to fall down and worship him." All traces of a smile faded. She crossed her arms over her breasts again. Her nipples were very stiff. "It's kind of worrisome, actually. Tahi and I have been trying to warn her to take it easy, but you don't know Zara." He blinked and forced his attention back on what she was saying. "Zara falls in love regularly, but I've never seen her get *this* worked up over a guy so fast."

Their gazes held for a few seconds. Suddenly, she ducked her head. His muscles tightened in restraint. He wanted to hold her.

Badly.

"Do you think your parents are going to find out you're out of the house?"

"We weren't sleeping at our cottage. We were at Zara's parents' place. Not that it matters. If they figure out we're gone, my parents will hear about it, eventually. But they usually never hear us, and we've been known to talk all night."

He stared out at a moonlit Lake Michigan and shifted on his feet.

"Asher?"

"Yeah?"

"Is everything okay?"

He focused on her face. "Yeah," he said after a pause.

He saw her swallow. "It's not, though. Is it?" she asked so quietly that he almost didn't hear her voice above the distant surf. "Have you changed your mind about what you said this afternoon? Would you rather not see me again, after everything I told you?"

"What? *No*."

"I'm not easy." She seemed to hear what she'd said and laughed self-consciously. "I mean, I know it's complicated. I'm complicated. *We* would be."

He stepped forward rapidly and wrapped his arms around her, the fronts of their bodies coming into contact. God, she felt better than he'd been anticipating. If that was even possible.

"I know it's complicated. I know it too well," he said, looking down into her upturned face. He stepped even closer, pressing their bodies tight, feeling himself spark to life. "It's worth it."

"But why are you acting so mad? Is it really just because of Eric?"

"I'm mad because I'm just as selfish as him," he admitted, his hands moving of their own volition along her supple back.

"What?"

"I'm pissed because your parents would hate the idea of you seeing me. I'm mad because this stupid plan of Eric's might be risking any chance of seeing you again. I'm furious because even though I hate my stupid cousin, I'm starting to think I'm being just as selfish with you as he's being with Zara. I *don't* like to be compared to Eric. Especially in my own head."

He saw her face go flat with amazement at his bitter recitation of facts.

"You mean that you think you're being like Eric, because all you want to do is have a vacation fling with me, no matter what the circumstances?" she asked, her voice sounding hollow. He cringed inwardly.

"I don't want to hurt you, Laila. I don't. And I'm *not* Eric. But I'm no saint either." He gritted his teeth in determination and palmed her ass, pressing her tight against his aroused body to make a point.

"Do you feel that? I want you . . . in a way I don't remember ever wanting anything," he stated hoarsely. "Where do you think this is going to go, if we keep this up? Is that what you want?"

He saw her mouth fall open at his display of crudeness. *Damn.* He was turning her off, but he only wanted to be fair—

"Let's go for a walk," she said softly.

"I'm . . . *what?*"

Starlight and moonlight gleamed in her eyes as she looked up at him. Or maybe it was just Laila herself. She shone all on her own.

"Down the dune a ways. Let's go find a private spot," she clarified, backing out of his embrace and taking his hand.

They walked for several minutes. She wasn't sure what had come over her, saying what she had. Her skin was flushed with heat and it felt like a hundred butterflies fluttered in anxious desperation in her stomach. If everything didn't look so crystal clear in front of her eyes, and if her senses weren't pitched to such a high degree, she'd think she was getting sick.

"How's this?" she heard Asher say beside her. He waved at an empty stretch of dune, the sand gleaming white in the moonlight. Laila nodded and started to sit.

"Wait," he said abruptly. She paused, still standing, and glanced back at him expectantly. "Your shorts. They're really . . ." He cleared this throat. "Thin."

She brushed her hands against her hips and buttocks, feeling the insubstantial cotton and her panties beneath it. Was the moonlight so strong Asher was seeing through her clothes? He started unbuttoning his shirt.

"What are you doing?" she asked. He didn't respond immediately, just whipped his shirt off his shoulders and down his arms. He was muscular, but lean. The ridges of his cut torso rippled in the pale silver light. He spread his shirt on the sand. "You don't have to—"

"I know it. My jeans are enough." He grasped her upper arm and urged her down. She sat on his shirt, bending her knees in front and setting her crossed forearms on them. He came down beside her and matched her pose.

"Thanks."

"No problem," he said, his gaze on her. His face looked mysterious, limned by shadow and moonlight. He suddenly looked out at the Great Lake.

"It's amazing, how bright the moon can make it," he said.

"It reflects off the white of the sand, making it seem even brighter," she murmured. For a moment, they just stared out at the glistening water.

"So . . . have you ever done this before?" he asked after a pause.

"Done *what*?"

"Escaped out into the night."

She laughed softly. "No, I can't say that I have. Not specifically like this, anyway."

"You always do what your parents want you to do?"

She scowled. "Of course not. I'm not that much of a prude."

"You're very dutiful. Very sweet." She glanced at him in surprise. "That's how Tahi described you. Last night at Chauncy's. She also told me you're smart. You got into both Michigan State and the University of Michigan, but your parents talked you into staying at home and going to Wayne State."

She rolled her eyes. Tahi hadn't told her she'd blabbed those particular details. Her cousin was going to be hearing from Laila about it. She didn't like being portrayed as a prim little goody-two-shoes. Just because she cared about other people—like her mom and dad and Mamma Sophia—didn't make her straitlaced.

"So what *do* you do? When you're not being dutiful? What's Laila's version of living on the edge?" he asked. His small, teasing smile distracted her. She cleared her throat and stared out at the lake, searching her brain for a good answer.

"I've arranged for Tahi, Zara and me to go to some concerts and music venues before . . . ones my mother wouldn't approve of."

"Why wouldn't she approve of them?"

"My mom loves music," Laila tried to explain. "If she's not

watching one of her soap operas, she's listening to her music on her iPod."

"But she doesn't like you going to concerts?"

Laila shook her head, still staring out at the midnight water. "Not to see the kind of music I like, anyway. She's crazy about traditional Moroccan and Arabic music, but she disapproves of most of my music."

"What kind of music do you like that she disapproves of?"

"All kinds. R&B. Pop. Jazz. The blues. Hip-hop. I even like my mamma's and Mamma Sophia's traditional music, even though Mamma doesn't like mine," she said, grinning and warming to the topic. "Zara, Tahi and I have been to some amazing concerts at Auburn Hills: Alicia Keys, Rihanna, Beyoncé, Sade. I really like this one singer, Djazia Satour—have you heard of her?" He shook his head. "She's this amazing French-Algerian singer who does trip hop, some jazz and bluesy stuff . . ." She realized how much she was gushing and laughed. "Sorry. I can get going on the topic. Most people tune me out, after a while."

"Never apologize for being passionate." A shiver coursed through her when she heard the warmth in his tone. She felt his stare on her cheek like a light caress. "All women singers? Is that because you're a singer?"

She blinked, taken aback slightly. She'd forgotten he'd heard her singing the afternoon at the secret lake.

"Not necessarily. I like Outlandish. Have you heard of them? They're a Danish hip-hop group, but they have an amazing Moroccan lead singer—"

She noticed his smile.

"What?" she wondered.

"You want to be a professional singer, don't you?"

"What? *No.* Maybe," she added lamely after a pause. She swallowed thickly. The truth hurt in her throat. "I don't think I could ever be a singer, really, but it would be so amazing if one of those women could sing my songs."

"The ones you've written?"

She nodded.

"How do you do that?" she asked slowly after a pause.

"Do what?"

"Read me like that." she replied softly. "Not one person in my family has ever recognized the things about me that you have. Not for my whole life," she said, looking at him. "And yet you've realized it in two days."

"That's because I'm seeing you. Not what I expect you to be."

His words seemed to vibrate in her flesh.

"Do you have any of the music you like here, in Crescent Bay?" he asked.

She nodded. "On my phone."

"Bring it with you the next time we meet. Bring your music too. The stuff you've written."

"You can read music?"

"No. But I can read your lyrics."

Her cheeks heated at the idea of him looking at something that had remained private for so long, of him experiencing her in such an intimate way. The idea both mortified and excited her. "Maybe," she hedged. "But like I said, I don't think I can come tomorrow in the afternoon. Zarif doesn't leave until four—"

"Tomorrow night, then? Rudy told me he asked your cousins and you to come over to my parents' place."

"I didn't say yes, though."

She saw his posture stiffen. "Why not?"

"Because *you* didn't ask, Rudy did. I wasn't sure if you actually were okay with it."

He exhaled a laugh. "I'm okay with it, trust me. And I'm asking now. Will you?"

"I'd like to."

"We'll take the boat out and swim."

"That sounds fun. We'll just say that we're going out to eat in town, after Zarif leaves."

"Excellent." For a moment, they just stared at each other. "Listen," he said after a charged pause. "About what I said back there, about being selfish—"

She put her hand on his forearm, cutting him off. He stilled beneath her touch.

"I don't think you're being selfish. I'm here of my own free will, Asher. Do you think I'm selfish?"

"No," he said grimly. "I think you're the opposite of selfish." He lifted her hand and pressed his lips to her knuckles. Shivers poured through her at the sensation of his mouth moving against her skin. Astonished at her courage, she reached and touched his face, her fingers trailing across his cheek and jaw. She saw the gleam of moonlight in his eyes, and suddenly he was bracketing her jaw with his hands and tilting her face up to his. His mouth covered hers. She moaned shakily, overwhelmed by a kiss that was both demanding and gentle at once.

Intoxicating.

The kiss deepened. She loved sensing his hunger. Feeling it grow. One of his hands continued to cradle the side of her head, but the other cupped her shoulder, his fingers sliding against the skin of her back, fully awakening her already-sensitized nerves. She glided her hands up the top of his naked arms and shoulders, a thrill going through her. She felt his skin roughen beneath her fingertips and knew he liked her touch. The fever that had been lingering in her flesh ever since she'd left him this afternoon spiked high once again.

He was so beautiful. She wanted to touch him everywhere.

His big hands spread around the side of her ribs, the ridge of his thumbs resting just beneath the lower curve of her breasts. He groaned roughly and sealed their kiss, keeping their lips in contact.

"I love the way you feel in my hands."

"I love the way I feel in your hands too," she breathed out against his lips.

He leaned back slightly, his stare spearing her. He moved his thumbs, caressing her nipples through her tank top. She shuddered slightly, a potent shock of pleasure shooting through her. She clamped her thighs together to alleviate the ache there, a soft moan escaping her lips.

"Shhh," he soothed, even though he continued to rub her nipples with his thumb, agitating her nerves. "Does it feel good?" he asked, his breath whisking across her lips.

"Yes," she replied through a tight throat.

"Do you have any idea how beautiful you look right now? How incredible you feel?" he asked, his thumbs continuing to rub her nipples. They were so sensitive to his touch, it was like a pinching pleasure. She bit off a moan, and then Asher was kissing her again, his mouth hungrier this time. He cradled both of her breasts in his hands, massaging her gently even though his kiss was fierce. Her hands moved anxiously on his back. She squeezed his rounded shoulder muscles and then his hard, defined biceps, the fire in her beginning to rage.

A spike of panic penetrated her intense, unprecedented arousal.

She broke their kiss, gasping raggedly against his seeking lips. "Asher, I feel so—"

"So fantastic, it's almost unreal," he muttered distractedly, nibbling at her mouth. She placed her hands on his sides, amazed at the feeling of his body, the strength coiling tight in him. She skimmed the length of his torso from the top of his rib cage to his waist, down and up and down, loving the slant from lean waist up to powerful chest.

"God," he muttered, and his hand moved, slipping beneath her tank top. She froze at the sensation of him cupping her bare breast. He stilled too. Anticipation swelled high in her. He pinched her nipple gently. She almost jumped clear off the sand.

"What?" he asked sharply. "Did I hurt you?"

"No. It felt so *good*. I don't know what's wrong," she moaned raggedly, seeking his mouth again. He pulled back slightly, studying her. He looked *worried*. Maybe he *should* be. She felt odd. Fevered. Dizzy. No . . . she was like a balloon being overfilled. The internal pressure was too much.

"I think I do. Luckily, it's very curable," he said suddenly.

He slid his hand between her legs, his manner striking her as matter-of-fact. Firm. Air rushed out of her lungs as he began to rub her sex through her shorts and underwear. She made a disbelieving sound as the friction inside her soared. A shock rippled through her flesh. His mouth moved on her neck and he spoke in a low, rough voice near her ear.

"It's okay. Just let go, Laila."

The feeling surrounded her, controlling her versus her controlling it. She made an anguished sound, twisting her hips against the pressure of his fingers. His free hand spread across her lower back and hip, keeping her steady while his fingers moved and agitated her flesh. The pressure built in her until she clamped her eyes closed in a hopeless attempt to stop it.

She shuddered in release.

He continued to touch her, even through the aftershocks. He pressed kisses against her ear and spoke to her. His deep voice melded with the sound of her pounding heart. It took her a few seconds to really interpret what he was saying.

"You're so sweet. So warm. I feel your heat, even through your shorts."

She drew up her knees abruptly, knocking aside his hand. She looped her arms around her knees and gasped raggedly.

What the hell had just happened?

"What's wrong?" he asked, clearly startled by her abrupt action. He was obviously confused. But he couldn't be as confused as her.

She pressed her forehead against her arms. She couldn't speak, so she just shook her head.

"Laila?" The sound of disbelieving concern in his voice swelled her pain. He put his hand on her back and moved it in a soothing motion. "Didn't it feel good?"

She nodded against her forearm, miserable. Suddenly, she couldn't take it anymore. She began to stand.

"Hey . . . *Hey*, where're you going?" he asked, sounding stunned. He caught her shoulders, halting her. She stopped trying to scramble off the beach and fell back on her butt, gasping. He touched her cheek. "Talk to me. Please. What's wrong?"

"I've never done that before," she blurted out. Her face pinched tight in acute embarrassment. His soothing hand on her back stilled.

"You're never had an orgasm?"

"Yes, I've done that," she mumbled, still clamping her eyes tight. She couldn't believe it had happened. Now they were *talking* about it, which was almost as bad. "Just not . . . with someone."

The silence felt like it lasted for an eternity, but probably was all of two seconds long.

"Oh. I see," he said, resuming rubbing her back. His tone was even. Confident. It told her that *he* did get it. He wasn't bullshitting her. "That's nothing to be embarrassed about. That's . . . that's amazing."

"It's not just that," she said in a choked tone. God, could this possibly be more horrifying?

"Then what?" he asked, sounding puzzled. Concerned.

She lifted her head. Did she really have to spell it out for him?

"You barely even touched me for *three* seconds, and I was . . ." She covered her hot face, drowning in shame.

He laughed softly. She lowered her hands and glowered at him. Here she was, shocked by her unprecedented physical reaction, the strength of it . . . the *quickness* of it, and he was *laughing* at her?

This time, she succeeding in shoving herself up off the beach. She made a beeline in the direction they'd come, fueled by mortified outrage. He caught her elbow.

"Laila, stop. Listen to me."

She spun around, his laughter still ringing in her head. She popped her palm against his shoulder. He started.

"You laughed at me."

"I wasn't laughing at you," he defended, grasping her shoulders.

"Yes, you were!" she sputtered, pointing to where they'd sat on the beach.

"I was laughing at *myself*. At both of us, more accurately." Even though what he'd said wasn't flattering, something about the helpless earnestness of his tone penetrated her mortification.

"What . . . what do you mean?"

"Do you think I wasn't worked up too? After being at the beach with you today?"

She just stared up at his shadowed face, her mouth hanging open. He lowered his head until their faces were just inches apart. "I came just as quickly as you did. It's nothing to be ashamed of. There's a lot of chemistry between us. More than I've ever experienced."

She blinked. She'd never had anyone say something like that

to her before. Yet from Asher's mouth, the words didn't sound coarse or dirty. Just private.

Exciting.

Still, she was confused.

"You mean . . . you mean, just *now*?" she asked hollowly.

He chuckled but immediately cut himself off. He must have felt her stiffen beneath his hands, and didn't want to offend her again.

"No. At the secret lake. After you left."

She pictured it suddenly, the vivid image striking her unprepared brain like a blow. Her flesh quivered in the aftermath.

"You just hadn't gotten a chance for any relief yet. Right?" he asked. He opened his hand at the side of her head, his thumb caressing her cheek softly.

She thought of how prickly she'd been all afternoon and night . . . how she couldn't stop thinking about him. She'd tried to touch herself in the shower but had been stopped by her mother and grandmother. That'd been why she'd been so primed to detonate when he finally did touch her.

"Right," she whispered hesitantly. Were they *really* having this conversation?

"Well, I had. Quite a few times, actually," he added in a distracted tone, as if he was counting the moments.

Laughter burst out of her throat. She couldn't believe him. She popped his shoulder again, this time in amused remonstrance. His deep laughter twined with hers.

"I'm just being honest. What can I say? Guys are pigs."

"You're not a pig," she managed to say between jags of laughter. He stepped closer, drawing her against him once again.

"I don't know," he said. Her laughter quieted at his more somber tone. "All I know is that I want you so much. And that you're so beautiful," he said, his lips brushing her temple. "*Especially* when you feel good. Never be embarrassed by who you are or what you feel. You're too special to ever run from anything."

"I wasn't running because of that," she whispered, turning her face up and nuzzling his chin.

His lips grazed hers. "Weren't you?"

"Ash."

The breath she'd been holding in her lungs when he'd asked her that pointed question popped out of her throat.

"Jimmy?" Asher asked, looking past Laila's shoulder.

"Yeah. We're all waiting at the car," Jim said in a hushed tone.

"Is everything okay?" Asher asked.

"Yeah. All is still quiet. Tahi just kicked us out, and told me to find Laila and send her back."

Relief swept through her at the news they hadn't been caught. *Yet*, anyway. She glanced up at Asher uncertainly as she stepped out of his embrace. She'd never answered his question. She wasn't sure if she could.

So somehow, it kept hovering around in her head.

Asher insisted on driving home, still pissed at Eric for hijacking them. Once they were all in the car and headed for the beach house, Eric reached to turn on the stereo to the aggressive rap music he'd been blaring earlier.

"Don't."

Eric glanced over at him from the passenger seat. "What's got your knickers in a twist?" he asked snidely, but at least he dropped his hand from the stereo.

If Asher couldn't be with Laila anymore tonight, then he craved quiet. He was desperate for privacy. He could barely tolerate his friends at that moment, let alone Eric and his loud music. "Or should I even ask what's wrong? Did Snow White leave you high and dry again? Snow *White*." Eric's snide laughter and dumb-ass racist joke broke through Asher's fraying attempt at calm. It would be one thing if it were the first time Eric had ever demonstrated prejudice and elitism. Unfortunately, Asher had experienced it dozens of times in the past. Hearing it leveled at Laila shattered his restraint.

Rudy yelped from the backseat when Asher jerked the car over to the side of the country road and braked hard. He leaned toward Eric.

"You are *gone* if you ever talk about her like that again, you racist pig. Do you understand me? And that face of yours isn't going to look too pretty when you fly out the front door either," Asher seethed, gripping the wheel in lieu of his cousin's neck.

Eric looked startled at his abrupt fury. But then he laughed roughly, choosing to take the threat as a joke.

"You wouldn't want to upset your mama like that, would you? She was so insistent that I come here."

"I don't care if my mother begged you. We both know I upset her all the time, so it won't be a new experience for her. I just want to make sure I'm making myself clear."

Eric's jaw tightened and he looked away. After a tense few seconds, Asher decided to take his sullen silence as a passive acquiescence. He rolled the car back onto the road.

"You *do* usually go for the brainy, smoking-hot, ballsy chicks," Rudy said cautiously from the backseat after a strained pause. Asher heard the hint of puzzlement in his friend's tone. "Laila's gorgeous, but . . . well, she's not your typical."

"I would have thought that was obvious," Asher said, staring straight ahead at the road.

Chapter Nine

It was a little after five the next evening when Zara turned her car onto the private road that led to Asher's parents' lake house. It hadn't been all that hard for them to get away. Laila's father and uncles had returned to Detroit for work, and the aunties and her mom were looking forward to taking it easy after the excitement of Zarif's visit. Laila had managed to get away without promising her mom she'd be home at a certain time. Since they'd told everyone they were going to play putt-putt golf in Crescent Bay, then go to dinner and a late movie, a wonderfully long stretch of the night was free.

The white house came into view on the horizon. Nerves and excitement flickered in Laila's stomach. She rubbed her belly nervously. In the front seats, Zara and Tahi were unusually quiet as they approached the house, as well.

"I can't believe we're actually going to the *white house*," Tahi said, glancing back at Laila and grinning. She looked especially pretty tonight, wearing a short strapless sapphire-blue dress, her long, highlighted brown hair spilling around her tanned shoulders. They'd all tucked their swimsuits and beach cover-ups in their purses, since they'd been invited for a swim.

Tahi had confessed to Laila earlier that afternoon that she liked Rudy. *"But not in an 'I-have-to-have-him-or-die' kind of way. He's cute, though. He makes me laugh. But it's not like Zara likes Eric, or you—"*

Her cousin had halted herself when Laila shook her head repressively once. She wasn't going to gossip to Tahi at the moment. Not about Asher, she wasn't. Something about what was happening between them was unique. So intensely personal. At least to Laila it was.

As Zara pulled into the circular drive, Laila replayed seemingly for the thousandth time how he'd touched her so surely last night. He'd known what she needed, even when she'd been ignorant. She recalled how she'd combusted after only a few strokes, and again experienced that wave of mixed mortification and pure excitement.

Zara parked. Almost immediately, the front door opened. Asher stepped out, wearing a pair of black swim trunks. He'd thrown on a white button-down shirt and was in the process of buttoning it while he walked toward them. Laila caught a glimpse of his chest and ridged, tanned abdomen. She pressed her fingertips to her hot cheeks.

"Yum. Eee," Tahi said succinctly.

"Down, girl," Zara said amusedly. She glanced back at Laila, hazel eyes sparkling. "I don't know how you did it, but you did it, little girl. He *is* smoking."

"I'm not a little girl," Laila muttered, most of her focus on Asher coming alongside the car. He opened Zara's door first, and then Laila's.

He bent and smiled at her before he reached out for her hand. "Hi," he greeted her.

"Hi," she responded breathlessly, getting out of the car. He didn't let go when she stood in front of him on the drive. His eyes looked sharp and brilliantly blue in the bright afternoon sunlight. They trailed down over her, his expression appreciative. Her heart seemed to lodge at the base of her throat. She knew she looked better than usual. Tahi had insisted she borrow a dress of hers: a simple, natural-looking ivory dress that showed off both her figure and tan well. With it, she wore sandals, a gold bracelet and earrings. Zara had done the traditional pullover into a parking lot a few miles after they'd left the cottages in order to make alterations on their wardrobes and put on makeup. Laila had uncharacteristically applied mascara and lip gloss.

"You look amazing," Asher said, squeezing her hand. His head dipped forward. "And you smell fantastic."

"Thanks."

"But you look too nice to go swimming."

"I brought a suit," she said, patting her bag.

"Brilliant." His head dipped even further, his mouth brushing hers. Electricity tingled just beneath her skin. Someone made an impatient sound.

"Can we just go in, Asher? It looks like you two might be at it for a while," Zara said drolly.

"Sure," Asher said, lifting his head. Still holding Laila's hand, he led them inside.

"*Look* at this," Zara muttered when they walked into a large entryway. Her stunned tone matched Laila's reaction. They walked into what would have corresponded to the second floor of the house onto an elevated balcony. In front of and below them was an enormous, airy great room. The lake side of the house was almost entirely floor-to-ceiling windows, overlooking the sun-gilded lake and a terrace with a pool. The sheer hugeness of the house, the wide-open space was what struck Laila the most, even more than the luxury of it. What would it be like, to have so much freedom to move in, so much glorious *space*?

"I'm bartending. What's your pleasure, ladies?" someone called out. Rudy stood behind a bar that stretched outside the kitchen area, near the terrace doors.

"This way," Asher said, pulling gently on her hand. He led them down some stairs. Through the terrace doors, Laila saw Eric and Jim lounging by the pool. Jim turned and waved, and she waved back. Tahi and Zara walked up to the bar and started talking to Rudy.

"This place is amazing," Laila said when she and Asher paused several feet away. "You must have loved coming here, when you were a kid."

"Most of the time, I did."

"*Most* of the time?" she asked curiously.

He shrugged. "Mostly when I was here alone. With just my nanny," he added when she gave him a puzzled glance. "Which was really just the same as being alone."

"You weren't lonely?" she asked quietly. As much as she admired all the open space, she knew she would have been lonely as a kid there. She couldn't imagine not having someone from her close-knit family around. Her family was always there, like some kind of protective blanket. Lately, she'd been feeling a little suffocated by that blanket, but family was still elemental to her . . . part of the weave of her life.

He paused, as if considering. "Maybe once in a while I was lonely. I usually like being alone, though."

"So do I. Mostly because I hardly ever am." He returned her smile.

"Do you want something to drink?"

"Oh . . . I'll have a Coke or something."

"Nothing harder?"

She shook her head. "No, I don't drink, really."

"Do you mind if I do?"

She blinked, taken off guard by his question.

"No, of course not."

"I won't drink much, I promise."

"Asher, do whatever you want," she exclaimed. "I'm not being judgmental. Alcohol just doesn't work well with my body. I get looped on half a glass of wine."

"Oh. So it's not a religious thing? Your preference?"

She shrugged, a little perplexed. "I don't think of it that way. We don't ever have alcohol at home, but that's not the issue with me. It's purely a personal thing. Case in point," she said amusedly, glancing over to the bar where Rudy was shaking a vodka martini—Zara's favorite—while Tahi sipped a glass of white wine.

"I don't want to do anything that makes you uncomfortable."

"You're *not*. Asher, where's all this coming from?" she wondered.

"We've got really different backgrounds. I just don't want to make any wrong assumptions, that's all."

She stared up at him, a little stunned. She wasn't used to it. Constantly, she walked a fine line between acting like her culture and background were of no account when she interacted with people at school or work. At the same time, she was very aware when other people ignored her ethnicity, or simply got it wrong. Some people assumed she was Hispanic, an error that was only reinforced by the fact that she spoke fairly fluent Spanish, because Darija contained a lot of Spanish and French words. Other people seemed to think it was impolite to ask her about her ethnicity. Some realized she was some strain of Arabic but never clarified what her specific ethnicity was, apparently thinking all Arabic cultures were one and the same. Or maybe they just found the topic an uncomfortable one.

And yet . . . Asher was willing to go there.

"Asher, that's really sweet. Thank you," she said sincerely.

He looked a little embarrassed. "I just don't want to do something wrong, and turn you off, that's all. Purely selfish on my part."

She squeezed his hand. "You're not selfish." She repeated what she'd said last night quietly.

He gave a doubtful shrug. "I've been accused of being insensitive more than once in my life," he said dryly.

"Did you deserve it?"

"Probably."

"Well, I haven't seen it so far," she stated honestly.

"Thank God," he muttered, his teeth flashing as he grinned.

She felt a pull toward him, like a magnet had been installed in her lower belly.

And he was pure iron.

Asher took them out on the sleek speedboat tethered by the dock. Afterward, they swam in the pool and lounged around on the deck, talking.

Laila knew that she liked Jim Rothschild from their first meeting, but her warmth toward him grew as she listened to him rib Asher and Rudy, and tell some hysterical stories. She'd already heard from Tahi that Rudy was a photographer. He wanted to specialize in celebrity photos. Jimmy described a few hilarious scrapes Rudy had hooked Asher and Jimmy into, all for the sake of a photo. She loved hearing the stories about when Asher was really young. Asher and Jimmy had known each other since they were six, and Jimmy had often stayed at the lake house with Asher when they were kids.

"*I* used to stay here too," Eric said, leaning up from where he'd been having a private conversation with Zara and frequently pausing to nip at her lips, neck, arms and chest. He seemed incapable of not touching her cousin while she lay there in her bikini, a fact that made Laila increasingly uncomfortable since they were all watching. Laila didn't know what was worse: him doing it, or Zara's smug little smiles every time he became more daring in his touches or kisses. "Our parents were always throwing Asher and me together. It usually lasted for all of a half hour before Asher ditched me. He's still doing it, right, Rudy?"

"Oh, *yeah.* You ditched us the other day in the woods," Rudy said, frowning as he recalled the event. "Where'd you go, anyway? You never said."

"Just for a walk," Asher said levelly, standing. His gaze flickered across Laila, and she saw his nearly imperceptible, knowing smile. Warmth expanded inside her. It was nice, sharing a secret with him. She glanced aside and noticed Eric watching her closely.

Asher grabbed his shirt. "I should go get the stuff for the grill ready."

"I'll help you," Laila said quickly, trying to shake off Eric's stare. She stood and scurried into her cover-up.

"They make you uncomfortable." Asher said a few minutes later as he unpackaged some chicken fillets and burgers, and put them on a platter. She was in the process of cutting a tomato and glanced over at him in puzzlement. "Eric and Zara," he clarified.

"Oh. Maybe a little, yeah."

"Why?"

She turned back to her task, thinking. "A couple reasons, I guess. One, you've mentioned he . . . wasn't your favorite person," she said cautiously.

"He goes through women like a lawn mower."

"That's kind of a brutal way to put it," she said, setting down the knife. "Why do *you* dislike him? You've never really said."

For a moment, he didn't answer. Laila turned toward him and leaned against the counter, watching him methodically setting out the meat.

"All my life, he was held up as an example of the right way to do things. '*See how Eric ties his shoes? Do it like that, the way you do it is wrong. See how Eric swings the bat? That's the way I've been trying to get you to do it. Eric is going to Harvard, why did you have to pick Stanford?*'"

"Eric is working for the family business. And you're choosing not to," Laila finished quietly.

He nodded once, picking up some salt and pepper from the counter. "That'll be what I hear at the end of this vacation, only it won't sound quite so nice as the way you put it. He's always showing this fake version of himself to my parents and everyone in the family. When no one was around that he thought he should impress, he showed his true colors. He was a rude, blackmailing little monster when he was a kid. Nowadays, he's a selfish. Two-faced. Bastard," he said, emphasizing each word with a hard shake of the salt shaker. Laila noticed the tightness of his jaw and went over to him. She put her hand on his wrist, halting his action. He glanced over at her in surprise.

"You're not Eric," she said softly. "You've known that your whole life, and everyone—most notably, your parents—seemed to know it too. They just didn't see the difference as a *good* thing. And that's what really gets to you, isn't it?"

"I guess," he said gruffly after a pause.

"But it *is* a good thing, Asher. It is."

Suddenly, he leaned down and kissed her. Hard.

And then sweet.

She blinked dazedly when he lifted his head a moment later. She felt flushed and flustered. "What'd I do to deserve that?" she wondered.

"You're you."

"Thanks," she said, smiling, extremely pleased by his answer.

"*Are* you worried about Zara?" he asked. "Because I can talk to Eric, if you are."

"I don't know. Zara has always been able to take care of herself. Maybe I should be the one to talk to her. She tends to get herself in too deep sometimes. And Eric isn't the guy she should be doing that with. This situation isn't," she said, thinking. She glanced up at Asher, suddenly uneasy.

"You're wondering how smart *you're* being. Aren't you?" he asked grimly, stepping over to the sink and turning on the tap with his wrist. "With me," he added, glancing over his shoulder.

She couldn't think of what to say.

He finished washing his hands and reached for a towel. He tossed it aside a moment later and walked over to her, standing only a few inches away. She looked up when he grabbed both her hands at once.

"You said earlier there were a few reasons Zara and Eric make you uncomfortable. Is one of the reasons that they remind you of us?"

He'd hit the nail on the head. She nodded.

"I worry about the same thing. That's what I was trying to say last night. But now . . . I think maybe I was wrong."

"You do?"

He nodded slowly. She stared up at him, caught by something she read in his eyes. He stepped closer to her, so that their fronts brushed together. As always, the feeling of his body against hers created a vacuum in her lungs. It made her flesh prickle with awareness and pleasure. It confused her too. He interfered with her common sense. He cradled her jaw and tilted her face upward. She could still smell the soap on his freshly washed hands.

"I know it seems like everything is against us. We're both only here for a short period of time. You have to lie to your family and sneak away to see me, and I can tell how much you hate that. I start a new job across the country in August. Neither of our parents would approve of us seeing each other."

She flinched slightly beneath his cradling hands. She'd assumed that his parents would never approve, given what she'd learned about them so far. But suspecting and hearing him say it were two different things. Had the truth hit him this hard, when she'd said her parents wouldn't allow her to date him? If so, she hadn't given him enough credit for his stoic reaction.

"I'm sorry," he said, looking regretful. He'd noticed her flinch. "I thought it would have been obvious. The only person my parents would probably ever approve of when it comes to me is some female version of Eric."

She laughed softly, the hurt fading a little. "That's a scary thought."

"You're telling me," he muttered. "It doesn't matter what my parents think. That's not why I said it. I was just—"

"Stating the facts. I get it."

A silence swelled between them, so full of unsaid things, so heavy with doubts.

So rife with longing.

He suddenly looked reluctant.

"What?" she whispered.

"We could stop now. That'd be the smart thing to do."

"No," she said emphatically, a frisson of panic going through her at the thought of never seeing him again.

"I'm not saying I *want* to. Just the opposite. But with everything stacked against us—"

"It *would* be the wise thing," she agreed against her will.

"Before we go deeper."

She looked up into his eyes. For a split second, she saw it all there. The promise. The glint of treasure.

The deeper.

Tears stung her eyes. How could she be expected to give up on *that*?

"Laila?"

She swallowed thickly, hearing his unsaid question.

"Just give me a little time to think about it," she replied thickly, ducking her head and moving away.

They barbecued and ate once it had cooled off on the deck. Laila was determined to enjoy herself . . . to forget for the moment Asher's suggestion that perhaps they should put a stop to what was happening between them. Besides, his warm glances at her and frequent touches told her loud and clear he was as torn about the decision as she was.

Asher asked her if she wanted to take a walk down to the beach at sunset, and she agreed.

"Look at all those colors," she murmured as they walked along the edge of the lake and she stared out at the fireball of the sun dipping into the pale blue water. "It's so beautiful . . . but I resent it a little."

"Resent it?"

She gave him a sheepish smile. "It's the ending of a day we'll never get back."

"Does that mean you had a good time tonight?"

"I did," she said earnestly, studying his somber, tanned face cast in the crimson and golds of sunset. "Did you?"

"Yeah. I did," he said, giving her hand a warm squeeze. But did his smile look a little strained?

"I brought some of my music."

She didn't know what made her say it then, when they were both wrestling with their doubts. Or maybe she *did* know. She resented the barriers that stood between them so much, it made her want to risk something . . .

"You mean recordings of some of the singers and bands you like?"

"I brought those too. But I meant that I brought some of the music and lyrics I've written myself."

He walked in front of her and stopped. She halted in front of him.

"They're back at the house?"

"Yeah," she said, smiling nervously. "In my purse."

"Those prized notebooks that you've never shown anyone before?" he clarified. A small grin tilted his mouth. She realized he looked tremendously pleased. It made her heart start to drum in her ears. He reached up and moved a lock of her hair away from her face, smoothing it against her shoulder. She shivered beneath his touch, feeling the heat of his fingers beneath the thin beach cover-up she wore. He felt her tremble. She could tell by the sudden smoldering quality in his eyes.

"That's right. Not another soul. Until you," she managed to say.

"I'm honored."

She pulled a face. "Don't say that until you've actually seen them. You might decide you're cursed. They're probably horrible."

"They won't be," he said. His finger caressed the side of her neck. The tiny, fine hairs on her nape and ears prickled at his touch.

"I don't know how you could possibly say that with so much certainly," she told him frankly.

"I don't either," he mused, sounding genuinely puzzled. His lips brushed hers. Their mouths rubbed together, clung and parted. "But I *do*," he whispered, before he pulled her against him, and their mouths fused.

Laila knew she'd always remember that kiss: Asher, the doubts of the dying day and the promise of tomorrow, all of it mingling to form a fragile, perfect moment.

They stayed on the beach for a while, walking and talking until they stood beneath a midnight dome sprinkled with thousands of stars. He told her why he'd always dreamed of becoming a foreign correspondent. "I want to learn about different people and cultures. I don't want to just read about history, or watch it pass by while I sit on the sidelines. I want to be on that boat. I want to witness it firsthand."

"You're not scared? Of going to strange countries and not knowing anyone? Of not even understanding the customs or the language?"

"A little," he admitted. "But that's part of the challenge. You can't open up your world and learn anything new without stepping into unfamiliar territory. That's how you know you're growing, when things get a little uncomfortable."

She thought of how nervous she'd been on her first day of class at Wayne State, and she hadn't even had to worry about moving onto campus.

"I guess I'm a coward," she said softly.

He ran his fingertip up and down her arm until she shivered in awareness.

"You're not a coward. You brought your music tonight, didn't you?"

She nodded.

"I know how hard that must have been, when you always keep it so private. Let's go inside. I want to see it. Hear it."

When they returned to the terrace, Zara and Eric were gone.

"Where's Zara?" Laila asked Tahi.

Both Rudy and Tahi pointed toward the house in the direction of the upper floor, wry expressions on their face. Laila knew they were referring to one of the bedrooms. Heat rushed into her cheeks. She felt a little nauseated. Zara and Eric weren't Asher and her. Still, their progressing intimacy—their obvious sexual chemistry—created some type of parallel to Asher and her. While she worried about both Zara and herself getting hurt, she craved closeness with Asher even more.

It stunned her to realize that was where her slight nausea originated. It came from acknowledging and confronting that need head-on.

Asher put his hand at the small of her back and moved his head in the direction of the house. She nodded in agreement. They walked inside together. She was highly aware of Tahi's and the guys' speculative stares on their backs.

Laila grabbed her bag. Asher took her hand and started up the stairs.

God, where was he taking her? A bedroom? She felt a little dizzy and weak in the knees. When he led her into a room and turned on several lamps, she sighed in mixed disappointment and relief. They were in a pretty sitting room with feminine, elegant décor. He waved toward a large bay window where a baby grand stood.

"Do you play?" he asked her.

"Yes," she said, walking over to admire the fine piano. "My grandmother taught me. Whose is this?"

"My mother's. This is her sitting room," he said, glancing around and taking in their surroundings. His vague curiosity made her think he hadn't been in the room in a long time.

"Does she play in here often?"

"No. She did when I was really little, but not anymore. This room doesn't get used much. Music just kind of . . . faded away from her life, I guess."

"That's so sad."

"Yeah. It is. Promise me you'll never let that happen to you."

She laughed softly.

"No, I'm serious. Promise me that even if you end up being some kind of business mogul, you'll never give up your music."

She snorted at the idea of her ever becoming a titan of business. Asher continued to appear dead serious, though. So she promised him.

"But only because I can't imagine music not being a part of my life. It would be like . . . giving up air or something."

He pulled back the piano bench. "Since I don't read music, I thought you might want to play some of what you've written."

She glanced back at the open door anxiously. Asher strode across the room and shut it. "They won't be able to hear out on the terrace. Neither will Eric and Zara. Eric's bedroom is on the northern corner of the house."

She felt her cheeks go hot at his matter-of-fact assessment.

"Okay. Well . . ." She inhaled for courage and walked over to the bench. "Here goes nothing."

"Can I sit next to you, so I can see the lyrics?" he asked once she'd sat and pulled one of her well-worn music notebooks from her bag.

"Yeah," she said, scooting over. She played a few notes, warming up. Her fingers faltered, causing a jarring chord. She glanced over at Asher apologetically. "I'm really nervous," she confessed. "No human ear but mine has ever heard this stuff before."

"Don't be nervous," he said gruffly. He ducked his head and kissed her, swift and potent. "Music is part of who you are, right? Never be embarrassed about any part of yourself. You're too special."

He'd said something similar last night, when she'd climaxed so thunderously at his mere touch. It was far too easy to remember every detail of that moment, feeling his body next to hers, breathing his scent, seeing the heat in his radiant eyes.

Straining to calm herself, she propped open the notebook. She chose a bluesy, soulful ballad she'd recently written in less than two hours in a manic burst of creative energy. It was one of those rare songs that had just clicked for her. Highly conscious of Asher's gaze on those virgin pages, she began to play. Her fingers loosened as the melody began to flow around them. Every once in a while, she'd sense his gaze moving off the pages of music and transferring to her profile.

"Sing," he said quietly when the music wound back to the refrain once again.

At his simple command, the words flew past her lips. They'd already been crowding there in her throat, eager to be released. A feeling of electricity pulsed through her. It wasn't just the words that'd been liberated from her throat.

She'd been freed. The music had liberated her.

Asher had.

The final chord hung in the air around them. Silence descended. A tightness started up in her chest. It grew hard to breathe. Slowly, she glanced over at Asher, eager for his response. Dreading it. His expression looked rigid. His stare blazed down at her.

"You're incredibly talented. It was amazing," he said.

Pleasure tingled in her limbs. She'd done it. She'd exposed her music, revealed a part of herself. And he'd liked it. "Thank you. I wasn't sure . . ."

"*Be* sure." She blinked at his fierceness. Nervous laughter bubbled past her lips.

"It's not that simple, Asher."

"Yeah. It *is*." Suddenly, he cursed heatedly under his breath. He reached for her. "Come here."

When she realized what he wanted, she went willingly. He slid to the middle of the bench and she came over him, straddling his lap. He opened his hands at the back of her waist and hauled her closer along his thighs. Her eyes sprang wide. He was aroused.

From listening to me play?

"Asher—"

He cut off her breathless query about his sudden intensity by reaching for the tie on her cover-up. She watched, her heart in her throat, as he solemnly drew on the strings. He parted the thin cotton fabric, revealing the tops of her breasts above her bikini top. Shivers poured through her. She went still at something she saw flash into his eyes.

"Believe me, I've been trying so hard not to touch you. I've been holding back all night. I can't do it anymore. Not after hearing you sing. Not after experiencing that part of you. You shine so bright in my eyes, it hurts, Laila."

Then he was pressing his lips against the swell of her breast. She whimpered softly. His mouth burned a place deep inside her.

"I don't think this . . . *thing* between us is going to come around every day. Do you?" he asked.

She saw him through a veil of tears. She didn't know where they'd come from, only that they were suddenly there when she'd watched his face as he told her how bright she shone.

"No," she whispered.

"I know what I said earlier. We *could* give up on it all. Or we could plow through. Hold on tight. Hope that an answer eventually comes to us. I know what I want to do. What do you want, Laila?"

"To hold on tight," she said without hesitation.

She saw something flash across his expression. Happiness. Triumph?

"Then that's what we're going to do," he said grimly before his mouth seized hers. His arms closed around her. She clutched onto his shoulders, feeling herself heating. Softening, until it felt like she was melting into him. Holding her tightly against him, he moved her, rubbing their sexes together until the friction made her moan shakily into his mouth.

He sealed their kiss. Holding her stare, he began to draw her cover-up off her. She lifted her arms, mesmerized by something she read in his eyes. He tossed the garment aside. His gaze dropped over her. She'd never been so aware of her body. Her skin tingled. Her nipples pinched tight. He lifted his hand and rubbed one distended tip through her swimsuit. Her hips jerked at the contact, her sex grinding down on his erection. A muscle flickered in his tense jaw. Heat swept through her cheeks, lips and chest.

"So sensitive," he murmured, as if to himself. She heard the awe in his tone. He reached behind her neck and drew on the tie of her bikini top. The fabric slithered off her breasts. For a few seconds, he just stared at her bared flesh while her heart hammered in her ears and she struggled to breathe.

"So beautiful," he whispered, before he leaned forward and kissed a nipple with such tender, focused passion, her entire body shuddered with feeling.

He'd never known anything like her. Her entire body was like a live wire. He felt the tension fly into her muscles every time he touched her. He felt her tremble, even at the lightest of his touches.

She was like a rare treasure, resting there in his lap, her face luminous, her eyelids heavy with arousal, the lamplight sheening her smooth, golden-brown skin. Her breasts were medium-sized, firm and high, the globes perfectly round and pale next to her tan. He'd never seen more beautiful breasts. He hadn't known a woman's nipples could get so hard and erect. Unable to stand it a moment longer, he leaned forward to feel her against his lips.

When he felt her tremble at the simple caress, he groaned and took his first taste.

Her flavor filled him. Laila, distilled. Sweet. Addictive. He rubbed his tongue against a rigid nipple, absorbing her tremors.

She grabbed at his head, the sensation of her fingernails scraping his scalp raising goose bumps along his arms. He cupped her ass, pulling her tighter to him. Her back arched. Her hips shifted subtly as she rode his rigid cock. Pleasure suffused him. She was so soft and supple here . . . but her nipple was diamond hard, he thought wildly as his lips and tongue charted her breast. He drew on her firmly, absorbing her precious, delicate shudder.

Pure lust made everything go black for a few seconds. The sounds of the piano keys being struck brought him out of his trance. His nose was buried in her soft, flat belly. She smelled subtly of honey and flowers. He blinked heavy eyelids and raised his head unwillingly. He held both her arms outstretched on either side of her. It had been her knuckles that'd struck the piano keys as he'd opened her wide for his consumption. She leaned back slightly, her eyelids closed, her lips and cheeks flushed, her spine arched, her beautiful breasts thrust forward.

A knot of need twisted so tight inside him, he winced in pain.

"Laila—"

Someone pounded on the salon doors.

"Asher? Laila? Are you in there?"

Her eyelids snapped open. He saw panic fly into her expression.

"Tahi? Yeah, what is it?" he yelled. As he spoke, he lifted Laila partially and slid out from under her, grimacing as her knees scraped across his erection. He stood and reached for her, hauling her up off the bench and setting her on her feet.

"I just got a text from your mother. She said she tried to text you, but when you didn't respond, she tried me. I told her you had your phone off for the movie. She wants to know when we're coming home. I think you better text her. We're going to have to get going," Tahi called through the door. He had the fleeting impression from Tahi's weary tone that she was used to Laila's mother behaving similarly. Asher bent and retrieved Laila's bikini top and cover-up. He handed them to her and nodded significantly toward a closed door. *Bathroom*, he mouthed. He watched, frowning, as she jogged across the room, her naked, elegant back and long legs gleaming in the lamplight.

He sat down again on the piano bench, blocking the view of his crotch.

"It's okay, Tahi. You can come in," he called after he'd raked his fingers through his hair.

The door opened cautiously. Tahi peered inside.

"Oh . . . this is nice," she said, stepping into the sitting room and looking around. Asher could tell she was relieved it wasn't a bedroom.

"Laila was playing my mom's piano," he said, closing the lid on the keys.

"I thought I heard a piano from down the hall. That's what led me here. This house is huge."

"Laila's in the bathroom. She'll be right out. So . . . Laila's mom texted?"

Tahi nodded, making a face.

"She does that a lot? Gets anxious about Laila when she's out?"

"I can hardly think of a time when she hasn't," Tahi sighed.

Tahi walked farther into the room, examining some of his mom's artwork. He covertly gathered up Laila's music notebooks and set them on the piano facedown. By the time Laila came out, looking flushed and flustered and very pretty, his body had cooled down sufficiently to stand.

She turned to him, a concerned look in her eyes, as they followed Tahi out of the sitting room. They paused next to the staircase, and Tahi walked ahead.

"Don't worry. I won't let anyone see your notebooks. I'll bring them with me tomorrow," he said very quietly, guessing what she was worried about.

"Tomorrow?" she whispered.

"Yeah. When we meet at the secret lake? At one?"

"I'll try," she whispered, and they continued down the hall. Asher willfully chose to focus on the excitement in her eyes at the prospect of them seeing each other again versus her reluctant answer.

Chapter Ten

The next day was unusually hot and muggy. He arrived at the inland lake a few minutes early, hauling a small cooler and sweating like crazy. Laila had mentioned last night that she loved the peaches that a farmer's wife sold at a roadside fruit stand down on Route 87. He'd driven there this morning and bought a dozen, then packed several along with some sandwiches and drinks for a lunch.

At one forty, he'd already swum twice and succumbed to eating one of the peaches. There was no sign of Laila, but he hadn't given up hope, recalling how she'd been late before. After he dried off, he checked his phone for the third time.

Sorry I'm not there yet. Mamma Sophia isn't feeling very well in this heat, and my mom wants me to read to her. I'll probably be able to get away as soon as she falls asleep, but I understand if you have to go.

He wrote back. No problem. I'll wait. The water is nice and cold.

Which was a good thing, because the heat of the day was *nothing* in comparison to his vivid memories of Laila last night—of her steady, brilliant inner flame as she played and sang her song; of her wearing nothing but bikini briefs, her arms outstretched, her breasts flushed, her nipples tight and hard. She'd been so deep in the moment, so lost in arousal, even the memory made him feel a little drunk.

Desperate.

Cursing under his breath, he threw down the towel and plowed into the cold water once again. He'd never restrained himself as greatly as he was with Laila. The last thing he wanted to do was offend her. Turn her off. It didn't take a genius to see she wasn't all that experienced with sex. But she was naturally sensual. So damn sexy.

He'd never felt so tested.

"And you failed last night," he muttered under his breath bitterly before he plunged his face back into the water and headed toward shore.

At a little after two, he got another text from her.

I'm so sorry, Asher. My mom just sprang it on me that we're having guests for dinner. I need to help her get things ready.

The sharp disappointment he experienced was tempered by the dismay he read between the lines of her text. He wrote:

Don't worry about it. Tomorrow at one?

Okay. Thank you for understanding.

It stormed that night. The next day dawned sunny but comfortably cooler. He grinned when he saw her already sitting on the beach when he broke the tree line.

"You're early," he said, soaking in the image of her. Her long hair was pulled back in the ponytail she always seemed to wear for swimming. Again, he noticed how the hairstyle emphasized the tilt of her pretty eyes. She wore some kind of sarong that twisted above her breasts and left her arms bare. It matched the color of her green eyes.

"To make up a little for yesterday?" she said, standing and smoothing the sarong.

"You don't have to make up for anything," he said, setting the cooler down on the beach. For a few seconds, they just soaked each other in. She stepped forward at the same time he did.

She tasted like peaches.

"You've been eating the peaches," he muttered against her mouth a moment later. He dipped his tongue between her lips, feeling every nerve in his body sizzle with excitement at the sensation.

"I just had one." She separated slightly from their embrace and pointed behind her. A plastic bag rested on top of her towel. Inside it, he saw several golden globes of fruit. "I thought I'd bring a few for you, since I was talking about them the other night," she said, her smile going all the way to her eyes. "I stole one while I was waiting. I hope you don't mind."

He grinned. "We have plenty. I brought some for you too," he said, hauling her back into his arms.

"What?"

He nodded his head in the direction of the cooler he'd brought, unable to peel his gaze off her. "In there. I went to the fruit stand you were telling me about and got some."

"I can't believe you did that. Thank you," she said, looking a little amazed. "They're sweet, aren't they?"

"You're sweeter."

"You know," she murmured teasingly, "somehow you manage to make it not sound like a line when you say things like that."

"That's because it's not a line. You know that." He touched her cheek. She was so soft. "I keep thinking about you singing that song the other night. You were incredible," he said, stroking her. "I brought back your notebooks. I hope you don't mind, but I read some more of the lyrics. Your poems too."

Her eyes widened. "You did? Which ones?"

"All of them. You really do have a gift. You should be studying music or poetry, not business."

"Thank you." She looked embarrassed, but very pleased. Which pleased him.

"Was it your parents' idea? For you to study business?"

She shrugged slightly.

"Laila?"

"Yes, but I agree with them. I have to study something practical. Something I can make some money at. I can't expect anyone to pay me for a song or a poem."

"Then you expect too little of yourself."

She blinked in surprise, and he realized he'd sounded very blunt. It's just that it bothered him a little. She was so incredible, and yet she hid her gift as a matter of course. "Anyway, I never got to thank you . . . you know. For putting it out there. Bringing the music. Playing for me. For trusting me enough to do it."

"I thought maybe you *did*."

"Huh?" he managed to say once her words penetrated and he peeled his gaze off her lips.

"Thank me," she whispered. "With what you said afterward. What you did."

The vision of her wearing nothing but her panties and leaning back on the piano lost in sensation flashed into his mind's eye. "I thought maybe you thought I was acting like a selfish pig."

Her eyebrows arched. "I would think you're being selfish by suggesting we should hang on to what's happening between us?"

"No," he insisted, frowning. His fingertip grazed across her full lower lip. "For wanting to eat you alive, and starting the feast without even warning you it was dinnertime."

Laughter burst out of her throat. The tension in him broke slightly at the sound.

"Asher, when are you going to get that I want to be in those moments as much as you do?" she asked, her sincere expression sobering him. "It seemed . . . natural, what happened. Especially after we decided to, you know. Go deeper." Her whispered two words hung in the air between them. She placed both of her hands on his upper abdomen. He held his breath at her touch . . . at something he saw in her eyes.

"I know I probably seem really young to you sometimes," she said, her eyes flickering downward. "I must seem really backward, compared to other girls . . . other *women* you've known."

He cupped her jaw and waited until she met his stare. She did so, albeit reluctantly. "The last thing you are is backward. I just don't want to push you into anything you're not ready to do. But even though I tell myself that, and really do want that, I still find myself doing it sometimes."

"I don't feel pushed," she whispered. Her cheeks were flushed. From embarrassment? Her hands began to move up and down on his abdomen, stroking him. *No.* She wasn't embarrassed. Or maybe she wasn't *just* embarrassed. She was turned on, he realized with a rising sense of wonder. His skin prickled beneath her hands. Tension leapt into his muscles at full force. "We decided not to back off from this, Asher. I don't want things between us to be one-sided."

"One-sided?" he repeated, confused. Wary. "What do you mean?" He sensed her hesitation. "Laila, just talk to me. Be honest. I'm not going to think badly of anything you say."

"I'm not used to talking about *it*."

"Sex?"

She nodded. Instead of meeting his stare, she watched herself stroking his abdomen. It didn't help his restraint much.

"Laila—"

"I haven't done it before," she blurted out.

He shrugged slightly. "Okay." She glanced up, clearly taken off-guard by his nonchalance.

"You knew?"

"I kind of figured, yeah," he admitted. He saw her face stiffen. "*Not* because I think you seem backward. Not at all. You're so responsive, it's like . . ." She looked up at him curiously—*suspiciously?* He paused, not exactly sure how to finish the sentence without possibly causing offense. He recalled all too well how she'd jumped up like she'd been stung when she'd climaxed so quickly beneath his touch on the dune the other night.

So *incredibly.*

He exhaled slowly, dipped his knees and leaned down, pressing his forehead to hers. The only thing he could think to say was the truth. "You're *perfect.* You make me feel like a fricking god, the way you respond."

Her eyes shone with emotion. He felt her beauty inside him, like the sweetest ache.

"I'll do whatever you want to do. Just don't tell me I have to stop seeing you. Kissing you." He nipped at her mouth. She craned her head up, kissing him back. He stroked the length of her smooth arms. "Don't tell me to stop touching your gorgeous arms."

She smiled beneath his seeking lips. "That's it? That's all you need is my lips and my *arms*?"

"Maybe," he said against her mouth. "A taste of you is better than a whole night with anyone else. Much. Better." He started to step closer and take her more fully into his arms. He paused when her stroking hands on his stomach stopped him. Glancing down, he saw the determination in her eyes. Then her hands were lowering over his swim trunks. Her fingers closed around his cock.

For several stunned seconds, she gripped him in her hand while he stared down at her in openmouthed amazement and shivers coursed down his body.

"I don't want this to be one-sided. I want to touch you too. I want to make you feel good too, Asher."

She'd never realized that distilled desire was the antidote to shyness. She felt dizzy at her boldness. Liquid heat poured through her veins at the sensation of holding his erection. He felt so amazing. It was like holding his male strength . . . his very power in her hand. She'd sensed the tension that leapt into his body at her touch.

Was her boldness somehow related to yesterday, to that abrupt, unexpected dinner her mother planned, and Ben Khairi's warm glances at her from across the supper table? To her mother's smug smiles? To her own drowning discomfort at the surprising situation into which her mother had thrust her with Ben?

No. That wasn't it. It was being deprived of seeing Asher yesterday combined with the memories of him touching her on that piano bench that had her so stirred up, pure and simple. It was the sharp realization of not just how *wrong* she felt with another man, like Ben Khairi, but how *right* she felt with Asher.

"I've wanted to touch you for . . . it seems like forever," she told Asher, her voice breaking. She moved her hand, stroking him through his trunks. A shudder went through his body. She stopped, her eyes widening in alarm.

"No," he said, his voice quiet, but rough. He put his hand on top of hers. For several seconds, their gazes clung while he guided her movements on his cock. She felt his shape pressing into her palm, the long, thick shaft. The flaring head. She tightened around the tip instinctively. He grimaced and hissed, his white teeth flashing in his tanned face.

"I'm sorry," she said, starting to jerk back her hand. He bit back a groan and kept her hand in place. "I don't know what to do."

"You're doing *fine*," he grated out. A film of perspiration had broken out on his upper lip.

"Show me," she said, desperation trumping mortification.

He nodded once but didn't move. He closed his eyes briefly and then pulled her hand off him.

"Let's sit down, okay?" he asked her, his voice sounding strained.

She nodded anxiously. He bent and withdrew a large beach towel from his backpack and spread it on a sandy portion of the beach. She saw his small smile as he turned to her. "Are you sure you want to?"

"*Yes*. Unless you don't want—"

"You can safely assume I'll *always* want to," he said, cutting her off with a dry glance. She grinned, warmth sweeping through her. His sexual honesty was just another characteristic about him she loved. It might fluster her, but it somehow freed her too. He took her hand, and she lowered down to the towel. When he came down next to her, his gaze swept over her face.

"Don't be nervous," he murmured, reaching for her jaw. He turned her to him and kissed her mouth softly. "It's like you said earlier. It's completely natural. Just let it unfold."

He covered her mouth with his, his taste, his maleness, his very essence filling her. She felt her body quickening. Maybe he was right, she thought as she dug her fingers into his short, thick hair. She felt herself unfolding for him. Blooming.

Her hands made a tour of his form, feverishly stroking his shoulders, chest and ribs. She bunched up the material of his T-shirt and dipped her hand beneath the hem. A thrill went through her at the sensation of his lean, muscular torso and bare skin against her fingertips. His tight abdominal muscles leapt at her touch. He made a rough sound in his throat. Emboldened, she ran her fingertips over his ribs and delved them into the hair on his chest, testing its texture. She found a flat nipple and rubbed it experimentally, arousal tearing through her when she felt the flesh tighten.

He broke their kiss abruptly but kept his lips in contact with hers. His warm breath fell across her mouth, his breathing slightly ragged. This time, she recognized the hard gleam of arousal in his eyes. She'd grown confident in her brief foray into seduction. She stared up at him, their mouths still touching, and wrapped her hand around his cock again.

"Like this?" she whispered, stroking him.

He nodded, their lips sliding together.

"Yeah. That's great." The tip of her tongue touched his upper lip as he spoke. She tasted his sweat. His arousal.

"Can I . . . can I put my hand?" Her fingers inched up to the top of his trunks. She felt that fever rising in her body again, like it had the other night on the beach.

"Be my guest," he said, the tension in his voice tempered by his small smile. "Here . . ."

He drew his T-shirt off with one rapid movement. He flicked the drawstring on his trunks and hooked his thumbs into the waistband. Her hand fell away from his crotch. She watched in amazement as he jerked the trunks down to his upper thighs, his actions striking her as matter-of-fact. He sat there, entirely nude save his swim trunks bunched above his knees.

For a few seconds, she just stared down at his lap. His pelvis and upper thighs were much paler than his ridged, flat abdomen. His erection rested against his belly. It too was pale, giving her the impression of vulnerability and rigid strength combined. A weird kind of fascinated euphoria swept through her.

"Laila?" She glanced up at him dazedly. "You're kind of giving me that uncomplimentary look again."

It took her a second to understand what he meant. She recalled how he'd said she'd looked terrified of him when she first saw him at the secret lake, and how he'd joked it wasn't the most complimentary expression a guy could see.

"*No*," she said emphatically. "It's not that at all." She wrapped her hand around the shaft of his cock to prove her point. A shudder went through both of them at once, as if they were joined. "You're so beautiful. I never thought I'd say that about a man," she said, stroking the length of him. The shaft was long, thick and straight. She mapped it with her fingers. When she traced a vein along the surface with her fingertip, he groaned softly. His skin was warm and soft, but he was so hard underneath.

"Jesus, Laila," he muttered roughly.

She glanced up. He was watching her as she touched him, his face rigid.

"Like this?" she whispered, running her fist up and down the middle of the shaft.

He nodded.

"Show me," she insisted. "Show me what you like."

He grimaced slightly but wrapped his hand just above hers. She watched him, fascinated, as he pumped the top of his cock, twisting his fist slightly around the fat cockhead. A moan slipped out of her throat. It was the most exciting thing she'd ever seen, Asher handling himself so knowingly. She began to move her hand on the bottom portion of the shaft, trying to imitate the pace and movement of his bigger hand. He groaned deep in his throat. His obvious pleasure at their mutual efforts emboldened her. Her fingers ran through his pubic hair. She cupped his testicles gently. He groaned again, more roughly this time, his hand moving faster on the shaft.

"Harder. You can do it harder," he said.

She massaged him more firmly, glancing up to see his reaction. Heat rushed through her when she saw his face. It was the first time she'd ever seen a man firmly in the grip of lust. Of need. It was the first time she'd witnessed Asher that way. It was like spying a whole new world.

"Let me," she said, her fist once again enclosing the shaft. He gasped and let go, placing both his hands behind him on the towel and bracing himself. She sensed him watching her as she stroked him. It excited her, his tight focus. Her entire arm moved now as she pumped him from tip to balls, her actions bolder now that she'd seen how he pleasured himself.

He felt even bigger in her hand than before, the flesh even more rigid. The tension in his body was palpable. His arm, chest and abdominal muscles flexed tight and hard. His small, brown nipples looked mouthwateringly erect.

"Is this right?" she whispered after a tense moment of jacking him firmly.

"It's so damn right," he said, his mouth hard. His eyes seemed alight as he peered at her face. "You've never done this before?"

She shook her head, her arm pumping faster.

"It feels so good." His nostrils flared slightly as he watched her with a feral focus. "You're going to make me come with that sweet little hand."

She started to say that was the point, but suddenly he lifted his right hand and caught her at the back of the head. He pulled her to him, seizing her mouth in a blistering kiss. Laila lost herself for a moment, his flavor, his heat and his need surrounding her, penetrating her, until she became one with it.

She concentrated her strokes at the top of the shaft, squeezing extra hard on the defined head. He groaned harshly into her mouth, his body tightening. She continued the brisk stroke, feeling the friction mount, made euphoric sensing the tension in him that surely must break . . .

A great shudder went through him. He broke their kiss roughly. He looked like he was in pain. She paused, unsure of what to do.

"No, Laila," he grated out. "Keep it up. I'm coming."

She resumed, staring down at his lap while she feverishly stroked him.

White semen jetted onto his belly. He gasped and tightened again. He ejaculated more on her next stroke.

"Asher?" she asked shakily, uncertain.

"Keep going. *Please*."

He hardly needed to say please. She'd never felt so powerful. She watched, enraptured, as each of the firm pumps of her hand made him tense and shudder again in pleasure. Until finally, he sagged back slightly, eyelids clenched tight, some of the tension leaving his rock-hard muscles. His semen now lubricated her strokes. It was everywhere, wetting his belly and pelvis, and even the left side of his ribs. He gleamed with it.

She couldn't take her eyes off the image he made.

Slowly, he opened his eyes, peering at her from beneath heavy eyelids. Their stares held.

"Wow," she mouthed.

He blinked, his stare sharpening on her.

"Wow *what*?" he wondered between pants for air.

She glanced down again at the intensely erotic image he made. "I don't know. I didn't know there'd be . . . so *much* of it."

She looked up at the sound of his choked laughter. He reached for her, bringing her to his mouth for a hard, hot, swift kiss. When they broke apart, she was breathless. She saw his smile.

"You had something to do with that." Her heart soared when she saw the warmth in his eyes. "Those hands of yours have talent for more than just the piano."

Her cheeks were hot—very—from arousal, but she felt them heat even more at that. He released her and leaned back, stretching to reach his backpack. He pulled out another towel and grabbed her hand, drying it. He started to dry himself.

"Let me clean up. Then we'll see to you," he said.

Her hips twisted on the towel at that, grinding downward. She frowned, trying desperately to control herself. The fever had spread over every inch of her body. Asher tossed aside the towel and jerked the waistband of his trunks up in a perfunctory gesture. He put out his arms for her.

"Come here," he said.

She hesitated. His gaze narrowed when she didn't move. "What's wrong?"

"Nothing."

"Laila?"

"It's just that . . . it's worse than it was the other night." She noticed his brows pinch even tighter. "On the beach," she explained reluctantly.

He closed his eyes briefly and pressed his mouth together in a straight line. She had the distinct impression he was commanding himself not to laugh. He scooted toward her and wrapped his arms around her. Despite her anxiety, she placed her cheek on a hard pectoral muscle. She felt him press his mouth against her temple.

"What do I have to do to convince you?"

"Convince me of what?" she asked, pressing her nose into his chest and smelling his male scent, now richer and headier because of his recent climax.

"The fact that you get that turned on when we're together isn't anything to be embarrassed about. It's fantastic. It's one of the things that I told you make me feel like a god."

She lifted her head, looking up at his face. He shook his head suddenly.

"I don't like it. I don't like it a bit," he said.

She blinked when she saw how fierce he appeared.

"*What?*"

"When you close yourself off. Shut off your gift. Hide who you are." His mouth slanted. "Try to dim your glory."

She stared up at him, speechless. He nipped at her opened lips.

"Kiss me like you mean it," he ordered quietly. "Come to me like you mean it, Laila."

And she did. What other choice did she have, with his blue eyes gleaming down at her, and her body sizzling like a live wire? She wrapped her arm around his neck and sank her fingers into a stony bicep, and she kissed him like he held the last oxygen in the universe in his lungs. When she felt his hand glide down the side of her body and slip beneath the hem of her sarong, she opened her thighs for him. It was like looking straight into the sun, but not caring.

Only wanting to burn.

His long fingers slid beneath her bikini bottoms. She made a choking sound of sharp anticipation. His fingers moved, and she could feel how wet she was, how naked her need. And he was whispering harshly in her ear, telling her how sweet she was. How wet. How desirable. Her entire world narrowed to the feeling of his rubbing finger. A splinter of anxiety penetrated her fever.

"Asher?"

"It's okay, Laila," he said, nipping at her lips forcefully. "I've never seen you more beautiful than you are right now."

She opened her eyelids sluggishly and saw his blazing stare. It hit her that he *saw* her. She was entirely exposed to him in that moment, turned inside out.

And he still thought her beautiful. Special.

She shuddered at the realization, her entire body seizing in a rush of bliss.

Chapter Eleven

Afterward, he laid her back gently on the towel and removed her clothing. Laila was too spent to question him. She was too enthralled by what had just happened and by his somber expression as he drew her bikini briefs down over her legs, and then came down over her. He palmed her sex so gently. Feeling swelled in her at his simple gesture of tender possession. She watched him, panting softly. His touch and his gaze as it toured her naked body sanctified her, somehow. It told her that everything she'd experienced in his arms a moment ago hadn't been a lie.

Far from it.

Then he kissed her lips. So gently at first, and then with mounting passion. And he touched her again, this time everywhere, until she was burning again in his arms.

She blinked open her eyes after surviving that solemn, piercing fire once again. His hand moved slightly between her legs. A residual tremor of pleasure shook her. The vibrant green canopy of the trees, the pristine blue sky, the sun-infused air, even: all of it looked different. Brighter. The world shimmered with life, just like her flesh did.

Asher was nibbling hungrily at her lips. She dug her fingers into the thick hair at his nape and scraped her nails against his scalp. God, he was so amazing. She wanted him . . . she needed him so much.

What's happening to me?

He groaned roughly, his hand falling away from her sex. He pushed himself into a sitting position beside her. She watched the in-and-out movement of his lean torso as he panted.

"I think I better take a swim to cool off," he said after a pause. He started to stand, and she realized the stiff movements of his body indicated renewed arousal. He'd brought her so much pleasure, made her lose herself not once, but twice. Now he was hurting again. She stopped him by grasping his wrist.

"No. Let me—"

"*No*," he said. He gave her an apologetic glance for his harshness. "You look like you've been put through the wringer. Rest a few seconds. I'll be right back."

She propped herself up on her elbow, watching as he plowed into the shallow water and then plunged into the lake, arms outstretched. He sliced through the water, his stroke powerful. Almost aggressive. By the time he'd reached the center of the lake, she'd gotten up and had put her bikini back on. She sat on the towel, her arms wrapped around her knees, waiting for him as he swam back to shore.

He sat down next to her on the beach towel, water dripping off his large body. He still breathed heavily, this time from the exercise instead of arousal. When he didn't speak, she grew uncertain. She touched his shoulder. He turned to her, and she saw the glint in his eyes. He'd banked the fire in him, but it was still there . . . waiting. Ready to leap up at any given moment. She brushed her lips softly against his damp, firm ones.

"Thank you," she whispered. She was thanking him for so many things. The pleasure. The sweetness. The glimpse of freedom.

"Thank you." She had the impression he was thanking her for his own reasons, and they were every bit as somber and amazing as hers had been.

They smiled at once, and their mouths met. A time would come, very soon, when she'd have to exist without his taste, Laila realized dazedly. He palmed the back of her head and tilted his face, deepening their kiss. She'd have to live without his hunger. She loved how demanding his kiss could be. How she lost herself in him. How she became somebody different.

Asher reached for her hand and squeezed it.

"I want to be friends, Laila. Someday, maybe we can be more. I'd like that."

She started slightly. The memory of Ben Khairi saying those words last night had leapt into her mind, unbidden. Ben had asked her to walk on the beach last night, and since he was their guest, she'd felt obligated to go. Despite her reluctance, they'd walked far enough to be out of sight of the cottages, and their mothers' gazes. He'd grasped her hand when he'd said those words. The feeling of Asher doing the same had made the uncomfortable memory spring into her consciousness.

Asher pressed his mouth to the back of her hand. She saw his puzzled glance. She realized he'd felt her start at the memory of Ben.

"You okay?" he asked.

"So good," she insisted hoarsely. "It was amazing. All of it."

"Yeah, it was," he agreed, studying her. "So what's wrong?"

She grimaced. He seemed to see straight through her. "It's nothing. It's just . . . my mother went and did something stupid last night, that's all. Sometimes she drives me crazy."

"What do you mean?" Asher asked, his brow creasing.

"There's this guy. Ben Khairi. He's the son of one of my mother's friends in Detroit. Our mothers have been plotting to push us together forever. He just graduated from Western Michigan, and he has a new job in Grand Rapids. He's an accountant there. Since Crescent Bay isn't too far from Grand Rapids, my mom arranged for him and his mother to come to dinner last night," she said in a rush before she could stop herself.

"So that was why you couldn't here come yesterday. Ben," Asher said in a flat tone. He still held her hand, but his body had gone stiff next to hers. "He's Moroccan, I assume?"

She nodded, finding it difficult to meet his stare.

"I thought you said your parents hadn't arranged for you to be with anyone."

"They haven't! Don't you think I'd know if I was arranged to *marry* someone? I swear, Asher, this wasn't about that. It was just my mother and his mom plotting for us to get to know each other, maybe date. She sprang it on me out of nowhere. I didn't *want* to have dinner with them."

He didn't speak for a few seconds. "Do you think she knows?"

Her head swung around. "My *mother*? About *us*?" she asked disbelievingly.

He stared out at the lake, his jaw tense. "Maybe not any details. But maybe she's catching a hint of what's going on with you, senses you pulling away from the fold a little, and is making moves to put a stop to it."

The idea startled her. "*No*," she said after thinking about it for a few seconds. "I don't think that for a second. She just saw an opportunity, with us being closer to Grand Rapids. I guess her friend—Ben's mom—had texted that she was visiting Ben in Grand Rapids, and she saw a chance to throw us together."

"Did he want to see you?"

She made a frustrated sound and backed out of his arms. "What has that got to do with anything?"

"If he's Moroccan, and your family approves of him, and his family approves of you, and he likes you, I would think it's got a *lot* to do with it."

"It doesn't matter," she said, hating the topic, despising the rigid expression on Asher's face, the hard slant of his mouth. "I told you my parents don't believe in arranged marriages. *I* certainly don't. I don't like Ben in any romantic sense."

"Then why are we talking about him?"

"Because I was trying to be honest with you," she blurted out. "About why I couldn't come yesterday."

"Do you feel guilty? About seeing him?"

"*What?* No, of course not. It was completely out of my control."

"Nothing is completely out of your control, Laila."

"You don't understand. They were guests in our home. Of course I had to be there. And I wasn't *seeing* him, Asher. He came to a family dinner. Haven't you ever had your parents try to get you together with someone they thought would be a good match for you?"

"Only a couple dozen times or so."

"Well, this is the exact same thing. I told Ben point-blank I only wanted to be friends, nothing else. What do you expect from me?"

"I don't know. What do you expect from me?" He leaned, reaching for his discarded T-shirt.

"What do you mean?"

"Do you think it's easy for me to hear about the type of guy your parents would approve of, knowing all along I could never match up? That there's not a damn thing I could do, no degree I could get, no job I could have, no perfect speech I could make to them, *nothing* that would *ever* make it okay for me to see you?"

"What they would think about you isn't important right now, Asher." He blinked, taken aback by her shout. Her burst of fury flew out of her as quickly as it had come. She pressed her hand near his heart.

"I want to be with you. So much. That's why I'm here," she said.

His rocklike expression broke slightly at that.

"This is hard," he said after a pause.

"I know. I told you it would be." She studied the rugged, handsome angles and lines of his face. How had the image of it become so ingrained in her mind so quickly? She'd dreamed of it for the past several nights. Passionate dreams. Joyful dreams. It was almost like some elemental part of her recognized his face. Like some part of her rejoiced at a reunion of their souls. Which made no sense, of course.

But there you had it.

She forced her mind back to the practicality of the moment. Did she see remorse in his expression?

"Are you regretting it?" she asked, dreading his response. "Deciding to be together, for as long as we can?"

"No," he replied emphatically, and she saw the blaze of truth in his eyes.

"Then let's forget about it," she said softly. "My mother's attempts at setting me up are just an annoying part of my life I have to deal with. Ben doesn't mean anything to me. I wanted to explain right away why I couldn't come yesterday but was worried you'd make a bigger deal out of it than it was."

He closed his eyes briefly, and this time she definitely sensed his remorse. "Which is exactly what I did. I'm sorry," he said after a pause, sounding sincere. His face tightened in anger. "It's just so frustrating, to think in this day and age that things like race or religion could actually keep us apart, that it actually matters when you compare it to this."

"This?" Laila asked quietly, searching his profile.

"This . . ." He waved between them. "Feeling," he finally said, staring out at the lake.

She felt tears prickle on the back of her eyelids. He'd said it, but he hadn't said it easily. It had been hard for him. She guessed the Gaites-Granvilles didn't speak of their deepest feelings easily. But he'd been breaking that rule with her, and not once.

Several times.

"I know. Trust me, Asher. I know," she said softly, pressing her hand more tightly to his chest, feeling his strong, steady heartbeat. He met her stare. "In everyday life, I've convinced myself it's not a big deal. I'm a third-generation American. In high school, I was on the volleyball team and in the French club and in chorus, and I played piano for concert band. I went to a huge, diversified high school. I had dozens of friends—white, black, Indian, Hispanic, Chinese, Arabic. I work as a waitress in a sports bar and restaurant, and I know just as much as, if not more than, any American girl my age about sports teams, the entertainment world, pop culture. For a lot of people, I'm just a typical American girl. But it's like I straddle two worlds, Asher." She sensed his attention fully on her. She wanted him to understand so badly. "At home, I speak a crazy mishmash of Darija and English, which would probably seem even more confusing to outsiders, since there's so much French and Spanish in Darija. I fast during Ramadan, and I like my mother's Arabic soap operas almost as much as she does. I crave both Mercury Burger sliders and Moroccan donuts. I love being invited over to my friend Jessica's house at Christmas and seeing all the decorations and drinking eggnog. I know *precisely* what to say about my life at work or at school in front of my parents, or my aunts and uncles. I know what not to say. I'm *good* at managing it. So are Tahi and Zara, and dozens of other friends and family members I know. I'm good at it because I love both worlds."

"But I don't fit there. There's a whole part of your life that I wouldn't be accepted into."

"There's a whole part of your life that I wouldn't fit into either. Can you imagine your parents' reaction if I showed up on your arm at their house?"

"I don't give a damn what they think. That's the difference between you and me."

She gave him an admonishing glance and laughed. He frowned, clearly surprised by her gentle sarcasm.

"*Please*. We all care what our parents think about us. I know how much you want their approval."

"I'd introduce you to them tomorrow," he stated unequivocally.

"I believe you would," she shot back, her spine straightening. "They hurt you as a matter of course, so you hurt them back."

"They'd have no *business* being hurt just because I want to see a gorgeous, smart, talented, incredible woman that I like being with. *A lot*."

She started to speak but then just made a frustrated sound. She smiled and shook her head, knowing when she'd been beat. "I can't talk to you about this. Especially when you throw sweet things like that into the argument."

He leaned toward her. "Is that what we were doing? Arguing?"

"Weren't we?"

"I don't want to fight with you. Our time together is too rare for that."

Her smile faded. "I don't want to fight either," she whispered feelingly. He placed his opened hand on the side of her head, tilting her face fully toward his. He leaned toward her, and she felt his intensity.

"*This* place." He nodded out at the still lake and the deep woods that protected it. "This is *our* place. When we're together, it's *our* world."

"Yes," she whispered fervently. "You're right. It is."

His mouth covered hers.

Here was the truth, right in front of her, burning her. Laila realized for certain she had a whole new, thrilling, amazing, scary world to deal with.

After she reluctantly left Asher on that golden afternoon that would forever be stamped in her memory, she went to Crescent Bay South beach to meet up with Tahi and Zara. Predictably, Jimmy and Rudy were there too. She saw Tahi, Rudy and Jimmy straddling a paddleboard and bobbing up and down in the rough surf, laughing as they tried to stay afloat. They all looked happy and sun-kissed, each as golden brown as the next. She went to the edge of the lake and waved at them. They waved back.

"Where's Zara?" she called.

She saw Tahi's sardonic expression as she gripped the board and rolled her hips with the waves. "With Eric," she shouted. "*Somewhere.*"

"We better find her. We've got to get back."

The three of them came to shore. Rudy said that Eric and Zara were probably in the car in the parking lot.

"Who's going to look for them?" Rudy asked amusedly.

"I'm not," Tahi stated flatly. "I've already seen way more than I ever wanted to when they're making out here on the beach." She gave Laila a conspiratorial glance. "I say *making out* loosely. It's actually like watching them have sex with their swimsuits on." She made a disgusted face. "*So* gross. Oh, guess what? The guys asked us over to Asher's again tonight. We were thinking of grilling out by the pool again, and then going over to that country-western place off Silver Dune Drive. Rudy and I are going to kill it on the dance floor," she drawled teasingly, reaching for Rudy's hand. The two of them did a surprisingly skilled little two-step in the sand. "You up for it, Laila?"

She and Asher had already discussed the possibility of them being able to see each other tonight. Her father and uncles were coming on Thursday this week instead of Friday. On Wednesday, there was always the chance her mom would ask Laila to help prepare dishes for their arrival, so she might not be able to get away then. Tonight *was* the best opportunity.

"We can probably get away," Laila said. "But I can't really promise . . ."

At that moment, she spotted Zara and Eric walking toward them. Her heart dipped in her chest. Zara's gait was wobbly. Eric was practically holding her up with his arm around her waist. Her cousin wasn't going to be going *anywhere* tonight. Which meant none of them would be. Zara certainly wouldn't be driving them to a meeting with Asher and his friends. As her cousin got closer, Laila saw the wildness of Zara's hair, the glassiness of her hazel eyes and her lopsided grin.

"What have you been giving her?" Tahi asked Eric angrily when they approached.

"Nothing controversial. Just some good old-fashioned Scotch," Eric replied glibly.

"Yeah, Glenlibbet. Glen . . . libbet," Zara tried again, bursting into laughter at her uncooperative mouth.

"Glenlivet," Eric corrected her. His stupid grin made Laila suspect he was nearly as far gone as Zara.

"I'll drive," Laila said, giving Tahi a grim once-over. "We're going to have to stop and get her some coffee and try to sober her up. Hopefully she can get through dinner tonight without giving away that she's wasted. We'll get her into bed after that, and there's a remote chance no one will notice."

Tahi sighed bitterly. "Nice job, both of you. Zara is the one with the car. Now we're not going to be able to go out tonight."

"You're a dick, Eric," Rudy stated bluntly. "Why'd you have to go and get her drunk?"

"Did I pour it down her throat?" Eric asked, scowling. "She drinks like a fish."

"Never mind," Laila said loudly when Zara irritably tried to contradict him. She wrapped her arm around Zara's waist and pulled her away from Eric. "Come on, Tahi. We've got to go. Now."

They took Zara to a drive-thru on the edge of town and pushed coffee, water and some food into her. Both Laila and Tahi got brushes out of their bags and took a side, each of them smoothing Zara's out-of-control hair. By the time they got back to the cottages, Zara looked like death warmed over, but at least she wasn't slurring her words, tripping over her feet and giggling manically anymore. The aunties accepted Laila and Tahi's cover story that Zara had eaten a bad fish taco at the beach concession stand. When Zara just stared down at the Moroccan tortilla on her plate at dinner that night and turned green, Nadine hustled her off to their cottage.

After dinner, the younger kids asked if they could go over to a carnival that had come to Crescent Bay North beach. Tahi and Laila volunteered to clean up and stay back with Zara, so the aunties could take the kids into town. Tahi and Laila found Zara passed out cold on her sleeping bag when they quietly entered the sleeping porch that evening at dusk.

"Eric is a bad influence," Tahi said, frowning as they lay down on their sleeping bags.

"It's not all Eric's fault," Laila murmured, studying her cousin's wan, pretty face while she slept.

"Yeah, Zara is being so irresponsible and selfish. She's kidding herself if she thinks Eric is going to so much as text her once he goes back to New York. Guess what Rudy told me today?"

"What?" asked Laila, propping herself up on her elbow.

"He heard Eric talking to another girl on the phone."

"How did Rudy know it was another girl?"

"He could tell," Tahi said wisely. "Besides, does it really surprise you? Eric's probably got a girl stashed away for every location and mood."

"No, I guess not," Laila said uneasily, thinking of some of the things Asher had said about his cousin. It suddenly struck her that Asher had never talked about a girlfriend. How likely was it that someone as good-looking, smart and sexy as Asher wasn't in a relationship?

"If Zara doesn't watch out, she's going to get herself pregnant from a summer fling. Nadine would die on the spot if she found out. *Amu* Reda would kick her out of the house. Then what's Zara going to do?"

"You really think Ami Reda would kick her out?" Laila asked, referring to her uncle, Zara's father. What Tahi had said about her aunt Nadine dying on the spot had been an exaggeration, although Laila could easily picture her aunt getting hysterical and at least *imagining* Zara had sent her to her deathbed. But what she'd said about Reda left Laila feeling a little ill. If her uncle Reda kicked out Zara, whom he adored, then surely her father would do something similar to Laila, if she ever found herself in similar circumstances. Her father and Reda were brothers, and very similar in their values and outlook on life. She'd never really had to think about it before. It left a gaping hole in her stomach, even considering the idea of her father or mother rejecting her.

"Of course. Are you crazy? Look what happened to that girl Amal, in high school, the one that got pregnant her sophomore year from that loser senior quarterback? They shipped her off somewhere, and we never saw her again."

Laila made a face. "Her family was a lot different than ours. I can't believe Reda would ever do that to Zara."

Tahi scoffed. "I can't picture her living with them and having a white guy's baby while she's single, can you?"

Laila placed her hand on her belly in an attempt to calm a swarm of butterflies. "Do you think I'm being irresponsible too? And selfish? With Asher?"

Tahi froze in the action of smoothing her long ponytail over her shoulder. Her gaze darted down to Laila's hands on her stomach. Her eyes sprang wide.

"Do you mean you could get pregnant?"

Laila blinked. "What? *No.* We've never . . . I just wanted to know if that's what you think? That I'm being selfish in getting involved with Asher?"

"No. Not as long as you're careful. There's nothing wrong with having a little fun, is there? That's what I'm doing with Rudy. Nothing serious," Tahi said matter-of-factly.

"But it *is* serious," Laila said quietly.

The sun had set minutes ago. The light was very dim on the sleeping porch. Tahi leaned forward, examining Laila's face closely.

"You mean like you're in love with him?"

Laila swallowed thickly. "I don't know. Maybe," she whispered. But the true answer rang in her head like a resonant bell. She lay on her back and stared blindly up at the beams on the ceiling.

I am so screwed.

"Tahi?"

"Yeah?"

"Have you ever felt like . . . like your whole world—the one that you've always known and loved—suddenly got too small? And you feel like you're going crazy? Like you're suffocating, and you just want to burst out of it?"

"Sure. All the time. Doesn't everybody our age feel that way? We're not kids, but we're not adults either. Not completely. It sucks."

Laila lifted her head. "So what do you do when you feel like that?"

Tahi shrugged. "Deal with it. It usually fades with a good night's sleep. It's all going to turn out, eventually. You and I will get our degrees from Wayne State. We'll get jobs. We'll get married. Then we'll be in a position to call the shots."

Laila laughed at her friend's practicality and rested her head on her pillow again. "It's just so hard to *know* sometimes, isn't it?"

"Know what?"

"What's selfish and what's courageous?" Laila said softly. "What's being naïve and immature, and what's being adult and strong?"

"I wouldn't know. You lost me. Let's get back to Asher. Are *you* worried you're being selfish when it comes to him?"

For a moment, she didn't answer. She just stared up at the beams on the ceiling, trying to find the right words. Maybe she was being selfish. But was being selfish *always* bad?

"He's so incredible. So *brave*. So independent. Fearless. He makes me feel so much. Not just in regard to him. About myself. He makes me want to take chances. Live *bigger*. Deeper."

"You mean like run off with him or something?" Tahi asked, sounding incredulous. Mystified. Maybe a little awed.

"I don't know. It's not just that. That's not what I'm trying to say," she said, frustrated that she couldn't make Tahi understand.

"I was half joking about Nadine keeling over if Zara ever pulled anything scandalous with Eric the Jerk. But I'm serious when I say *Khal-ti* Amira would have a stroke if you ran off with Asher. That's definitely *not* what Auntie has in mind for her precious little girl," Tahi said drolly.

"I know," Laila whispered, hiding her wince at the mere thought of her mother's pain if she ever did something so drastic. Her shame. And Laila's subsequent shame, at exposing her need . . . at making her dreams and desires more important than those of the ones she loved.

What was selfish, and what was brave?

That question made her dizzy. How was it that when she asked that question from one point of view, the answer was so drastically different than when she asked it from another?

Chapter Twelve

Wednesday morning, she and Asher texted.

I missed seeing you last night.

I missed you too, she wrote.

Eric is a jerk, getting Zara drunk like that. Is she okay today?

She's pretty hungover still, but surviving.

Do you think you can meet me at the sl at one?

SL was their abbreviation for *secret lake*.

You know I'd like to. I'll try my hardest to be there.

I'll bring some peaches.

Are you trying to bribe me? she texted jokingly.

I'd do just about anything to see you shining again on that beach this afternoon.

Her cheeks had grown hot at that. His words had sounded intensely sexual in her head . . . but somehow sacred too.

After lunch, Laila helped her mother clean up and then said she was going to put on her suit for the beach.

"No, I need you here this afternoon," her mother said.

"But Tahi and Zara are going—"

"I know, but it's your *khal-ti* Nora's birthday tomorrow. That's why your father and your uncles are coming to Crescent Bay early. You and I need to get busy and make Nora some of her favorites for her party. Plus, we need to decide what we should do for decorations. I thought we could run into town this afternoon and pick out some things."

"But, Mamma, I can do that tomorrow—"

"We still have plenty to do tomorrow. Think of all Nora does for you. She's your favorite auntie," her mom said, looking hurt and a little put out. "Have you even gotten her a gift yet?"

"No, but I was going to get her something in time for her party. Tahi is her *daughter*, and *she's* going to the beach this afternoon," Laila exclaimed heatedly.

"Tahi isn't *my* daughter. You are. And Nora and I are very close. We'll show her the respect and the love she deserves."

Her mother turned away to shut a cupboard with a sharp bang. Laila stood there, fuming and helpless, understanding that not only the cabinet door but the conversation had been closed.

She walked away from her mother, hiding tears of anger and desperation. Hating that she had to do it yet again, she texted Asher and told him she wouldn't be able to meet him at the beach.

The next day, her father and uncles were due to arrive from Detroit in the late afternoon. Mamma decided to have Nora's birthday celebration on the beach. Laila, Tahi and Zara got a long table ready, decorating it with the bright tablecloth, pretty lanterns and fresh flowers Laila and her mother had purchased yesterday in town.

She grew increasingly anxious and discontent as the day progressed and she helped her mother in the kitchen, thinking of

Asher waiting for her at the beach yesterday and how she'd had to disappoint him, ruminating about the questions she'd been asking herself over and over again about her life.

Was Asher right? Should she be living her passion, instead of taking the safe path? Should she be studying music or poetry? Were her dreams about composing and even performing her songs the fantasies of a child? Or were they the potential of her true self, the poet in her . . . the artist?

As one o'clock approached, she grew increasingly restless and short-tempered as she cooked with her mom. All she could think about was that she was missing her time with Asher *again* at their secret beach. What was he doing?

As she was pulling an orange and almond cake out of the oven, she felt her phone vibrate in her pocket. She'd gotten a message. Somehow, she just knew it was from Asher. She almost dropped the cake.

"What's gotten into you?" Mamma demanded, coming up beside her. "You've been as jumpy as a nervous rabbit for days. There," she said, taking the cake from her and setting it on the counter. "Should we do powdered sugar or icing for it?"

"What? Oh, I don't know, whatever you want," Laila replied distractedly, removing the oven mitts and tossing them on the counter.

"Where are you going?" her mother demanded when she started to walk out of the kitchen.

"To the bathroom, is that okay, Mamma?" she seethed, exasperated.

Her mom took off her oven mitts and approached her, a worried expression tightening her features. She touched Laila's forehead with the back of her fingers.

"Stop it. I'm not sick!" she said, unable to keep the irritation out of her voice. She stalked out of the kitchen, worried she'd say something else to further insult her mother in her frayed mood. Only when she was in the dim hallway did she pull her phone out of her pocket. Her throat ached when she saw the text was from Asher.

Hey. I was just thinking about you.

She typed rapidly.

I was just thinking about you too. One o'clock. ☺ Her smiley face was to hide the way she was really feeling: miserable.

Do you think you can get away tomorrow at one?

I'm going to try. It's just hard, with my dad and my uncles here, and it being my auntie's birthday weekend and everything.

There was a slight pause.

I miss you, he wrote.

She swallowed back the ache in her throat and typed.

I miss you too.

We only have one more week.

His words had sent a spike of pain through her. Misery pressed hard against her heart, making it difficult for her to breathe for a few seconds. She wiped at the tear hastily before she started to type again.

I'll be there no matter—

"Laila?"

She spun around and saw her mother standing in the hallway.

"Who are you texting to?" her mom asked, taking a step toward her, her eyes narrowed in curiosity.

"No one," she snapped, shoving the phone in her shorts pocket.

"No one," her mom said sarcastically. "You were texting awfully fast to *no one*."

"Leave me alone, Mamma. Stop spying on me. You're driving me crazy," she said in a burst of frustration. She lunged for the bathroom. She slammed the door in her mother's face and locked it.

"What's gotten into you?" her mother shouted through the closed door. "What will your father say when I tell him you've accused me of spying?"

Laila plopped down on the closed toilet seat and made a sound of pure frustration. "What will Baba say when *I* tell him you're invading my privacy?" she shouted back.

There was an uncomfortable silence.

"*Oh* . . . is it Ben?" her mother asked, her tone completely altering from being angry to excited. "Is that who you're texting with?"

"*Mamma*," Laila growled. "That's none of your business."

"It's entirely my business. I'm the one who asked him here, aren't I?" her mom said, her voice sounding calmer now. Smugger. "Listen, don't tell your father about Ben and his mother's visit a few days ago until I get a chance to talk to him about it tonight. I'm going to invite Ben back this Sunday. I'm sure your father will like him as much as we did. But don't mention it to Ben until I smooth the path with your father."

Laila rolled her eyes. She couldn't believe this. She wanted to scream until her throat was raw.

"Don't be too long, now," her mother said amiably, as though they hadn't just been shouting at each other. "I need you to make some cookie dough."

That night, after helping clean up following the birthday party, Laila walked down the terrace stairs of their cottage. She made out a large shadow relaxing on the steps in the darkness and paused.

"Have things been busy at the shop, Baba?" she asked quietly, sitting down next to her father. Her dad, Anass Barek, was one of her favorite people in the world. He worked so hard for them at his collision and glass repair shop, putting in long, grueling hours both during the week and on weekends. Yet he'd never failed to attend even one of Laila's volleyball games or concerts when she was in school.

"It's an especially nice summer. Lots of people are traveling. That means more wrecks. The shop is packed." He glanced over at her. From the lights glowing through the kitchen window, she was able to make out his small, amused smile. "Your mamma has been telling me about this young man she invited over. Ben, isn't it?"

"Ben Khairi."

"Is he nice?"

"Sure, he's nice," Laila said, failing to keep the frustration out of her voice. "But Mamma is making a much bigger deal out of him than she should. I don't like Ben that way, Baba. And I don't like having someone thrown at me either. You should have seen the way Mamma and Ben's mom were watching us like hawks that night at dinner. I felt like *we* were the meal instead of the mrouzia."

Her father chuckled. "Your mother just gets a little carried away sometimes, that's all. She just wants you to be happy. Don't worry. I'll talk to her about it."

"Really?" Laila asked hopefully. "Can you make it so she doesn't ask Ben over again? It made me so uncomfortable."

He nodded. "I'll take care of it with her. But are you sure you don't want to give him another chance?"

"Another chance at what? I'm nineteen years old. I'm not looking to get *married*," she insisted.

Her dad put up his hands in a surrender gesture. "Okay, okay. No one says you're going to get married tomorrow. These things take time. I'm just saying, a young man like that: he sounds decent. He might be worth keeping on the hook."

"Why, because he's got a good job as a CPA? Because he's Moroccan? Do you *really* believe that, Baba?"

"Ah, probably not," her dad said after a moment, waving his hand. "You're right. You'll know when the right one comes along."

She hesitated for a moment, listening to the rhythmic sound of the surf breaking on the beach. She'd never really trod on this ground with her father before.

"Baba? How do you know he'll be Moroccan? The right one, I mean?"

"Marriage is a tricky, lifetime business," he said thoughtfully after a pause. "It's hard enough to make a successful one when the man and the woman have so much in common. Without shared values and culture, it gets difficult. And it's not fair to the children of the marriage, because that strife is passed on to them. Now, I'm not saying that every Moroccan male out there is good enough for my Laila. Far from it," he said with a smile in his voice. "I'm just saying this Ben sounds like the type that'll provide a good, solid life for his family someday."

"Like you have for us with the shop?" Laila asked softly.

"My family is everything to me. It wasn't just my duty to provide. It was my joy, little girl."

She gave him a quick kiss on his cheek. "And you have done it so well. Thank you." He smiled and patted her hand fondly.

"Baba? Remember when you and *Ami* Reda were thinking about starting that business together, custom-building those luxury sports cars?" He made a sound to the affirmative. "Do you ever regret not doing it?"

"No. It would have been a very risky business, starting a niche company like that."

"It was a wonderful dream. And you and *Ami* Reda are so talented when it comes to building cars."

"Family is forever. Dreams come and go. And they don't put food on the table either."

Laila gave an uncomfortable laugh. For a moment, she just stared out at the lake, her mind whirring with thoughts, that horrible friction building in her. Something occurred to her.

"You said I'd know when the right one comes along. Did you? Know it when Mamma came along?"

"Oh yes," he said without hesitation.

"Right away? Really?"

"Really."

"That must have been some first meeting," Laila said, grinning despite her chaotic mood. "What did Mamma say that blew you away so completely?"

"Oh, it's not what she *said*. It's what she sang," her father said, his teeth flashing as he smiled. "The first time I ever saw your mamma, she was singing. And I was a goner."

Later that night, Zara fell asleep faster than either Laila or Tahi. Their beach picnic had been delicious but filling—not to mention eternal, as far as Laila was concerned.

Her conversation with her father had been unexpected and so sweet in some ways, but it had only added to her volatility. Part of her felt as if she'd been fooling him. She was becoming someone different than her father thought she was as they conversed together on those steps. The fact that he didn't seem to recognize she was any different, when she felt it so acutely, only increased her agitation. She was going to explode through her own skin. Or escape. One of the two.

Tahi stared at her disbelievingly when Laila stood from her sleeping bag at eleven thirty and quickly began to change out of her sleeping clothes into a simple white button-down sundress.

"What the heck do you think you're doing?" Tahi asked quietly, clearly stunned.

"I'm going over to Asher's," Laila said, shoving her sleepwear into her pillowcase.

"*What?* How are you going to get there?" Tahi demanded, scrambling up onto her knees.

Laila walked over to Zara's purse and reached in. She held up Zara's car keys. Tahi's eyes grew to the size of saucers.

"You're as crazy as Zara is," Tahi declared. Laila shoved the keys into her own purse. "You don't seem crazy, though," Tahi amended. "You seem dead serious. Laila, what's wrong?"

"Nothing. I just—" Her voice broke. She knew she looked calm on the outside, but inside, she was about to break. "I have to see Asher. I can't take this anymore."

"I'm coming with you, then," Tahi whispered, standing.

"No," Laila said, gagging. Her mouth filled with saliva. "*Oh God.*"

"Laila—"

She flew past Tahi and silently opened the screen porch door. She wasn't sure how she got to the edge of the lake, but suddenly she was retching, and the contents of their huge feast were going into the waves.

A miserable moment later, she realized Tahi was standing next to her, her hand on her back, the surf washing across their ankles.

"Are you sure you're not pregnant?"

Laila heard the fear in her cousin's voice. The wave of anxious nausea had passed completely. She felt hollow. Cleansed. Her head had cleared. Everything about the star-filled, sultry summer night seemed sharp and luminous. She turned and hugged her cousin.

"I'm not pregnant. Don't worry. It's just this . . . this friction inside me. I feel better now," she said next to Tahi's soft hair.

Tahi leaned back. "You're not used to breaking the rules, that's the problem. You were always the good one. Are you still going to Asher's?"

Laila nodded.

"And you're *sure* you don't want me to go with you?" Tahi asked.

"You need to be here to explain that I'm okay, and that I took Zara's car, in case Zara wakes up, or someone else finds out I'm gone. I don't want people to worry. Can you do that for me?"

For a few seconds, Tahi didn't answer. Laila found herself wondering what her cousin saw on her—Laila's—face. Then Tahi took her hand and urged her out of the surf.

"Let's go get you cleaned up. There's some mouthwash in the bathroom off the porch."

Laila squeezed her hand. "Thanks, Tahi."

Eric, Jimmy, Rudy and Asher went over to Chauncy's at around ten. The local dive was packed. Asher got nauseated from the loud music, the warm beer, the increasingly drunk crowd . . . and listening to Eric talk. He sank lower and lower into a black mood. All he could think about was how Laila was only a few miles away, but she might as well be in a different universe.

They got home around eleven thirty and went out to the pool deck. They'd only been there for two minutes when Eric got a message on his phone and read it. That smug smile Asher despised spread on his mouth. Eric got up and walked inside.

"Who is she?" Asher asked bluntly a half hour later when Eric rejoined them. They had a fire going in the pit. Asher suspected it was his dark mood lending to the effect, but the firelight made his cousin's face look a little demonic.

Eric started at the question but quickly got hold of himself. He grabbed his glass of Scotch and nonchalantly took a sip. "She *who*?"

"Whoever you've been slinking off to have phone sex with for the past few days."

"Asher's right," Jimmy said. "You've been sneaking off to powwow with someone on the phone a hell of a lot. And it's not Zara, since Zara has been there a few times when you did it."

"Fuck you. Get your own life, Rothschild." He shook his head in disgust and noticed Rudy's glare. "What's *wrong* with you tools? What do you think? I'm going to *marry* Zara Barek, give my mom and dad the priceless gift of a few little African grandkids—"

Asher lunged up from his chair, causing Eric to flinch back and spill Scotch on his shirt.

"What did I *tell* you, you smug motherfucker—"

Jimmy caught Asher at the shoulders.

"Stop it. Get a hold of yourself, Ash," Jimmy demanded. But Asher was furiously focused on Eric's perfect face. He craved the feeling of sinking his knuckles into it. The prospect of violence would help him focus on something else tonight. But distraction aside, it would feel *fucking* fantastic to wipe that smug look off Eric's face.

He jerked out of Jimmy's hold, fist and jaw clenched, and lunged again. This time, both Rudy and Jimmy caught him. Eric flew up from his chair.

"I didn't say anything about your precious Laila. I was joking . . . *joking* about her cousin. I don't get you, Asher. Your father gave you this vacation to have a summer fling before you start the grind. From what I know about Clark, your dad expected you to bag not just one, but quite a few babes. Any other summer, that's exactly what you would have done. Since when did you become such a self-righteous son of a bitch?"

Asher strained in the hold, his teeth bared. He started to drag Rudy and Jimmy with him.

"Get out of here, Eric," Rudy shouted with effort. "I mean it, man. He's going to kill you. And if he doesn't, I just might."

Eric gave them all a superior, disgusted look. "Like you'd ever stand a chance." He turned and sauntered away, but his pace picked up as he reached the terrace doors.

"Pretty Boy is in an awful hurry all of a sudden," Rudy observed after Eric had slammed shut the screen door behind him.

"Let go of me, damn it," Asher grated out, sick of inching along the deck with his friends hanging on him. As soon as they loosened their hold, he lunged toward the doors.

"Asher—"

"Just let him go," Jimmy said.

Eric was already long gone when he got inside, probably pulling away in his Aston Martin or in his room with the door barricaded to keep Asher out. Jimmy's weary, exasperated tone echoed in Asher's ears as he took the stairs two at a time. His friend sensed Asher's wound-up state. Jimmy knew there was nothing that could be done or said that would calm him down.

Once he got to his room, he searched for his cell phone in his pocket. Maybe Laila had texted. If not, he'd call her.

He cursed when he realized he must have left his phone in the pool changing room earlier. He jogged back down the stairs, making a beeline for the pool house.

"Have either of you seen my phone?" he asked Jimmy and Rudy after he'd searched the changing room and come up empty-handed. Both guys shook their heads. Maybe it had slipped out of his pocket. They helped him look around on the lounge chairs and terrace.

"Never mind. Screw it," Asher said after a minute, frustrated. He hated how sharp he sounded. He despised himself for his foul mood. "Thanks for helping me look," he told his friends, feeling guilty. "And sorry. About that before."

"Don't worry about it. Get some sleep, man. You look cashed out," Jimmy said.

But Asher knew he was too wired to sleep. Once in his room, he flung open a dormer window and unhinged the screen. A few seconds later, he climbed out onto the shingled roof.

He sat with his knees bent, looking out at the expanse of the black lake across the horizon. God, he hadn't come out on the roof to calm down and be alone since he was fourteen years old. There was something about being up so high . . . about being that much closer to the stars that gave him a little perspective. Plus, he'd known his parents would have hated it back then, him being out here on the high, slanted roof. That knowledge had often helped soothe whatever had gotten him riled.

He pressed his forehead against his forearms, willing this feeling inside him to fade. It wouldn't. He realized what he was feeling wasn't anger. It was desperation.

Six nights. That was how many he had left here in Crescent Bay. And he was wasting this one.

"Asher?"

He started and lifted his head, sure he'd imagined her voice. He wanted her so much he was hallucinating her presence.

"Asher? Are you out there?"

Adrenaline shot through him, making his veins seem to burn. He saw a flash of movement at the edge of the window eight feet below him.

"Laila?"

"Yeah. What are you doing out there?"

Her flat, incredulous tone brought it home. It really was her. He gave a bark of disbelieving laughter and started to crawl down the roof. He noticed the outline of her shoulders as she leaned farther out the window. Her long hair rippled in the breeze off the lake.

"Don't come out, Laila," he insisted. "I'm coming down."

"Asher, be careful."

She disappeared behind the pane when he reached the dormer. A few seconds later, he clambered across the sill into his bedroom. He saw her pale dress glowing from the shadows. He turned on a bedside lamp. She was *definitely* here. No ghost or hallucination could possess Laila's singular, luminous face or smooth, toned arms or lush, sexy hair. He hadn't seen her in days. He experienced a wild urge to yell like some kind of savage. She was so damn beautiful, he wanted to *absorb* her.

Her eyes looked huge in her delicate face.

"Is everything okay?" he demanded, concern penetrating his euphoria at seeing her so unexpectedly.

"Yeah."

"Then . . . what are you doing here?"

She pursed her lips together. She looked anxious. *Miserable.*

"Laila?" he asked, stepping toward her. He took her hands in his. His head dropped and he brushed his mouth against her cheek. "What is it?"

"It's just . . . it *wasn't* okay," she whispered, glancing up at him. He realized she was trembling slightly all over. His arms closed around her.

"Shhh," he murmured against her temple. "Just tell me what's wrong."

"I've been feeling like I was going to jump out of my own skin for days. My mom kept giving me one thing to do after another, after another. She saw me texting you and assumed I was texting with Ben. She wants to ask him back for dinner on Sunday, but Baba said he'd talk her out of it. We had this big picnic on the beach, and I threw it all up."

"What? Are you sick?"

"No. I'm fine. I just . . . I feel like my insides are scraping together. Like my *worlds* are," she said, looking up at him entreatingly. He smoothed back her hair, hating witnessing her distress, wishing like hell he could say something to help . . . knowing he couldn't, because he was the *cause* of it. "After dinner, my dad started telling me all this stuff about how important it was to find someone that you shared common values with, because relationships are hard enough as it is. And then he told me how it would've been irresponsible for Uncle Reda and him to build sports cars and how you can't buy food with dreams . . ." She paused and gasped for air.

"*What?*" Asher asked, very confused and concerned at how worked up she was. *Christ, she looks as tense as I feel.*

"It doesn't matter," she sniffed. "None of it matters. My point is, the whole day, I felt so . . . *trapped*, because I couldn't speak the truth out loud, and I knew you were here, so *close*, but I couldn't see you."

He pressed his mouth to her temple again, and then to her hair. Inhaling her scent made his throat hurt. His chest. Everything.

"I had to come. I snuck off the sleeping porch. I stole Zara's car. Jimmy told me you were up here in your room," she recounted shakily. "I've never done anything like this before. I don't know what's wrong with me—"

"Shhh," he whispered, kissing her cheek. "There's nothing wrong with you, baby. I felt the same way all day."

"It was . . . it was you saying that thing about us having only a week left that really . . ."

"I know. I know," he murmured, skimming his lips against her jaw. She turned her face toward him. Their lips brushed together.

"You do?" she whispered.

"I know I've fallen in love with you."

He hadn't been prepared to say it. He'd never felt it, let alone said it in his life until now. It had just popped out of his mouth, a simple, huge, inarguable truth. She stared up at him, her eyes shimmering. Since he was acknowledging it for the first time, he thought maybe he looked just as amazed by his declaration at that moment as she did.

"Is that what this is?" she asked him slowly, wonder tingeing her voice.

"Granted, I'm new to it, but yeah. *I'm* sure."

Her throat convulsed as she swallowed. "I am too. That I love you, I mean. What else could be making me so crazy?" she said, as if it had all just become crystal clear to her.

He gave a sharp bark of laughter, feeling some of the tension he'd been carrying around seep out of him. "This is a good thing. This is a *very* good thing."

"Right. I mean . . . it's never bad, to love someone. To be loved. Is it?" she whispered, stepping closer to him. His arms tightened around her. "It's always a good thing." Her gaze traveled over his face. "It's always . . . an *amazing* thing."

He cradled her jaw and lifted her mouth to his. "In the case of you, it's nothing less than a miracle." Unable to take it a second longer, he swooped down to claim her mouth.

Chapter Thirteen

She drowned in him, every cell in her being flooding with Asher. She succumbed willingly to the onslaught. Joyfully. He placed his hands at the top of her bottom and leaned over her, making her back arch, while he kissed her with furious intent. There was something so sharp about her need tonight. Something unbearable that clawed at her insides. Maybe it had to do with what they'd just confessed to each other . . . the revelation.

She gripped his rib cage, her fingertips sinking into the dense muscles of his back, her nails digging through the fabric of his shirt. When he groaned into her mouth and broke their kiss, she sought him again, craning up to nip at his lips. She saw his small snarl.

"Come here, Laila."

He lifted her off her feet, and he was kissing her again, wild, deep and wholesale. She clung to his neck, feeling herself moving. Sailing. But mostly, her entire awareness was dominated by his hot, hungry kiss. He laid her down on her back. She blinked her eyes open when his mouth left her. He stood by the edge of the bed he'd laid her on, his expression fierce as he looked down at her.

"From the moment I first saw you, heard you even, something told me you were mine," he said. "I didn't realize it at the time, but now . . . it seems so obvious."

She held her breath when he leaned down and traced her skin along the top of her dress, his fingertips gliding over the tops of her breasts. With his other hand, he caressed her arm so lovingly, it made her ache. "I'm going to make you mine, Laila."

"Yes," she said, the single word saying it all: yes, to the risk . . . to the deeper . . .

. . . To him.

Holding her stare, he began to unbutton her dress. It would have been easier for her to just slip it over her head, but she didn't say anything, enthralled by his expression as his fingers descended down the middle of her body.

Finally, he parted the fabric and just looked down at her. She wore only her panties beneath the dress. Her skin felt flushed, her breasts tender and sensitive. But she experienced no shame beneath his possessive stare.

"I wish I could tell you what you do to me."

"Show me," she whispered, holding up her arms for him.

He knelt, sliding off the sandals she wore and kicking off his own shoes. He drew his shirt over his head. Placing his hands on her knees, he parted her thighs and sank down next to the bed between her legs.

She was like a dream, lying there with her long, dark hair spread around her head, her dress opened to reveal her breasts and the smooth, erotic span of her belly. That was where he kissed her first, pressing his face to her softness. She whimpered. He felt her hand at the back of his head, holding him to her as his lips skimmed across her fragrant skin. He nuzzled the area just above her panties, that stretch of exquisitely soft skin. He inhaled her scent: flowers and honey and the sweetness of her arousal. That fullness inside him, the one he'd wanted to describe to her but couldn't put into words, swelled high.

He lowered her panties down to her ankles, sliding them off her feet. She shifted restlessly on the mattress beneath his stare. He glanced up at her face, his hands bracketing her hips. He recognized what glistened in her eyes and leaned down to kiss her mons.

"Such a gift," he told her gruffly, before he dipped his tongue into the distilled essence of Laila.

He'd said it like she was presenting him with a gift, but as pleasure flooded her in a wave, Laila knew it was the reverse. Surely it was his mouth that was the gift, his focused desire.

Oh God. It felt like heaven on earth when he touched me with his hand, but this . . . this is almost unbearable, it's so sweet.

Her entire body tensed tight at the sensation of his tongue moving in her most intimate flesh. He was firm but tender; hungry but somehow worshipful, as well. One of her hands gripped the bedspread, the other at his head, her fingers delving into his thick hair. She made a wild, helpless sound in her throat.

He lifted his head and pressed his warm, damp lips to her thigh. She felt the deprivation of his mouth like a pinching pain. "Okay?" he asked her hoarsely.

"Yes. God, *yes*. Please . . ."

But his mouth was already back on her, the tip of his tongue finding her clitoris, rubbing and agitating her until her eyes rolled back in her head. He sealed his lips to her flesh, providing a slight suction, while his tongue dipped and pressed and circled. She moaned his name, her hips twisting against the sharp pleasure.

He firmed his hold on her hips and lifted his head.

"Does it feel good?"

"Yes . . . I never knew it could feel like this," she managed to say, biting her lip to silence an anguished cry. She shook slightly from the absence of his touch.

"I never knew anyone could taste so good. Hold still. I want more. So much more."

He groaned, and the pleasure was stealing her breath again.

He was hungrier now, but so was she. Her entire world swirled in a cyclone of sensation. She called his name as she rose to the pinnacle, and she thought maybe she sounded a little afraid . . .

. . . Because she was, she realized. It had never felt like this before, like she was about to commit herself to some scary initiatory flames.

And then his finger was at her entrance, piercing her. She heard his voice. She trusted in it.

"Come for me. There's no going back."

His tongue found her again. His head twisted subtly but firmly between her thighs while his finger sank into her to the knuckle. She ignited, her entire body blasting with pleasure. She gave herself to the fire, feeling the old world falling further and further away.

When she came back to herself, Asher stood again next to the bed, shedding his shorts. He came down over her, helping her scoot farther onto the bed. She let her dress slip off her arms and fall away. She caressed his face when he came down over her, mouthing his name, wonder still clinging thick in her dazed consciousness. He touched his mouth to hers, and she tasted her desire mingling with his.

"I love you," he said.

"I love you too."

"Tell me how to say it in Moroccan."

"*Kan hubek*," she whispered feelingly.

He flexed his hips against her, and his heavy erection slid against her thigh. He looked so beautiful in the dim lamplight, his skin gilded from the sun, his muscles bulging and tight.

"*Kan hubek*," he said.

It's like a god came down to love me.

"I'm going to wear a condom," he said.

She nodded, her throat too tight to speak.

"But I'm not going to come inside you either. The consequences are too big to play with the odds," he said thickly.

For a few seconds, she wanted to weep. She had a wild, crazy urge to tell him no. She wanted him in her naked, for them to surrender to this completely.

All or nothing.

But then reality took hold, and she recognized her childishness. The selfishness of her impulse. They were committing to each other in a very deep sense. But the future was still far from certain. She couldn't afford to get pregnant.

Asher couldn't risk his future either.

"Yeah. You're right," she whispered. "Thank you for thinking of it."

He leaned down and kissed her mouth. In typical Asher fashion, his kiss started out tender and quickly turned hot and fierce, melting her.

His mouth blazed a trail down her neck and chest. She lay with her head fully back on the pillows, feeling like she'd never felt in her life, like she'd discovered an additional sense. He touched her so reverently. So knowingly. His tongue swept across her nipple, and she gasped in wonder. His mouth enclosed her, warm and wet and hungry. She felt his firm suck tugging at her core. His hand moved at her sex. She called his name, raking her hands through his hair and squeezing the muscles of his shoulders with her palms. She could feel his cock pressed against the side of her hip. He felt so heavy . . . so stark and blunt and unapologetic in his need. She leaned up slightly, eager to return the pleasure. He caught her mouth in a hot kiss and her wrist with his hand.

"Let me touch you right now," he said against her mouth. "It'll be better for both of us this way."

She wasn't sure what he meant but gasped in relief when his hand returned to her sex. For a moment, she closed her eyes and swam in pure, decadent pleasure. Her eyelids fluttered open. He watched her closely while he took her to the brink again. She accepted his gaze into her private world, melting into it. Everything was blending and burning, and she wondered where he began and she ended.

"This is why they call it making love," he said as if from a distance, a small smile of wonder curving his mouth. It was as if he was just getting something that had always seemed mundane that was, in actuality, one of the most profound truths of the universe.

And she felt it too.

"Asher—"

"Shhh, it's okay," he said, calming her, because he'd just removed his hand when she was so close to climax. He stretched, opening a bedside table drawer. He rolled away slightly and she realized he was putting on a condom. Rolling between her thighs, he leaned down to kiss her mouth. She felt him shift his cock until he pressed at her entrance. She winced in pleasure at the feeling of his hardness against her melting, sensitive flesh.

"*Kan hubek*," she told him softly, opening her thighs wider. "*Kan hubek.*"

The words were new to his tongue, but the expression on his face made them ancient, somehow. Eternal. He flexed his hips, and she gasped.

"I don't want to hurt you," he said, his face pinched as if he were in pain.

She reached for him, cradling his face. "It hurts far worse being separate from you."

He pressed again.

It was like all the emotional friction in her became a solid reality, like it found an outlet in the flesh. It hurt her, to feel it so vividly, so harshly. It felt like being reborn.

Remade.

He made a rough sound of misery, his chin dropping to his chest. He held himself off her with his straightened arms. She touched him, trying to soothe his pain. His muscles were hard as stone.

"Asher, it's okay. Go deeper."

"*Laila.*"

He thrust, his face breaking in agony.

She was so full, she couldn't speak. Think. Only feel. He reached between their fused bodies. His touch made her burst with pleasure.

Through the roar in her ears and the convulsions shaking her world, she felt him moving, doing battle with their shared desperation, slaking his own hunger. She held on to his shoulders, urging him to her. Their bellies pressed tight. He rolled his hips, his strokes in her shorter and harder.

"You feel like heaven. *God*, Laila."

She grasped his hips and then his buttocks, mounting the pressure of his thrusts. Her body began to move in tandem with him, recognizing the dance by instinct. She stared fixedly at his face, enraptured by what she saw there. The pain had left her. His driving cock created a whole new pressure in her. He rocked them fiercely now, his actions causing his bed to bump in a sharp tempo against the wall. It was a new rhythm for her, a whole new cadence, one rife with power. She touched his face with her fingertips. She'd never seen another human being so tormented by pleasure.

"Let go, Asher."

He clamped his eyes tight and let out an agonized groan. A knocking sound penetrated her dazed awareness. At first she thought it was the headboard against the wall, but then she realized it was another, discordant sound.

"Asher."

She started at the male voice, gasping. Someone was at the door, knocking. Asher withdrew from her abruptly. He came down next to her on his hip. His hand moved between his thighs. He cursed fiercely under his breath. He tensed and shuddered.

Laila sat up partially, disoriented by their abrupt separation. She realized he was climaxing. *No*, it shouldn't have been this way. They should have been joined. The knowledge pierced her.

"Asher. I have your phone, man."

Asher lifted his head. He looked so disbelieving, he seemed crazed. "Get the *fuck* out of here, Eric!" he bellowed so loudly, Laila jumped.

There was a pause.

"I'll leave it down on the kitchen counter. You can get it when you're finished," Eric said knowingly through the door.

Asher hissed and jerked, his hand falling away from his cock. She grabbed his arm when he started to roll off the bed.

"Asher."

He looked around at the sound of her voice, his blazing gaze landing on her.

"Jesus. I'm sorry, Laila. I'm going to kill him—"

"It doesn't matter," she said, reaching for him with her hands on his shoulders. He resisted at first but rolled against her at her insistent urging. "It doesn't *matter*," she repeated intently, running her lips against his whiskered jaw while she rubbed some of the tension out of his back muscles. Their mouths brushed together.

"It was amazing. Don't let him ruin it. What is Eric, compared to this?" she whispered. He lifted his head slowly. "Don't let anything ruin it, let alone him. *Our* world, remember?"

She saw the hard glitter in his eyes. He was still angry at Eric's interruption, she could tell. Agitated. *Worried?* But then she saw his sharp focus return as his gaze moved over her face.

He leaned down and kissed her mouth tenderly. She felt the frayed filaments of their connection reweaving.

"Our world," he swore next to her lips.

Chapter Fourteen

They succeeded in blocking out the rest of the world, at least for the next three and a half hours. It wasn't hard, when Asher's skin was pressed tight next to hers, when she was looking into his eyes and listening to his deep voice . . . when he was making love to her again and she was spiraling in bliss.

He walked her out to Zara's car at four fifteen a.m. She shivered in the damp night air. He wrapped his arms around her.

"Do you feel okay?" he murmured.

"I'd give anything to stay," she whispered, clutching him close, as if she thought his hard body could staunch the ache mounting inside her at the idea of separating from him after the most special night of her life.

"I'd give anything to have you stay," he said, pressing his mouth to her temple. "But I didn't mean that. I meant are you okay, physically. You said you threw up earlier. And then . . ." He nodded at the upstairs of the house, and she understood. He meant was she in any discomfort. From her first time.

And the second.

She pressed her warm cheek to his chest.

"I'm fine," she said honestly. True, there was a little discomfort. But she strangely welcomed the sensation. It was a reminder of what it had been like, to be fused so tight with him, the boundaries between them evaporated.

He nuzzled her cheek. "What if I got a job at a Detroit paper?"

She started and leaned back, examining his face to see if he was serious.

"You would *do* that?" she asked, incredulous.

"We could see each other that way."

"But you told me you did an internship in L.A., and know the editor. He thinks if you work hard, he can get you a foreign affairs post within a year or two. If you came to Detroit, you'd be giving up your dream."

"Maybe not giving it up. Just postponing it a little. What, Laila?" he asked, his brow creasing. He'd noticed her anxiety.

"I can't ask you to do that, Asher. Postpone your dream? And for what? It would be just as hard for me to get away in Detroit as it is here," she said miserably.

"You're getting older, Laila. You're not going to be at your mother's beck and call forever."

"I'm not at her beck and call. You don't understand. I know she can be a pain sometimes, but I love her—"

"Okay," he said, cutting her off by kissing her mouth. "Maybe that's not the solution. We said we'd keep trying to hang on. That's all I was doing. Brainstorming."

"I know. I know you were. Asher, it means so much to me. Thank you. You're right. I'll try to come up with some ideas too," she said, smiling up at him brightly. Inside, she was cringing a little. It dismayed her because she couldn't imagine a scenario where they could be together.

He reached to open the car door. "You better get going," he said. "Everyone's going to panic if they find out you're gone."

When she was seated, she glanced up and saw him through the opened door. He was peering fixedly at the driveway.

"Asher? What's wrong?"

"Nothing," he said distractedly, dragging his gaze back to her. She looked at where he'd been staring.

"What is it?" she repeated, nothing about the darkened driveway standing out to her as significant.

"Eric's car is gone," he replied in a flat tone. He leaned down to kiss her once more, but she noticed the tension had returned to his face.

She parked Zara's car in the predawn darkness and came around the front of the cottage. Relief swept through her when she noticed no lights anywhere. She hadn't been caught, it would seem. When she reached to push open the screen door, it flew away from her hand. Someone grabbed her forearm and pulled her inside.

"Tahi?" she whispered, brushing past her cousin while Tahi silently shut the door. Something about her tense actions sent an alarm going off in Laila's head. The alarm started blaring when she saw Zara sitting up on her sleeping bag, her posture tense.

"Thank God you're here," Zara whispered.

"Why? What's happened?" Laila asked, going down on her knees on her sleeping bag.

"Did you see your dad's car on the way in?" Tahi asked, lowering to her air mattress.

Shivers poured down Laila's arms. "*What?* No. There wasn't a car on the entry road."

"You must have just missed them," Tahi muttered.

"They just left here three or four minutes ago," Zara added.

"Who? My *father*?" Laila asked, straining not to shout in her rising panic. Had she been caught after all, and her father had left to go looking for her?

"Calm down," Tahi shushed. "We covered for you. We said you were in the bathroom. Your dad was in such a hurry, he didn't seem to notice there wasn't a light on under the door," she said, pointing to the distant closed bathroom door.

"Why was he in a hurry? What's *wrong*?" Laila demanded.

"It's Mamma Sophia," Tahi whispered, her face looking wan and tight in the dim light. "She was having chest pains. Your father came over to tell us that he and your mom were taking her over to the emergency room in Grand Haven. He wanted us to tell you what was happening, and for all of us to let everyone know in the morning when they wake up. Your mom was over at our cabin, waking up my mom. The four of them just pulled out minutes before you got here."

"Oh my God," Laila said. A trembling had started up in her limbs and she couldn't seem to control her shaking hands. "Did you see Mamma Sophia?"

"Tahi did," Zara whispered. "She went out and saw them taking her to the car."

"Was she *conscious*?"

Tahi nodded. "It didn't seem that bad, Laila. She was walking, with your mom's help. Mamma Sophia told your mom and dad she'd refuse to get an ambulance if they called it. Then *Amu* Anass insisted they drive over to the emergency room, if she wouldn't go with the ambulance. You know how stubborn Mamma Sophia can be when it comes to her health."

Laila started to stand. "Let's go. Let's drive over to the hospital."

"*No*, *Amu* Anass says we should stay here. He'll text us as soon as they know anything," Tahi exclaimed in a hushed tone, grabbing Laila's arm again and halting her. "Hurry up, and get changed back into your pajamas before someone wakes up. You barely missed being caught the first time; you don't want to chance it again."

Laila collapsed back onto her sleeping bag, feeling like the power plug had just been pulled on all her muscles. From the moment Tahi had mentioned Mamma Sophia, she'd forgotten how close she'd been to being discovered. The concept of being "caught" seemed utterly empty. Irrelevant. The only thing she could think of was Mamma Sophia waking up alone and in pain in the room they shared, while Laila had been miles away in Asher's arms.

At around ten the next morning, Rudy paused in the action of shoveling some Captain Crunch in his mouth with a spoon when Asher entered the breakfast nook. Jimmy glanced around his newspaper.

"What's wrong?" Jimmy asked, noticing Asher holding up a key and a piece of paper. Or maybe he saw Asher's angry expression.

"He's gone," Asher said bitterly, tossing the key and note onto the wood table. "I found those and my cell phone"—he placed his cell phone facedown next to the key—"on his bedside table."

"Eric, you mean? He had your phone?" Rudy asked before he swallowed. He picked up the piece of paper. "This says he had to drive over to Chicago for business. But he's probably not gone for good, is he? Maybe he just drove over for a few days—"

"He's in Chicago on *business*," Asher grated out.

Rudy and Jimmy shared a bemused glance at his intensity.

"*He* took my damn phone!" Asher told them, giving Jimmy a half-panicked, half-furious glance. "He must have taken it last night on the terrace. He's been reading my messages. That means he knows about my job at the *Times*," Asher bellowed. "He knows about—" He cut himself off with a curse, wincing. The very idea of Eric going through his private texts with Laila made him want to punch something. Since it was Eric he wanted to pound the most, and that snake had slithered away in the night, there was nowhere to put his fury.

"You don't think he'd go and . . ."

"What?" Rudy asked when Jimmy faded off.

"That's exactly what I think," Asher fumed, reading Jimmy's mind. "He's going to get back at me for going after him last night. He's going to go and tell my father I'm not working for GGM before I ever get a chance to."

"Fuuuck," Rudy muttered, looking floored. "He'd really do that?"

"Yeah. I think he would," Jimmy said quietly.

"He really is every bit of the asshole you said he was from the start," Rudy told Asher.

"What are you going to do?" Jimmy asked.

Asher unclenched his grinding teeth. *Damn that stupid, interfering fuck*. It was bad enough that he had plotted to further damage Asher and his parents' already shaky relationship. But because of Eric, Asher was going to have to cancel his meeting with Laila at the secret lake this afternoon. It was that, as much as anything, that had him ready to explode.

"I'm going to have to drive to Chicago and either try to stop him . . . or mop up the mess he's already made with my parents," he said to Jimmy and Rudy. "It sounds like Eric is going to try to ambush my dad at his office downtown, but my dad has been away on business in Boston. He called me from there a few nights ago. Maybe there's a chance I can get to him before Eric does."

"Your dad should be back already . . . or back soon," Jimmy said, standing up and looking worried.

"What makes you say that?" Asher asked.

"The Summer Soiree at the Blackhawk Country Club. I heard my mom mention last week that our parents were all going together, and that's tomorrow night."

Asher cursed. "You two just stay here and try to enjoy yourself. It's only a three-hour drive to Chicago, four to Winnetka. I'll be back as soon as I can."

He felt his phone vibrate as he turned to leave in order to throw a change of clothes in a bag. He glanced at the screen and saw that the message was from Laila. Pausing, he read it, and then picked up his pace.

It wasn't enough for it to just rain trouble. Fate just *had* to pour it down like a shitstorm.

She was waiting for him when he arrived at the secret lake just twenty minutes later. It was strange—a little jarring—to see Laila there not wearing a swimsuit or beachwear. Instead, she perched stiffly on the big rock, wearing a pair of jeans that were rolled up at the bottom, sandals and a loose short-sleeved light blue top that highlighted her even tan and smooth skin. Her long hair spilled around her shoulders, but the front had been pinned back. Her face looked tight with worry, but it lightened some when she saw him walk onto the beach.

She stood to greet him. "Thank you for coming as soon as I texted," she said as he approached her and tossed his backpack onto the beach. She looked so earnest . . . so scared, it made him feel like something had been rubbed raw inside his chest.

"Of course I'd come," he said, putting out his arms. She came into his embrace, squeezing him tight. For a few seconds, he nuzzled her fragrant hair and absorbed the feeling of her in his arms. "Have you had any more news? How's your grandmother?"

"She was resting when I left the hospital," Laila said, moving back in his arms a little but keeping in contact with his body. "My mom and dad, and Aunt Nora and Uncle Taha stayed, but they said we should all go home. Knowing all her grandkids were around would likely keep Mamma Sophia awake. We're all going back at one thirty, so that's why I asked if we could meet early. Mamma Sophia's blood pressure is still high, so the doctor doesn't want her to be discharged until they can get it under control."

"And it was definitely a heart attack?"

She nodded. "Not a bad one. Not a mild one either, though. My dad told me the doctor reported she responded well to the emergency room therapies. She should be fine, once they get her blood pressure down." She blinked back some tears.

"What?" he asked, rubbing her back, sensing her spiking unrest.

"They could have given her aspirin and oxygen therapy right away if she'd been in an ambulance, but Mamma Sophia refused to get in one. My parents and *Khal-ti* Nora had to drive her to the hospital. They called at around seven this morning and said she'd been admitted, so we all drove over." She glanced up at him, and he saw her misery in her clear green eyes. "I sleep in the same room as Mamma Sophia while we're here on vacation. If I'd been there, I might have been able to convince her to take an ambulance. We're really close. I can talk her into things sometimes, when Mamma and Baba can't. Things might have gone better for her."

"Don't blame yourself. You told me it's normal operating procedure for Tahi, Zara and you to sleep on the porch on hot nights . . ."

"But I wasn't there at *all*," she said, her voice thick with emotion. "If I'd been on the porch, I could have run over when Baba came to tell us what had happened before they left for the hospital. As it was, Tahi and Zara had to lie and say I was in the bathroom.

Baba never noticed anything different, because he was so distracted about Mamma Sophia. But all the while, I was with you—"

He pulled her tighter to him, his hands at the curve of her back. "You don't *know* that you could have changed your grandmother's mind if you were there, or that the earlier treatments would have made that big a difference." She looked up at him uncertainly through thick, damp lashes. He brushed his mouth against her eyebrows. She closed her eyelids. He kissed her, his lips coming away damp with the tears on her lashes. He lowered his face, pressing their foreheads together. "It's natural in a crisis to wonder what you could have done differently, to imagine what things would have been like if you'd done this or that," he said quietly. "But stuff just happens, Laila. All we can do is deal with it the best we can when it does."

"You're right. I'm just so worried about her. Mamma Sophia has always been a part of my life. I can't imagine things without her—"

"Shhh. You don't have to worry about that. Not yet," he said, kissing her mouth. "From what the doctor said to your dad, her prognosis sounds good."

She swallowed thickly and nodded. A tiny smile flickered across her lips. "Thanks."

"I only say it because it's true."

Her smile widened. He nipped at her lips. He couldn't help it. Her smile after seeing her fear was like watching the dawn breaking after a stormy night.

"Not just for that. Thank you for dropping everything and coming so quickly. I hope I didn't interrupt anything."

"Nothing at all. I told you before I'd come, anytime you wanted to see me."

"It's all I could think about, once I saw Mamma Sophia and heard she was going to be okay."

"What's that?"

"Seeing you," she whispered. "Having you hold me."

There was something about the way she was looking up at him that made his head automatically dip in preparation to kiss her. Sink into her. He felt his body harden at the mere flashing, vivid thought. Now that he knew what it was like to be inside her, it was like he'd been programmed—hardwired somehow—with a mandate to get back there. He stepped back, feeling extremely guilty about his uncontrollable reaction in this situation. Laila needed his support right now, not for him to jump her while she was vulnerable.

"Here, let's sit down," he suggested, waving over at the big rock.

They sat side by side. She curled into him, her cheek against his ribs, her arms encircling his waist. He pulled her tight against him. The singular scent of her hair and the feeling of her soft, curving body against his stroking hand didn't help much in his nonselfish course of action.

"What were you doing?" she murmured quietly, her mouth near his chest. "When I texted?"

He thought of finding his cell phone, Eric's note and the key to the beach house. A vivid imagined picture popped into his head of Eric walking into his dad's office in Chicago, that smug smile Asher hated plastered on his face. He tamped down a flare of fury and opened his hand at the back of her head.

"Nothing. Just eating breakfast with the guys," he said, stroking her hair.

She placed a hand on his abdomen. He stilled beneath her touch, his nerves flickering in awareness.

"I guess Rudy and Jimmy knew. About me staying with you last night," he heard her say.

"They didn't say anything about it. They're not like that."

"They aren't?"

He resumed stroking her hair. Her hand caressed his stomach ever so slightly, but his brain charted every minuscule shift.

"Well, Jimmy isn't. Rudy *can* be. In other situations, maybe. But he wouldn't be. Not about you," he tried to explain, finding it difficult to focus with her touching him.

"Not about me?" she asked, lifting her chin and meeting his stare.

"Yeah. He knows better by now." He jerked his gaze off her full, pink mouth when he noticed her eyebrows arch in a query. "He knows better than to say anything crude about you in front of me."

A smile curved her mouth. Much to his horror, he felt himself go rock hard at the sight. His cock tingled and tightened.

"Because he knows you'd defend my honor?" she asked him.

He shrugged uneasily. She laughed and shook her head, looking a little sad.

"What's wrong?" he wondered.

"After last night, I haven't got much left."

"Got much left of what?" he asked, confused.

"Honor."

He stiffened. He put his hand on her chin, lifting her face to his. "You don't really believe that, do you?" he demanded. "I honor you more now than I ever have."

Her mouth fell open, and he could tell he'd surprised her by his intensity.

"Does that mean you're regretting it? Last night?" he asked, finding the idea reprehensible . . . just *wrong* on so many levels.

She shook her head rapidly, her long hair whisking across his hand at her back, some of it spilling onto his crotch. "No. I'm sorry. I shouldn't have said that. It was stupid. Of course I don't regret it. How could I ever regret something so amazing?"

"You sounded like you regretted it just a minute ago," he said slowly. "When you were talking about your grandmother."

"It was hard, finding out about Mamma Sophia the way I did," she said quietly. "I know I sound confused. Upset. Mostly because I *am*. But I'd never change last night, Asher. Not even if I had the power to go back and do things differently. I'd never change *us*."

Her hand moved again on his abdomen, gliding lower. He gritted his teeth and caught it at the wrist.

"Don't," he told her in a strained voice. He felt beads of sweat pop out on his forehead. "You have no idea what I want to do to you right now. It's not . . . appropriate, I know, given what's happened to your grandmother and everything you're feeling. But I can't seem to stop it." When he noticed her slightly incredulous glance, he closed his eyes wearily. There was no point in trying to hide it from her. His shame was as flagrant as his arousal. He nodded down toward his crotch. When she didn't speak, he pried open his eyelids.

She was staring directly at where he burned. His erection tented his shorts, his need for her a huge, inescapable red flag.

"I'm sorry," he said, miserable at the idea of her being exposed to his crudeness while she was suffering. If he couldn't comfort her, then he should leave. She shouldn't be subjected to this. He started to stand, but she halted him in an instant by placing her hand between his legs. She cupped the head of his cock through his shorts and met his stare. Color spread on her cheeks, but he knew by the fierce glint in her clear green eyes she wasn't embarrassed.

She'd just caught fire.

"You think it's wrong? That you want to make love to me? That I want to make love to you?" she asked.

"I want to comfort you," he grated out, because her hand was moving on his cock, and *God*, it felt good. He started to sweat in earnest. His head fell back and he stared up at the sky through crossed eyes. "I've never felt this way about someone, so I don't know how to do it right . . . how to be there for you."

"I think you know how to do it *more* than right," he heard her say through the roar in his ears.

"Jesus, Laila," he hissed, because she was unfastening his shorts with fleet fingers. The feeling of her knuckles brushing against his balls made him tense hard. He caught both of her wrists at once and jerked her against him, her fists pressing against his chest and her mouth just inches away from his. His head dipped. He caught her scent and snarled slightly. All he could think about was penetrating her parted lips with his tongue.

"I don't think there's anything wrong with you wanting to make love to me right now. I want it too," she said shakily. "I've thought about it all morning. At first, I thought it was . . . indecent or something, to keep imagining it, to keep remembering last night. I couldn't stop thinking about being with you again, even while I was at the hospital. It felt selfish. Dirty." She twisted her forearms gently but firmly. Slowly, he released her, compelled by something he read in her eyes. She cupped his face in her hands and moved her mouth to within inches of his. "But I was wrong, Asher. It would never be selfish or wrong. Not with you."

Her mouth brushed against his. His body leapt in response. Holding his stare, she dropped her hand again between his thighs and caressed him through his clothing. He winced at the sharpness of the pleasure.

"I know you want to comfort me. This *will*. It's all okay, Asher. Because it's us."

She stood and faced him. He watched, utterly captivated, as she began to undress in front of him.

She wanted to cry, seeing him sitting there, so tense. So torn. His handsome face was flushed and rigid. She sensed his torment and his need doing battle, swaying on some imagined balance beam inside him.

She whisked her panties—the last of her clothing—down her thighs and stepped out of them. When she stood before him, naked, she wasn't exactly sure what to do next.

Or what he'd do. She knew he was holding himself on a fraying leash. She wasn't trying to test him. It was just that she needed him so *badly* in that moment. She never felt so exposed in her life . . . so vulnerable as she did, standing there in front of him.

But then he stood, and without saying anything, began to undress. A few seconds later, they faced each other on the beach, naked. He'd taken a condom from his wallet and now held it in his right hand. Her gaze trailed down over him. Her lungs locked. He was so beautiful to her.

"My mother has always said I was selfish," he said, and she knew he'd noticed her staring at his heavy erection.

Her throat grew tight and achy at what she saw in his eyes: sharp desire and a kind of tired acceptance. The latter killed her a little. She stepped forward and took the condom from him. She ripped open the package, holding his stare.

"She's wrong. What you're doing is the exact opposite of selfish," she insisted, stepping toward him.

They both rolled on the condom together.

A moment later, she came down over him. He sat on the big rock, their clothes beneath him. She clutched his hard shoulder muscles. He opened his large hands beneath her bottom, taking much of her weight. She felt his muscles flex tight as he lowered her slowly onto his cock. Her tissues still stung a little from last night. But the overall feeling that pulsed in her brain was pure relief at the sensation of him filling her.

He was so tense, she sensed a slight shaking in his powerful body.

She touched his face gently, a feeling of awe swelling in her.

"*Kan bghik*," he grated out. *I want you*. "So damn much, Laila." He pulled her closer, sheathing himself in her to the hilt.

Laila gasped as sensation swelled tight in her.

"And I've never honored you more for it," she told him fiercely, before she rolled her hips, riding him. He hissed. His hold on her tightened.

He finally let go of his restraint. She felt it with every cell in her being. He pulsed her over him, taking the lead, controlling their dance with his powerful upper body. Pleasure inundated her. For a few blessed minutes, their fire reigned supreme, incinerating everything . . . making everything clean.

"You're so beautiful right now," she heard him say as if from far away. She cracked open her eyelids and saw that he watched her narrowly as she moved up and down over him. He grasped her hip in his big hand and reached with his thumb, rubbing her slick clitoris. She cried out shakily. "Come here," he said, his mouth hard with mounting lust. He held her tightly to him, sucking a nipple into his mouth. He pumped her onto his cock in short, firm strokes, his muscles bunching hard with the effort. All the while, he sucked and pressed and pleasured her until she sizzled with the friction and heat. Just as she was about to light up, he grabbed her head and brought her mouth to his.

She screamed into his possessive kiss as pleasure blasted through her. Clutching him for all she was worth, she shifted her hips, desperate to bring him deeper. Pain fractured her shuddering bliss. He broke their kiss.

"What?" he demanded, glancing down to her leg.

"It's nothing," she moaned, her body still vibrating in aftershocks of pleasure.

"It's not nothing. You scraped your knee on the damn rock," he said, his face tight with concern. She glanced down dazedly, seeing that his shirt had slipped out from beneath them during their more heated moments. Blood smeared her knee.

"Here," Asher said, lifting her off him.

"No . . . don't, Asher," she wailed. He was still hugely erect. It felt horrible, having their connection so abruptly broken. His face went tight with something that looked like pain, but he seemed determined. He set her on her feet next to the rock and stood next to her.

"You're bleeding."

"Barely. It's a little scrape," she moaned, feeling feverish. His cock jutted out between his thighs, impossible for her to ignore. She fisted the shaft and tugged on him boldly. He shut his eyes and groaned deep in his throat. "I'm *fine*, Asher. Make love to me."

She fisted him tighter and pumped him briskly. He grimaced in pleasure, but she still sensed his hesitation. He was still concerned about a tiny scrape on her knee and a little blood. Her hand still on his cock, she reached behind his head and pulled him down to her. She nipped at his lips and stroked him with her hand. He was as hard as stone and slick with her juices.

Then it happened. She felt his restraint break. He grabbed her upper arms and hauled her against him. His tongue sank between her lips. His groan was guttural. Primal. Mixed triumph and arousal flooded through her.

"Laila," he muttered thickly a moment later, his hot mouth against her neck. "You make me crazy."

She was too dazed with arousal to answer logically. She tightened her hold on his erection, wanting so badly to be joined with him again. Then he was turning her in his arms and tensely giving her instructions. She leaned over the rock. He entered her from behind. Then there was only him, filling up her world.

"Asher," she moaned, inundated. Overwhelmed.

All of his hesitation had vanished. He took her with a focused, deliberate abandonment. She loved his greediness. In that moment with him on that beach, she learned to crave his single-minded, complete possession of her.

She existed with him at the heart of a fire. He was the source, his long, powerful thrusts building the friction so perfectly. The sound of their bodies crashing together and his low growls of pleasure pulsed in her ears, faster and faster, louder and louder. She screamed through her clenched teeth and ignited again, wave after wave of release pulsing through her.

The sound of his roar penetrated her climax. She felt his cock swell inside her, then heard his ragged, rough groan as he began to come while he held himself deep inside her.

Suddenly, he cursed and jerked his cock out of her.

"*God*, Laila," he groaned, and she heard the abject misery in his tone. She tried to turn around, startled, recognizing in a dazed way that something was wrong. He held her hips in place, though. She felt his cock brush against her ass . . . and wetness.

"The condom broke," he said tensely between pants.

Chapter Fifteen

"What?" She was too disoriented to fully absorb what he'd said, let alone become worried about it.

"Come on," he said, gently but firmly urging her to stand.

"Asher, I don't—"

"Get in the water, Laila. You need to wash off," he insisted. She turned, studying his face. He looked fierce. Panicked? "I withdrew when I realized something didn't feel right. When I did, I saw the condom had broken. I probably came some inside you. I'm not sure . . ."

His anxiety finally penetrated her sated brain. She let him lead her to the water's edge. They waded in together, the cold water helping to clear her head. He helped her to rinse off. After she'd washed herself as best she could, she turned to face him. The water level was at her neck, but much of his chest was exposed. For a moment, they just stared at each other as they stood in the calm water.

"I'm sorry," he said.

"It wasn't your fault."

He closed his eyes briefly, and she sensed his intense regret. "Yeah, it was, actually. I was going at you like a madman. It's not surprising it broke."

She placed her hand on his chest. She could feel his rapid, strong heartbeat. "I was just as into it as you were. It felt so good."

Tears stung her eyes when she witnessed his misery. "I wanted to comfort you," he said, frowning. "Now look at what I did."

"You *did* comfort me. You made me forget everything in those moments. It was an accident, Asher. They aren't supposed to break. You know that."

"Do you think the timing is right?" he asked her reluctantly.

She blinked. It took her a moment to understand his meaning. No *wonder* he looked so worried.

"No," she said after thinking a moment. "I should start my period in a few days."

He exhaled, looking a little relieved. He grabbed her wrist and pressed the palm of her hand against his lips.

"It's weird, isn't it?" she whispered, watching him kiss her.

"What?"

"Thinking about being pregnant."

Her quietly uttered words seemed to hang in the air between them. For a few seconds, she vividly imagined it: a new life growing inside her. A person. A child—Asher's and hers. There would be no more secrets. A baby would force their hand. It would demand that they burn all their bridges . . . forge a new path toward the future, one where they were together. A flash of euphoria went through her.

His face was rigid with worry. She looked down, averting her eyes. What if he'd read her mind? What if he'd sensed her momentary selfishness? How could she fantasize about something that would be such a nightmare for him and his future? How could she dream about something that would wound her family so deeply?

He squeezed her hand. "I'm sure you're not. I don't think I actually came that much inside you. But if you *were*—"

"I'm sure I'm not too," she interrupted him breathlessly. She smiled to cover her unrest. She didn't want him to feel sorry for her. "It's stupid, to worry about it, when the chances are so small. I've got enough on my plate as it is." She stared up at the position of the sun behind a bank of clouds.

"I should probably be going. We'll be going to the hospital in a little while."

"Laila—"

"It's okay, Asher," she said, going up on her tiptoes and kissing his mouth. She didn't think she could stand it if he apologized again . . . if she saw his regret. "I asked you here because I knew you'd make me feel better. And you did," she assured him quietly. "I love you."

"I love you too."

"That's all that matters right now," she said, kissing him once more before she turned and waded to shore.

Late that afternoon, Tahi plopped down next to her in the hospital waiting room, her cell phone clutched in her hand. Laila's family was taking turns visiting with Mamma Sophia. The hospital rooms weren't large, and her grandmother shared hers with another woman. The nurses asked that only two people visit with her at a time. Presently, Laila's and Tahi's mothers were in there. Everyone else—including Tahi's brother Zarif, who had just arrived from Detroit—had gone down to the cafeteria for an early dinner. Laila and Tahi weren't hungry, though, and had opted to stay in the waiting room.

Tahi glanced over her shoulder, making sure they were alone, before she spoke.

"What did Asher tell you earlier about Eric leaving last night?"

"Nothing. Eric left?" Laila asked, confused.

"Yeah. Rudy just told me. Asher found out this morning. He didn't say anything when you met?" Tahi knew that Laila had snuck off to see Asher earlier today, before they all planned to leave for the hospital.

Laila shook her head. *Why didn't Asher mention it?* "Where'd Eric go?"

Tahi made a face. "That's the thing. Rudy told me that he's gone to Chicago. Asher thinks he's going to tell his father about Asher going to work for the *L.A. Times*, not GGM, before Asher gets a chance to. Asher was really pissed off when he got the note from Eric."

"But how did Eric find out about the *L.A. Times*?"

"Apparently, Eric got hold of Asher's cell phone. Rudy said Eric stole it on purpose. Anyway, he was probably nosing around in Asher's texts. If he was, he found out about Asher's job, and must have wanted to be the one to break the news to Asher's dad. You know how jealous he is of Asher. He probably thought he'd just hit the jackpot, finding out about Asher's plans when Asher's parents don't know about them yet. He gets to be the messenger of bad news and look like the hero in comparison to Asher. Slime-ball," Tahi muttered in disgust.

Shivers poured down Laila's arms as she recalled how Eric had interrupted their lovemaking last night . . . how smug he'd sounded about Asher's phone.

"Rudy said Asher was headed to Chicago to try to stop Eric, or at least try to smooth things over with his parents if he couldn't get there before the damage was done," Tahi continued. "When I talked to Rudy, he seemed to think Asher was driving to Chicago, not meeting with you. So I didn't say anything different."

"I texted Asher about Mamma Sophia," Laila said numbly,

thinking about the chain of events. "He must have come and met me instead of driving to Chicago."

She recalled asking him what he'd been doing when she texted about her grandmother, and how he'd casually responded that he'd just been eating breakfast with the guys. He'd hidden the truth about his own anxiety regarding his family because he knew she was worried about Mamma Sophia.

Her throat ached. She stood abruptly and grabbed her purse.

"Where are you going?" Tahi asked.

"Just to call Asher." Her feet faltered and she came to a halt.

"What?" Tahi wondered.

"Zara," Laila whispered. She thought of how her cousin had looked just now as she'd left the waiting room for the cafeteria. She'd been teasing her little brother about something and laughing. "She doesn't know yet about Eric. Does she?"

"I haven't told her," Tahi said. "I just found out. I wouldn't be surprised if Eric skipped town without so much as a good-bye text. Would you? And now he's burned his bridges with Asher. He's not going to be coming back."

"She's crazy about Eric. This is going to kill her. We'll have to tell her together, okay?"

Tahi nodded, looking grim.

A few seconds later, Laila sat on a step in the silent, empty hospital stairwell. He answered on the third ring.

"Hey. How's Mamma Sophia?"

"She's doing okay. Her blood pressure is coming down. They're talking about discharging her tomorrow or the next day."

"That's great."

"Yeah. Asher . . . where are you?"

"Out by the pool. Why?"

"Tahi told me about Eric taking off last night . . . and about where he went."

"Oh."

"You should have *told* me. I was hoping when I called, you would have left for Chicago already." She winced when she realized she'd sounded sharp in her anxiety. "I mean . . . I know you didn't tell me because you were worried about me. *Thank* you for that," she said feelingly. "But your family . . . your mom and dad. You should go to Chicago and try to explain things to them. Even if Eric has told them about your job at the *L.A. Times* already, they deserve to hear the truth from you."

He didn't respond immediately. Her anxiety doubled in the silence.

"Asher?"

"I already told my dad," he finally said. "Well, I *tried* to explain, anyway. I called him after I got home from the secret lake."

"Oh no," she whispered, cringing inwardly. She could tell by the resigned, bitter tone of his voice that the conversation with his dad hadn't gone well. "Had Eric already told him about your job?"

"No," he stated flatly. "Eric had made an appointment to see Dad this afternoon, but he hadn't actually broken the news yet. So the joke was on me, in the end. I ended up telling my father before I was ready to. And on the phone instead of in person."

"The conversation went that bad?"

He gave a dry bark of laughter. "*Bad* is an understatement. He was so shocked . . . and then so pissed off, he was having trouble putting more than three words together at a time."

So disappointed. He hadn't said the two words, but somehow she'd heard his thoughts.

"Asher, you have to go to see your parents."

"I only have a few more nights here. I only have a handful of days left with you. Why should I waste them on a lost cause? They aren't going to understand."

She squeezed her eyelids tight, hearing his desperation beneath the cracks of his calm voice. "But it's your family. Your mom and dad love you. Underneath their anger, they're probably hurt." She swallowed back the lump in her throat. "I don't want to miss any time with you either. I *hate* the idea. But you should go and try to explain to them why you want to work at the *Times* and why you don't want to work at GGM . . . tell them why you want to follow your own path."

"My dad accused me of being a traitor on the phone. They'll never accept it, Laila."

"But you have to *try*. If they don't understand today or tomorrow or next year, maybe they will *someday*. There has to be a beginning to healing sometime. You have to be honest about who you are in front of them, no matter how hard it is."

She heard his soft laugh.

"What?" she asked.

"You give that advice so convincingly, but you won't take it from me."

"It's not the same situation, Asher."

He exhaled heavily. "Yeah. I guess you're right."

"Are you going?"

"Yeah. I'll leave as soon as I can," he said.

"It's the right thing to do."

"How can driving away from you be right?"

His bitter, solemn voice echoed in her head. A tear splashed down her cheek. He made a good point. Nothing about being separated from him at that place and time felt *right*.

"It'll only be for a night or two. We'll see each other soon," she managed to say after she'd gotten hold of herself.

Neither of them said anything further about it. Somehow, Laila thought Asher was thinking the same thing she was at that moment, however. Maybe they'd see each other again in a day or two. But both of them knew a longer, farther separation loomed close. They still hadn't come up with anything to solve that horrible reality.

She was hanging up her phone, her heart feeling like a heavy stone in her chest, when the stairwell door opened.

"There you are," Tahi said. "Mamma Sophia wants to see you."

"She does? Is everything okay?"

"Yeah. She just wants to see her little *kibdi*," Tahi said, grinning at the familiar Moroccan endearment. "We'll tell Zara about Eric after you finish with Mamma Sophia?"

Laila's small smile vanished at the reminder of Zara.

"Yeah," she agreed. "I guess the sooner we get it over with, the better."

Zara's reaction to the news that Eric had left Crescent Bay wasn't at all what Tahi and Laila had expected it to be.

"So what if he left for a little bit? Why do you guys look so serious?" Zara wondered, nonchalantly sipping the coffee she'd brought up from the cafeteria.

"It's not for a *little* bit," Tahi said uneasily. "Rudy said Eric's gone for good."

Zara slid her cell phone out of her pocket and held it up pointedly. "Then how come we're meeting tonight over at Chauncy's?"

"Eric said he'd meet you tonight?" Laila asked disbelievingly.

"Don't look so surprised," Zara said, rolling her eyes. "Just because he got sick and tired of Asher being rude to him all the time over at his house doesn't mean he wanted to leave *me*. He's still on vacation, you know. He's got a hotel room in Crescent Bay."

Laila and Tahi shared an uneasy glance. What was Eric up to?

"If Asher was rude to Eric, it was probably with good reason," Tahi stated bluntly. "Eric went to Chicago specifically to tattle to Asher's dad that Asher wasn't planning to work for the family business. *Eric* wanted to be the one to break the bad news. He loves to gloat over making Asher look bad. He's been doing it to Asher his whole life. That's what Rudy told me."

"Oh, *poor* Asher," Zara said scathingly.

"Zara, listen . . . I really think you have to be careful about Eric," Laila said, growing more and more unsettled by the second.

Zara's laugh made a chill go through her. There was something in her cousin's face in that moment that she'd never really seen before, a bitterness, distrust . . . even *disgust* toward Tahi and her. Was *this* what falling for Eric had done to Zara? Turned her against them, Zara's cousins and best friends? It was like Laila was watching this whole situation with the guys—their carefree summer—begin to unwind.

Grow rancid.

"That's *funny.* You preaching to me about being careful with Eric, when you've jumped into a grave far deeper than any of us with Asher. Sweet little Laila isn't so innocent anymore, is she? And yet you sit there and try to throw the blame on *Eric*?"

Laila flinched back, thinking of how Eric had interrupted Asher and her in bed last night. He'd apparently told Zara about it.

"And *you've* been listening to that little weasel Rudy too much," Zara said, turning to Tahi, malice twisting her pretty face. "What if Eric *did* go to Chicago with the intention of telling Asher's dad about Asher's plans? Eric *does* work for GGM. He probably thought Asher's father should know Asher was never planning to come on board. Eric is loyal to the business *and* to his family. What's so horrible about that?"

"Because *Asher* should have been the one to break the news."

Laila defended Asher hotly. "He planned to do it in person next week. Now Eric has ruined everything with his interference."

"Eric hasn't ruined anything. Asher's a liar. How is that Eric's fault?"

"Oh, and Eric is just an angel in all this," Tahi seethed, her cheeks flushed. "And since when do *you* get off, acting all holier-than-thou. Like you don't lie through your teeth dozens of times a day—"

"Shut up. *Zarif*," Zara warned in a hiss under her breath, her white teeth bared.

Tahi and Laila glanced over their shoulder. Tahi's older brother, Zarif, entered the waiting room. Laila waved self-consciously at her cousin. Zarif waved stiffly, a puzzled expression on his face. He went over to the vending machine without saying anything, but Laila thought he'd looked a little suspicious about their hushed, charged conversation.

Zara was cool toward Tahi and Laila for the rest of the evening. Tahi was furious at Zara. Laila was angry too, and worried, and . . . sad. What had seemed like a tiff to Tahi felt like a tear to Laila, somehow, like something elemental had ripped in her family life. Zara was changing.

So was Laila. And that had her scared as much as anything.

After they'd returned to the cottages, Laila texted Asher. She wasn't sure if he'd met up with his parents yet. But she wanted to give him the information that Eric had returned to Crescent Bay, in case he didn't know it.

Where's he staying in Crescent Bay? Asher texted her almost immediately when she wrote about Eric.

There was something about the terseness of his texted question that sent off an alarm in her head.

I don't know. Some hotel. Asher . . . promise me you won't look for him.

A short pause ensued.

I'm close to my parents' house. We'll talk about it later, he texted.

A vivid picture popped into her head of Eric and Asher pounding on each other.

Okay. I understand. But promise me you won't look for Eric before you go. Please?

I just pulled up at my parents' house. I promise. I'll call soon.

A feeling of relief went swept her at his promise, but she was anxious for him too because of the imminent meeting with his parents. She didn't want to bother him while he was trying to explain his decision to them. Determined to give him space, she set aside her phone.

Since Zara was mad at them, Tahi and she decided to sleep at their own family cottages that night instead of on the sleeping porch. After Laila got into bed, she found herself staring at Mamma Sophia's empty bed, that increasingly familiar ache expanding in her belly. Her grandmother had been more alert, but very emotional, when Laila had gone to see her that evening. She'd reached for Laila's hands, beaming at her.

"*My little* kibdi . . . *The light of my life. Beautiful Laila*," Mamma Sophia had uttered quietly in Darija.

A poignant feeling of love unfolded inside Laila at the memory. What would she do without her grandmother? What would Mamma Sophia think, if she knew about Asher . . . about her granddaughter's lies?

She realized that her hand was moving nervously at her belly. Graphic, erotic images flooded her mind's eye, memories of her and Asher's moments at the secret lake this afternoon. She thought of how he'd ignored his own family crisis in order to be with her during hers.

She clamped her thighs together tightly and moaned in misery. What if she *was* pregnant? It was like a blade in her side, imagining her mother's bewildered reaction at her secrecy and betrayal. Her father's. Mamma Sophia's.

She envisioned their subsequent worry and anguish, and their anger at her betrayal of their trust. It tormented her, considering it. And yet . . . somehow that cutting pain freed her too. Because even though she imagined hurt and disappointment on her family members' faces, she knew they would see her without blinders on. They would see Laila truly.

They would likely reject her.

The very idea made it hard for her to draw air. Her family was her whole world. The idea of being cut off from them felt like suffocating.

But being without Asher? Well . . . imagining it made her feel as if her heart were freezing in her chest. It would have to turn to ice.

Because otherwise, she wouldn't be able to stand the pain.

When she got up the next morning, there was a text from Asher. He said that his mother was insisting they all have lunch before he left for Crescent Bay. They wanted one more opportunity to talk him around to their point of view, but Asher was resolute in his decision. Grimly so. He texted:

I know I'm disappointing them. I hate it. They think they know what's right for me so well, and that I'm just being stubborn in going against them. But it's them they know about. Not me.

She'd sensed his loneliness in those words. It made her ache for him.

He wanted to meet with her at the secret lake at four or five o'clock. But Laila was forced to tell him that she wasn't sure if she could go. There was a possibility Mamma Sophia would come home this afternoon. She wanted to be there to get her grandmother settled, and to support her mother too. Her mom had been energetic and vigilant about Mamma Sophia's care since the heart attack, but Laila, who knew her so well, sensed how strained and anxious she was beneath her smiles. To add to everything, her father had been forced to travel back to Detroit, just for the day, in order to see to an emergency situation in his shop. So he wouldn't be there to assist her mom.

But won't your mom's sister be there to help her with your grandmother? Asher texted.

Yes, but Mamma will want me here. Laila paused in typing, torn. It was so hard to convey to him the elemental bonds of her family.

She started to text: But I'll do what I can to meet you later . . . if not tonight, then tomorrow. I promise. I'll get back to you when I know more.

Mamma Sophia was discharged that afternoon. Everyone pitched in to make her as comfortable as possible. All their efforts must have worked, because Mamma Sophia was fast asleep by five o'clock.

Laila put down the book she'd been reading to her grandmother and turned out the light in their bedroom. Her mother, aunties, Zarif and Tahi were all drinking tea in the kitchen when she entered.

"Have you told Laila yet, *Khal-ti* Amira?" Tahi asked Laila's mother. Laila paused next to the table when she saw the anxiety in Tahi's eyes.

"We're all going back to Detroit tomorrow," her mother stated, calmly taking a sip of her tea.

"But . . . but what about Mamma Sophia?" Laila asked, stunned.

"Zarif has kindly arranged for a friend of his—a man who owns a private ambulance service—to transport Mamma Sophia back home. She'll be much more comfortable at our house, and we need to get her in to see Dr. Boulos," she said, referring to Mamma Sophia's regular doctor in Detroit. "Are you sure your friend is doing this as a favor, Zarif? I wouldn't want you paying for this out of your own pocket."

"She *is* my grandmother, you know," Zarif said, smiling. He noticed Laila's mom's intensified worried expression and added quickly, "It's a favor, *Khal*-ti Amira. *Honest.*"

Laila heard all of this through a ringing in her ears. This was it. The end. It had come sooner than she'd thought. She wasn't prepared—

"Laila? You okay?"

She blinked and focused on Zarif's handsome face. He looked concerned.

"It looks like all the blood just dropped out of your head," he said, standing.

She realized she gripped tightly at the corner of the table.

"No, I'm fine," she mumbled. She gave Tahi a wild glance. "Do you want to take a little walk?"

"Sure," Tahi said, setting down her tea abruptly and standing. They headed for the beach.

"What's *with* those girls?" Laila heard Zarif say through the screen door.

"It's Mamma Sophia," Laila's mother said with a sigh. "You have no idea how much Laila has been worried about her."

Laila strained to overhear more, but Tahi was pulling her

across the terrace. She heard Zarif say something about Zara before the sound of the surf silenced the conversation.

"What are you going to do?" Tahi asked her tensely once they put some distance between themselves and the cottages.

Laila stared out at the white sand and the shimmering periwinkle-blue water, seeing nothing but Asher's face.

"I don't know," she said. She'd never been so scared.

Chapter Sixteen

At eleven forty-five that night, Laila rose from her bed. She silently and methodically stuffed some pillows beneath the bedclothes to make it look like she was still in the bed. For several seconds, she lingered by the side of Mamma Sophia's sleeping form, assuring herself that her grandmother was breathing and peaceful.

Then she snuck out of the room.

Her heart pounded faster tonight than any time when she'd escaped from the sleeping porch. There was a good chance her parents would hear her tread in the hallway. One misplaced step on a squeaky floorboard would betray her. What she was doing tonight was a far greater risk than she'd ever taken before. She didn't dare to even breathe until she'd made it through the house. When she finally made it out the door and down the terrace steps, she felt dizzy. She paused, bending over and gasping for air.

A moment later, she raced up the white, moonlit dune toward the road. Toward Asher. They'd agreed by text to meet. Three quarters of the way up the dune, she paused and glanced backward at the cottages. A light in the communal parking area told her that Zara's car was missing.

She's with Eric.

Both she and her cousin were rebels tonight.

Her cousin Zarif's car was missing too. Had he decided to go back to Detroit?

"Laila."

Asher's hushed call jerked her out of her thoughts. She resumed jogging up the dune.

It felt like her heart was going to burst out of her chest by the time she reached the summit of the dune and the road. It gave another leap when she saw his tall form leave the shadows and step into the moonlight. He wore jeans and a dark-colored T-shirt that showed off his cut, muscular torso. A shiver passed through her when she saw his lean, hungry expression as he stared at her. For the past several days and nights, she'd been so chaotic emotionally, so scattered, so uncertain about what she should do . . . about what was right, about what was *true* for her.

But in that moment, Asher struck her as almost savage in his focus. He had enough single-minded intent for both of them . . . for a thousand people.

For a few seconds, she just stood there, panting, a little in awe of him. He came toward her and reached out with one hand, caressing her cheek. He cupped her shoulder and leaned down, capturing her mouth in a quick, blistering kiss.

"Let's go," he breathed next to her mouth, nodding toward his parked roadster.

She just followed him, made speechless by the heat of his kiss.

Asher could hear explosions and gunfire emanating from the television set in the family room when they entered the beach house.

Rudy and Jimmy were watching a movie. Chances were, they hadn't even heard Asher leave to pick up Laila, let alone realized he was returning. He led Laila up the stairs to his bedroom. They'd barely spoken since they'd met up on the dune road. A strained silence had reigned between them. She'd texted him about her mother's proclamation that they were leaving in the morning for Detroit. He'd sensed her panic. He'd insisted that they meet tonight, and she'd agreed. But he still had no idea what she was thinking about the fact that her parents expected her to leave tomorrow. He was scared to ask her.

But he would.

A few seconds later, he shut the door and turned, taking her into his arms.

She wore a sleeveless blouse and her hair was down around her shoulders. He pressed his face against her neck, inhaling the subtle floral scent from her hair and skin. He trailed his hands down her slender, lithe arms.

Laila.

He couldn't stand the thought of not seeing her again. Touching her.

He wouldn't accept it.

"Your father came back from Detroit tonight?" he asked her, lifting his head.

She looked up at him and nodded. Her eyes looked huge, and her face seemed paler than usual. He cupped the side of her head, his thumb brushing against the silky skin of her cheek.

"I'm going to come over and meet them—your mom and dad—in the morning."

"*No*, Asher. That would never work."

"I don't want to keep sneaking around like this."

She shook her head rapidly. "You don't understand. That would be the worst thing you could do. Especially with Mamma

Sophia's heart attack and everything. My mom is already worried sick."

He cupped her head more firmly. "I'm *not* going to just let you go," he stated unequivocally.

"It's not that simple, Asher."

"It *is*, Laila. You're an adult. You have the right to see whomever you want. Your mom and dad would be upset if we told them we wanted to see each other, just like my parents were when I told them about my job. But they'd come to accept it. Eventually. You have a choice in this, Laila. This isn't about them. It's about you. Us."

"*Don't*," she blurted out, her eyes going wild. "Don't make me do that. Don't make me choose. It's . . . it's *cruel*." She twisted out of his arms and fled across the room, pausing in front of the dormer window. It felt like she'd just slapped him.

It took him two seconds to realize she'd felt exactly the same way about what he'd said.

He inhaled, trying to calm his choppy emotions, and went to her. She stood with her back to him, her head lowered. He couldn't decide where her misery ended and his began. He put his hands on her upper arms. When he tried to turn her, she resisted at first.

"They *are* me, Asher. Don't you get that? I can't discount my family like you do your parents," she said bitterly.

He stiffened. "Wow. That was a low blow."

Regret tightened her face.

"I'm *sorry*. I'm sorry for saying that. It was mean. Horrible. I know it," she said in a strangled voice. "I'm sorry I can't explain myself right to you. I'm sorry if it means I'm still too young to stand up for myself, or that I'm not brave enough, or that I'm weak." She reached up and took his face in her hands. "I love you," she said fiercely, her eyes shimmering with tears. "I don't know what's right, but I don't want to give up on us. But I don't want to hurt my family either. Can't you understand that?"

"I'm trying," he said. "But I don't see how you can have both without bending."

"You're not bending me," she said so loudly, he started. Her face suddenly collapsed. "God, Asher, you're *breaking* me."

The way she looked in that moment nearly brought him to his knees. She was like a cornered animal, and there was no way out of facing the truth. *He* was one of the people cornering her. Torturing her.

"*No*, I'm the one who's sorry," he muttered, pulling her to him. He pressed his mouth to her temple, running his hand through her soft hair, his palm at her back absorbing her trembling. He was an asshole for pushing and prodding at something so sweet. So precious. "I'm so sorry. Shhh," he pleaded softly. *"Laila—"*

And then—he wasn't sure how it happened, if she'd craned up for him, or if he'd swept down for her—their mouths fused. All their volatility and blind uncertainty found a channel in that kiss. It hit him like an explosion. Somewhere in the back of his brain, he realized he probably could have stopped himself if Laila hadn't reciprocated completely. But she seemed every bit as wild as he was. They fell onto the bed, Asher coming down over her. Laila clutched at him like she thought she was drowning.

And he knew this wasn't just lust. It was love, and need . . . and the desperation that comes from fear, because a brutal loss was drawing near.

Afterward, they lay there, holding each other fast. They hadn't even taken off most of their clothes before they'd made love. He regretted that now, sliding his hand beneath her dress and caressing the supple curve of her hip. He pressed his mouth against the silky skin of her belly and felt his airway tighten, like there was a hand at his throat.

"I'll fly back in a few weeks," he said, trying to sound calm. "To Detroit."

He felt her fingers in his hair. "It'll be even harder for me to see you in Detroit than it is here."

He lifted his head, hearing the flat, hopeless quality of her voice.

"Don't give up, Laila."

He saw her throat convulse and thought maybe that invisible, choking hand had transferred to her. He pressed his mouth to her neck, her small moan of misery vibrating into his lips. Her arms surrounded him, beckoning him to her. He rose up over her, seeking her mouth. The sound of several car doors slamming—three or four in quick succession?—reached his ears. His head jerked around.

"What was that?"

"I don't know," Laila whispered.

He rolled off the bed. Jerking up his jeans and underwear, he hurried over to the window and drew back the curtain. Four tall men were walking in the driveway toward the house. They didn't speak. Something about their somber intent and rapid, long strides sent an alarm going off in his head.

"Shit," he muttered.

"Asher?" Laila called from behind him. "Who is it?"

He turned to her. The grim reality of the situation had settled on him like a lead jacket, grounding him in the inescapable moment.

"I've never seen your family before, but I'm guessing it's them. Or at least four of the guys in the family." He waved toward the window. She rushed across the room. She peered cautiously out the window, and then stepped back, her face frozen in shock.

"It *is* them. My father, my uncles and Zarif, my cousin," she whispered, disbelief making her voice sound hollow. "How in the world—"

He grabbed her shoulders. She glanced up at him, startled.

"Tell me one thing, and be honest, Laila. I'll know if you're lying. Are they going to hurt you?"

Her blank stare told him she wasn't computing his meaning. "I won't let them see you, if they're going to hurt you in any way," he clarified. The muted sound of knocking on the front doors reached their ears. He shook her softly. Her glazed eyes sharpened on him. "Are you going to be safe?" he demanded.

"Of *course* I am. My father would *never* hurt me in any way, no matter *how* furious he is." Her lips trembled, as if she'd just heard what she'd said about her father's fury.

The knocking below them grew louder . . . more insistent.

He cursed bitterly, seeing no way out of the situation but to face it head-on. He finished buttoning his jeans and led Laila over to the bed to retrieve her underwear.

"What are we going to do?" she whispered after she'd scurried into the panties he handed her.

He smoothed her hair, then took her hand in his. "We're going down to meet them."

Laila couldn't breathe. She couldn't understand how Asher seemed so calm as he led her down the stairs.

"Who the hell is *that*?" someone said.

Laila realized it was Rudy, standing in the entryway and peering through the cut-glass windows on the double front doors. Someone on the other side pounded extra loud, making Rudy start back in alarm.

"Open up. Now!"

"Laila."

Laila started at the sound of her father's bellow.

"Stand back, Rudy. It's Laila's family," Asher said. He flipped several light switches in the foyer. Rudy stepped away from the door, looking confused. Laila could tell by his surprised glance at her that he hadn't even realized she was in the house.

"Asher." It was Jimmy, just entering the foyer. "Don't you think—"

But Asher flipped the lock. She felt Asher push her behind him before he swung open the door.

It was surreal, seeing her father's, uncles' and Zarif's tense faces illuminated by the entryway lights.

"Baba, what are you *doing* here?" Laila asked in a strangled voice, peering around Asher's wide shoulders. Her father's gaze jumped from Laila to Rudy and Jimmy standing behind them. It landed on Asher. His jaw clenched tight.

"You ask me what I'm doing at this place in the middle of the night, when I thought my daughter was sleeping soundly in her bed?" her father asked bitterly. Laila cringed at the wild hurt she saw in his eyes. "I didn't believe it was true, until this minute. Not even when Zarif woke me up and told me that he'd followed Zara to some bar, and the man she'd been with claimed that *you'd* been sneaking out at night, as well. Coming here." He pointed aggressively at Asher. "To be with this one. But here I find you. Step aside," he ordered Asher.

"Mr. Barek, if you could just calm down, this isn't—"

But Baba stepped across the threshold aggressively, reaching around Asher for Laila. Asher moved to block him. Zarif lunged, grabbing Asher's shirt and jerking him in the opposite direction of Laila. Asher slammed into the door frame and bounced off it. Laila's dad's hand closed around her upper arm.

"Baba—Asher . . . *no!*" She shouted the last because Zarif shoved Asher again, then stepped into him, blocking him from Laila. When Asher started to move toward Laila again, her cousin restrained him. Rudy stepped between them, pushing back on Zarif.

"Get *off* him," Rudy seethed.

"Let's go, Laila," her father said, pulling on her arm and urging her through the opened door. Her uncle Reda reached for her. Both of them pulled her down the steps, one of them on each side. For a second, she couldn't see what was happening behind her. She heard scuffling and cursing, and then the sound of a thump and a grunt of pain. She twisted her chin over her shoulder.

"*Asher*," she screamed. She strained in her father's and Reda's grip, desperate to go back. Rudy held his hand over his eye and was wincing in pain. Asher's face looked tight with anger and helplessness.

"Just go, Laila," Asher yelled. "Just go with them, for now."

"What do you mean, for *now*, you son of a bitch?" Zarif shouted. He grabbed Asher's shirt and drew back his fist.

"*No*, Zarif," her uncle Taha shouted.

"Zarif, *don't—*"

"Laila, stop it," her father said angrily, because she was straining in their hold now, trying to get back to Asher. It was like she was seeing the whole catastrophe in slow motion, like a dream she couldn't wake up from. Zarif's punch landed on Asher's jaw. Asher's chin swung around, but his feet remained planted firmly on the ground. He turned back slowly. Laila called his name in rising anguish, seeing the glint of fury in his eyes as he focused on Zarif. Zarif threw another punch, but this time, Asher grabbed her cousin's fist, halting him in midair.

His other fist sank into Zarif's abdomen.

"*No*," she shouted hoarsely. Helplessness hit her in a drowning wave. She caught the horrible, fleeting image of her uncle Taha bending over a slumped Zarif. Her cousin seemed too hurt or stunned to stand on his own.

Then her dad and Reda were hustling her toward the car. Even though it felt like she was flailing underwater, she strained to see over her shoulder. She thought she saw Jimmy and Rudy pulling Asher inside the house.

She fell more than sat in the dim backseat, and her father was coming down next to her.

"You shouldn't have done that, Baba," she exclaimed bitterly. "You shouldn't have come here and hurt Asher. You don't even know him!"

Her breath caught when she took in her father's rigid profile. He sat very still. He looked like her father, whom she loved dearly, but bizarrely like a stranger too.

"He wasn't the only one who has been hurt by this, Laila," her father said without looking at her.

Her mouth snapped shut. It dawned on her with dread that he was right.

And the hurt was just beginning.

Chapter Seventeen

The next morning, the sun was overcast with dull gray clouds. Her father pulled his car into the turnabout in front of the beach house, braked and twisted his wrist in the ignition. For a moment, he and Laila just sat there with the silence billowing around them. She saw movement and turned to see one of the front doors opening. Asher stepped out onto the front steps. She'd called him a half hour ago and told him they were coming. He wore jeans, a button-down ivory shirt and a tense expression.

"I think I should go in with you," her father said.

"I'll be fine, Baba," she said, her tone weary. Her throat hurt. Her eyes felt dry. It hurt even to blink.

There had been a lot of yelling—from both her parents and herself upon her return last night. There had been no rest for any of them. There'd been a lot of tears too, and then the tears had dried up. Then Mamma Sophia had fallen as she'd tried to get out of bed, and they'd had to take her to the emergency room. It had been a night straight out of a nightmare. Laila's insides felt abraded . . . scraped raw.

"He hit your cousin—"

"Zarif hit Asher first, and was about to do it again," Laila said, irritation rising in her voice even though she'd said the same thing dozens of times last night. She'd never seen Zarif behave that way. She hadn't even known he had it in him to be such an aggressive caveman.

"I don't think this is a good idea, coming here."

"It was *your* idea. The only thing I'm doing now is finalizing it. You told me a thousand times last night how dishonest I was being by sneaking around." She met her dad's gaze squarely. "All I'm trying to do now is be honest."

"We're doing this for your sake, Laila."

"No. *I'm* doing this for *you*," she corrected coldly. "I love him, Baba. I'd *never* do this for myself."

Her father closed his eyes briefly, and she felt his pain. She felt *everyone's* pain on that gray morning. She wished like hell she could make it stop.

"You're nineteen, Laila. You're young. This will pass," he said quietly. "You *have* to believe me when I say that I'm thinking only of you in this. Of your happiness. I'm going to allow you to speak to him this one time. But understand this. Never again."

Laila said nothing. She'd heard it so many times last night, the words felt like hollowed-out missiles. They still hurt, but they weren't penetrating as far. Something had hardened inside her.

She peered out the window at Asher's face and saw the discoloration on his jaw where Zarif had hit him. She saw the worry in his eyes. A numbness settled on her. She turned to her father. He looked different to her. Older. Had last night aged him? Or maybe it was just that he was looking at her—Laila—differently?

"I'll only be a few minutes. Stay here."

She opened the door and stepped out onto the driveway. She

slammed the car door. For several seconds, she stood there, her gaze locked with Asher's.

The she started to walk toward him. That was when she first felt it: the icy hand of fate gripping her heart.

". . . and so that's how it all happened," Laila was saying in a flat tone. They sat in his mother's sitting room, Asher at the corner of a couch. Laila perched on the edge of a chair. As she talked, she rubbed her hands together in a nervous gesture. Asher was growing more and more concerned by the pallor of her face, the dark circles under her eyes and the frozen quality of her usually animated expression. When they'd entered the sitting room earlier and shut the door, he'd tried to take her into his arms. But she'd just walked around him and sat down on the chair, where he couldn't sit next to her.

"My cousin Zarif is really smart, and he's close enough to our age to know when something's up," she continued, still refusing to make eye contact with him. "He noticed Zara sneaking out last night to meet Eric and followed them to Chauncy's. From what I gather, he didn't find them in the most beneficial of circumstances. They were in an empty back room alone at Chauncy's, fooling around. Anyway, accusations were flying between them, and suddenly Eric blurted out all this stuff about you and me. I don't know why he did it then—"

"To deflect your cousin's attention off kicking *his* ass onto kicking *mine*," Asher said, his mouth curling in disgusted fury. Laila gave him a startled glance at his concise, bitter evaluation of things. "I know how Eric works," he stated simply. "Then what happened?"

"Zarif hauled Zara back to the cottages and woke up her

parents. My mom and dad, and Tahi's too, got up because of all the shouting at Zara's parents' place. In the midst of all the chaos, Zarif told my dad about what Eric had said about you and me. They stormed into my and Mamma Sophia's room and saw that I was missing." She paused, her face tightening briefly in pain.

"Laila?"

"My grandmother got confused and scared by all the shouting and confusion," she continued in a muffled voice. "She tried to get out of bed by herself, and she fell—"

"Jesus," Asher said, sitting forward and taking her hand. "Is she okay?"

Laila's chin fell down to her chest. Wild concern swamped him when he realized she was shaking, her entire body quaking in a fine tremor. She wasn't actually cold and distant in those moments, he realized. She was in misery, and barely holding it together. He went down on his knees and moved before her in the chair. He cradled her head and lifted her face gently.

"She's okay," Laila said. "We took her to the ER, just to be sure. There's some bruising, but she's okay."

"It wasn't your fault, Laila," he said, knowing her well enough by now to know precisely what was going through her head.

She clamped her eyelids closed, shaking her head in his hands. "I have to go. I can't keep putting this off by talking about last night," she said, her voice so thick with emotion he could barely understand her. "It's done."

"What's done?"

She opened her eyelids. He glimpsed through a crack that deep inside, she blazed like she was burning . . . like she was in the pain of a person at the center of a fire.

"We're over."

"We're not over," he said, laughing slightly after a stunned pause, sure he'd misheard her. She just stared at him, the blaze of pain slowly leaving her eyes, the window to her soul shutting tight. His thumbs feathered her cheekbones. Despite the tension of the moment—despite the impossibility of it—he wondered again at how beautiful she was. How rare. "Laila, you *can't* let them get to you. We'll find a way to keep talking. To see each other. You can't let them turn you away from what you want."

"What I want," she stated, "is to not hurt my family anymore. The only way I can do that is to try to respect the rules they've laid out for me while I live under their roof. I hate it. I *should* do it, though."

He shook his head. "That's your parents talking. Not you. They're forcing you to say that."

"*Please.* Try to understand, Asher. I love my family. I'm nineteen years old. I depend on them, and not just in some existential way either. I can't afford to live on my own. I live under their roof. I eat their food. They expect certain things of me—"

"I have money. Plenty of it. I've never told you before, but my grandfather left me a trust. I've had control of it since he passed when I was twenty. I try not use it, because . . ."

"You've wanted to stand on your own two feet. Don't you think I know that about you?"

He blinked at her concise interruption. Apparently, she'd come to know him as well as he knew her. "The point is, I have plenty to support us. Come with me to Los Angeles."

"What am I going to do there? I don't have a college degree yet. Do you want me to waitress my whole life? Or maybe you're going to pay my way for everything, make me into a kept woman or something? You'd come to resent me."

"I wouldn't. Because that's not what would happen—"

"You're starting out your life, Asher. The last thing you need is me hanging around your neck. Standing on your own is important to you. You want to know you can make it on your own, without resorting to inheritances and trust funds. You deserve to know you *can* do that. If I were there, you couldn't really know that. If you had to sacrifice a personal standard like that for me, you *would* resent it. You'd resent *me. No.* I know you think my parents are forcing me to say this—"

"I don't think they're threatening you with force. I think they're intimidating you in a way that feels even worse to you. They're threatening to take away their approval. Their love. Their acceptance. Do you think I don't know what that's like, Laila?"

"I think you *believe* you do. But I'm different than you, Asher. My family is different. That's something you've never *gotten* about me. We come from two different worlds. Your ways of dealing with things just won't work for me. Maybe Baba isn't a hundred percent right in saying interracial stuff *never* works. Maybe it can work sometimes, for some people. But right now, at this point in my life, I don't know how to do it. I don't know *how*, Asher. And neither do you. It's just that you're too stubborn, and too determined, and too strong, and too . . . wonderful"—she choked softly—"to admit it."

His caressing fingers paused. She met his stare. Despite the misery he sensed flowing off her like a freezing fog, she remained unflinching. Asher started to feel that frigid cold penetrate him. But he fought it like crazy.

"What about what we talked about? About fighting through? About not giving up?" he asked.

Her lower lip trembled.

"Laila," he whispered, caressing her again, willing her to bend. To unfreeze. To come to him in the way only she could . . . so sweetly. So completely.

Instead, he saw her delicate jaw clench hard. She wrapped her hands around his wrists and pulled. Tears swelled in her eyes when his fingertips slid off her face.

"I love you, Asher. So much. It's been like a dream, being with you these past couple weeks. I will *always* love you." A spasm went through her beautiful face. Dread swooped through him, making everything seem to go dim for a moment. "But this hurts too much," she said in a strangled voice. "You suggested last night I needed to decide. To choose—"

"No," he said rapidly, wild to make her stop talking. To make this *moment* halt. To undo itself. "I told you I was wrong about saying that, about trying to make it black and white—"

"I choose for us not to see each other anymore."

"*No*," he roared, making her start. He stood in front of her, feeling off balance.

"It's *not* just because of my family, Asher. It's for you too—"

Anger pierced his helplessness. He pointed at her.

"*Don't*. Don't try to spin it that way."

"It's true," she said, leaping up from her chair. "I can't be with you in the way you want. The way you deserve. And what about your parents? Things are rough enough between you three as it is without you having to worry about dating a woman they'd disapprove of."

He turned away from her. "You *know* my parents don't even factor in to any of this."

"Well, maybe they *should*," she exclaimed.

He spun around.

"So this is it?" he asked, his voice ringing in rising anger and disbelief. "You're choosing your family over me."

Her spine straightened. He didn't know what he hated more, the blaze of pain he'd witnessed in her expression earlier or the lifelessness in her eyes as she looked at him now.

"If that's the way you want to frame it all. It's not how *I* see it. But we both already know that we look at this situation differently. There's no point in arguing about it more." She lowered her head. "I have to go," she said thickly. "My father is waiting for me."

"God forbid we should keep him waiting," he stated bitterly. He couldn't believe this was happening.

"Good-bye, then," she said softly.

He clamped his mouth shut tight. He refused to say it, denying her the clean breakup that she so clearly craved.

"What about the possibility that you're pregnant?" he demanded harshly when she reached the door. "What are you going to do if you are?"

She turned to him slowly, her hand on the doorknob. The sadness on her face made him want to roar at the unfairness of life, to beat his fists until he'd pounded the world raw.

"I'm not pregnant. I started my period last night, after we took Mamma Sophia to the emergency room."

He stood there, the soft click of the door shutting behind her resounding like an explosion in his head. He wasn't sure how long he remained there, numb with disbelief.

Suddenly, anger sluiced through him. It galvanized him. He lunged toward the door, one clear target in mind. Crescent Bay wasn't a big town. There were only three hotels in it. He'd find Eric. What better outlet for his fury? He'd beat that bastard to a pulp for betraying him . . . for putting the wheels in motion that led to the pain he was feeling right now.

Yeah, he'd promised Laila he'd leave Eric alone, Asher acknowledged bitterly as he sped out of the driveway a moment later. But Laila had turned and walked away, hadn't she?

As far as Asher was concerned, all promises were null and void.

PART TWO

Chapter Eighteen

Present Day

As she unlocked the front door to their condo, the brief, graphic image of his face through the train doors flashed into Laila's mind's eye. The vivid blue eyes. The unmistakable determination.

Asher.

Here. In Chicago. It was too incredible to believe.

Once again, an electric charge passed through her at the memory. She shivered. The door swung open and she stepped into the foyer. She saw the flicker of the television in the distant, darkened living room. Her heart sank. Her roommate was awake.

"Laila?" Tahi yelled.

"What are you still doing up?" Laila called, straining to keep her voice even. She wished her cousin were in bed, like she usually was when Laila came home late from performing at the State Room. Once in a while, Tahi would attend her performance with a date. But she and Tahi had lived together in Chicago for the past five years now, ever since they'd both graduated from Wayne State.

Laila had started singing publicly six months after their move, so the novelty of watching her cousin perform five nights a week had undoubtedly worn thin for Tahi.

"Michael got a new espresso machine, and he kept experimenting on me," Tahi called from the living room. Laila knew Michael was the guy Tahi had been seeing for the past few weeks. He was a lawyer who had relocated to Chicago from San Francisco. Or was it Seattle? Tahi had left their first jobs out of college at Microsoft soon after Laila had, wooed away by a young, hip, skyrocketing tech firm. As the manager of that company, Tahi met a boatload of eligible guys. Laila got Tahi's men mixed up as a matter of course.

"I have enough caffeine in me to keep me awake for a week." Laila could tell by the sound of Tahi's that voice she was walking toward her. She barely had enough time to try to wipe the anxiety off her face and appear nonchalant before the foyer light switched on.

"What's wrong with you?" Tahi wondered with her usual sharp observance and blunt manner of speaking. "You look like you just saw a ghost."

Laila refrained from rolling her eyes. So much for appearing calm and nonchalant. She pushed the hood off her head and unzipped her jacket.

"Nothing's wrong. It was a busy night at the club."

"It's always busy. You're a smash hit," Tahi said frankly, her gaze narrowing on Laila's appearance. "Did you take the train *again*?"

Laila laughed and hung up her hoodie. "You can tell by my clothes?"

"That, plus Rafe called earlier and wondered if you were home yet."

Laila grimaced and walked past her cousin toward the kitchen.

Rafe was Rafael Durand, the owner of the State Room and several other hot music venues on the East Coast and in the Midwest. He also had managed and promoted Laila exclusively for the past year. He was extremely good at what he did. Despite Laila's firm resolve not to expose her face to her audience, Rafe had managed not only to make her live performances a hot ticket but to get her a valuable indie recording contract. He still regularly tried to talk her into moving out from behind the veil and reminded her he could do much, much more for her if she didn't insist on anonymity. But he also respected and protected her choice for privacy.

Rafe had also pursued her romantically since the moment they'd been introduced by a mutual friend. It had been after one of her performances at a Gold Coast club fourteen months ago. But Laila had only made the decision to date him last month. Even before they'd started dating, Rafe hated when she took the L home. He insisted it was dangerous at the time of night her performances ended. He hired a driver for her. But Laila always took a perverse pleasure in slipping through the dark tunnels at night and blending into the shadows.

"Didn't feel like hanging out with Rafe tonight, huh?" Tahi asked wisely, following her. Laila flipped on a light, illuminating the kitchen. It was one of her favorite rooms in the Near North Side condominium Tahi and she had bought last year. Laila had started to do well with her singing, and Tahi had landed a really good job two years ago. They could afford the condo, and then some. The rest of the apartment was sophisticated urban chic, but the kitchen was cozy and warm. It had been the room Tahi and she had fallen in love with immediately.

"Rafe can be a little . . . intense," Laila said, opening up a cupboard.

"Intense? That can be so sexy in the right guy, and a total turnoff in the wrong one."

"He means well. Do you want some atay?" Laila asked, referring to the staple Moroccan tea they'd drunk since they were kids and had never outgrown.

"I better stick to some chamomile. I'm wired enough."

Laila nodded, distracted by the persistent image of the man on the other side of the train doors. He'd looked so fierce. Almost savage. It was as if the young man she knew so many years ago—all of his focus, his determination . . . his sex appeal—had become distilled.

"Hey. *Hello*. Laila?"

Laila blinked and looked over at Tahi.

"You just gave me a bag of atay, but I want chamomile," Tahi said, nodding at their tea glasses..

"Oh, I'm sorry," Laila mumbled.

"Never mind. I'll get mine," Tahi said, laughing. "Why *are* you so out of it? Is it something to do with Rafe? Is he crowding you?"

"No, it's not that."

"What is it, then?"

Laila turned on the gas burner, searching for words. The language for talking about Asher Gaites-Granville had slowly left her in all the years of forbidding herself to speak of him.

"Laila?" Tahi prompted. Laila glanced at her cousin, who was giving her a puzzled look. For a few seconds, she nearly quashed the urge to tell Tahi. But somehow, she just *knew* if she didn't speak now, she never would. She'd grown too accomplished at the skill of denial. The pain would slowly fade, as it always did. Tonight there was little relief in the idea of being numb, however.

"You said earlier I looked like I'd seen a ghost," Laila said, busying herself with pulling some cookies out of the cupboard. She handed the cookies to Tahi while she retrieved a plate.

"Yeah. So did you see one?" Tahi joked, putting a few cookies on the plate to have with their tea.

"In a manner of speaking," Laila said slowly. "I saw Asher tonight. Asher Gaites-Granville."

One of the cookies slid off the plate. Tahi gave her a wide-eyed, startled glance.

"Asher?"

Laila smiled wistfully. "It feels weird, to say his name, doesn't it?"

"You haven't talked about him for years. . . practically since that *night*," Tahi said significantly, picking up the cookie and putting it back on the plate.

"You haven't either," Laila reminded her.

"I thought you didn't want me to bring him up, so I didn't. Things between you and my brother have never been the same since that night when he hit Asher."

"I'm always polite to Zarif," Laila defended.

"Yeah. Politely cold," Tahi said, rolling her eyes. "Anyway, I knew why your mom and dad wouldn't mention Asher, and Zara's parents. . . why *everyone* avoided the topic, my parents included."

"You mean because my deep, dark shame might spread to you, the innocent one, if someone so much as said his name?" Laila muttered dryly.

Tahi laughed. "Maybe that is what they thought, in some weird way. You have to admit, with everything that's happened to Zara in the past few years, anything that was related to that summer in Crescent Bay has become even *more* hush-hush and charged with our family. I mean, you and I both know Asher had *nothing* to do with Zara or the train wreck of her life, but—"

"But Eric did. Asher and Eric might as well have been the same man, in our parents' eyes . . . both of them interfering with their daughters. Corrupting them." Laila sighed, regret and sadness filling her, as it always did, at the mention of Zara. They weren't even sure of Zara's exact address at this point. Last Laila had heard was from a high school friend from Detroit. He'd seen Zara working at a "gentlemen's club" downtown. When her friend had noticed Laila's expression at the news, he'd hastily explained that Zara had been cocktail waitressing, *not* stripping. The additional information helped ease Laila's worry a little, but not much.

After Laila told Tahi about it, the two of them had ventured into the club one night, determined to confront Zara since she'd left home when she was twenty-one—and hopefully haul her away from that seedy place. They'd gotten tips on Zara's whereabouts and gone out to find her on four other occasions before this one. Each time, they'd failed. Zara always seemed to keep one step ahead of them. The news at the strip club had been that Zara Barek hadn't shown up for the past five nights she was scheduled to work. According to the rude club manager, she definitely didn't have a job anymore.

So Tahi and Laila lost the trail of Zara again.

"Do you think Zara could have really loved him? Eric?" Tahi asked, and Laila knew Tahi had been thinking about Zara too. Zara could be a handful at times, willful and insensitive. But she also could be fun, warm and loyal. She'd been at Tahi's and her sides their whole lives. She was both sister and friend. You didn't just wash your hands of someone like that . . . even if Zara's parents tried to every day. Laila knew they never succeeded. Reda and Nadine had thought they'd been heartbroken by Zara's promiscuity with a white guy. But they hadn't known *true* anguish until Zara had left and never come back.

"I think she thought she loved him," Laila said softly.

Tahi seemed to hesitate.

"What?" Laila prompted.

"It's just . . . *I* didn't not say Asher's name in front of you because I was going along with everyone else in our family. I wouldn't want you thinking that. I didn't mention Asher after a while because I could see how much it hurt you."

"Thanks," Laila said, watching Tahi bite into the cookie. "I appreciate that."

"So you saw him? Actually *saw* Asher? Tonight?"

She shook her head slightly, for a second wondering if, indeed, it had all been a dream. But then she remembered his eyes as he'd pinned her with his stare. The full beard. She'd seen him all right. And he'd seen her.

"I really did."

"What'd he say?" Tahi whispered.

"My name. Just my name." She saw Tahi's puzzled look and quickly told her about their brief encounter down in the subway, and how the train closing between them had interrupted their meeting.

"Wow," Tahi said after she'd finished. "Asher Gaites-Granville. It seems like so long ago, doesn't it? That summer in Crescent Bay? But also like—"

"It happened yesterday?"

Tahi swallowed and tossed down the remainder of her cookie onto the plate. "I know he became a persona non grata with our family . . . kind of a he-who-shall-not-be-named?" Laila gave a bark of bitter laughter in agreement. "Even though you never talked about him much after that night, I want you to know that I *knew*."

"Knew what?"

"That it wasn't a teenage infatuation. It wasn't like Zara and Eric. It was special. You really loved him. Once."

"How can you know that?" she asked Tahi, smiling to cover her unease and opening a drawer to get a spoon.

"For one thing, I know you followed his career. Closely."

She gave her cousin a surprised glance. Tahi shrugged.

"We shared a computer for the first two years of college. I wasn't being nosy, but I noticed a few times that you were searching his name. His articles. His bio. Tracking his progress as he moved around in the Middle East, working as a correspondent." Tahi paused and Laila gave her a questioning look. "Did you know he's been nominated for a Pulitzer Prize for the piece he did, following that family in Aleppo during the Syrian civil war? They say he was able to get it past censorship by never mentioning the government. Instead, he just focused on the family's everyday experience, their struggles, the horrors they experienced and their little victories. He let the story about what was happening there tell itself."

Laila placed her hands on the counter. She had to remind herself to breathe.

"I knew about it," she admitted after a pause. "I've read the piece. It was brilliant."

"It really was. *Hey*."

Laila realized Tahi was gripping her arm. She stood close. Her brown eyes were filled with compassion. Anxiety. Understanding.

"*Don't* tell me," Tahi whispered. "After all these years?"

"No, don't be ridiculous. I was nineteen years old," Laila said, laughing through the blockage in her throat. But then she thought of all his stories she'd read over the years, his fierce honesty, the compassion he somehow injected into his lean, concise prose. She wiped away a tear from her cheek. "Of *course* not. Right? That wouldn't make any sense."

"It didn't make any sense to you back then either. That's one thing that always stood out to me. How confused you were, like you couldn't understand this . . . this *force* that had come over you, but how you couldn't deny it. Asher was just as caught up in it. He was nuts about you. It was like watching something epic, seeing you two together." Laila gave her a startled glance. "Everyone said so, not just me. Rudy. Jimmy. Even Zara, when she wasn't too busy glowing green from envy about you two. Personally, I think Eric saw it too. He knew by betraying Asher that night, by creating the possibility of you two being ripped apart, that it was the purest, meanest way to get back at Asher."

Laila shook her head. "It's so strange, talking about it . . . hearing all their names again."

"Yeah. Laila?" Tahi asked quietly.

She looked up and met her cousin's stare.

"I've always wanted to ask you, but I didn't. Because I knew how much it hurt you, to think about him. But seeing as we're on a roll tonight, maybe now's the time."

That old, too-familiar mixture of dread, helplessness and longing rose in her belly. *Oh God, I was just a kid then. How could those old feelings still be inside me?* She'd known that pain many times in the past eight years. Most recently, she'd experienced that rise of emotion when she'd followed his story about the Syrian family, the one for which he'd been nominated for a Pulitzer. But even then, the pain had been muted to a dull ache. Presently, it felt sharp. Piercing. It alarmed her, knowing the loss of him still lived in her . . . that it had been burned somewhere deeper than flesh.

She was a successful twenty-seven-year-old woman with her whole future in front of her. She might not have known at nineteen how to balance the demands of family, culture and her own desires and goals, but she'd learned that hard lesson now.

"What did you want to ask me?" she asked Tahi, determined to ignore the anxiety rising in her.

"You regretted it, didn't you? That summer . . . you regretted letting them all talk you into not seeing Asher or talking to him ever again?"

It was on the tip of her tongue to deny it. But denial wasn't what came out of her mouth.

"Yes," she whispered hoarsely. "I've regretted it."

"You would have done things differently if you'd known what you know now?"

Laila shut her eyes. They burned. "What difference does it make?" she asked, feeling trapped by Tahi's question.

"It does matter, I think," Tahi said slowly. Laila opened her eyes at something she heard in her cousin's tone of voice. "If you wish you'd done things differently, then maybe it's not too late for you and Asher. He's here in Chicago. Why not try and find him?"

"Because things *are* different, Tahi," Laila insisted. "I broke things off with him. I hurt him. Even if I did decide I wanted to be with him, it'd *never* happen." She saw the question and confusion in Tahi's eyes. "Because he'd never want to be with *me*, given what I did."

The teapot started to hiss. She pushed herself away from the counter and busied herself preparing their teas, trying to reign in her chaotic emotions. Tahi didn't say anything when she placed their delicate tea glasses and the cookies on the cozy table surrounded by an upholstered booth, but Laila sensed her waiting patiently.

"I wrote to him," Laila admitted after they'd sat, and she took several sips of atay.

"You did?" Tahi asked.

She nodded. "Six months or so after Crescent Bay. By that time, I realized it had been a mistake to cut all ties to him. I still didn't think I should sneak around seeing him, when Mamma and Baba had expressly forbidden it and I still lived in their house. But I regretted breaking all contact with him. That had been wrong of me. I understand why I did it back then. I was young, and I was scared. I hated hurting everyone. But I hated hurting him too. It hurt so much more than I thought it would, living with that pain day in and day out," she said quietly, setting down her cup. "It ended up being a worse hell than I'd ever imagined. And it only seemed to get worse as time went on. I tried to phone and text him. He never replied. So I found his e-mail at the *L.A. Times*, and I wrote to him. I told him I knew I'd hurt him badly. But would he consider at least talking to me again?"

"What did he say?" Tahi asked.

Laila tried to blink away the memories. "Say? Nothing. He never said anything. He never responded to any of my messages."

"Ever?"

Laila shook her head. "I don't blame him. He'd moved on. He was young. Driven. Extremely talented. He'd gotten promoted to a foreign post in Istanbul less than a year after starting at the *Times*. His dreams were coming true. Even if he did still think of me, it was probably with anger. Why would he want to risk being hurt again? Who was to say I wouldn't reject him again, when backed against a wall?"

Tahi frowned. "But you changed so much in that time period. You seemed like you got ten years older overnight. It's weird, I never really thought about it before . . . but your relationship with Asher changed you so much, but in a positive way, you know? While Eric had the *opposite* effect on Zara. When Eric cut all ties with her after that summer, she got bitter, like she was pissed off at the world and determined to flip it off at every turn. You got a backbone too, but in a completely different way. You were as respectful as ever to your parents, but you still found your own voice. You started working more hours at the restaurant, even though your mom hated it. You took those extra courses in poetry and music at the junior college, paying your own tuition. And you never told your parents about it, just like you've never told them you started singing. Even though you got your degree in business from Wayne State, just like *Khal-ti* Amira and *Amu* Anass wanted you to, you were different when it came to their demands. You tried to give them what they wanted when you could, but you didn't let their preferences for your life get to you as much. *Khal-ti* Amira stopped having the power to push your buttons, a fact that I know bugs the crap out of her to this day," Tahi said with a weary, but fond laugh. "When we graduated, they gave you such a hard time about moving to Chicago with me, but you wouldn't bend. You started singing at O'Rourke's a couple months after we got here. Even though you didn't want to hurt your mom and dad by having them find out from someone else about you singing in public, you didn't let it stop you from following your dreams. Our family doesn't know about your career—true—but you haven't let the fear of their disapproval stop you. Not this time, you haven't."

Laila smiled sadly. "It was because of him I've been able to do it . . . try to make things work in different areas of my life."

"Asher?"

"Yeah," she said, sipping her tea. "Somehow, as horrible as giving him up was, it made things clearer to me. I still live in two worlds, in a way. But I stopped feeling guilty about not sharing things with Mamma and Baba that I know they'll make me feel bad about . . . that I know we'll fight about. I wish they'd be part of my professional life, but I've accepted that they wouldn't want to be. My lyrics and my performances would be just too . . . *difficult* for them. They'd never accept what I do. I do my best to respect them, but I know what I want now . . . what I'm willing to sacrifice. What I'm not. Or, at least I know *better.* I sacrificed what felt like everything for them, once. That's enough for a lifetime."

They continued to talk for hours. Both of them seemed liberated and energized by the idea of talking about topics they'd considered taboo for years.

"He was there," Laila said suddenly at one point at around three in the morning, the realization hitting just before she said the words.

"What?" Tahi asked, turning from the stove where she'd been checking the kettle.

"Asher," Laila said, amazement tingeing her tone. "Tonight. At the club. He was there. I just realized . . ."

"In the audience, you mean?"

She nodded. "You know how I've told you I can't see the audience really well through the veil?"

"Yeah," Tahi said, stepping toward the booth. "You've said the veil works both ways. People can't identify you. Since you're becoming so big, and nobody in our family knows you perform but me, that's a good thing. But since you're sort of shy, it works the other way too. Not being able to make out people's individual faces helps you to lose yourself in the music . . . escape your self-consciousness about performing in front of all those people."

"Right," Laila said, thinking. "But tonight, my attention kept going to this one man . . . he was sitting at a table up front, all by himself. I could only see his outline, but he was big. Imposing . . ."

"Asher." The kettle started to wail. Tahi turned back to prepare their tea. "If he was waiting for you in the underground tunnel that leads from the State Room, then he must have known it was you, right?" Tahi asked, setting their tea down on the table and sliding into the booth.

"How could he know that?" Laila wondered.

"You were aware of him in the audience, even though he was just a shadow to you. You haven't laid eyes on him in years, and you said he was wearing a thick beard. But you also said you recognized him in an instant when you saw him. Don't you think there's a possibility he could have recognized you, as well? Even through the veil?" Tahi speculated.

Laila cleared her throat and took a sip of her tea, made very uneasy by the suggestion behind Tahi's question.

"Well?" Tahi prompted.

"I don't know. Maybe, I guess. He heard me sing once, a long time ago. I'm not sure what else makes sense. It's pretty unlikely he just happened to be in that tunnel at the exact moment I was passing, and that he somehow recognized me, even with my hood up."

"That's not what I meant," Tahi said. "I meant, *well* . . . what are you going to do about it?"

"About what?"

"About the fact that fate has thrown you two together again."

Laila made a scoffing sound, irritated and anxious that Tahi was pressing the subject again. She glanced around the large kitchen. "Do you see him here? Asher and I aren't *together*."

"Fate can't do everything. It expects some sweat." Tahi gave her a significant glance over her delicate tea glass as she sipped.

"*No*," Laila said emphatically after a pause, shaking her head. "Time moves on. Crescent Bay was a long time ago. I'm a different person. So is he."

"So how come you both recognized each other through the veil, without even seeing each other's faces?"

Laila's tongue felt knotted. She couldn't think of how to respond to Tahi's provocative question. Tahi took another sip of tea, frowned and set down her glass. She yawned widely. "I think my espresso high just gave out. Just think about what I said, Laila. I'm going to bed."

The next afternoon. Laila hesitated on the sidewalk outside an elegant, Art Deco high-rise on West Webster Avenue. Lincoln Park was just across the street. It was ablaze with autumn color. She couldn't believe she was here.

Abruptly, she turned and headed in the opposite direction. This had all been a mistake. What had she been thinking, stalking her first love after all these years?

A tall man entered her vision, walking toward her. Her heart seized. She stumbled in her boots. She steadied herself almost immediately, noticing the man's expression. A *stranger's* startled expression. She'd never seen the man in her life. He passed her on the sidewalk. Laila just stood there, stunned.

The random encounter had made another event jump into her mind's eye: standing outside Crescent Bay's downtown ice cream parlor at twilight, music from the park bandstand filling the summer night air . . . seeing a tall, dark young man and her body's automatic, visceral response. All because for a split second, she'd thought it had been *him* . . . the man who had seen her naked at the secret inland lake.

A feeling of poignancy rose in her. *Still*, after all this time, just the idea of him made her uncontrollably excited. Maybe Tahi was right. Maybe there was some kind of connection between Asher and her, something that bypassed the years.

But what about all the hurt?

She turned and gazed up at the luxury high-rise again. The address had remained intact in her memory all these years. She recalled Asher telling her once, in an offhand way, that his parents owned a condo in downtown Chicago, and that he stayed there often during breaks from school. At the time, she remembered thinking that he was downplaying the scenario out of embarrassment or modesty or both. She suspected that the condo had actually been purchased exclusively for him. Having learned what she had about his parents, she wondered if they hadn't provided the desirable living arrangement for their son in order to increase the chances of him visiting them.

Maybe the reason the address had stuck in her head all these years was that she was a little familiar with the neighborhood. Her family liked a pizza place, Mamma's, nearby. They'd gone there three or four times after Chicago shopping trips when Laila was young. Mamma's was long gone now. A nail and eyelash boutique had taken its place. When she and Tahi had bought their condo last year, the family had turned out in en masse to help them move. One night, her mother had suggested they return to Mamma's. Laila had been hesitant about returning to the neighborhood. She hadn't been there since that summer in Crescent Bay. She'd agreed, however.

It had been sad seeing Asher's building, knowing from her online investigations that he wasn't there, but instead on the opposite side of the globe. The chances of Asher's parents still owning a place here, and that Asher was actually *staying* there on his visit to Chicago, were very thin.

But it couldn't hurt to check it out, could it? What about that incredible connection Tahi mentioned? What about the fact that, presumably, they'd recognized one another . . . even through the veil?

The fact that her feet *still* didn't move made her face the truth. She was afraid. Had he thought about her much, over the years? She'd hurt him. Time hadn't dimmed her vivid recollection of his anger on that last day in his mother's sitting room. His disbelief. His bitterness.

Chances were, he'd resent seeing her now. Maybe he'd reject her . . . walk away. Just like she'd walked away from him eight years ago.

Recognizing the source of her hesitation—of her fear—helped, but it didn't lessen it a bit. Nevertheless, she began to walk toward the high-rise. Yeah, he might refuse to talk to her. Maybe she deserved that.

The doorman's face remained wooden when she said Asher's

name. For a second, disappointment swooped through her. Asher wasn't staying here—

"Asher Gaites, you mean?" the doorman asked.

"Oh . . . yes. Asher Gaites." She'd forgotten he'd dropped the hyphenation of his last name. She knew that from seeing his byline on his articles.

The doorman smiled suddenly and stood from his chair, reaching for the phone. "That's okay. I've been here a long time. I knew him when he was just a kid, and the *Granville* was still stuck to his last name. If you're his friend, then you must know he's come a long way since then. Not that he brags. I got a brother in L.A. who e-mails me links to his stories. You know he's up for a Pulitzer?"

Laila nodded. She heard the pride in the older man's voice. She recognized it because she'd felt it herself so many times, reading Asher's words.

"Something else, that kid," the doorman said. "Who shall I tell him is here, beautiful?"

She swallowed thickly. She experienced another wild urge to run.

"Ma'am? Sorry about the *beautiful*. You *are*, though."

Laila laughed at his unexpected combination of sheepish gruffness. Her amusement penetrated her anxiety.

"Laila. Laila Barek."

He nodded once and dialed the phone. A muted roar started up in her ears in the silence that followed. He wasn't answering. Thank God, he wasn't there.

Shit. Now I'm going to have to find the nerve to do this all over again.

"Asher." Her stomach lurched. "It's Pete down at the desk. There's a young lady here to see you." He glanced up at Laila and

winked. “A real looker. You always did have the prettiest girls coming to visit. Uh . . . Laila. Laila Brek, wasn’t it?”

“Barek,” Laila said through a sandpapery throat.

The ensuing silence was unbearable. A slightly confused expression came over the doorman’s weathered face. He cast her a curious glance. Laila felt ill.

“He says he’s in a rush to make an appointment with his attorney,” Pete said awkwardly as he hung up the phone a moment later.

“Oh, of course,” Laila said, backing away, hiding her mortification and hurt as best she could. “It was just an impulse thing, stopping by. Well . . . have a good afternoon.”

Pete nodded once. She could still picture his sympathetic expression as she plunged through the revolving doors and rushed down the sidewalk.

Chapter Nineteen

She usually arrived at the club an hour and a half before showtime. Rafe had installed a small spa in the performer dressing room area, which included a dry sauna and steam showers. The spa helped her relax before a performance, something she sorely needed tonight. She'd been so tense and nauseated after that trip to Asher's condominium, she hadn't been able to eat again all day.

Rafe must have noticed her tension that evening when she arrived at her dressing room. He came up behind where she sat at a vanity and began rubbing her shoulder. Laila winced. Whether it was from her wound-up state or a reaction to his touch, she couldn't say.

"What's got you strung so tight?" Rafe asked, his handsome, thin face tightening with concern in the mirror.

"I might have overdone it at the gym." She sidestepped the question, smiling. She reached up and grabbed his hand, a polite way to stop his massaging fingers. Their stares met in the mirror and she squeezed his hand reassuringly. "I'll go and sit in the sauna. It always melts away all my knots."

"Maybe I'll join you," Rafe murmured, his French accent thickening a little, as it always did, when he became aroused. Not that she knew the full extent of his amorous tells. They hadn't made love yet. Laila was determined to take it slow with him. In fact . . . she usually took things slow with all her boyfriends. It was her modus operandi, and probably the chief complaint of a majority of her exes.

She watched in the mirror as he leaned down. Her stomach muscles clenched. He pressed his mouth to the side of her neck. Her hand drifted up and clutched at his head as he kissed her neck and the slope of her shoulder.

"How would you like that? A nice. Hot. Sauna. Only Phoebe, Jared and Miguel are upstairs," he said thickly between kisses, referring to a waitress, a cook and the club's audio tech, who were there prepping for the night. None of the other members of her band had arrived yet. His well-trimmed goatee tickled her skin. Laila found herself wondering, off topic, what it would be like to be kissed by a man with a full beard.

"And there's a nice thick lock on the spa door," Rafe continued. He looked up and met her gaze in the mirror, his dark eyes smoldering. "What do you say, *mon ange*? I can't afford to have you tense tonight. That reporter from *Entertainment Weekly* has said he'll be here. That'll be huge coverage for you."

"Even if he *does* do a feature, it might not be a positive one. He could hate the show," she said dryly.

"Impossible. You're incredible. You have the richest vein of talent I've ever known. And the world is about to discover you." He clutched her shoulders tighter. Again, she flinched. Rafe didn't seem to notice this time. He just pressed his mouth to her neck again. "I can't think of a better way to relax, can you?"

"It might be a little too relaxing, not to mention dehydrating," she teased, to defray the topic.

He growled deep in his throat and lifted his head. He smiled at her wryly in the mirror. "I think I just struck out again, as you Americans would say." She laughed. Rafe had lived and worked as a club owner and artist manager/promoter in the United States for ten years, so he was pretty Americanized. Nevertheless, she'd learned recently that he'd never experienced baseball. So she'd taken him to a Cubs game.

"I'm sorry," she said, grinning. "I'm just not picturing it in the sauna. Not for . . . you know."

"Our first time?" he asked gruffly, planting one last kiss on her neck and standing. Laila swallowed thickly and nodded, watching him in the mirror. Relief swept through her when he finally removed his hands.

Snap out of it. What's wrong with me?

Maybe she'd never been in a rush to get into bed with Rafe, but she'd always enjoyed his touch before. Asher's reentrance in her life, and then his impersonal rejection of her this afternoon, had rattled her, whether she liked it or not. No, it had done more than rattle her. It had hurt her. Badly. It felt like there was a place deep in her chest cavity that had been rubbed raw. She couldn't ignore it. The sting only grew worse by the minute.

"At least I got you to admit there will be a first time," Rafe said, interrupting her ruminations. "I'll leave you to find relaxation in your own way, then." He straightened his tie while watching her in the mirror. "And I'll just go on imagining the day when I can *relax* with the most beautiful, talented woman on the entire planet."

She shook her head in amusement at his shameless flattery. He planted one last kiss on the top of her head and walked out of her dressing room. She stared at herself sternly in the mirror.

Get over yourself. You didn't lose anything today that hadn't been lost years ago.

Her self-lecture, a muscle-melting stint in the dry sauna and a long, hot shower helped her regain her equilibrium a little. It lasted until about an hour before showtime, when there was a knock at her door.

"Yes?" Laila called, setting down a bottle of lotion on her makeup table. A blond woman stuck her head around the door. "Hi, Phoebe," Laila said, startled. No one but Rafe, and occasionally one of the musicians from her band, ever came to her dressing room. She'd met Phoebe briefly a few times when she'd ventured up to the kitchen before or after a performance, to get a cup of tea or a bite to eat.

"Hi," Phoebe returned. She looked behind her, seeming a little flustered. Laila stood slowly.

"Phoebe? Is everything okay?"

"Someone wants to see you," Phoebe blurted out. She gave Laila an apologetic look before she opened the door wider. Laila froze when she saw the tall man standing behind her in the door. He seemed to tower over Phoebe. His appearance was made all the more intimidating by an opened black overcoat. Beneath it, he wore a pair of jeans and a pale blue button-down shirt.

She straightened and lifted her chin, recognizing his formidability. He'd shaved. Seeing his lean, handsome face exposed made her experience her defenselessness like a knife's edge pressing subtly against her skin. His face looked strangely vulnerable, due to the lack of the beard, and yet harder than stone all at once.

"He said that he knew you years ago, and . . . well, I hope it's okay that I brought him down." Laila jerked her gaze off Asher Gaites and focused on a nervous-looking Phoebe. Had Asher bribed her to bring him down here? Was that why she was so anxious? Or was it just Asher's good looks, seething sexuality and aura of power that had convinced her to break the steadfast club rule about guarding Laila's privacy? Either way, Rafe would probably fire Phoebe on the spot if he found out what the waitress had done.

"It's okay, Phoebe," Laila said, her gaze flickering back to where Asher stood. "I do know him. Come in, Asher."

Phoebe seemed relieved when Laila said his name. She backed out of the room.

"Phoebe," Laila called. "You don't have to tell Rafe about this."

The waitress looked a little stunned, and then relieved.

Asher stepped across the threshold, and Phoebe shut the door. For a few seconds, they just stared at each other silently. She'd always thought her dressing room was relatively roomy, but he shrank it just by standing in it. She realized she was absorbing every detail about him, soaking up his image like a sponge even though her mind was blank as to what to say. It took her a moment to realize he was doing the same. Even though his face remained impassive, his eyes gleamed as they moved across her face and dipped down over her body. She self-consciously tightened the belt on her robe, the movement of the fabric amplifying the prickling sensation his gaze had ignited on her naked skin. She felt her nipples stiffen. It wasn't the most opportune time to be caught wearing nothing but a robe.

"You changed your mind?" she said. She noticed his dark brows arching in a questioning gesture. God, he was just as beautiful to her as he ever was. More so. His body was as lean as it ever was, but his chest and shoulders looked a little broader. He'd grown harder with age . . . more distilled. Infinitely more compelling. "About seeing me," she added.

Her anxiety ratcheted up when he didn't respond immediately.

"I told myself I didn't want to see you," he finally said bluntly.

A shadow of self-annoyance crossed his bold features. "But some things don't change much, apparently. I told you once that I'd come whenever you could see me."

Her smile was forced. "That was a long time ago."

"You're right. It was."

The way he was studying her face made her jumpy. She couldn't decide if he was angry or . . . hungry.

"And yet here I stand," he said. She could tell by the way his mouth slanted slightly that he wasn't exactly pleased about that fact.

She felt her strained smile wavering. "Please. Sit down." She waved at the seating area of her dressing room, where there was a couch and two chairs.

"I'll stand."

She nodded, floundering for what else to say. This brooding, simmering, mature Asher wasn't one she knew how to relate to, and yet he was surprisingly familiar, as well. The contrast only increased her awareness of him until it was cuttingly sharp.

"I've followed your career. I've read a lot of your articles. Whatever I could find online, anyway. They're so amazing, Asher. You're very talented. I always knew you would be, but actually reading your stories . . . well . . ." She realized she was prattling on nervously when he didn't speak. "I just . . . I wanted you to know. Every time I read one, I felt so—"

She cut herself off when he tensed perceptibly. A muscle jumped in his cheek. She swallowed back the praise on her tongue, realizing her mistake. She'd been about to say she'd felt so proud of him, reading his writing, glimpsing between the lines and the words into *him*. His soul. That was too personal . . . too intimate of a thing to either say or suggest, when they hadn't seen each other in almost a decade.

"Why did you come to the condominium today?" he asked.

She shrugged, wrapping her arms around her waist in an attempt to diminish her vulnerability. "Because of seeing you on the subway, of course. Once I realized you were in Chicago, I thought maybe you'd be staying there. You mentioned that building a few times." Her gaze flickered up to his stoic expression. "When we were young," she added hoarsely.

Against her will, a vivid memory popped into her brain of lying on the beach, Asher staring down at her with a hooded, hot gaze while she shook in orgasm. She flinched slightly at the intrusive, intensely intimate memory.

"Are you sure you won't sit down?" she asked him again.

"When I saw you up on the stage," he said, ignoring her hollow attempt at politeness—she'd forgotten how he always cut to the chase. No idle chitchat for Asher. "I knew it was you. Or at least part of me did. The other part couldn't believe it."

"Why not?" she asked uneasily.

"The Laila I knew was too shy to ever put on a performance like that. So raw. So sexy," he added in a quieter, gruffer voice.

She swallowed thickly and looked away from his stare. It burned her.

"But then I *got* it. The curtain. That's how you figured it out. How to show the world your talent. Your gift. How to express it safely. Without hurting anyone?" he asked, and she heard the sarcasm in his tone. "I'm assuming your family doesn't know that the Veiled Siren is you?"

"Tahi knows. She and I own a condo here together."

"How long?"

She blinked. "Since Tahi and I bought our condo?"

"No. Since you've been singing in public."

"Oh . . . it happened slowly, over time. The sports bar I worked at during college started a karaoke night. A club owner in Detroit heard me singing one night, and offered me a job. But I turned him down."

"Too close to home for comfort," he stated.

She wasn't sure she liked his certainty when he talked about her motivations. Wasn't there an edge of bitterness in his tone? Nevertheless . . . he was right. It had been too much of a risk in Detroit. Word would eventually circulate back to her mother or father or a family member about her performing professionally.

"Yeah. Tahi and I both landed customer service jobs at Microsoft right after college. Tahi thrived in the technology sector, but I really struggled. I was bored stiff. I thought it was mind-numbing work." She cast him an uneasy glance, recalling how he'd told her so confidently as a young man that she wasn't the business type. She was an artist. Even then, he'd known her better than she'd known herself. That the same man who had once seen down to the heart of her now stood before her like a cold stranger caused that familiar ache to swell in her chest and throat.

"Anyway, Tahi and I used to go to this blues bar in the underground, not too far from our first apartment. It was a grimy little dive, but they'd get some amazing musicians there. We got to know the club owner, and when he found out I could sing, he gave me a Monday night—their slow night—to perform."

"And before long, he was offering you Fridays and Saturdays, and any other night you'd take. I'm surprised your parents let you move to Chicago."

Her heart jumped a little, then began to drum in her ears at his mention of her parents. "They put up a huge fight about it, that's for sure." *And you actually fought back?* He didn't say it, but the imagined caustic question, asked in Asher's voice, echoed in her head. "They couldn't argue with the jobs we got or the salaries they offered us," she continued. "I ended up hating the work, but I have to admit, they paid us well for entry-level work, just out of college. And Tahi was moving to Chicago too, so—"

"The Laila I knew would have caved in that fight."

Her chin went up higher at that. For the first time, anger pierced her anxiety and self-consciousness at standing face to face with him again. "The Laila you knew has grown up," she stated unequivocally.

He frowned. She thought maybe he'd realized he'd gone too far.

"You never really answered me. About why you came to the condo this afternoon."

She arched her eyebrows and dropped her arms, standing tall. "Why did *you* come *here* tonight?"

He stepped toward her.

It was like a wall of flames suddenly leapt up between them. She was scared of the heat. She was undeniably drawn to it. Something about his stare made her want to back away, but she held her ground. "Are you telling me the reason you came to the condo was the same reason I showed up here tonight?" He said it quietly, but it was a demand, somehow. A command for honesty.

"I came because I wanted to see you," she admitted breathlessly after a pause.

"I came because I couldn't stay away."

He shook his head tensely and cursed under his breath.

"Asher—"

"I wouldn't have thought it was possible for you to grow more beautiful, but you went and did it, didn't you? You're still the most beautiful woman I've ever laid eyes on."

A whimper leaked out of her throat. He'd looked so naked, saying it, like her appearance pained him somehow. It made her want to cry. But then he was stepping into her, and she recognized that look on his face. That determination. That fire. He cupped her face in his hands possessively, but he needn't have urged her. She was already lifting her face to meet his kiss.

He blistered her from the start, seizing her mouth with his and then parting her lips boldly with his tongue. He sank into her, and she felt that silky, bold caress all the way to her sex. His tongue had trained her in pleasure. Her body hadn't forgotten those ecstatic lessons. Every cell in her body seemed to leap with joy at his touch. It felt so achingly familiar, yet so blessedly new. This was a man in his prime. He was so much . . . *more* than he had been once, and what he'd been at twenty-two had forever changed her.

The taste of him, the feel of him pounded into her chaotic awareness. Her arms surrounded him. Her hands and fingers moved in a desperate search to remember the familiar . . . to discover the differences. He dropped his hands to her hips and pulled her tight against him. He bent over her, making her back arch, his kiss becoming more demanding. Hotter. And she responded the only way she'd ever been able to with Asher.

Wholesale.

From his first glimpse of her standing there in that dressing room, Asher recognized it. He was defeated before he could even make a first move. Hers was the face to which he'd compared all others, and found them wanting. And the years had made her even more stunning. Like the way she'd grown into her sultry, resonant voice, she'd grown into her body. She'd filled out, and not just in the flesh. She owned her beauty now. Yes, she was clearly anxious about his unexpected arrival, but she stood straight and tall. Standing there with that robe draped around her slender, curving body, and her long, lustrous hair spilling around her shoulders, she looked like nothing less than a goddess. It made him bitter. His hunger for her was his helplessness; his need his Achilles' heel.

But it was undeniable. Once he tasted her, he gave in to it with a fierce abandon.

She tasted of fruit and honey. She tasted like sex. He sank into her, drowning in her flavor like a starving man sitting down to a feast fit for a king. Her mouth fed him, and yet it made him so much hungrier. He spread his hands on her hips, feeling the taut curve of her naked skin beneath the thin covering of her robe. He rubbed her, his throat vibrating in a growl. His cock lurched at the sensation of her, and suddenly he couldn't take it anymore.

"Jesus," he rasped, nipping at her upturned, parted lips while his fingers found the belt of her robe. He leaned back slightly, looking down at her face as he jerked at the tie. He parted the fabric and stared down at her exposed body. His throat knotted. A pain went through him, one of pure lust and longing. Her breasts were a little fuller than he remembered, but still high and round and firm, the nipples small and mouthwateringly erect. She was paler than she had been during that sun-drenched summer so long ago, but her skin was still flawless and smooth, with a golden hue. Clenching his teeth, he pushed the robe off her shoulders. It slid down her back and legs to the floor. He touched both of her shoulders and trailed his hands down her beautiful arms.

Laila's arms.

Bending his knees, he pulled her tight against his aroused body. He pressed his mouth to her biceps, feeling her silky skin against his lips. He gently scraped his teeth against the firm muscle and clamped his eyes tight against a surge of emotion. The sound of her hoarse whimper penetrated his awareness, and then she was digging her fingers into his hair and saying his name. He shifted his chin, finding a hard nipple. He latched onto it, shivers running beneath his skin at the feeling of her nails dragging against his scalp.

She started against him. He lifted his head, dazed. Had he hurt her? Her wide eyes and obvious anxiety penetrated the flash fire of his arousal. He heard the sound of footsteps in the far distance. Suddenly, Laila bent and scooped up her robe from the floor.

"That's a bathroom," Laila said in a low, hoarse voice. She pointed to a door. "Can you please go in there?"

"Am I *hiding*?" he asked incredulously.

"Yes," she replied shortly, closing her robe and cinching the belt. The sound of footsteps approaching grew louder. "*Please*, Asher."

"Okay, okay," he muttered, frowning. Jesus. Had nothing changed? They weren't kids anymore. It was like they were nineteen and twenty-two all over again, and about to be caught red-handed by her parents. Someone knocked briskly on the dressing room door.

"Laila?" a man called.

"Yes?" she replied, her eyes broadcasting a silent plea to him. She nodded pointedly at the bathroom she'd indicated, her beautiful face tight with anxiety. "Just a second, Rafe."

Asher moved, his feet dragging a little as he glanced behind him at Laila. He went into the dark bathroom. He shut the door but left it open a few inches. He watched through the crack as Laila did something similar to her dressing room door, opening it only a few inches.

"I'm in the middle of dressing," she said breathlessly to the man on other side.

"Oh, I thought you'd be finished. Lance Meyer, the reporter from *Entertainment Weekly*, came a little early. It's a good sign. He was hoping to meet you."

"What? You know I prefer not to meet anyone in person."

"He's not going to bring his photographer to the meeting. I thought we'd have some champagne sent down here and have a drink with him before the show," the guy—Rafe—said in a French-accented voice.

"No," she said, shaking her head adamantly and causing her long hair to slide against her robe.

"Laila, we *need* this. If you'd let me sign you with a big name recording studio for your first contract, a well-organized publicity blitz would have come with it. As it is, this reporter from *EW* might be all we get before you begin recording next month—our only chance."

"That's one of the reasons I picked Sunday Records, and you know it. No huge publicity. You know my stance on this, Rafe. I don't want to be interviewed or have the media connect my face with Yesenia's. That was my condition from the beginning, and you agreed to it. I thought Meyer was just coming here to see my performance."

"But this is your chance for some major exposure from one of the top music and entertainment magazines. Most artists would kill for this opportunity."

"No, Rafe," she said firmly.

"Your privacy is still going to remain intact." Asher's muscles tensed so hard they hurt. What was this guy's problem? He was going at Laila like a battering ram. Couldn't he *hear*? "But it's only going to fuel the flames of fascination about Yesenia, even if you allow Meyer just to see you," Rafe continued. "He's bound to be blown away by the way you look. Even though he won't have a photo, he'll likely write tributes to your beauty that will only make your legend grow." A hand came through the door. Asher stiffened, watching Rafe caress first Laila's tumbling locks of hair and then her cheek. Laila started back but then stilled herself.

Asher recognized a lover's familiar touch. A burning sensation started up in his belly.

"You're flushed, *ma cherie*. Did you stay in the sauna too long?"

"No. But I'm not feeling all that well. Rafe, I wish you hadn't suggested it was a possibility I'd meet with Meyer," Laila said.

"You aren't feeling well? Do you think you'll be able to perform?" Rafe asked, suddenly sounding nervous.

"Yes. That is, I *will* if you give me time to get ready."

"Of course. Please don't worry yourself about it now," Asher heard Rafe say after a pause. "But sometime soon, we're going to have to talk again about this absolute need for privacy on your part, Laila. It's in direct opposition to you growing as an artist. It would be one thing if you were some kind of troll behind the curtain, but you're the most stunning woman—"

"You said you didn't want me to worry about it now," Laila interrupted tensely. "Do you want me to get ready for the show, or not?"

"Of course."

Asher ground his teeth together as he watched Laila turn her cheek for Rafe's kiss. It shocked him a little, how his entire body seemed to recoil at the vision of another man touching her.

It had been a mistake to come here.

Chapter Twenty

Laila hurried to the bathroom door after Rafe had gone. It was shut tight. She wanted to knock and call Asher's name, but it felt like an intrusion. How could it feel like an intrusion when she'd been naked and pressed against his aroused body just minutes ago?

All of this was crazy.

She recalled their impulsive, intense make-out session earlier . . . the feeling of his hot, firm mouth pulling gently on her nipple. Against her will, need tightened her sex. She placed her fingertips on her hot cheeks, willing the memory to fade.

Had he heard her talking to Rafe?

"Asher—"

The door abruptly opened. She started. His face was hard again.

She only had to take one look at it to know. He'd definitely heard her and Rafe talking. He walked over the threshold, seeming to tower over her. She stepped back.

"I'm sorry about that," she said breathlessly. "That's Rafe.

Rafael Durand. He's the club owner and my manager and promoter."

"He's more than that."

Without saying another word, he started to walk toward her dressing room door. Anger and confusion rose in her.

"What do you expect from me, Asher?" she called out bitterly. He turned around, his jaw tight, eyes blazing. "I didn't know you were going to come here. My life hasn't frozen in time since Crescent Bay. I'm not some kind of prop to your life, ready to fawn all over you the second you return."

Heat scorched into her cheeks upon hearing her own words. Maybe she hadn't fawned all over him, but she'd certainly been about to get *under* him in about three minutes flat. But that wasn't the point, she told herself, rallying.

"Are you going to try to tell me you've been celibate for eight years? No. Of course not," she said, her mouth slanting in irritation that she'd asked the question. Her own brain had answered it, making her picture the long line of fascinating, beautiful women a man like Asher had likely been with over the years. She threw up her hands in a helpless gesture. "I didn't know this was going to happen any more than you did, Asher. Don't blame me for the unexpected."

He closed his eyes briefly.

"You're right. I'm sorry." He said it stiffly, but she thought she sensed genuine regret on his part. If she'd had to guess, she'd say he was as confused and overwhelmed by what had just happened between them as she was. They'd *both* been stung by the lash of lust.

Feeling the chink in his armor, she stepped toward him. "Can't we please just sit down together? Talk? Catch up. Act like *most* people would, after not seeing each other for eight years?"

"I guess that's the problem. You're not most people to me," he stated, his eyes piercing her.

Exposing her.

"God, Asher." She exhaled shakily after a stunned pause. "I'd forgotten."

"Forgotten what?"

"Your honesty," she said through a congested throat. Her eyes burned. "The way you strip me bare."

For a moment, neither of them spoke, but silent truths seemed to swarm around them. It was like standing on a ledge in the pitch-black. She didn't know what was in front of her, an amazing path or a frightening abyss. She wavered.

"I have to get ready for my show," she finally said, resorting to the obvious and mundane in her bewilderment.

He nodded once, his mouth hard. "I'll go, then," he said. He started to turn.

"Asher."

He paused but didn't turn around.

"You're not most people to me either," she said shakily. "You never will be."

He faced her slowly. For several seconds, they just stared at one another. She felt like she was crazy, wondering what was going on behind those brilliant eyes of his.

"You're still existing behind the curtain. That hasn't changed," he said.

Her breath hitched with unwanted emotion. She struggled not to break down in front of him . . . to keep it locked inside.

"Things *have* changed, Asher."

She wanted to say more. She wanted to tell him that she'd never sacrifice something so precious again. Not her music. Not someone she loved with every fiber of her being. She kept her profession separate from her family life because she *could*. She and Tahi still went to Detroit frequently. Their parents, aunts, uncles and cousins visited them in Chicago. Her family would be very distressed by the idea of her performing in public, especially her modern, sexy compositions. The fact that she herself had written the music and lyrics wouldn't help matters much. They didn't even know she wrote her own music. It was a conflict and a pain that she could spare them. It was manageable. She'd been managing it for the last five years of her life.

She wanted to say all those things to Asher in that moment, but her throat had tightened, and the words were trapped. She sensed his reluctance in those dragging seconds, and that cut as much as anything.

"I'm leaving Chicago in a little over a week," he said. "I've taken a position as the *Gazette*'s new European bureau chief."

Some of the clogged emotion rushed out of her throat at that. Here it was: the inevitable barriers.

"Well. Time never was on our side," she said with a mirthless laugh. *So many things were against us, from the beginning.* She strained to smile, knowing all along she wasn't kidding him. His large, dark figure shimmered in a veil of tears. "I'll be going to L.A. in a month, as well. Not on a permanent basis, but probably for a good chunk of time."

"For your first recording contract," he said.

She nodded. He'd heard Rafe mention it just now. She inhaled, willing herself to remain calm.

"Will you at least stay for the show?" she managed to say, surprised at how even her voice sounded.

"I wouldn't miss it," he said.

The door closed quietly behind him.

She just stood there, scared as hell she'd never look at him full in the face again.

He didn't leave. He stayed, like he'd said he would. She sensed him out there during her performance. Or at least she *thought* she did. Maybe she *hoped* she did. Unlike last night, she couldn't make out his solitary, formidable shadow sitting at a front table through the stage lights and crimson veil. But she felt him, somehow, to the left of the room and toward the back.

As the music flowed through her, and her entire body became a conduit for it, her awareness of Asher Gaites only amplified. It was like some invisible cord joined them. As her performance progressed, that thread grew tighter. It surged with some magical, unnamed energy, fueling her voice, expanding her heart . . . pulsing in her sex.

It wasn't until the final note of her last number resounded and the audience exploded with thunderous applause that she really fully came back to herself. She'd been so lost in the electricity. She blinked in disorientation.

It was like waking up after years of being in a coma and realizing she was fevered with blinding hunger. She walked off the stage rapidly.

"Laila. *Laila*."

She turned around. She was in the hallway outside her dressing room. A loud roar was emanating from above them.

"My God, you brought the house down," Rafe said, his face lit with glee as he approached her. She glanced down at his expectant outstretched arms blankly. Confusion crossed his face. "What's wrong? Are you still not feeling well? You'd never have guessed it," he said, his smile returning full force. "You were *fantastic*. Lance Meyer is ecstatic. He wants to try to get a cover for you. I don't blame him. I've never seen you so on fire. Listen to them up there. They're going to tear the place down if you don't get back up there, tout de suite."

"I'm not doing an encore," she said, turning and continuing her trip to her dressing room.

"Are you out of your *mind*?" Rafe shouted from behind her. "Laila, *listen* to them up there."

She reached for her dressing room door. “I’m not doing an encore,” she repeated distractedly.

“Laila, you’ve *got* to—” His sudden sternness penetrated her single-minded focus. She spun around.

“I’m not going back up there. Not tonight,” she told him fiercely.

“But what about Lance Meyer?” Rafe asked incredulously.

“What *about* him?” Laila muttered before she entered her dressing room and slammed the door.

Thirty minutes later, she pressed her ear against her dressing room door. Several of the members of her band had come to check on her. Laila usually did several encores, so her behavior tonight was unusual enough to cause concern. She’d assured first her bass player through the door, and then her saxophone player, that she was fine and that she was just feeling a little under the weather.

Rafe had come back, of course. She’d managed to get rid of him by telling him she thought she had a fever and was coming down with something. He seemed mollified, although she half expected him back at her door any minute. He’d said something earlier about driving her home once she’d showered and dressed.

It sounded like the coast was clear. For now, anyway. She slipped out of the dressing room, slung her backpack over her shoulder and hastened down the hallway toward a distant door. Seconds later, she was racing down old cement steps in a dimly lit stairwell. When she reached another door, she jerked the hood on her sweatshirt up. She plunged into the tunnel, her breathing coming fast and erratic. Her pace escalated to a jog. A strange franticness had overcome her.

Up ahead, she spied the chipped white-painted column in the dimly lit tunnel. Even though she was half expecting it, not to mention full-on *praying* for it, she still halted and gasped when Asher stepped out from behind the column.

"I'm not sleeping with Rafe," she said between erratic pants. "We just started dating a few weeks ago. It's not serious—" She cut herself off when he stepped into her and she saw that familiar glint in his eyes.

"I don't think it would have mattered if you'd told me you planned to marry him tomorrow," Asher said. "Tonight, you're mine." He cupped her face in his hands. Air seemed to roar past her ears.

An intense emotional release rushed her at his hot, possessive kiss. She gripped his shoulders, feeling dizzy with relief. Fevered need.

Absolute joy.

Asher. She couldn't believe he was in her arms.

"Come to my place," he said next to her mouth a moment later.

"Yes."

"We'll take the train to the Fullerton stop and cab it the rest of the way."

Maybe fate was a little repentant about her cruelty to them in the past, because they heard the sound of a train approaching in the distance. She saw his small, special smile and wondered if he'd had the same thought.

He grabbed her hand, and they ran for the distant platform. They flew onto the train just before the doors closed.

"Both of us on this side of them this time," he said.

She glanced around at him, knowing he was referring to last night, when the door had slammed shut between them.

"Both of us on the same side," she repeated softly.

It was nearly midnight. The car was empty. Asher urged her into two empty seats. He helped her remove her backpack and set it on the floor. Almost immediately, he was kissing her again, his fingers threading under her hood and delving into her upswept hair. She kissed him back eagerly, all the while stroking his angular, newly shaved jaw with her fingertips. It was like neither of them could fully believe the other one was there, and needed to absorb that reality with every sense to convince their brains.

Her other hand worked its way beneath his overcoat and button-down shirt. She moaned into his forceful kiss at the sensation of crinkly chest hair, smooth skin and dense muscle. He abruptly broke their kiss. His eyes glittered down at her as he swept back her hood and then grabbed at the tab of her zipper on her hoodie. He lowered it to just above her navel and then swept the fabric over her shoulders in two swift movements. Beneath the hoodie, she wore a white tank top. She was braless. She stared up at him, enthralled by the heat and focus in his eyes. He opened his hand along her neck and swept it slowly along her shoulder, and then her upper arms.

"You get to me like no one else can. Still," he said gruffly.

"I missed you."

It was impulsive of her to say it. Crazy. But this *moment* was crazy. There was nothing else that would come out of her throat but the truth while she sat there, drinking in every detail of his rugged, handsome face . . . a face she adored. A face she'd anguished over, thought she might never see again.

"*Laila*," he growled, as if her name were some strange, exciting combination of a curse and a prayer. Suddenly, his mouth was on her bare skin, everywhere he touched awakening and exciting her nerves. One hand enclosed her breast. She felt his heat through the thin fabric of the tank top. He massaged her firmly, his fingers finessing the nipple, until she grabbed at his shoulders and then his jaw and brought him to her. The rattle of the train roared in her ears as their mouths fused in a kiss so hungry, so electric, it was nearly unbearable. She felt Asher's hand moving on the fastening of her jeans, and realized he felt the same way.

"I can't wait," he muttered tensely next to her seeking lips a moment later.

"I don't think I can either," she whispered.

His hand plunged inside her opened button fly. For a few seconds, she couldn't breathe as sensation pounded into her and Asher's mouth seized her again. His need was so raw, so focused, it was like being kissed by a blowtorch. She was just as hot. It was flame fusing with flame, or she wouldn't have been able to take the force of his need. He wouldn't have been able to stand her desperation. She clutched at his head, her hips grinding against his hand at her sex. He shifted aside her panties, his finger sliding into the cleft of her labia. She broke their kiss, staring blindly up at an ad for free legal services. He rubbed her clit with the ridge of his finger.

"You're so wet," she heard him say roughly before he kissed her ear and applied suction. Bands of shadow and light were flickering past her vision. She realized they were slowing for the Clark and Division station—her usual stop. She started in alarm.

"Shhh, it's okay," he said. He removed his hand from her sex, making her tense in pain at the deprivation. He grasped the edge of his overcoat, leaned into her and pulled the coat over her, draping the front of her body. Hiding it. His hand was back at her sex almost immediately.

"Oh God," she moaned as the train slowed, because he was stroking her again in a way only Asher could. She'd forgotten how shockingly accurate his fingers could be. If someone got into their car, it would be agony to have him stop.

"It doesn't matter," he rasped near her ear. "Even if someone gets on, they won't see anything." His soft kiss on her flushed cheeks belied the way his hand moved so firmly beneath the obscuring coat. "You look so beautiful right now," he hissed near her ear. "I love to watch you come. Still . . . raise your hood. No one else is going to see that."

She caught the edges of her sweatshirt and drew it up over her shoulders as the train rolled to a stop. The doors sprang open, and she drew the hood up.

"Pull it forward all the way," Asher said beside her, his finger sliding faster against her clit. She followed his instructions, grimacing in pleasure. Her clit sizzled beneath his touch.

The doors slammed shut. No one had gotten onto their car. She whimpered in relief, turning her face to find Asher's mouth. But suddenly, his hand was gone.

"Asher—"

"I know. Help me get your jeans down. I'm going to cover you with my coat," he said tensely, whipping the overcoat off his shoulders. She hastened to comply, too fevered to be surprised by her bizarre willingness to have sex on a train. She came up off the seat and managed to get her panties and jeans down to her ankles. Before she knew it, Asher was sliding beneath her and pulling her into his lap, her back to his front. He whisked his black overcoat over both of them. Beneath the cover, he lifted her tank top over her breasts, fondling one. Liquid heat surged through her at how good it felt, how tense and exciting. She felt his cock surge against her buttock. He'd freed himself from his clothing before he'd pulled her into his lap. He groaned deep in his throat, grasping both her bare breasts in his hands and rocking her against him. In contrast to the furtiveness of their lovemaking, his erection against her skin struck her as baldfaced. Burning.

"Lift up a second," she heard him say through the sound of the train's rumble off the side of the subway tunnels. She placed her hands on the metal bar above the seat in front of her and put her feet on the floor. Bending forward, she rose several inches off his lap. She gritted her teeth in anticipation, hovering over him, feeling him rolling on a condom.

He placed his hands on her buttocks, squeezing them tautly in his palms. He slapped one cheek briskly, making her start in surprise. He gripped her hips and pulled her back. His cockhead nudged at her channel. He entered her slowly.

"Oh God help me," she moaned. He felt huge. Hard. Like he'd split her into a million glorious pieces.

"Shh, it's okay," she heard him say behind her through the roar in her ears. He firmed his hold on her ass, balancing her weight on the end of his cock. She held her breath, her knuckles growing white as she clutched onto the metal bar like her life depended on it.

Slowly, he urged her down onto his cock. A low, plaintive sound escaped her throat as he carved into her inch by inch, and her flesh melted around his rigid length. Finally, she was sitting fully in his lap while he clutched her to him, his cock buried deep inside her.

"I'm not hurting you, am I?" he asked her in a strained voice. She knew what he was probably getting at. It embarrassed her a little. She hadn't had intercourse for over a year and a half.

And even then, it hadn't been anything like this.

"No," she managed to say through a tight throat. "It feels so good."

"Good. Because you feel like a sinner's version of heaven," he grated out, his fingers digging deeper into her hips and ass cheeks. She sensed his rising desperation and responded without thought. Holding on to the bar in front of her, she rose off him several inches and ground down with her hips. He groaned and tightened his hold on her, guiding her.

She'd been primed for climax by his hand. Now, she was so deliciously full of him. *Asher.* Time stood still as the train barreled down the underground tunnel and she took her fill of him, her hips moving in a firm, fluid rhythm.

At one point, she turned and saw their reflection in the train window, their image illuminated against the black background of the tunnel wall. Her face was tight with ecstasy. His was rigid. As their stares held, he lowered the coat, exposing her bare breasts. They looked pale and vulnerable, thrusting out from beneath the bunched fabric of her tank top. He cupped both of them and squeezed firmly.

"Still the prettiest breasts in existence," he muttered thickly, lifting them and releasing them, watching the flesh bounce softly before he repeated the action. She started to pump her hips faster, intensely aroused. For a moment, he let her ride him at a frantic pace while he played with her breasts and they both watched, spellbound.

But then she felt him grip at her hips again. He stilled her frantic movements, holding her in his lap, his cock fully piercing her. She whimpered at the loss of divine friction. She'd been about to come. But he was pulling his coat up and around her shoulders again, and she realized they were slowing for the North and Clybourn stop.

"Asher," she whimpered, trying to shift her hips. He held her fast against him, not allowing her to move. The throb of his cock inside her maddened her. She was about to explode. Light and shadow fanned across them, and the train rolled to a stop. "Oh, God," she whispered, her arousal peaking and then halting at the precipice. Throbbing. Unbearable.

She made out four or five people dispersed on the platform. The train slowed to a stop. The doors sprang open. A long-haired, youngish guy wearing earbuds loped toward the door in front of them. Asher made a sharp, cutting gesture in the window. It caught the kid's attention. For a split second, he stared at them through the window. Laila dazedly absorbed Asher's forbidding frown at him in the reflection.

The kid veered and jogged down the platform toward another

car. The doors slammed closed. The train started to roll down the tracks again.

I can't believe I'm doing this. We could be arrested.

But then the train zoomed into the black subway tunnel again, and one of Asher's hands slid between her thighs. She cried out, her doubts incinerated in an instant. He urged her with his strong hands and body.

She rose and fell over him in a fast, harsh, staccato rhythm. She climaxed so hard that everything went black for a moment.

When she came back to herself, Asher was gripping her hips and ass tightly, pumping himself into her and groaning. She recognized he was right on the edge. The train began to rise on an upgrade. They were leaving the subway and rising to the elevated tracks. The next stop was Asher's. They didn't have much time.

She firmed her grip on the metal bar and came to her feet in the bent-over position. Bending over, she bounced her ass and sex up and down on his cock. He gave an incredulous growl and tightened his hold on her hips. His arms bent and straightened as he powered her efforts, creating a ruthless pace. She gritted her teeth at the sensation of his cock swelling in her.

"Ah, God. *Laila*."

His roar as he came obliterated the rattle of the train on the tracks. They zoomed out of the tunnel into the landscape of the glittering city.

Chapter Twenty-one

He closed the front door of his shadowed apartment. His fingers slid beneath the strap of her backpack. It fell to the floor with a dull thud. He pressed her back into the door. She turned her face up to him, as if she knew by instinct what he expected. What he wanted. He swept down, nipping at her gorgeous mouth, penetrating her lips with his tongue. He couldn't stop touching her. The capacity for restraint just wasn't inside him.

Not when it came to her.

They'd held each other fast in the backseat of the taxi on the short cab ride from the L station, as if they each thought the other would disappear if they let go. The city looked hyper-real to him, the lights against the black night sky sharp and beautiful. They had spoken hardly at all, but the spell that she'd woven during her performance—the one she'd cast on him from the first moment he'd ever heard her resonant, smooth voice and seen her naked body glistening with water eight years ago—clung around them in the backseat of the cab and on the hasty trip up to the condo.

"I can't believe we did that," she said breathlessly, her lips brushing across his hovering ones. He knew she was referring to their spontaneous, explosive sex on the train.

"Do you regret it?"

"No." Her emphatic whisper pleased him. So much so that, distantly, he knew he should be concerned.

She walked away from you once. You know damn well she could do it again.

But tonight wasn't for worrying. Because there was nothing . . . absolutely nothing to complain about in the way she came to him. Her responsiveness, her eagerness, her sweetness, she was everything he remembered times ten.

She looped her arms around his neck and went up on her tiptoes to kiss him. He lifted her off her feet, bringing her more surely to his mouth. She tasted so good. Always. He started to move through the shadowed condo, carrying her in his arms. A moment later, he spilled her back on the bed and came down over her. The master bedroom was unlit, but the city lights spilling in from the two windows next to the headboard allowed him to see the sparkle in her eyes and her curving lips.

"*Again?*" she asked.

He cupped her sex warmly through the canvas pants she wore. A small puff of air left her lips.

"It felt like you haven't done this in a while," he said. "Am I wrong?"

She shook her head.

"Are you too sore?"

"No." The sound of her soft laughter made him smile widely. "I'm just amazed at your potency."

He matter-of-factly pushed back her hood and unzipped the sweatshirt she wore. He slipped it off her chest and then cupped her sex again. Gently stroking her, he tried to focus on their conversation. "Maybe it's not a surprise."

"What do you mean?"

"When we were young, back there in Crescent Bay, we never had this. The freedom."

"Just to be with each other," she agreed quietly.

"For as long as we wanted. As much as we wanted."

He leaned down and kissed her mouth deliberately, savoring her.

"So . . . how are you, Asher Gaites-Granville?" she whispered when their lips parted a moment later. "Have you been happy for the past eight years?"

"I've lived. I've seen a lot."

"I'll bet you have." She reached up and touched his forehead. "Some of it was really hard to witness, wasn't it?" His eyebrows arched in a query. "I can see it on your face. Your experiences have changed you. Matured you. Maybe hardened you," she added softly. "Has there been room for happiness? Do you *like* your life?"

He paused for a moment, considering. "I wouldn't have changed anything, given what life has thrown me."

He wondered what she thought of his answer in the brief silence that followed.

"How are you, Laila Barek? Have *you* been happy for the past eight years?"

"I've lived."

She looked so beautiful to him in that moment, her face luminous even in the dim light. He'd forgotten how she shone in his eyes. Or maybe it had hurt him too much to remember. She stroked his jaw. "I've learned how to make myself happy. As happy as I can be."

He hesitated for a few seconds, but then he pushed past it. He'd worried about it for years, and then cursed himself just as many times for being stupid enough to anguish over it.

"Did they give you a hard time? After that night? Your family?"

Her stroking hand paused on his cheek. Had she heard the dread in his tone?

"No, Asher. It wasn't horrible. I mean . . . it was difficult, of course. Stressful. I won't lie. There were some epic yelling matches, especially between my mom and me. She was very hurt by my dishonesty. But my mom's emotions operate in explosion mode versus low boil. That situation may have taken longer to get out of her system than most, but she got to a point where she could forget it more easily. My dad was more . . ." She shrugged slightly, her expression a little sad. "Things *were* strained between him and me for a while, but we sort of reached an equilibrium. That is, until . . ." Something flickered across her expression.

"What?" he asked.

"Zara left," she said after a pause.

"Your cousin? Where'd she go? Her leaving didn't have anything to do with *Eric*, did it?" he said, frowning when she didn't immediately respond. He hadn't had to say his cousin's name for years while he'd worked in the Middle East, and it had been great. Since returning to Chicago, he'd been forced to say it way more often than he'd like.

"No. Not directly, anyway. But that summer in Crescent Bay *was* behind her leaving. The start of it all. But as for actual contact, I think Zara and Eric only texted for a few weeks after we went home to Detroit that summer, before he—"

"Dropped her like a hot brick."

"Yeah," Laila said. "Things didn't go as well for Zara and the family after that summer as they did for me. Not that they went smoothly for me, by any means. But Zara has always been more rebellious than me."

His hand shifted off her sex. He cupped her hip instead. "You mean she resisted her parents' attempts to bring her into line?"

He thought she tensed beneath him. She started to say something, but only air puffed past her lips.

"That wasn't what I meant. Not exactly," she said after a pause. "Zara started fighting more and more with my uncle Reda and aunt Nadine. She always had a chip on her shoulder. She never *wasn't* angry. It was like all of us were responsible for her losing Eric, even though that wasn't true. Didn't Eric get married three or four years ago?"

"Yeah. To some toilet paper heiress from Newport. Fitting," Asher said, his lip curling in amused disgust. He recalled his parents' anger and cold disbelief when he told them during a phone call once in Damascus that there was no way in *hell* he was flying to the States to attend that weasel's wedding. His parents still didn't know about Laila, or Eric's betrayal.

His mom and dad still didn't know Asher had gone past despising his cousin to grinding his teeth in white-hot hatred at the mere mention of his name. His mother had kept calling and needling him persistently about the wedding. He'd finally lost control. He'd informed his mom bitterly over the phone that the last time he'd seen Eric in Crescent Bay, he'd been beating his pretty face to a bloody pulp in a hotel room. He'd gone on to tell her he very much doubted Eric was going to lose any tears over Asher not being at his fucking fake-ass high-society wedding.

He'd ended up feeling guilty for being so tactless and insensitive with his mom. But she *had* stopped mentioning Eric and his stupid wedding.

"Anyway, about nine months after Crescent Bay, Zara packed up her things and walked out," Laila continued. "My uncle Reda and aunt Nadine don't say her name anymore, and we don't speak it in front of them. But Tahi and I have looked for Zara over the years, without our parents knowing about it. Apparently, she's been working as either a waitress or a maid at places all over Detroit. She's always moving on. Tahi and I have never seen her, let alone spoken with her. It's like she's always staying two steps ahead of us. We haven't been in contact for seven years."

He heard the crack in her voice. He sensed her sadness. The largeness of the issue, the far-reaching impact of that golden, supposedly carefree summer, hit him unpleasantly for the ten-thousandth time in his life. He rolled onto his back and came down beside Laila on the bed. For several seconds, they just stared silently up at the ceiling.

"You still think it, don't you? That I didn't show any backbone. That I wasn't rebellious enough," she said softly. He rolled his head on the pillow and met her stare in the semidarkness.

"No. I don't *think* that. Logically, I understand why you did what you did," he could say honestly.

She nodded once. "But you *feel* it."

"I wouldn't have wanted you to become like Zara, if that's what you mean. Cut off from family and friends. If it weren't for your family supporting you and giving you a home those years while you were in college, you might not have turned out so well. I'm sorry. I know how close you, Tahi and Zara were. It must hurt."

"You have no reason to be sorry. You never did anything to Zara."

"No, but a white guy with the same last name as me did. My cousin did. That's how your parents and your aunts and uncles saw it. Isn't it?"

"They don't know you, Asher. They never did. I tried to tell them."

He swallowed back the bitterness that had risen at the back of his throat. He stared back up at the ceiling. "It's not the end of the world."

She didn't reply immediately. He knew his weary, indifferent act hadn't fooled her.

"You're still angry with me." Her voice clung in the still air and echoed around his head. He couldn't admit to her that what she said was true. He didn't like to admit it to himself.

"It was a long time ago," he said levelly. "It feels like a lifetime ago."

"It's okay. I understand," she said. He blinked, taken aback by her earnestness. He rolled his head on the pillow. Her eyes glittered with fractured light. Reacting entirely on instinct, he reached and touched her soft cheek. She smiled, but she looked so sad. "I'm still mad at myself too."

"You are?"

She nodded. A single tear wet his caressing finger. "Not for telling you I couldn't see you while my parents forbade it and I lived in their home. But for cutting off all ties with you. For giving up entirely. Or at least for giving up in my head," she whispered. She cleared her throat. "My heart didn't let go so easily. I told you about it. In the e-mail I sent," she said after a pause where her quietly uttered words vibrated inside him. Finally, her final sentence penetrated his consciousness.

"*What* e-mail?"

She rolled over on her hip, facing him.

"I wrote to you," she said. "Six months after Crescent Bay. I told you I'd realized I'd made a mistake. I asked you if you could forgive me . . . if we could keep in touch. You never wrote back." Her mouth fell open, and he realized she was reading his blank, stunned expression. "I thought you didn't write back because you were too mad at me. Or that you'd just realized it was all a mistake. An infatuation. A summertime indiscretion better left in the past. I assumed you'd moved on."

"I never got any e-mail," he assured her, rolling toward her and propping himself up on his elbow.

"I tried to call you and text too, but—"

"I changed phone numbers when I moved to L.A.," he interrupted. "I didn't think it would matter."

"When I couldn't reach you by phone, I looked online to see if you had an e-mail listed at the *Times*. You did, and I wrote there."

Bitterness washed over him. "Jesus," he muttered.

"What?"

He fell back on the pillows. "Nothing. It's just always one thing or another."

"Asher?" He heard her confusion.

"About three months after I started at the *Times*, the paper was bought by a different company. All of our e-mails were changed."

"Oh."

He hated the sound of her shaky sadness. He rolled off the bed. "I think I'm going to take a shower," he said.

He'd startled her. He could tell by her tense expression and big eyes as she pushed herself into a sitting position.

"Maybe I should go," she said.

"*No*, don't." He cursed under his breath when he saw her start at his emphatic denial. He raked his fingers through his hair and strained to calm himself . . . to tamp down his anger. "I'm just pissed," he admitted.

"At me."

"At you. At me. At the whole damn situation. But don't go anywhere. I just need a minute. Please?"

She nodded, but he didn't move. He felt awkward in the ensuing silence. Stupid, for having exposed his vulnerability so abruptly, like a lightning strike from the blue. Finally, he forced his feet to move. He spun around when he reached the corner of the bed.

"I lost my phone soon after I moved to L.A. I could have gotten a replacement with the same number on the new phone. I just figured it didn't matter, though, you know? Why not get a new number? I wanted to wipe the slate clean. I could tell my friends and family the new number. No one was going to try to reach me that I hadn't given the new number to. *You* certainly were never going to try."

She remained utterly still. He had the impression she didn't even breathe.

"I'd like to call it fate," he said with a harsh laugh, "or bad luck or wrong timing on our part. But the truth is—at least in this instance—it was my own dumb-ass pride."

When he came out of the bathroom five minutes later, pulling a clean T-shirt down over his chest, he froze on the threshold. The blood seemed to drop out of his head in a free fall. The bedroom was empty.

He stalked down the hallway. "Laila?" he called. *"Laila?"*

"I'm in here."

Relief rushed through him, the distilled form of it leaving him light-headed. He entered the kitchen. She turned to him as she pulled two cups out of his cabinet. She was heating a kettle on the stove.

"I thought you'd left. I'm glad you didn't," he stated bluntly. "I'm sorry. I shouldn't have said those things."

"Why not?" she asked, her smooth, calm voice both soothing his agitated state and increasing his bewilderment.

He threw up his hands. "Because I don't *want* you to go, that's why."

"You were just being honest before," she said, opening another cabinet and looking inside. "I don't expect you to walk on eggshells around me. Where's your tea?"

"Laila," he said, frustrated because her face was blocked by the cabinet door.

She looked around the edge of the door. He started to speak

but paused when he saw the compassionate expression in her beautiful eyes.

"I know you're angry, Asher. I know you're mad at me for walking away back then, after I'd told you I'd fight for us. I'm plenty mad at myself too. But I can't go back and change it. I only have right now. I know you're mad at yourself, and at the world a little too, when it comes to all of it. But—" She dropped her hands from the cabinet and faced him. "The thing of it is—don't take this the wrong way—but—"

"What?" he asked, taking a step closer.

She gave him a helpless glance and shrugged. "Part of me is glad you're mad. Part of me is happy that it still hurts," she said, touching her chest with her fingertips. She noticed his dubious expression. "Because it means we still care. Doesn't it?" she added, a shadow of anxiety flickering across her expression.

He stepped into her, holding her face with his hands. His mouth closed over hers. He lifted his head a moment later. Her smile sliced right through him.

"All I know is we're together right now," she said tremulously.

"All I know is there's no place in the world I'd rather be," he said, leaning down to taste the miracle of her again.

When he finally got around to showing her where the tea was located, she exclaimed happily when she saw some Moroccan mint tea.

He smiled at her reaction. "It's my favorite, actually."

"Really?" she asked him in amazement, grinning. Excitement shone in her eyes. "Did you ever go to Morocco, like you hoped to?"

"Three times, actually. Did you ever go?"

She nodded. "I've been twice with my family and Tahi's parents." She saw his eyebrows knit together.

"What's wrong?" she asked him.

"It's just . . . back then, one of the reasons you said you hadn't gone to Morocco yet was your grandmother's illness." She saw the question in his eyes and understood.

"Mamma Sophia died six years ago."

"I'm sorry. I know how much she meant to you."

"She did. I miss her every day. And thank you," Laila said.

They talked about their experiences in Morocco while she made them a pot of atay. Afterward, they sipped the tea at the kitchen table and talked about everything and anything. They had eight years to catch up on.

He told her about his routines as a foreign correspondent in the digital age, explaining how he constantly had to balance being tied to his phone and computer to keep abreast of breaking news with getting out into the field, interacting with colleagues and sources in order to work original and unique stories.

"Aren't you going to miss it?" she asked him at some point. He'd already told her about his future job in London. She'd felt a little melancholy, thinking of him leaving, but she couldn't help but feel proud of him too when he spoke about his career with such calm confidence and purpose.

"Probably," he admitted. "But I'll still be able to do some reporting. It's just that now, I'll have a team helping me investigate leads and writing. Besides, I felt like I'd reached the peak of my learning curve, being a correspondent. As the bureau chief, I'll be responsible for directing a team of American and European reporters in several countries. I'll be traveling a lot still, mostly between the U.K., France and Germany. I'm nervous about starting, but it'll be a new arena for making a difference . . . for learning about another side of the newspaper business . . . for gaining a bigger perspective on getting a story out to the public."

"A whole new learning curve. You never were afraid of trying something new. Even when you were young, you told me that we didn't grow unless we stepped into unfamiliar territory. '*That's how you know you're growing, when things get a little uncomfortable.*'"

He grinned slowly, his teacup wavering in the air.

"Did you just *quote* me?"

She laughed at his incredulous amusement. "Oh, I remember all sorts of things about you. You'd be shocked if you knew."

"If it's anything close to the details I remember about you, I doubt it," he said, giving her a hooded, smoky glance that made her heart give a little jump.

She had the impression that his mother or a decorator had furnished the elegant, luxurious condominium, including purchasing the dishes. It felt strange to Laila to use cups, and not the pretty, fragile glasses with which she was used to drinking Moroccan tea. The teacups and saucers they used were fine china, the muted floral pattern hardly one she'd imagine Asher ever choosing. But she loved the way he held the cup in his big hand—not by the delicate handle but with his fingers cupping the bowl. There was something sexual about it: his masculine handling of the delicate, feminine cup; the way he brought it to his firm, well-shaped mouth; the vision of his strong throat as he swallowed.

His hair had still been wet when he'd come into the kitchen. The strands had dried spiky and mussed. After his shower, he'd put on a pair of black cotton pajama bottoms and a simple white T-shirt that molded his powerful torso. She liked to look at his strong forearms sprinkled with dark hair and long, blunt-tipped fingers.

She could never get tired of watching him.

"What about you?" he asked her, resting his elbows on the table. "You've taken some chances, haven't you? Stepped into new territory?"

"You're talking about my performing?"

He nodded. "And you write your own music, I understand."

"I do a cover now and then, but yeah. It's mostly all mine."

She took a sip of her tea, watching him over the rim. "After that summer in Crescent Bay, I took your advice and signed up for some writing and music classes."

His dark brows rose. "What did your parents think about that?"

"They never knew about it." She took a sip of tea, examining his reaction closely. She wanted to try and convince him that she was an adult now . . . that she'd make very different decisions today than she had when she'd known him years ago. But part of her felt foolish for wanting to plead her case, maybe even a little unworthy. She'd sacrificed him once. Maybe he didn't deserve to bear witness to her defense, especially when he'd thought her actions indefensible.

"Your family still don't know that you're a poet and songwriter?" he asked after a pause.

"They still think I work at Microsoft." A weary smile curved her mouth when she saw his stunned reaction.

It was hard, living the lie. She only knew it would be even harder, to hide who and what she really was. "Tahi has generously promoted me three times now in her stories to the family. I'm now an account manager for a huge restaurant chain. We chose restaurants carefully. It was a business that could conceivably have me work a Tuesday through Saturday workweek."

"It matches your performance schedule," he said as understanding hit. "Wasn't it hard for you? Going behind your parents' back?"

"Oh, yeah. It still is. Every day. I'm still very involved in family life. I try to visit whenever I can. My mother either texts or calls me more days than not. But I'm not willing to give up something that's so crucial to who I am." She set down her cup. "Not anymore," she added softly under her breath.

"It *would* be a crime. You were clearly born to share your gift. I told you back then how talented you were."

Her heart fluttered. He wanted to keep the conversation focused on her singing . . . on the sacrifice she'd refused to make in regard to her family versus the one she'd made *for* them eight years ago. She'd given *him* up then.

"But even I couldn't have imagined back then just how amazing you'd become," he continued. "You grew into your voice."

Her gaze dropped over him. "You grew into yourself. Everywhere."

A small, distracting smile shaped his mouth. She smiled back. It was so wonderful, being able to relish a quiet, adult moment of sensual appreciation and awareness with him.

"I was blown away at your performance tonight. I didn't get a chance to tell you," he said.

She smiled wider, despite her earlier anxious thoughts.

"What?" he asked her.

"Nothing," she said, unable to hide her grin. "It's just . . . I thought you *did*. Tell me. There, on the train tonight." She waited for a moment, wondering if he'd recall how he'd told her something similar once, and how she'd responded in the same way. It had been that first time he'd heard her sing in his mother's sitting room. He'd grown extremely passionate with her while they'd sat at the piano afterward. She saw recollection spark in his expression. He leaned toward her, holding her fast in his stare.

"Are you telling me it's okay with you that your gorgeous voice and artistic brilliance make me hornier than a stag?" he asked her quietly.

"I'm telling you that coming from you, it's the best kind of compliment," she said, taking a sip of her tea and watching as his eyes caught fire.

They talked until five thirty in the morning. Finally, feeling warm and content after having communed with him all night, but also fatigued and grubby, she asked him if she could shower. When she left the bathroom wearing a towel five minutes later, she saw that he was lying on the bed in the dim bedroom. He tracked her progress as she walked toward him and sat on the edge of the bed. She touched his whiskered jaw softly. He caught her wrist and held her against his skin. The full silence rang in her ears and seemed to swell her heart in her chest cavity.

"It seems so unreal . . . so amazing, seeing you lying there. Touching you," she murmured.

He reached and pulled on the end of the towel she wore. The fabric fell and pooled around her hips. He ran his hand in a solemn gesture along her shoulder and down her arm, pausing to gently cup a breast.

"You seem like a miracle," he said.

He sat up and hugged her against him, sliding her over him and onto her back on the bed.

When he finally entered her body again later, Laila realized their entire nighttime talk session had been lovemaking, of a sort. Every glance had been a hungry, intimate caress. Every word they'd uttered had been a delving into the other's spirit. And the thousands of words *not* said—the hovering knowledge of how short and impermanent their time together was, the exquisite and excruciating memories they shared—had created its own brand of desperate longing, as well.

Of course, she realized as dawn peeked around the corner of the curtains and started to soften Asher's rugged features as he slept, she wasn't exactly sure if he experienced things precisely in the same way.

Chapter Twenty-two

She awoke in a split second, knowing precisely where she was, despite the relative unfamiliarity of the room. She'd been dreaming her phone was ringing, but all was silent in Asher's luxurious condo.

Her phone was in her backpack, she recalled. Asher had discarded the bag onto the floor almost immediately when they'd entered the condo. Asher continued to sleep as she slid off the mattress. She snagged his discarded T-shirt from the carpet and pulled it down over herself. She closed the door behind her softly and rushed down the hallway.

Her phone was set to silent. Even though it didn't ring out loud, she saw that someone was indeed calling at that very moment. When she saw the caller identification, a prickle of anxiety went through her. It was her mom. Her concern wasn't because of her mother calling, precisely. It was the realization that she'd never texted Tahi and told her she would be away for the night. They usually did that as a courtesy so the other one wouldn't worry.

She shouldn't worry, though. Even if her mom had talked to Tahi first, Tahi would have covered for her.

Rafe had also undoubtedly called last night, she realized. Several times. She pushed the anxious thought out of her brain.

"Mamma?" she said quietly into her phone. She walked into the living room. It must be nine . . . maybe ten o'clock? Sunlight poured into the east-facing bank of windows.

"You sound out of breath," her mother said. "Did I catch you at a bad time?"

"No, no, I just couldn't find my phone." She sidestepped the question. "What are you up to this morning?"

"Nadine and Nora are here, going over the menu for Driss's visit next weekend. You and Tahi are still planning on being here, aren't you?"

A feeling of trepidation swept through her. Crap. The Detroit visit. She'd almost forgotten about it, with the rush of adrenaline and excitement of being with Asher again. Asher was scheduled to leave the Wednesday after next. But the Detroit visit had been scheduled for months now. It was important for Laila and Tahi to be there for obvious reasons, but for some unspoken ones, as well.

"Of course. We'll be there Sunday morning," Laila said uneasily.

"I still don't understand why you can't have a normal weekend like everyone else," her mother said. "Tahi gets off on Saturday and Sunday."

"I know Tahi does. But her business follows a different work week than mine does," Laila repeated for the thousandth time.

"But Driss and Sara get here on Friday night and leave on Monday morning. You'll miss almost their whole visit."

Her mom referred to her cousin Driss's new fiancée. Her mother and the aunties were in full-out excitement mode, given the fact that they'd never met Driss's intended. What they *did* know only fueled their anticipation—Sara had a good job as a senior analyst at a financial consulting firm, was very pretty and was Moroccan.

Of course.

"I'm sure one day with Tahi and me will be plenty for Sara," Laila said drolly. "Poor girl. She's going to be worn out by the time they go back to San Diego."

"It's her first visit to her fiancé's family. She's got to expect—"

"Uncles and aunts and cousins and neighbors thrown at her from every direction?"

"You know it would help things to go smoother for her if you and Tahi were here. You're all bound to become friends with Sara. You two girls are the family members closest to her age. What I say is even more true, given—"

"*Mamma*," Laila warned softly. She knew her mother's impulsiveness, rambling train of thought and her habits so well, and she realized she was about to indirectly refer to Zara.

Or more correctly, to Zara's absence.

As Driss's sister, Zara would normally have been expected to bond with Sara and make her feel welcome in the family. Both Laila's mother and her aunt Nadine, who was undoubtedly within hearing distance of this phone conversation, were aware of that fact. Aunt Nadine was especially sensitive and pained by Zara's absence during her son's and his fiancée's visit.

"I just wish you and Tahi could be here sooner, that's all," her mother said.

"I know it. But you and the aunties will do just fine welcoming Sara." Movement caught her eye and she turned. Her mother continued talking about the menu and plans for the visit, but she might as well have been talking in Chinese, for as much as Laila comprehended. Asher walked into the living room. He was dressed only in the pajama bottoms he'd had on last night. His hair was mussed and dark whiskers shadowed his jaw. Sunlight gilded his tanned, muscular torso. He looked like he'd just rolled out of bed. Delicious. Sexy as hell.

Every inch the miracle he'd seemed like last night.

"That all sounds fantastic, Mamma. I've got to go."

"But wait, I called to get your opinion on chicken or lamb for the tagine on Sunday night."

"Both would be great," she said, taking a step toward Asher. Despite his disheveled, newly-risen-from-bed state, his gaze on her was sharp. She recognized that fire in his blue eyes.

"Laila, are you listening? We're not doing *both*. I'm asking your opinion on *which*, chicken or lamb?" her mother scolded.

"Chicken, I guess. I've got to go, Mamma," she said firmly. "Someone is knocking at the door."

She hung up the phone a second later and immediately walked into his arms. The hair on his chest felt good against her pressing cheek. His skin was smooth and warm beneath her lips, the muscle beneath so hard. "Good morning," she whispered. She kissed a small, dark brown nipple. His low growl thrilled her. He delved his fingers into her hair and pushed her head against him as she charted the stiffening flesh with the tip of her tongue. She felt him harden against her lower belly. He bent his knees, slid his big hands beneath the T-shirt she wore, cupped her bare ass and pushed her more firmly against his hard body. Liquid heat rushed through her sex.

"I woke up and you were gone," he said gruffly from above her. "I didn't like it."

"I don't think I like it either. Let's go back," she murmured. She glanced up as she went back to finessing his nipple with her tongue. His hand went to the back of her head, holding her as she licked the hardening disc of flesh. He watched her, his stare hot enough to melt through metal. She saw herself as if from his eyes, experienced her red, wet tongue. She felt his heavy cock bump against her belly. He lifted her against him, his mouth slanted in arousal, and walked toward the bright sunlight. He lowered her down onto the couch.

"I don't think I can make it to the bedroom. I want you right now," he said.

"We seem to be saying that a lot to each other," she replied, smiling.

She knew exactly what he meant. The hunger—the need—had slammed into her like a locomotive upon seeing him walk into the room. Even her mother's voice in her ear hadn't dampened it. She lay back and he came down over her. Their mouths fused and clung in a liquid, heated kiss. The sun warmed his bare back. It felt so good against her wandering, massaging fingertips.

It was as if they were encapsulated in some kind of sunlit cocoon. Only they existed, their seeking lips and exploring tongues, the pressure and heat of each other's bodies. He slid his T-shirt up over her chest, baring her and caressing her with his large hand. She moaned, feeling herself soften for him, growing wetter. Hotter. Their bodies pressed tight. She loved the feel of him against her skin. She adored how heavy his cock felt behind the thin layer of his pajama bottoms. He was so big and blatant. So amazingly male.

Her hand slid between their pressing, grinding bodies. He felt what she was doing and braced himself on his arms, lifting slightly off her. She cupped his full testicles in her palm and squeezed gently. He groaned into her mouth and broke their kiss. He came up on his knees slightly, still crouching over her, giving her free rein. She glided her hand up the thick, long shaft, watching his handsome face tighten in pleasure.

"Do you have any idea what I want to do to you right now?" he rasped.

She saw the answer in the feral glint in his eyes. She opened her thighs, feeling the air tickle at her wet sex.

Her hand slipped beneath the waistband of his pajamas. She

grasped his beautiful cock tighter, gritting her teeth in arousal at the sensation of the soft skin gloving the long, rigid shaft. She pushed his pajama bottoms down over his ass. Gripping his cock with both hands, she began to pump him. She met his stare as her arms moved up and down.

"Tell me. What do you want to do?"

His nostrils flared slightly. A snarl shaped his mouth. "Something I shouldn't."

Excitement rippled through her at his words. Wincing in pleasure, he glanced down between their bodies to where she jacked his cock. "God bless it, you're good at that."

"I should be. You taught me how to do it."

He gave her a sharp glance. She pumped him faster with both hands.

"Laila—"

"Tell me what you want to do," she entreated. She could feel her pulse throbbing at her throat. He still stared down between their bodies, but this time, she knew he wasn't looking at her jacking his cock. She felt his stare on her sex and spread thighs. She pumped him more determinedly.

"Jesus," he groaned. "I'll go get a condom."

But she wouldn't let up on him. A fever had seized her body. Her brain.

"Asher." He met her stare. "Tell me. Say it."

"You know what I want," he grated out between white, bared teeth. She sensed his anger in that moment, his cutting frustration. It sent a perverse thrill through her. "You *know* I want to dip my cock into this." He moved abruptly, rearing back on his bent knees. He grabbed her hips and roughly pulled her lower body onto his thighs. He slid a long finger into her sex. She gasped. His hand circled on her outer sex, applying pressure to her clit.

"So damn creamy," he muttered. "So warm and tight." He drew

his finger out of her and plunged it deep again. He pushed another finger between her labia and applied direct pressure on her clit. She whimpered and twisted her hips against the divine friction.

He grasped a hip with one hand and held her in place as he thrust his finger in and out of her. "Do you hear that? Do you hear how wet you are? I could die in this pussy," he grated out darkly. He was right. She was soaking wet. She could hear him moving in her flesh. "You know I fantasize about it. About fucking you raw. You know it, but you wanted me to say it. Didn't you?" She cried out in unbearable excitement as he stroked her harder and her clit sizzled beneath his rubbing forefinger. His dirty talk was driving her crazy. So was the sensation of his thick erection pulsing next to her bare ass.

"No barriers between us. Just my cock sinking into your wet little pussy and fucking you until I don't know where you start and I end . . . feeling you squeeze the living daylights out of me while you come—"

"Oh *God*." She lifted her head off the pillows, her face tight. She was mindless with pleasure, desperate with need. Not fully aware of what she was doing, she instinctively began to bob her ass up and down, popping his erection with her ass. His growl would have been intimidating if she weren't so turned on by it. Everything had grown hot and sticky and delicious. She was about to go off like a lit firecracker.

"Do it," she whispered fervently. She splayed her legs open even further and lifted her pelvis from his lap in a flagrant invitation. She popped her bottom against his cock again, once, then twice. "Put your cock in me," she begged.

He abruptly grasped her hips with both hands, holding her ass down on his cock. She cried out at the loss of his fingers at her sex. She'd been on the verge of coming.

"*Stop* it, Laila."

His hard, tense voice barely breached her trance of lust.

"Stop writhing around. You're killing me." This time, his fury penetrated. She blinked open her eyelids and stilled her wiggling butt. She saw the wildness in his eyes. It killed *her* a little.

"Just for a little bit," she whispered. "I'm healthy, Asher. I swear it. I just had a doctor's appointment last month, and I haven't had sex since then."

He winced. He looked like he was in considerable pain.

"I'm healthy too. That's not what I'm worried about. What about—"

"You won't come in me," she interrupted. Part of her couldn't believe she was saying this. But it had been what he'd said earlier—in addition to a whole hell of a lot of lust, of course. "I won't get pregnant. I want to feel what it's like without any barriers between us too. I always have, Asher."

A muscle ticked in his lean cheek.

"I'm not sure I'll be able to stop, once I'm inside you. I've never done this before . . . let alone with *you*," she thought she heard him mutter under his breath. Yet she couldn't help but notice that the whole time he spoke of his uncertainty, he stared down hungrily between her thighs.

"You'll stop," she whispered, putting out her arms for him. "I trust you."

He didn't know what he'd done to deserve it, but he saw the truth of her words shining like a beacon in her green eyes. She trusted him without a doubt . . . trusted him to taste heaven and then walk away.

The problem was—the thing he didn't want to think about at that moment—she hadn't been correct about what he'd wanted to do to her in those golden, tense seconds. Not *entirely*, she hadn't been.

If she'd accurately guessed his fantasy, she wouldn't be allowing this.

The impulse that had come over him had been completely irrational anyway, the crazy impulse of a savage, the residue of the caveman that usually slumbered deep in his twenty-first-century male brain.

As he came down over her, he honestly couldn't have said if she'd made a mistake in trusting him or not. He ached so much. He only knew he needed her more in that moment than he'd ever needed anything. This was the kind of sexual hunger that could turn a man into a lunatic . . . or quite possibly kill him, if it wasn't pacified.

He guided his cock to her liquid entry. He opened his mouth to tell her it wasn't too late to change her mind, but nothing came out but a groan at the sensation of her channel squeezing his cockhead. Concentrated excitement tickled at the base of his spine, and he abandoned his feeble attempts at reason.

When it came to Laila, his need had always been overwhelming.

He sank into her slowly, grinding his teeth together at the exquisite sensation. She hugged him so tightly . . . like she'd never let go. She was so warm and wet and sweet.

"Laila," he muttered in agony as he pressed his balls tightly against her outer sex and she encapsulated every inch of him. He glanced at her face. She stared up at him, her pink lips parted in wonder, her cheeks flushed and glazed with perspiration.

"This is how it's supposed to be," he said. She just nodded, her lush mouth trembling.

Holding her stare, he began to dip his cock in and out of her. He was deliberate. He forced himself to absorb every sensation. Every stroke felt like it would be his last. He balanced precariously on a ledge between agony and bliss.

She began to move in synchrony with him in that liquid, sensuous roll of her hips that he loved. She lifted her head off the pillow and stared down between their bodies, watching them fuse. He followed her gaze, gritting his teeth hard at the erotic vision of his naked cock penetrating her, her juices glistening on the naked shaft. The silence seemed to surround them, embrace them, interrupted only by Laila's soft whimpers. For his part, he held his breath. He had some vague, irrational idea that if he sucked his lungs full of air, he'd combust into a million flaming pieces.

He came up on his knees on the couch and opened his hands at the back of her thighs. He lifted her legs into the air, urged them wide and began to thrust. She stared up at him as though mesmerized, her firm breasts bouncing slightly as his pelvis smacked into hers.

"You're so beautiful," he said. Distantly, he realized he sounded a little angry. She disarmed him so easily, turned his entire body into a single, quivering, exposed nerve. He realized he could feel her shaking, feel her trembling with his hands and even his pounding cock. She was on the edge. He craved her release, but dreaded it too. He knew he couldn't survive, naked as he was. Armorless. He'd burst into flame the second she started to come.

But a heaven like this wasn't meant to last.

He held her hips tightly and thrust hard, causing her body to jerk.

"Jesus," he groaned miserably. He reached with his thumb and rubbed her lubricated clit. He felt her surge against his fingertip. A huge shudder went through her. He knew he should withdraw, but then he felt it: her heat pouring into him, the exquisite, tiny, rippling convulsions of her vagina as she climaxed. Instead he pumped into her rapidly. It was like fucking fire . . . like rushing between the closing gates of heaven. His balls felt like they were caught in a vise.

He pulled out of her, a vicious roar ripping at his throat. A fog hazed his consciousness for a moment. When he came back to himself, he was frantically pumping his cock. He shuddered again, and another white, ropy strand of ejaculate jetted onto Laila's smooth belly. The vision struck him as intensely erotic, and yet *wrong* somehow.

He resisted a wild, primal urge to plunge back inside and leave his seed at the deepest reaches of this woman's body.

He blinked dazedly at the sound of the house phone ringing. His head went up. His face had been planted at the juncture of Laila's neck and shoulder. Their pressing bodies were wet with his semen.

He jerked up at the realization.

"Damn," he muttered, staring down at her damp belly. Even her lower breasts glistened with his ejaculate. *Are you out of your fucking mind?*

"What's wrong?" she asked, her voice low and a little rough. She lifted her head from a couch pillow when she noticed his anxious expression. She glanced down at her wet stomach. The phone had stopped ringing, but then it started again.

"None of it went inside me. It's okay, Asher."

"It doesn't take much," he stated grimly.

He stood rapidly from the couch, the abrupt action making him feel a little light-headed. Or maybe what had just happened, that inexplicable, intense rush of primal possessiveness, was what had left him dizzy in its wake. He jerked up his pajama bottoms.

"Let me get you something. Don't move," he muttered, stalking toward the hallway. He wouldn't allow his brain to focus on what he'd just done . . . the crazy things he'd just been feeling and thinking. He returned a few seconds later and handed her a towel from the bathroom. She sat up.

"Aren't you going to get that?" she asked him uneasily.

He blinked, breaking his mesmerized stare from her naked body gilded with sunlight and his semen.

"Yeah," he muttered thickly, making a beeline for the phone. He needed to rein in his brain . . . bring himself back into the present. Into reality.

Because he'd sure as hell checked out of it during those moments on that couch with Laila.

Laila watched him as he picked up the receiver. His expression as he'd stared at his semen on her body had alarmed her a little. He'd been shocked at what they'd just done . . . at having sex without using protection.

She was pretty surprised herself. But her disbelief didn't begin to approximate what she'd seen on Asher's face just moments ago. It had been something close to horror. He'd been stunned that he'd allowed himself to be so vulnerable with her, that he'd let his guard down, given the inevitable impermanence of their affair.

She heard him curse. She finished drying herself and stood, pulling Asher's bunched-up T-shirt down over her.

"No, it's okay. You can send him up." Asher glanced back at her. "I just completely forgot he was coming by, that's all."

"That was the doorman," he said a moment later as he hung up the phone. "Rudy's downstairs. He's on his way up."

She blinked. "Not *Rudy*, Rudy." He nodded once. "Rudy Fattore . . . from Crescent Bay?" she asked in amazement.

"He's from Los Angeles, nowadays. I canceled dinner with him the last few nights because—" He gave her a swift glance, and she understood he'd canceled because he'd gone to see her at the club both nights. "I told him I wasn't feeling great, and suggested he come by this morning. I forgot about it. With everything." She saw his gaze shoot to the couch behind her. His mouth tightened. "I would have made another excuse just now, but he flew in from L.A. just to see me for a few days. I didn't want to—"

"No, it's all right. Of course he should come up. I'll just go and shower, if that's all right?" She edged toward the hallway. She felt awkward, beyond the unexpected situation of Rudy Fattore suddenly springing out of her past, just like Asher had. Something seemed wrong with Asher. He was regretting the intense intimacy they'd just shared. She just knew it. She hesitated. "I'd like to see him again. Is it . . . okay if I come out after I shower?"

"Of course."

She nodded once, her uneasiness escalating. She started toward the hallway.

"Laila?"

Her heart jumped and she turned around anxiously.

"Do you remember how Rudy wanted to be a celebrity photographer back in Crescent Bay?"

"Yeah."

"Well, he became one. A pretty major one, actually. He'd love to get a photo of Yesenia. That's why we first showed up at the club on Thursday night," he explained tensely.

"Oh." She glanced nervously toward the foyer and the front door. Rudy would arrive any second.

"He won't get that Yesenia and Laila from Crescent Bay are the same person." A loud knock resounded from the front door. She jumped. "And *I'm* not going to tell him," Asher continued in a firm, hushed tone. "So don't worry about it, okay? I'll just tell him we met up accidentally yesterday. You're an account manager for Microsoft, just like you tell your parents."

"Where?" she whispered.

"Where *what*?" he asked, looking around when Rudy knocked louder.

"Where did we meet?"

He glanced back at her.

"The subway, of course," he replied with a small smile.

She felt self-conscious walking out into the living room fifteen minutes later, fully dressed after her shower. But she'd forgotten Rudy's no-nonsense friendliness and charm.

"Well, will you look at that," he said, spinning around when she said hello. "It's Laila Barek. I don't believe it."

She laughed. "Didn't Asher tell you I was here?"

"Yeah, but I didn't believe him. I just figured he'd grown a little delusional in his old age, wishing up some old fantasies from his past," Rudy said bluntly, approaching her. Laila put out her hand to shake in greeting, but Rudy wouldn't have it. He gave her a big bear hug, making her shriek in surprise. He lifted her feet several inches off the floor and swung her around. She snorted with laughter, noticing Asher's mildly amused, forbearing expression over Rudy's shoulder. "Look at you. You grew up *good*," Rudy told her, giving her a frank assessment once he'd set her back on the carpet. "Asher says you live in Chicago now?"

"Yeah. With Tahi. You remember my cousin Tahi, right?"

Rudy's expression flattened. He looked very much the same to her, with the exception of a few added pounds, a slightly receding hairline and his expensive-looking clothing.

"Tahi is *here*? In Chicago?"

"Yeah. We have a place on the Near North Side."

"Is she still single?" Rudy demanded.

Laila nodded, grinning.

"Well what are we *waiting* for?" Rudy asked disbelievingly, spinning on his heels to look at Asher. "Get your clothes on, Ash. We're gonna go find that girl and have ourselves some *fun*."

Chapter Twenty-three

Although Rudy's plan sounded like a good time, Laila had her doubts as to it panning out. She tried to text and call Tahi while Asher showered and dressed, but her cousin didn't respond immediately.

"She's probably getting ready or something," Laila explained, wondering privately if her cousin had a date that Sunday.

"No problem," Rudy insisted once Asher had rejoined them, looking mouthwatering in a pair of jeans, casual boots, a button-down shirt, gray hoodie pullover sweater and a rugged brown jacket. "We'll just go over to your place and hunt her down."

Laila gave Asher a doubtful glance.

"Will Tahi kill us for barging in on her?" Asher asked her with a small smile, seemingly reading her mind.

"I don't *think* so," Laila replied uncertainly.

"Because if not, I'd love to see your place," Asher said.

She couldn't refuse him after he'd said that. She couldn't refuse him much of anything, apparently.

They drove to her condo in Rudy's rental car. Rudy protested when instead of getting in the passenger seat, Asher got into the backseat with Laila.

"What am I, your chauffeur or something?" he complained. Asher didn't bother to reply, just put his arm around Laila and pulled her against him. Rudy rolled his eyes in the rearview mirror.

"Jesus. Some things never change," he said in a long-suffering, beleaguered tone before he started the engine.

Laila was a little worried as she unlocked their front door. What if Michael was there with Tahi? That would be awkward.

"I'll just go and look for her—" she told Asher and Rudy as she led them into her living room.

"Tahi!" Rudy bellowed, making Laila start before she ever got to the hallway. "Get your butt out here, girl."

Laila heard something drop heavily onto the floor in the vicinity of Tahi's bedroom.

"Tahi, it's me. Everything's okay," Laila called anxiously, all too aware of how shocked Tahi would be hearing a man yelling at her in their condominium. A few seconds later, Tahi came rushing into the living room wearing a robe with a towel wrapped around her head.

"Laila? What's—" Her brown eyes grew to the size of saucers when she focused on all three of them standing there. Rudy started toward her.

"*Rudy Fattore?*" she exclaimed. A huge grin broke across her face. Rudy grabbed her hand.

"None other. Come *on*, woman. What are you *doing*? Put on your dancing shoes. Let's go have some fun," Rudy urged. Much to Laila's amazement, the two of them started a two-step at the exact same moment. Tahi laughed out loud as Rudy spun and dipped her so energetically, her towel fell off her head.

Laila glanced up at Asher, her grin widening when she saw the amusement and warmth gleaming in his eyes as he watched the other two. For a moment, it was like nothing had changed since that summer eight years ago.

And yet . . . *everything* had changed. Now they were free . . . free to spend a sunny autumn day together. Free to dance. Free to laugh. She put her arms around Asher's waist, hugging him close. He held her tight in return. Turning her nose into his sweatshirt, she inhaled his scent, feeling his hardness. His strength. She listened happily to Tahi and Rudy laughing and catching up in sporadic, breathless phrases while they kept dancing. Asher's hand cupped the back of her head, and she looked up at his handsome face.

Free to love?

A lump formed at the back of her throat as she stared into his eyes. His head dipped, his mouth brushing hers. *Maybe?* At least for these sweet, precious moments they were free . . . perhaps even for that.

That Sunday was one of those days that would remain forever vivid and happy in her memory. It was a beautiful October day: crisp and cool, but warm in the sunshine. The trees in Lincoln Park were a riot of yellow, gold, red and orange. They had lunch at Zizi's and then walked over to the zoo. Afterward, they strolled through the park and came upon a little Oktoberfest. A band was playing oompah music interspersed with some modern covers. Asher and Laila sat in the grass and watched as Rudy led Tahi in a bouncy polka.

"Rudy better watch it, or he's going to yank her arms off," Asher joked.

Laila grinned. "I'd forgotten how much fun they had together in Crescent Bay. I haven't seen Tahi smile and laugh so much in years."

He took her hand in his and rested it on his jeans-covered thigh. He wore a pair of sunglasses, so she couldn't see his eyes. "You've been smiling a lot today. Just an observation."

"That's because I'm happy. I'm with you," she murmured. His sunglasses blocked much of his expression. She, on the other hand, knew her heart was on display in her eyes. She couldn't help it.

His smile faded slightly and he leaned forward. Their lips met and clung.

"What do you say we ditch those two and go back to my place? I don't like sharing you. I want you all to myself," he muttered next to her lips a moment later.

"No, we shouldn't." She noticed his frown and laughed. "You said you've hardly seen Rudy since he's come to Chicago. It would be rude."

"I only have so much time here, Laila. I care about Rudy a lot, but I won't let him stand in the way of us being together." She leaned back a few inches, studying every precious line and rugged angle of his face. What he'd said, and the seriousness with which he'd said it, had sobered her. "I suppose I'm being selfish. Again," he said.

"No, I wasn't thinking that," she whispered.

"Will you spend it with me?"

"What?"

"Will you spend as much time with me as you can before I leave for London?"

She hesitated. It wasn't that she didn't want to—she wanted to be with him with every fiber of her being. It was his putting it so explicitly into words. Maybe she'd been imagining it would be easier if they'd just fallen into it all, spending every hour they could together impulsively, just letting it unfold without a plan. That way, she wouldn't have to deliberately think about how it would feel when they had an ocean separating them.

"I'm not sure that'd be wise on our part," she whispered.

"Do you think I don't know that?" he asked, his mouth going hard. "This isn't about wisdom. I thought you got that eight years ago. This is about us, and what happens when we're together. This is about the way you make me feel. I come alive when I'm with you. Sometimes I wish it weren't true, but that doesn't change the fact that it *is*."

She opened her mouth, stunned and moved by his customary blunt honesty but entirely unexpected declaration of feeling. His mouth covered hers again. She clutched onto his jacket, feeling herself being swept away by him.

Letting it happen.

"Jesus, they're just as bad as they were in Crescent Bay. *Worse*," someone said loudly next to them. "Get off your ass and ask the girl to dance, Ash."

Laila blinked the sunlight out of her eyes and saw Rudy and Tahi standing over them. A ballad resounded around them. Tahi grinned down at her knowingly, but her eyebrows were arched in a silent query. She and Laila hadn't had much of an opportunity to talk in private since they'd pounced on Tahi in the condo earlier. She was curious about what was happening between Asher and Laila. She wasn't sure she had a great answer . . . or at least, not an easy one. What happened between her and Asher had always been inexplicable. Undeniably powerful. She watched as Rudy and Tahi began to dance and talk once more. They moved away from them.

Asher stood swiftly, startling her. Still shielding her eyes from the sun, she looked up the considerable length of him. She noticed his somber expression. He put out his hand and she took it. He pulled her up, and she fell against his chest with a thud and a bark of laughter. His arm went around her waist, holding her tight against him. He grabbed her hand. They immediately began to dance to the modern song the band now played.

"We've never danced before," she said after a few seconds. Something about his stark honesty before, the bright fall sunlight, the brilliant fall foliage, the plaintive ballad and the feeling of moving so intimately with him had left her dazed.

"There's a lot of things we've never done before," he said.

Keeping her body pressed against his, she reached up and removed his sunglasses. She tucked them into his jacket pocket and put her hand back in his. "There. That's better," she said, looking directly into his blue eyes. They were fierce and smoldering, just like she'd known they would be. But she caught a hint of expectation in his narrowed gaze, as well. He was still waiting for her answer.

"*Yes*," she said breathlessly. "I'll spend every minute with you that I can. Because you always make me feel a way I've never felt in my life. So full. So happy I feel like I'm going to spill over with it."

He bent and kissed her hard on the mouth, moving her in double time to the music for a few bars of music. When he broke their kiss, she realized he was smiling down at her. She smiled back and shook her head.

"What?" he asked as they spun to the music.

"The song," she said hesitantly. It was Ed Sheeran's "Thinking Out Loud."

"*People fall in love in mysterious ways*," she echoed the young man singing on the stage.

She watched as Asher's eyes darkened and his smile vanished. Regret instantly filled her. She shouldn't have said that loaded word. He'd recognized the lyric as well, heard the echo of their feelings in it . . . their history. For a second, she recalled it vividly, the moment she'd looked up from bathing nude in the secret lake and seen him standing there on the shore. His stare had gone through her like an arrow.

He pulled her tighter against him, lowering his head and pressing his lips against her neck . . . hiding his expression from her. There was so much more she wanted to express. All the words and feelings swelled inside her until she felt like she'd burst.

She *had* sacrificed the right to speak so intimately to him when she'd walked away eight years ago. Was that what he subtly told her in that moment? She'd hurt him badly. She understood if he wanted to protect himself, at least in part, from her. This time, he'd be the one to walk away. Maybe she owed it to him, to carry out their short affair with as little drama and heartache as possible?

The last thing she wanted was to hurt him again.

Neither of them said anything else for the remainder of the dance. Laila suspected he didn't want them to speak . . . to make things messier than they already were.

Yes, they'd agreed to spend their time together before Asher left the country, to enjoy their uncommonly strong connection to one another. But Laila recognized that the uncertainty of their future and the heartache of their past prevented them from risking saying that single haunting word: *Love*.

She was determined to live every moment with him to the fullest, despite her rush of doubt. Asher treated the four of them to dinner at Oriole that night. Afterward, they all went to Laila and Tahi's condo. Laila had them sit at the cozy booth in their kitchen while she prepared tea. After a few minutes of moving around furtively at the counter, trying to hide what she was doing, she turned and headed toward the table, carrying a plate of Moroccan donuts and cookies in one hand and a large slice of orange cardamom cake with a lit candle stuck in it in the other.

"I'm sorry I don't have a whole cake, but this one is still fresh," she told Asher. She started to sing "Happy Birthday." Rudy and Tahi joined in as she set the slice of cake in front of a nonplussed Asher.

"How did you know it was my birthday tomorrow?" he asked Laila once he'd blown out the candle at the end of the song and Laila had sat down next to him in the booth.

She reached to pull the single candle out of his slice of cake. She sucked the cake off the end between a playful smile.

"I told you before. You'd be shocked at the details I remember about you."

Asher and Rudy inhaled the cake, cookies and donuts, both of them repeatedly saying how good they were, both of them amazed that Tahi and Laila had made them.

"You don't get anything about being a Moroccan female if you don't believe we could have made these things blindfolded by the time we were twelve," Tahi teased.

They sat at the table long after all the sweets were done, drinking tea and then decaf coffee. Rudy had a collection of entertaining stories about celebrities he'd photographed, both as a hired photographer and as a member of the paparazzi. Tahi milked every detail about some of her favorite celebs. Asher talked some too about his work overseas. But the stories he relayed were light and humorous, anecdotes that hardly began to explain the shadow that fell over his face at times over the topic of his coverage in the Middle East, especially Aleppo, or the hint of sadness in his eyes as he recalled certain memories. She knew he'd experienced some horrors there. She felt the difference those years and those tragedies had created in him. From reading his stories, she understood he'd witnessed both unimaginable terror and incredible moments of kindness and humanity. Instead of becoming aloof in order to deal with what he'd seen, he'd grown tougher—true—but also more compassionate. She didn't need him to spill every detail of his ordeals in order to know that.

She leaned over to kiss him when it turned midnight. "Happy birthday for real, this time," she whispered, smiling against his lips.

"Let's go back to my place and celebrate for real," he said quietly, just for her ears.

"Yeah. Let's do that. For *sure*," she murmured, nibbling again at his firm, sexy lower lip.

"Laila, my mom called this morning," Tahi called from across the large round table. "She was needling for us to try to get to Detroit on Saturday night next weekend. I told her we couldn't leave until Sunday morning, but she kept suggesting it, like if she said it enough, it would become reality. I told her for the millionth time that you worked on Saturday nights, but be warned. The aunties are starting to get really worked up about this visit." Her cousin gave Rudy a sideways glance. Laila had whispered to Tahi earlier while they dressed to go out with the guys that Laila's true career was to be kept a secret from Rudy.

"I know. I talked to Mamma this morning," Laila said uneasily. She felt Asher's stare on her cheek. She wished Tahi hadn't been the one to first bring up the visit. Laila herself had planned to break it to him in her own way and time.

"What's this? You're going to Detroit next Sunday? For how long?" Asher asked in a low voice. She had a sickening feeling of the familiar.

"Just until Monday," Laila said.

"Our cousin Driss is bringing his fiancée to Detroit. It's the first time for her to meet everyone, and the aunties are going overboard, as usual, planning gargantuan feasts and parties. Everyone in town except for the mayor is coming over at some point, but it's not because the aunties didn't ask him," Tahi told Rudy with a grin.

"I'm leaving for London early Wednesday morning," Asher said tensely, for Laila's ears only.

"I know," she whispered. Feeling torn, she started to explain about how the weekend had been planned for months now, ever since Driss had called to say he was bringing Sara to Detroit. She wanted to tell him how important it was for Tahi and her to be there, given Zara's absence and her uncle Reda's and aunt Nadine's vulnerability over that situation. Before she could get out a word of explanation, though, she heard the sound of distant knocking. Someone was at the front door. Tahi's blank look told Laila she didn't have a clue who it could be either.

"I'll get it," Laila said, sliding out of the booth. "Someone probably has the wrong unit."

A few seconds later she looked through the peephole on the front door. Her stomach dropped. Rafe stood in the hallway wearing a dark overcoat. She hesitated but only for a few seconds. Firming her resolve, she swung open the front door.

"Hi," she said breathlessly.

Rafe's mouth looked tight with anxiety. Or was it anger?

"I've been trying to get hold of you all last night and today," he said. "Is everything all right?" His gaze flickered off her face to the left of her. Instinctively, Laila turned. Asher stood behind her, his brow lowered, his jaw hard, his expression unreadable.

He looked intimidating as hell.

"Yeah. I'm fine. I'm so sorry for not getting back sooner. Uh . . . Rafe Durand, I'd like you to meet Asher Gaites."

"I sat you at the club the other night," Rafe said after a stunned pause. "You wanted a front-row seat."

"Yeah. That was me," Asher stated flatly.

"Asher and I have known each other for years," Laila said,

clearing her throat. Neither man said anything else. Talk about awkward. Asher's stare on Rafe was so unwavering and cold, she was surprised Rafe didn't freeze to the spot.

"Rafe," she said. "We need to talk. Can we go outside?"

"In the *hallway*?" His incredulous, panicked expression warned Laila he had an idea what was coming.

"I just . . ." She waved toward the interior of the condo. In the distance, she saw Rudy and Tahi coming out of the kitchen. "Wanted someplace private, that's all."

He stepped back into the hallway. Laila gave a silent, brooding Asher an apologetic, desperate glance over her shoulder before she shut the door between them. She turned to Rafe, struggling for what to say. Finally, only the simple truth came out of her throat.

"I've loved him since I was nineteen years old," she said softly. "He's a foreign correspondent for the *New York Gazette*. He just returned to Chicago for a short visit before he takes another job overseas, and we—"

"Hooked up?"

She sensed his anger. "It's more than that, Rafe. I'm not saying it'll last forever, but this thing between Asher and me is far from a casual hookup."

He gave a sharp bark of laughter. "So that's it? Things are over between us before they really ever got started? I don't stand a chance, is that what you're saying? One second, you're available, and then he walks onto the scene, and you're not? What about when he walks out of your life again, Laila? What then?"

"I don't know that I *was* ever available. Not while he's alive somewhere. Anywhere." He looked a little taken aback by her stark admission. The truth had just come out of her. She herself hadn't fully understood it until that moment. Yes, she'd dated over the years. But she'd never truly committed herself to anyone, never truly shared all of herself. Just like she'd once predicted would happen, her heart had frozen eight years ago.

She sighed, hating to see the dawning hurt on Rafe's face. She cared about him. He'd been good to her, as her manager and promoter. He'd made a success of the impossible, a woman in show business who wanted to remain partially in the shadows. It was unheard of. Few other promoters and managers would have ever touched her, seeing it as too big a boundary to overcome in the high-profile entertainment industry. Regular public appearances were as necessary as an in-your-face, constant social media presence. Rafe may not have liked her choice for privacy, but he'd gone along with it. He'd helped her make the impossible possible.

"I'm sorry, Rafe. I really am," she said sincerely. "You've been a good friend to me. A good manager. I wouldn't be where I am today if it weren't for you. I hope you know how grateful I am, you made my career possible. My *dreams* possible. It's just—"

"What?" he asked.

"Well . . . you've always asked me about the inspiration for the passion in my songs, the sexual tension and longing in my lyrics." His expression stiffened in understanding. He glanced at the door behind her, to the foyer where Asher had just been standing.

"Him? You're telling me your inspiration was *him*?"

"Yes," Laila replied softly. A strange, mixed feeling of joy and sadness went through her, a sense of inevitability. "I think it always will be."

After Rafe left, Laila went inside and shut the door quietly. She wasn't surprised to see Asher standing in the hallway outside the living room. He'd already put on his jacket. He had her coat draped in the crook of his elbow. She approached him, unoffended that he'd assumed she'd still want to spend the night with him.

She couldn't imagine being separated from him in that moment, even though unspoken currents of emotion seemed to ebb and flow between them. He held up her coat and helped her put it on.

They didn't really talk until Rudy had dropped them off at Asher's condo. After they'd removed their coats, Asher grabbed her hand and led her down the hallway to the bedroom. He turned her to face him in the shadowed room.

"Did Rafe take it all right?" he asked her as he began to unfasten the button-down sweater she wore.

"As well as can be imagined," Laila replied softly, staring up at his shadowed face.

"He wanted to be with you ever since he first saw you perform, didn't he?"

She heard the edge to his tone. "It doesn't matter. I was never really invested in seeing him romantically. It never felt right." He silently drew her sweater over her shoulders. She wore only a bra beneath it. She caught the sweater with her hands and tossed it onto a chair in the bedroom suite. He touched her chest with his fingertips.

"What is it, then?" he asked. "What's wrong?"

She glanced up, unsurprised she couldn't fool him. "It's just something I said to Rafe, out there in that hallway," she said in a hushed tone. "Something I hadn't realized was true until I said it."

"What?" he asked, his head dipping downward until their faces were only inches apart. She swallowed back the lump in her throat. If she could say it so simply to Rafe, why was it so hard to say it to him, whom it most concerned?

"I told him that as long as you were somewhere on this earth, even if it was on the other side of the globe, I was never really going to be available to another man. I never really have been. Not for all these years."

His gliding fingertips paused on the upper swell of her left breast. She saw his eyes glitter in the dim light as he searched her face.

"You said that?"

She smiled and nodded. Her eyelids burned when she closed them. "You don't have to sound so surprised."

"I am, though."

She glanced up sharply. "Why?"

"Because saying it," he murmured, brushing the line of her jaw with his fingertip. "It's like . . . stepping out from behind the curtain a little bit, isn't it?"

She was confused. "I use the curtain for my professional life, because I want to protect my anonymity. It has nothing to do with my relationships. Nothing to do with you."

His quirked his brow. "You use it to keep your family life intact, to protect the people you love, to remain respectful of your culture and way of life, and to live out your dreams at once. I'd say there's some parallel."

She shook her head, feeling agitated. She stepped away from him. "No. You're wrong. I don't just use the curtain to protect my family. I use it to protect *myself*. I don't want to be anyone else's property. I'm never going to spend my days at publicity events getting my picture taken thousands of times, or sending off tweets about every personal moment of my day. My singing is an important part of me, but it's mine to share as I choose. I've found a way to make it all work, by singing behind the curtain."

She saw his small shrug and doubtful expression. Emotion surged in her until it boiled over.

"What are you *saying*? Are you mad because I found a way to make music and performing a part of my life when I couldn't find a way to do that with you when I was nineteen years old?"

"I'm saying that there are similarities with how you've managed your gift as a songwriter and performer and how you manage being with me. Not eight years ago. I understand you were barely an adult then. I'm talking about right now."

Realization hit her. "You're mad about the Detroit visit next weekend, aren't you? I'm sorry about that, Asher, but it's been planned for months. I didn't get a chance to explain about it."

"I wouldn't say I'm mad, exactly. Disappointed, maybe. Don't you see? You're still doing it, Laila. Trying to live in both worlds, never really committing to either one."

"That's not fair! What exactly would you have me do, Asher? You're here for another week. Do you want me to drive you up to my parents' house and explain to them how we're sleeping together every chance we get, because apparently we have no self-control when it comes to each other?"

"No," he bellowed so abruptly, she gasped in surprise. He exhaled and closed his eyes. "All I was saying before," he said in a quieter, strained voice, "is that I was surprised you were so honest with Rafe about how you felt about me." He opened his eyes and met her stare. "I was surprised you were so open with *me*. I didn't mean to start a fight. I shouldn't have said that about the curtain. I just meant that you can be careful at times, Laila. Part of you is always a bit of a mystery to me. Uncommitted. Unavailable. A little bit of you is always veiled."

The burning in her eyes amplified. "I honestly don't know why you feel that way. I've told you how much I regretted cutting all ties with you. You must know I'm crazy about you. I care about you in a way that I can't completely put into words, but I feel it here," she said, pushing her fist against her chest. "I feel it so much, I *ache* with it, Asher."

"I do know that," he said starkly. "But I also know you walked away."

A pocket of air popped out of her throat. She looked up at the ceiling, helplessness nearly choking off her voice. "You're never going to forgive me for that, are you?"

"Yes," he stated emphatically, coming toward her and grasping her shoulders. "I think I *have* forgiven you. There was probably nothing to forgive. You were a teenager, for Christ's sake. I get that. I understand the expectations a Moroccan Muslim family would have for their young daughter. But I'm talking about right now. You *still* have it in you to walk away, Laila."

"*I'm* not walking away! I'm right. *Here*," she told him with succinct fierceness. She reached up and grabbed his dense biceps, squeezing them for emphasis. "If you want me, then here I am. What more can I do or say?"

A shudder coursed through his tense features. "I wish I could stop it, but I can't. *Ana kan bghik bezaf, gulbi ki darni.*"

She winced in pain. Tears jetted down her cheeks. He'd said it better than her, both what she was feeling and what he was. *I want you so much, my heart hurts*. She'd never taught him that entire phrase in Darija. He'd learned it in the years they'd been apart. Somehow, she knew he'd learned and remembered it because of her. She began to tremble.

"Asher."

They crashed together, their mouths battling, surrendering; their bodies straining. They fell onto the bed a moment later, clawing to rid each other of their clothing. Laila had the strangest sense of déjà vu. She didn't understand why that was until after the storm of need had raged between them and left them exhausted and spent in each other's arms.

It had reminded her of their intense anxiety once, long ago in Crescent Bay. They'd argued, and she'd expressed how confused she was. How torn. They'd made love wildly afterward. They'd been so mindless with desperation . . . so fearful of loss.

They'd been right to be scared. They'd been split apart within hours.

"It's different now, Asher," she whispered next to his neck.

She raised her chin and saw that his eyes were open, and that he was watching her. “Please let it be different for us.”

He lifted his hand and cupped her face in that tender, focused way he had. She felt her heart swell and ache.

“I’ll let it be any way you want it to be, as long as you agree that there’s an *us*.”

“There will *always* be an *us*,” she promised in a choked voice before she pressed her lips to his.

Chapter Twenty-four

Asher awoke with a start. Sunlight streamed between the edges of the closed curtains. Someone was knocking persistently on the front door in the distance. He felt Laila rustle next to him, her silky, naked skin and long hair sliding against him. His body flickered with pleasure. Flashes of memory trickled across his consciousness, dragging emotion along with it. He delved his fingers into her long, unbound hair and cupped the back of her head.

"Asher?" she whispered sleepily.

He pressed his lips to her temple.

"It's okay, beautiful. I'll get it. Just relax." He reluctantly released her, carefully covering her bare shoulders with the blanket. He slid along the mattress, getting out on his side of the bed.

Was he surprised when he opened the front door a few seconds later to see his mother standing there with a large box in her hands? Not entirely. No matter how bad the fight between them had been the other day, his mother had never missed one of his birthdays.

Besides. A birthday was an excuse to get together and bring him around to her way of thinking.

"Happy birthday," she said brightly, stepping over the threshold and kissing him on the cheek. "Did I wake you? It's past ten o'clock."

"I was up late," he said, accepting the box she thrust into his hands. "What's this?"

"Oh, just a little something Lettie made for you." Lettie had been working in the Winnetka residence as their cook since Asher was eight years old. He should have known his mother wasn't responsible for the personal gift. "Lettie knows just what you like. She had it all boxed up and ready for you first thing this morning when I came down for breakfast."

"So you're here because Lettie remembered it was my birthday and made me a cake," Asher said dryly, taking the box and walking with it toward the kitchen. He gave a silent nod of respect to Lettie. The cook clearly understood the undercurrents of strain between her employers and their son, despite all of his mother's constant admonishments to not talk in front of the help. His mother would be floored if she ever actually understood how much the people she employed knew about her personal life.

"That was nice of Lettie," he said neutrally.

"It wasn't Lettie's idea for me to come downtown and wish you a happy birthday," his mother said as she followed him into the kitchen. He set the cake on the counter. Despite the fact that he didn't want to, he heard the hint of hurt in his mother's tone. He turned and kissed her cheek.

"I know that. Thanks, Mom."

He hugged her. She reciprocated, albeit clumsily. His mom had never been much of a hugger. She squeezed his upper arms.

"My goodness, you've grown," she said, sounding flustered as they separated. He laughed.

"I'm the same size as I was the last time you saw me."

"Well," she said, smoothing her bobbed brown hair even though not a strand was out of place. "You *have* grown, nevertheless. You've become quite an accomplished man," she said, staring everywhere but at him. He opened his mouth to thank her. It had been the closest thing to a compliment that he'd heard from his mother in years. "Asher, go and put on some clothes," she scolded before he could say anything. "You shouldn't be answering the door naked."

"I'm wearing pajama bottoms, Mom. What do you expect? I was sleeping," he muttered, rolling his eyes at the fact that she had to revert to scolding instead of letting the warm moment unfold.

"Well, go and shower and get dressed anyway. I've scheduled a birthday brunch for us at the club."

"Mom, I'm not alone."

"What?" Her wide-eyed, askance look transferred to the entryway of the kitchen. Asher turned and saw Laila standing in the entryway, looking uncertain as to whether she should stay or try to escape. She wore the button-down shirt he'd been wearing yesterday. The shirt fell on her pretty legs at midthigh. Her long hair spilled around her shoulders. She looked mussed and radiant and amazingly beautiful.

"Hello," she said in her low, resonant, singular voice. "I'm sorry. I didn't mean to interrupt—"

"You're not interrupting," Asher assured her. Part of his brain absorbed his mother's stiff, increasingly imperious expression. It embarrassed the hell out of him, as usual. The familiar feeling was even stronger presently, because it was Laila witnessing it all. Out of long habit, another part of him was already determinedly ignoring his mother's arrogance. "Mom, this is Laila Barek. Laila, this is my mother, Madeline Gaites-Granville."

"Well. It's a pleasure to meet you," his mom said, giving Laila a puzzled, frigid once-over before she stepped forward and shook her hand. The formal gesture struck Asher as ridiculous, given Laila's and his rumpled, just-rolled-out-of-bed condition.

"It's nice to meet you as well. I've heard so much about you," Laila said breathlessly, shaking his mother's hand.

"That much? Really?" his mother said, stepping back and giving Asher a speculative, coldly amused glance. "You work fast, son. You've only been in town a few days."

"I've known Laila for eight years," he said, all too happy to puncture a hole in his mother's superior bubble. It worked. She started and blinked, glancing at Laila more sharply this time.

"Eight *years*?"

"Yeah. In fact, I have you and Dad to thank for it. We met at Crescent Bay, that summer after I finished college," Asher said evenly. He noticed Laila's disbelieving, concerned glance, but it didn't stop him from his mission of bringing his mother down a notch or two. "We fell hard for each other, back then."

"And you've been in contact ever since then?" his mother asked in a high-pitched voice.

"No. We ran into each other unexpectedly a few days ago, here in Chicago," Asher said. He stepped closer to Laila and put his arm around her, rubbing her hip. "You can imagine how happy we were to see each other again."

"Yes, I can imagine. Barek, is it?" his mother asked, as if suddenly politely fascinated. Asher clenched his teeth hard at her sudden change of behavior.

"Yes," Laila said.

"Laila Barek," his mother mused. "I'm trying to recall if Asher has ever mentioned you, but I'm coming up short. I'm sure I'd remember the name. It's lovely. Is it Spanish, by chance? You have a look I associate with traveling along the Mediterranean coast there—"

"Mom—" Asher interrupted impatiently, seeing where this was headed.

"Just on the other side of the Mediterranean from Spain, actually. My family comes from Morocco," Laila said, cutting off Asher in turn.

"Morocco," his mother said stiffly after a pause. "How . . . exotic."

Asher refrained from rolling his eyes again. Instead, he pulled Laila closer. His mother noticed his protective gesture. She inhaled, as if to clear her head of the image of the two of them, and smiled widely. "Well, I can see you're not available to celebrate your birthday with your mother. You have much more interesting company. Would it be too much of an inconvenience if I were to ask you to the house tomorrow for lunch? I'll ask your father to be there, as well."

"To celebrate my birthday?" Asher asked.

"Of course. And to talk, as well. We have some unfinished business," she said briskly, buttoning her coat.

"I told you we were done getting together for *business*," he reminded her quietly. Firmly.

His mother's mouth trembled slightly. Guilt swept through him, the feeling annoyingly familiar. "Just to celebrate your birthday, then. You are still our son. Aren't you?"

"Of course. If you still want to be my parents."

"Don't be ridiculous."

"So it will just be a pleasant lunch? No talk about the trust fund or my job?" Asher pressed.

His mother lifted her chin. He could see her mind whirring, trying to come up with a loophole.

"Mom?" he asked warningly. "And you'll remind Dad of all that?"

"Oh, all right. Fine," she snapped. She glanced at him skittishly. "I'm just worried about your father and you. It's not right, this falling-out you've had. I don't want you to disappear to the other side of the world again with things the way they are."

"I don't want that either," Asher admitted honestly.

He spied her anxiety, her vulnerability . . . a fragility that was usually masked so well behind her cool indifference. He glanced quickly at Laila while his mother fussily rearranged her purse on her forearm. One look at Laila's compassionate expression, and he knew Laila had noticed it too.

"You'll come, then?" his mother asked crisply, her armor back in place.

"I'd like to bring Laila."

His mother's fiddling fingers froze. He was aware of Laila looking up at him in disbelieving surprise, but he didn't meet her stare. He just continued to stroke her hip as a means of assurance.

"I don't think I can," Laila said. He looked down at her. "My agent is in town, and I have a rehearsal scheduled tomorrow at twelve thirty."

"Can I come and watch?" he asked earnestly.

She glanced over at his mom, clearly tongue-tied as to how to respond.

"What about the *next* day for lunch, then?" his mother snapped before Laila could reply. Asher just raised his eyebrows expectantly as he looked down at Laila.

"Um . . . I'm so sorry, but I'm busy then too. But please . . . don't not go on my account," she told Asher.

"I'd like Laila to be there," Asher told his fuming mother calmly. "Is there any other day we can make work?"

His mom looked scandalized and furiously tight-lipped. Laila appeared totally confused. He prompted both of them until they came up with a day they agreed upon.

"Friday for lunch, then," Asher finally said. "It's all settled. We'll be there, Mom."

"You shouldn't have done that, Asher," Laila said quietly once the door had closed behind his mother and they were alone.

"Why not? I want them to meet you," he said, walking past her and picking up his phone to check messages.

"They won't want me there. Did you see the way your mother was looking at me?"

He gave her a sideways glance. "I did. I'm sorry about that," he said honestly.

"You invited me to go with you to get back at her for being rude," Laila said, her mouth tightening into an angry line.

He tossed down the phone onto the desk and walked into her. He took her into his arms and dropped a kiss on her mouth, softening it from the anxious frown she wore. "You're right," he admitted. "But only partially," he interrupted when she opened her mouth to scold hm. "Mostly, I want them to meet you because they're the only family I have. I want them to know the woman who is so important to me. It's probably just like your cousin Driss wants your family to meet his fiancée. It's not so strange, Laila."

He took advantage of her lips parting in disbelief and leaned down to taste her.

Later that afternoon, Asher hung up his phone and checked the time. He'd just gotten off the phone with the *Gazette*'s managing editor. Apparently, his father hadn't been successful in his threat to call in a favor and have Asher's new job taken away from him. Avery Sennet, his new direct boss, sounded as firm and enthusiastic as ever about Asher reporting for work in London in a few weeks. Sennet's secretary had even gotten on the phone and described some details about how he could pick up the keys for the flat they'd arranged for him to lease near Leicester Square.

Sennet had given him some good news during the phone call. Maybe that news had contributed to Sennet's enthusiasm about him starting work. Maybe it also related to Sennet's apparent willingness to ignore Asher's father's intrusions into him taking the job, if his father had indeed tried to interfere as he'd threatened.

At any rate, the phone call made his impatience to see Laila again spike. He wanted to share the good news. Talking to Sennet and making plans for his move to London also made him anxious.

He'd be leaving Chicago so soon. Leaving Laila's arms.

He checked the clock on the desk and frowned. Where *was* she? She'd left after she'd showered and dressed earlier, insisting she just needed to run a couple errands downtown. She'd been elusive about what the errands were and why they were so important. It had been nearly three hours since she'd left. Had she been put off by that comparison he'd made to him wanting her to meet his parents and Driss bringing his fiancée home to Detroit?

He was in the process of trying to call her when a call came in from the front desk. It was his doorman. Laila had arrived.

He opened the front door a moment later. The question he'd been about to ask her about where she'd been and what had taken her so long faded from his tongue when he saw her glowing expression and the bag hanging at her side. A plaid gift-wrapped box stuck out of the top of it.

"I'm sorry I took so long," she exclaimed, crossing the threshold and going up on her toes to kiss him. She smelled like autumn air and her fresh floral perfume. He resisted an urge to pull her closer and bury his face in her neck when she backed away. "I was having trouble finding exactly what I wanted." She dangled the bag in front of him. "Happy birthday, Asher."

"That's where you were this whole time? Looking for a *birthday* present? For *me*?"

"Who else, goofy?" she asked, grinning and unbelting her long suede coat. She paused as she slid her coat off her shoulders. "Why are you frowning like that?"

"I would have rather spent the time with you," he told her bluntly. "That would have been the gift I chose."

A shadow passed over her radiant face. Regret spiked through him. "Picking out a special birthday gift for someone I care about is important. To *me*, it is. My mother spends months researching and thinking about perfect gifts for my dad and me for our birthdays. I only had a few hours."

"I'm sorry," he said, feeling stupid for his crassness. His damn insensitivity. He'd never get rid of that character flaw. "I'm not used to having anyone giving me presents."

"I thought your parents were always giving you things."

"Not things like this," he mumbled, eyeing the elegantly wrapped gift with wary curiosity. He saw her questioning glance as they walked into the living room. He shrugged. "Not things that they took half a day to shop for personally. More like things they asked their secretary or lawyer to procure for me."

"Like a car or this condo?" she asked as they sat down on the couch.

"I guess."

"This isn't anything like that. It's not a big deal. It's a new Burberry trench coat and an umbrella. I had to make sure you looked the part of a London bureau chief, didn't I?"

"It is a big deal," he realized, humbled. "That sounds great. If you picked it out, it is. I'm sorry. Just ignore me. You're incredibly sweet," he said, kissing her to underline his apology. Still, he was uncomfortable for some reason. He couldn't help it. He was used to giving women presents and usually enjoyed it. It hit him that he'd never *once* given her anything—Laila, whom he'd most like to spoil. He needed to rectify that. The idea of her shopping for a gift for him made him feel weird. Awkward, but also . . . special. It wasn't really a feeling he'd ever experienced before.

"Aren't you going to open it?" she asked, her sexy, curling lips and bright eyes making him forget for a second what she was talking about. He leaned over and palmed her jaw, kissing her without restraint this time. She moaned softly. He felt her melting against him. He reached for her, and the bag dropped to the floor.

"Asher, what are you *doing*?" she mumbled when he pressed her back on the couch and palmed a breast. He groaned. She felt so good beneath the thin sweater she wore, so firm and soft. He'd never get enough of her beautiful breasts. He felt the peak harden beneath his stroking fingers. Her reaction enflamed him. He went to kiss her mouth again. She twisted her chin.

"*Asher Gaites-Granville*, you aren't going to get out of opening that birthday present!"

He blinked in surprise at her scolding. She sat up, forcing him to straighten. She slid the gift out of the bag and plopped it unceremoniously into his lap, directly onto his erection. He started and grimaced.

"You are so *odd* sometimes. Who doesn't like presents? Now open the damn thing," she ordered, shaking her head, a smile peeking around her frown. She sighed and laughed when he began to unwrap the present in a desultory fashion.

"Then maybe we'll see about giving you the birthday gift you clearly would have preferred," she added drolly.

He grinned and started to rip the paper more enthusiastically.

They lay together side by side later that night on a mussed bed, Laila in the cradle of one of Asher's bent arms. His fingers moved lazily in her unbound hair. They'd made love with the lamp on. He'd wanted to see every nuance of her giving herself to him.

"I got a call earlier today from my new boss at the *Gazette*," Asher said quietly.

"You did?" Laila asked in a hushed voice. Had she stiffened a little when he'd brought up his job? It seemed more and more that they were veering away from the topic of his leaving next week.

"Yeah. You know how I told you that my father threatened to contact the head of Mandor Media Group and get me blackballed from my job? Well, either he backed off from doing it or Mandor decided it was worth the risk to make even more of an enemy of Clark and GGM."

"They recognize how good you are and want you working for them. *You* made it worth it for them, no matter what your dad can threaten," Laila said softly, stroking his jaw. He didn't respond. "Asher?" He turned his head and met her stare in the dim room. "Was there something else? About the call or your job? You seem preoccupied."

"I can't keep much from you, can I?"

"I hope not," she said, smiling. He reached up and traced the line of her plump lower lip.

"Avery Sennet told me something else. Something great," he said.

She spun over on her belly and propped herself up on her elbows. "What?" she asked breathlessly. He dragged his gaze off the vision of her firm, suspended breasts gilded by soft lamplight. Before he could answer, she spoke.

"You won the Pulitzer Prize. Didn't you?" she asked tensely.

He blinked in surprise. "How did you know that?"

She laughed, the sound clear and joyful. She scooted up on the mattress and started planting kisses all over his face and chest.

"I *knew* you'd win. That piece was so amazing. So honest and strong and compassionate, just like you." He laughed when she started to kiss his ribs, her enthusiasm and soft, falling hair tickling him. His fingers cupped her scalp and she looked up at him. Air popped out of his lungs at what he saw on her radiant face.

"I'm *so* proud of you, Asher."

A full, throat-gripping feeling rose in him. It mortified him, a little—her heartfelt reaction and the pride shining in her eyes.

It also pleased him more than he could put into words.

"Your parents are going to be so proud too," she said tremulously. "How wonderful, that you'll get to give them the news when we go there for lunch. I bet your father will especially be proud, given how he's in the newspaper business too. I hope he doesn't find out the news first!"

"The winners' names were announced to their editors and publishers earlier today, but a general announcement won't go out until next week."

"So it will be a wonderful surprise for your parents too." She looked so happy, he didn't have the heart to correct her about his parents' probable cool or dismissive reaction. Suddenly, she was scrambling out of bed.

"Where are you going?" he asked, not at all happy with the loss of her warmth and her naked, silky skin pressing against his.

"I saw some champagne in the refrigerator," she told him with a grin. "We're going to celebrate."

Chapter Twenty-five

It was one thing to watch Laila perform behind the curtain. It was even more mind-blowing to watch her without the veil, Asher realized the next day as he observed her rehearsing at the State Room. The amount of talent she possessed, the sheer magnitude of her stage presence and her sex appeal was a little intimidating for him to consider.

She made eye contact with him now as she sang on the stage, a small, shy smile curving her full lips. She was dressed casually in jeans, a purple T-shirt, a scarf and boots. Her long hair was pulled into a high ponytail that emphasized her almond-shaped green eyes. He hadn't seen her wear her hair that way since Crescent Bay. Since the secret lake.

The way she subtly moved her hips to the music and the knowing shine in her beautiful eyes went straight to the heart of him. Not to mention the crotch. He shifted his legs uncomfortably beneath the cocktail table. He was growing hard, watching her.

Wanting her.

He recalled perfectly that she'd had a similar effect on him the first time he'd seen her perform here at the State Room, when her true identity had been only a vague, seemingly impossible suspicion.

"She's phenomenal, isn't she?" a woman asked him quietly, fracturing his focused attention on Laila. "I just wish I could convince her to forget the veil. With that voice, face and body, she'd become one of the most recognized names in the world."

Asher frowned slightly. It bothered him that he both agreed with what the woman next to him said and yet felt irritated at the pat, arrogant assessment of Laila, as well. He shared the table in the otherwise empty club with a woman named Charlotte Morris. Laila had introduced them before she'd begun to rehearse, explaining that Charlotte was her newly hired agent.

"I thought Rafe was your agent," Asher had said earlier.

"Rafe is her manager," Charlotte had interrupted. She was the kind of pseudo-blond, no-nonsense, brassy middle-aged woman he associated with the entertainment industry. "Up until now, Rafe has been doing a lot of things that an agent would normally do."

"I needed to hire a professional like Charlotte to negotiate my contract with Sunday Records," Laila explained. One of the musicians on the stage had called her name. She'd leaned forward and kissed him on the mouth before she hurried onto the stage to rehearse.

"Laila is a very private person," Asher responded to Charlotte presently. The band broke midsong and Laila went over to confer with the musicians. "Public displays like this aren't condoned by her culture, generally speaking. Plus, she's very reserved, by nature, aside from cultural expectations. It's incredibly courageous of her, performing at all. The curtain helps her to manage things."

"What things, exactly?" Charlotte asked.

"The different worlds she lives in," Asher replied without pause, his gaze once again on Laila.

"I realize she's Moroccan and Muslim. Her lyrics and performance *are* very sexual. Of course it might be a challenge," Charlotte said brusquely. "But I mean, in this day and age, how big a deal could it be?"

"A very big deal," Asher stated unequivocally. "To Laila, it is."

"But surely it's one she can overcome, given the probable result. She could become an epic star . . . a legend."

"Just a word of advice, if you're trying to sway Laila to your point of view, I wouldn't try to convince her with flattery like that."

The music resumed. Asher turned his attention back to the stage. Laila's velvety smooth, resonant voice filled the large club once again.

"But I mean, listen to her. *Look* at her," Charlotte muttered next to him, awe tingeing her tone. "Is a force of nature like that, is something so beautiful, *meant* to be veiled?"

He ground his teeth together, annoyed . . . sort of at Charlotte, but mostly at himself. Because he agreed with the agent—in part. Charlotte's sentiment echoed something Asher had told Laila once, years ago.

"I don't like it. I don't like it a bit. When you close yourself off. Shut off your gift. Hide who you are. Try to dim your glory."

The memory and the present moment created a friction in him. Because while he did agree with Charlotte in part, he also understood Laila. He got the conflict she constantly experienced between the different worlds she carefully and thoughtfully negotiated. It dawned on him, maybe fully for the first time, just how much strength and fortitude and courage it took for her to balance those worlds. He admired her for it.

He loved her like crazy for it.

He exhaled slowly at the admission. He still loved her. Now, more than ever. Of course, he'd known it all along. It was just too big a truth for him to consciously dwell on much.

And yet . . . he still *did* hate the fact that she felt the need to dim the incredible light inside her. Would he love her more if she'd rebelled, if she'd blatantly defied and denied her culture and family? No. He couldn't love her more than he did right at that moment, watching her radiant face as her talent—her spirit itself—so effortlessly filled that room.

But he couldn't help but feel frustration too. Yes, she'd told him that the curtain didn't just protect her bonds with culture and family, but also shielded her personal privacy. But he wasn't entirely convinced. Just as she felt the need to block her gift from a part of her world, he worried she'd feel a similar need to keep *him* separate from a good part of her life too. He didn't want to have a half relationship with Laila. He wanted her fully, with no reservations.

He knew he was selfish. According to his mother, he always had been. Recognizing his fault didn't help matters any.

He wanted all of her, without barriers. Without constraint.

The friction of his emotions only built as the afternoon wore on and he watched the evidence of her talent mount, until it felt like he drowned in its abundance.

He felt a little edgy and uncomfortable in his own skin as he followed Laila down the hallway to her dressing room later, after the rehearsal was finished. It didn't really hit him that she hadn't spoken either, or that she was feeling almost as wired as he was. Not until she shut her dressing room door, locked it, turned and slid her arms around his neck. She pulled him to her. The fire she'd started with her performance smoldered in her kiss. She passed it to him, until he hauled her up against his body and burned alongside her.

He broke their hot and heavy kiss a moment later when she cupped his cock boldly in her palm.

"Were you getting hard out there, watching me?" she asked throatily, moving her hand.

His gaze narrowed on her beautiful, exultant face. "How did you know that?"

"I can tell by the look on your face," she said, an intoxicating smile tilting her lips. She began yanking on his button fly. "I can read your mind."

"Oh yeah? What was I thinking about, exactly?"

"Dirty stuff," she grinned.

He laughed and cupped her face. As he looked down at her, his amusement faded. "That's *all* you imagine I was thinking about, watching you light up that room?"

Her smile faded. He kissed her deep and thoroughly. When he ended the kiss, she opened heavy-looking eyelids.

"Maybe not," she replied. She jerked his jeans down over his ass abruptly, planting a kiss on his chest. She looked up at him, her gaze mischievous—sexy as hell. "Is it okay if I was the one thinking nothing but dirty thoughts, then?"

She went to her knees. A rush of heat went through him.

"I suppose I could forgive your lechery this once," he told her sarcastically, palming the back of her head. She cupped his balls through his boxer briefs, lifting them slightly. He groaned at her touch, feeling himself stiffen even more. The head of his cock poked lewdly against stretchy white cotton. She slid her cheek against it, moaning softly. Then she placed a chaste-seeming kiss on the tip, her green eyes shining as she looked up at his face.

"I was thinking about giving you this birthday gift yesterday," she said, her lips moving against his cock. "But you kept taking over in bed. You have a habit of doing that, you know."

"I am a controlling jerk," he admitted, watching her, spellbound, as she removed his erection from his briefs. She'd never sucked him off before. He'd thought about it, of course. A lot. He liked fellatio as much as most men, and Laila was the most desirable woman he'd ever known. But despite the fact that she was an innately sensual, incredibly responsive lover, there was something that remained untouchable about her. He held back with her a little. He wasn't as demanding as he might be with another experienced woman. Maybe it was because her beauty, her fire—her very spirit—were so refined. So pure. His male hunger sometimes seemed coarse and blunt in contrast to her.

She held his now-naked, pulsing cock in her hand, her lips just inches from the head, and looked up at him soberly.

"If you're a controlling jerk, why haven't you asked me to give you pleasure this way?" She stroked the shaft of his cock with her soft hand. He shivered with sharp excitement. "Don't you like it?"

He ground his teeth together as she continued to caress his erection. "I like it," he said in bald understatement.

"Then why haven't you asked me to?" she whispered.

"I don't know."

"Yes, you do," she said, her entire arm moving as she steadily stroked him from tip to balls.

"I'm not stopping you now," he pointed out, mesmerized by the vision of her full, pink lips hovering just inches from his swollen cockhead.

"Tell me how you like it," she whispered, her warm breath tickling his sensitive flesh. "Teach me, like you taught me how to touch you at the secret lake."

He felt his cock surge in her hand. It was a potent memory. The prospect of repeating it with a different mode of making love inflamed him. He shut his eyes briefly and groaned.

"Asher?"

He heard the uncertainty in her tone. He found himself gripping her thick, soft ponytail. "Just . . . do what you want, Laila."

She stopped stroking, gripping him at midstaff. "No. Tell me. Please?" He saw the desperation in her eyes. "I've never really done it before," she whispered, looking a little embarrassed. "Or if I have, not well," she added under her breath resignedly.

He started to sweat. He gently pulled her hand off his cock and replaced it with his own.

"Open your mouth," he said gruffly. He felt blood rush into his cock at merely saying the words. Watching her follow his instructions was even worse. Grappling for restraint, he told her matter-of-factly how to use her lips to stroke him firmly and protect him at once from her teeth.

"Like this?" she asked.

She dipped him into her warm mouth. Excitement tingled at the base of his spine at the feeling of her sliding along her warm tongue. His balls pinched in pleasure. He groaned.

"That's good. Tighten your mouth some," he muttered, watching her like a hawk as she began to bob her head over the first several inches of his appreciative cock. She followed his instructions so precisely, he hissed in mounting pleasure. She slid her warm mouth off him, a concerned look on her face. He caught the back of her head and his cock at once, firmly reinserting himself into her mouth.

"You were doing great. That felt fantastic," he assured her. "God, yeah," he muttered as she resumed even more enthusiastically. "That's so good, Laila. Now suck." Again, he hissed at how well she followed his instructions. His eyes rolled back in his head at the sharp blast of pleasure. She was amazing.

"Just use your tongue for a minute," he urged, needing a break from the emotion boiling inside him and the forceful stroke of her mouth.

He watched her with a tight focus as she charted his cock with a red, wet tongue. This was no break. This was yet another wicked source of torture. The pleasure she gave him was every bit as pure and distilled as she was . . . as what he felt for her.

Without a word, he reinserted his cock between her lips.

"You can be aggressive, beautiful," he told her a moment later, watching her every move. Her eyes killed him as she looked up at him and her head bobbed back and forth. She began to take him more strenuously, observing his reaction as closely as he watched her. His face tightened in pleasure.

"Now use your hand as well as your mouth," he instructed. He wrapped his hand around hers and guided her, until she took over, her hand squeezing him in tandem with her hot, eager mouth. Air rushed past his lips and burned his throat. For a stretched moment, he existed on a blissful, sharp edge.

He felt so raw, so flayed by pleasure. All the feelings and thoughts he'd been having about her as he recognized the immensity of her talent combined with the razor-sharp pleasure she gave him so unselfishly. He gripped her ponytail and moved her head. She kept pace eagerly, the vision of her bringing him near to climax. He wanted to come in her sweet, hot mouth.

He wanted to explode inside her, anywhere . . . anyhow . . . break through all the barriers, leave himself so deep inside her that there could be no doubt.

They were one.

The logical part of his brain never told him to move. It was that deep, primal aspect that had him lifting her against him and carrying her over to the couch. While he did it, he feasted on her mouth again. Even when he bent to set her down on the cushion, he couldn't stop delving his tongue into her sweetness, feeding on her heat and her reciprocated need.

He heard a ripping sound as he undressed her. He cursed. Laila didn't seem to notice he'd torn her shirt, though, as she frantically assisted him. When he'd pulled off her jeans and underwear and she was finally naked, he didn't stop there. He reached and slid her hair band off her long, smooth hair. He greedily grabbed handfuls of it and spread it around her shoulders. The perfume from the long, smooth strands permeated the air. He inhaled a lungful of it before he forced himself to stand.

She looked up at him with glistening green eyes, her cheeks and lips flushed, her hair spilling around her shoulders and chest, an erect nipple poking out from the soft tendrils. Her thighs were parted. Harsh arousal tore through him at the vision of her soft-looking pubic hair and tender, flushed labia.

"*Laila*," he said, his voice sounding thick and grim with lust. He reached out and swept her hair behind her shoulders in a deliberate, slow movement despite his anticipation, baring her entirely to his gaze. He contained a shudder of emotion. God, he could probably come just from staring at her.

"Asher." She lifted her beautiful arms, the gesture going straight to the heart of him.

He couldn't stop it anymore. The frenzy. If he'd had to think about the mechanics of getting his clothes off his body so rapidly, or finding a condom, it would have taken twice as long. But that primal part of him had taken over, and it knew exactly what it wanted.

A moment later, he put his hands on the back of the couch and looked down at her while she spread her smooth thighs, lifted her feet and bent knees and rolled her hips back, positioning herself at the edge of the couch to take him. He braced himself, leaning down over her with his thighs spread, his toes digging into the carpet for traction.

He watched his cock sink into her inch by inch, listening to her soft moans, feeling her sweet heat encapsulating him, squeezing him mercilessly. His throat hurt. He met her stare.

"I love you," he said.

Her face tightened with disbelief.

"You do?" she whispered.

"I've never stopped. I knew that for certain, watching you on that stage today. That's what I was thinking about, Laila," he said, because nothing else would come out of him in that moment but painful honesty.

"I love you too. I've never stopped." The words tumbled past her lips, like she'd been storing them in her throat, wanting to release them. Afraid to do it.

He understood that feeling all too well.

A tear skipped down her cheek. The truth was so sweet. Why did it ache so badly? He wanted to howl like a savage.

He pressed his balls tight against her damp outer sex, grimacing in pleasure. Her soft whimpers cut right through him. His eyes rolled back in his head. God, he wasn't going to survive this torture for long. He began to thrust, mindless pleasure pummeling him in every direction.

He lunged with his legs, pushing with his planted feet, powering himself into the sheer heaven of her. Yes, he was greedy. Yes, he was forceful. It was an orgy of sensation—of feeling—and he reveled in her to the fullest.

Her voice and the brisk slap of their bodies crashing together entered his lust-dazed awareness. She chanted his name again and again, the single word rife with lust and longing and love. Her hands gripped his ass, and she was pushing him to her, adding her strength to his thrusts. They groaned in unison, pleasure spiking as he slammed into her to the hilt. His body screamed at him for release, but he couldn't heed the call. Not when he wanted this to last forever.

He pulled out of her, his entire body shuddering at the absence. He knelt before her and pushed her legs wider.

"Asher," she moaned when he pressed his face to her belly. She was warm silk against his lips and nose. He smelled her arousal.

"I had to have you," he mumbled against her fragrant skin. "From the very first, I had to have you. Sometimes I wish it had changed, but it hasn't. It *can't*. It'll only grow stronger. Sweet, beautiful girl."

He lowered over her, dipping his tongue into the creamy cleft between her labia. The essence of her in its purest form filled him. Fed him. For a moment, he lost himself as his tongue played in her sweetness and he absorbed her delicate shudders. Her shaking mounted, and she was clutching at his hair and repeating his name.

Her release went through him like a shearing wave. He braced himself and absorbed it, eating up her pleasure. Craving more.

He rose to ravish her mouth. She'd slumped against the back of the couch following her climax. He pressed down on her in his need, her body dipping between the two cushions. His cock found her unerringly. He carved into her, the walls of her vagina hugging him tightly even as she seemed to melt around him. A scream began to vibrate in her throat. He silenced it with his mouth, absorbing it . . . wanting to shout in crazy abandon right back.

He took her harder now, faster, the sound of their bodies smacking together outpacing even his charging heart. But his desperation only mounted. He'd never get enough. He wanted deeper.

More. Always more.

He encircled her with his arms and hugged her to him, lifting her upper body and thrusting her up on his raging cock.

Climax ripped through him. Brutal. Electric. He seized and shuddered, vibrating like a hammered gong. Her name scraped at his throat.

"Love," he heard her mutter against his throat. "Love you so much."

Dazedly, as the moments passed, he recognized that another barrier had been at least partially hurdled—that of their own caution and fear. They'd entered more dangerous territory. The words had been said. Their hearts fully exposed. He knew what path that led to last time.

All he could do was pray this time would be different.

Chapter Twenty-six

The next few days flew by in a whirlwind of ecstatic contentment. Laila had never felt so alive in her life. She and Asher spent every minute they could together. He came to all of her rehearsals and her shows.

Rafe was still a little distant following their breakup. But after he witnessed her show on Tuesday night, some of his former enthusiasm bounded to the forefront again. When he saw Asher in her dressing room after the show, he frowned at first. But when Asher just met his stare unflinchingly, a change came over Rafe. He seemed to surrender to practicality. He'd been Laila's manager before he'd ever dated her, after all. If Asher was the reason for her extra-passionate, emotional performances, then he couldn't be entirely bad, in Rafe's mind. He gave a small shrug and hugged Laila.

"Even I can't argue with results like that," he said quietly near her ear. "You were beyond magnificent tonight."

She and Asher couldn't get enough of each other. They expressed their love for each other so frequently, Laila wondered if unconsciously they thought the words were like a ward against a curse, a staving off of the inevitable. Their time was running out. Asher would be flying to London in seven days, six . . . five. It was like some giant clock of doom was growing closer and closer every day, ticking louder and louder in Laila's dreams every night that she spent in Asher's arms. She wanted to ask him what he was thinking and feeling about their separation, but she was afraid of his answer.

She'd walked away from him once. Had she forsaken the right to beg him for a future?

On Thursday, Asher said that he couldn't attend her rehearsal because he had some errands to run. She missed him that afternoon and was extra eager to see him when she entered his Lincoln Park condo that night. When he led her into the living room, she paused in disbelief at the threshold. There must have been twenty or thirty wrapped packages dispersed throughout the room.

"What in the world is *this*?" she asked him in stunned amazement.

"Happy birthday," he said, a slow smile spreading across his sexy mouth.

"My birthday isn't until June," she exclaimed.

He leaned down and kissed her, making her forget her incredulity for a minute.

"I got one for every birthday I've missed," he told her against her mouth a few seconds later. She saw his eyes gleaming in amused warmth. "And I picked them all out myself too. You taught me the importance of that."

She laughed. She couldn't believe him.

Each gift was as amazing as the last: a beautiful gold bracelet, a rare signed vinyl recording of Ella Fitzgerald, a gorgeous white silk negligee, a collection of leather-bound music notebooks . . .

the treasures went on and on. Laila was overwhelmed. He gave the last one to her with a solemnness that made her wonder.

"Why do you look like that?" she whispered as she ripped open the paper on the flat, rectangular box.

"Because. I got this two years ago, on my last trip to Morocco. I don't think I consciously got it for you. It just struck me yesterday, that maybe I *had* . . . even if it was only wishful thinking. At the time, I just told myself it was pretty, and wouldn't think much beyond that . . ."

She held her breath as she opened the box. She gasped, shivers pouring down her spine and arm.

"It's a hamsa," she whispered, glancing up at him in disbelief. The hamsa was a popular symbol in Morocco and Northern Africa. It depicted the open right hand and was often used for jewelry. Asher's gift was an especially rare and lovely necklace of a hamsa, made from finely wrought silver and some sort of jade or peridot stones—she couldn't be sure—that had been carefully inlaid to make an intricate, delicate pattern.

"I've never seen one so beautiful," she told him, her heart in her eyes. "I can't believe you got me this."

He scooted over on the living room floor, where they sat. "Here. Let me put it on you."

She smiled widely a few seconds later as she met his stare, tears skipping down her cheeks. She touched the hamsa below her throat with her fingertips.

"Thank you. Thank you so much, Asher."

"You're welcome," he murmured, his gaze roving over her face. He used his fingers to dry her few tears. "It matches your eyes. That should have been the dead giveaway why I was buying it. It's supposed to ward off bad energies, I understand. Perfect thing for you to wear when you go over to my parents' house."

Laughter burst out of her throat at that. She threw her arms around him, love swelling so tight inside her, she couldn't speak.

Moments later, they made love heatedly on the floor in the midst of a sea of torn wrapping paper. She felt like she drowned in decadence, not just from Asher's incredible, thoughtful presents, but from the richness of the love that seemed to enfold them.

"You're the best gift in the world," Laila told him feelingly afterward.

A pang of fear and loss went through her. She hugged him tighter to her, but the pain didn't ease as much as it had in the past. She suspected it was because that ticking of the clock had grown even louder and more ominous in her head.

Friday dawned sunny, cool and crisp. Laila was up at dawn, jumpy as a skittish cat about the lunch appointment at Asher's parents' home in Winnetka. She met Asher in the living room at eleven o'clock. He looked very handsome in a pair of jeans, a button-down shirt, and a sports coat. She smoothed her skirt nervously.

"Is this all right?" she asked him. "I thought this skirt would look nice with the new boots you got me," she said, referring to the beautiful pair of supple, russet leather boots he'd given her—he'd informed her last night with adorable solemnness—for her eighteenth birthday.

His gaze dropped down over her. "You look gorgeous. I like that sweater," he said, his gaze lingering on her breasts warmly.

"Is it too tight?" she asked, sounding a little shrill.

He walked toward her, holding his arms out and laughing gruffly.

"Of course it's not too tight. You can't help it that you have beautiful breasts." He wrapped his arms around her and placed a kiss on her nose. "Or the prettiest face in the world or stunning eyes," he continued, dropping two kisses on her eyebrows.

"They're going to hate me," she whispered, her voice thick with dread.

"Not hate. *Hate* is too passionate. Much too common. Insufferably middle-class. *Dislike*, maybe. *Disapprove* with a white-Anglo-Saxon-Protestant arrogance, which is like an ice-cold blast of air," he murmured nonchalantly. He planted a kiss on her mouth. "It's unpleasant, but not deadly. It's just something you have to forbear. Brace yourself for it, and then just count the minutes until you can leave. It's the best you can do. Trust me, I know."

Her brows pinched tight. His levity on this topic pained her. "How can they dislike you? You're the very picture of an ideal son."

"Never mind," he said, briskly moving back and taking her hand. He pressed her knuckles against his lips before he led her toward the door. "It's their way of loving me. It's warped, but that's WASP love for you."

His voice still rang in her head when he turned his car down a tree-lined drive forty-five minutes later. Despite his teasing manner, she knew that his parents' opinion of him mattered . . . that their cool disapproval pained him deeply.

"Asher," she began determinedly. "Please don't get too . . . sensitive about anything your parents do or say today when it comes to me."

"What do you mean?" he asked, frowning slightly above his sunglasses.

"It's just that I sensed how much your mother wants to patch things up with you. And she seems really concerned about your father's and your relationship. I just don't want to be the thing that gets in the way of you guys making up before . . . Well, I just don't want to stand in the way," she continued, shying away from mentioning the fact that he was leaving for London in a few days. They mentioned it less and less to each other, as their time together dwindled away. She fingered the hamsa at her throat in a nervous gesture. "Will you promise me you'll try to keep things as smooth as you can with them?"

"Do what *you* do? Is that what you mean?" He noticed her confusion. "Like you told me when we were young? How you knew just what to say in front of your family, and what *not* to say, in order to keep everyone happy?"

"Is that so bad?" she asked him quietly.

"I don't know. I used to think so," he said, his expression hard and guarded as he stared forward at the road.

"Just try to be patient with them, Asher? For me?"

He glanced over at her. "All right," he said, grasping her hand. Relief swept through her. "If it's important to you."

As the house came into view, the butterflies in her stomach transformed to what felt like a swarm of bees.

"Is that it?" she asked through a tight throat.

"That's it. Home sweet home. Cozy, no?" he muttered dryly.

They zoomed toward an enormous, intimidating-looking, pale limestone French Provincial–style mansion. In the distance was the pale blue lake. Asher pulled the car up to what appeared to be a six-car garage at the rear. A youngish dark-haired man jogged out to greet them. He opened Laila's car door for her.

"Thank you," Laila said as she alighted.

"How's it going, Jerry?" Asher said, coming around the car and shaking Jerry's hand.

"Well, sir. It's good to see you again," Jerry said.

"Hopefully I'll make it for longer than an hour this time," Asher said under his breath.

"Yes, sir," Jerry replied with a brief knowing glance and a compassionate smile.

Asher took her hand and led her to a large double-door entryway. At that moment, one of the doors opened and Asher's mother stepped out onto the upper step, followed by a tall, handsome, gray-haired man wearing a dark suit and open-collar button-down shirt. He was much younger and handsome-looking than Laila expected. He looked like Asher . . .

. . . Except that Asher didn't have that cold, arrogant expression.

"Are you ready for this?" Asher asked her quietly under his breath.

"No," she whispered shakily.

He glanced over at her, a flicker of concern crossing his face. He stopped her abruptly on the gravel path and stepped in front of her.

"Asher—"

He cut her off by seizing her mouth in a quick kiss.

"Don't let them get to you. You're too special for that, Laila. You're worth a thousand of them. A million."

A hushed, nervous laugh left her throat. "Oh, really? To whom?"

"To me," he said without pause. Her smile faded.

"Asher?"

"Coming, Mom," Asher called, squeezing Laila's hand before he turned.

They sat in a pristine, luxurious room that overlooked a wide terrace and the lake in the distance. It was a room meant to intimidate, and it did its job well. At least on Laila, it did. It was decorated in blackwood and white upholstery, with silver and crystal accents. Laila didn't think she'd ever been so uncomfortable in her life. The sound of a magnificent blackwood grandfather clock ticked loudly in the oppressive silence.

"So you perform in a nightclub," Asher's father said, interrupting the horrible silence. Asher had just explained to his parents that Laila was a singer. They'd agreed beforehand to be honest with his mom and dad about that, without revealing any details that might tie Laila back to Yesenia. It had been Laila's choice not to mislead Asher's parents from the first about her career. It had been an intuitive decision, one that she was now actively dreading.

"That's right," Laila said breathlessly.

Madeline and Clark shared a swift glance that somehow spoke volumes of puzzlement and vague disapproval. She might as well have just revealed that she flew to Mars for a living.

"She writes her own music, as well," Asher said from where he sat next to Laila on a stiff, stylized white couch. He reached for her hand and squeezed it. "She's the most talented musician I've ever heard."

"You're hardly much of a judge, son," Madeline said. Her superior, knowing glance at Laila seemed to say loud and clear that no one knows a man better than his mother. "His piano teacher practically had to chain him to the bench during his lessons. He always wanted to be playing football or out on his sailboat."

"I didn't know you took piano lessons," Laila said, turning to Asher.

He shrugged. "I might as well not have, as much as I actually learned." He waved at the gorgeous Steinway at the corner of the room. "Why don't you play something, Laila?"

She flushed in embarrassment.

"Don't put the girl on the spot, Asher," Clark said.

"He's not always the most sensitive of men," Madeline agreed.

"I think Asher is incredibly sensitive."

All eyes zoomed to Laila.

"I mean . . . he's always thinking about my needs. He understood I was an artist even before I did. He's the one who encouraged me to sing and write. He knew I wouldn't be happy, being anything else," she said, looking at Asher. Relief swept through her when she saw his small smile and the warmth in his eyes. He reached up and touched her cheek briefly, and for a moment, they might have been the only two people in the room.

Clark cleared his throat loudly. "Well, he always *was* more sensitive to his lady friends' needs than he was his parents'. I suppose that's not uncommon for a young man."

Laila felt heat flood her cheeks at the subtle innuendo.

"I don't know how you would know that, Dad," Asher said. "I've never brought any of my girlfriends around the house before."

"We *have* met several of them, though, at various functions. And one hears things," Clark said, frowning pointedly at his son. "It's not as if you've ever been lacking in female companionship."

Asher sat forward, eyes blazing. "What's that supposed to—"

"Lunch should be ready in ten minutes or so," Madeline said loudly, cutting off Asher's angry query. "Asher, why don't you take Laila out onto the terrace and show her the gardens down by the lake?"

Madeline cast a nervous glance between father and son. There was something in her eyes Laila recognized in that moment: a mother's worry. Maybe Madeline Gaites-Granville would never win an award for Warmest Mother of the Year, but she was genuinely concerned about the rift between her husband and son. More than that, she did love her son fiercely, despite Asher's doubts on that front. Asher and his father looked incredibly alike at that moment, both of their handsome faces cast in an angry, stubborn expression. Laila felt a little guilty, knowing he was holding in whatever he longed to say because she'd asked him specifically not to roughen the waters.

"I'd love to see the gardens," Laila told Asher.

Frowning, he stood and put out his hand for her.

They reentered the French doors that led to the terrace a while later. At first, Laila thought the stunning room was empty. But then she noticed Asher's parents standing near the Steinway in the distance.

". . . I'm telling you, she *must* be a Muslim if she's Moroccan," Clark Gaites-Granville was saying to his wife as he pointed at his phone, as if he'd discovered some proof there and was showing her.

Laila looked up at Asher's face and immediately knew he'd heard as well. She squeezed his hand tightly. He blinked and looked down at her. Her heart sank when she saw the fury building behind his eyes.

Asher shut the French doors loudly on purpose. Clark and Madeline both turned toward them. Laila was stunned—and a little impressed—at how cool and unruffled they were as they asked Laila and Asher about their walk, and Madeline ushered them into the dining room.

If the prelunch attempt at polite conversation was a bad dream, then luncheon itself was an all-out nightmare. The four of them sat at the most opulently set table Laila had ever seen. Asher felt so far away from her, on the opposite side of the table. She had the random impression that the distance and all the silver, crystal and china between them had been purposefully set there to separate them.

She was having trouble remembering what heavy silver fork or what spoon to use, especially when Clark was shooting questions at her from the end of the table.

"What is it that your father does for a living in Detroit, Laila?"

She paused awkwardly in the action of biting into a shrimp. "He owns an automobile collision and repair shop," she managed to say.

"Madeline has explained to me that you're Moroccan?"

She set the shrimp down onto her plate. "Yes, that's right."

"But you *are* a U.S. citizen?" Clark continued.

"Laila was born in the U.S.," Asher interrupted impatiently, tossing down his silver fork onto the china. "She's as much a U.S. citizen as you are."

"I've never met a Moroccan before. I was just trying to understand," Clark defended.

"She's Moroccan-American, Dad. That's not *all* that she is. Why are you focusing on it so much? You really need to get out of your lily-white world a little."

"No . . . it's okay," Laila interrupted when Clark opened his mouth to retort angrily to his son. "I don't mind you asking about my background. It's only natural. I mean . . . it's kind of mind-boggling for me to imagine what it was like for Asher to grow up here, in this spectacular place," she said, glancing around the opulent dining room. She attempted a smile at a stunned-looking Madeline. Laila realized with a sinking feeling that his mother thought it was tactless of her to specifically point out their wealth. "Asher and I come from really different worlds. It's going to take a little bit for us to learn about what the other one is used to."

"You make it sound like that's important," Madeline said, leaning forward. "For you to learn about each other's worlds."

"We're in love, Mom. I'd say it's pretty damn important," Asher stated bluntly.

The color washed out of Madeline's face. She sat back in her chair. Laila held her breath, her gaze zooming over to Clark's face. He didn't look pale like Madeline did. He appeared positively ashen.

"Do I take this to mean," he said slowly, "that Asher has met *your* parents?"

"No, he hasn't," Laila said as calmly as possible, even though it felt like an explosion was about to occur at any moment. She sent Asher a pleading glance. It was no use. She could sense the conflagration building.

"May I ask why not?" Clark asked.

She swallowed thickly and placed her hands in her lap. There would be no more attempts at eating. She didn't think she could keep the food down.

"My parents are a little old-fashioned. Moroccans tend to be a very close-knit community, as a rule," she tried to explain as tactfully as she could. "At least when it comes to matters of romance."

"Are you saying that your parents wouldn't approve of *Asher*?" Madeline asked, sheer disbelief spreading on her pretty face.

She saw Asher close his eyes briefly in obviously peaking frustration. Laila swore she could hear all the crystal in the room giving off an eerie, barely audible ring.

"*Your* parents wouldn't approve of *my* son?" Clark abruptly repeated loudly.

"Clark—" Madeline muttered, sounding alarmed at his tone of voice.

"I don't *believe* this," Asher said, his mouth slanting in fury. He tossed down his napkin. "*You* don't approve of me. Why should Laila's parents?"

Clark looked positively apoplectic. Laila gave Asher a wild, worried glance. What if Asher's father had a heart attack, right there at the head of the table? Asher's father abruptly stood from the table, as well.

"Asher, I demand to talk to you. Right now. In my study," he said, pointing toward a door.

"Clark, *please*," Madeline implored.

Asher laughed. Laila couldn't believe it, given the off-the-charts tension level in the room. He pushed back his chair and stood.

"It's not easy to hear, is it, Dad? That someone else could possibly be on the judging end of things. It's usually Mom and you who are sitting in the judges' chairs, isn't it?"

"Asher, please. Stop this," Madeline said, her muted voice shaking.

"It's true, isn't it?" Asher asked his mother. "Do you know why I brought Laila here today?"

"Because you wanted to hurt us, as usual?" Clark bit out between a tight jaw.

"I brought her because you're my only family, despite the fact that you constantly wish I were something different. Still, I was stupid enough to believe you'd want to know someone who is important to me. I'm used to you disapproving of me, but I mean . . . *Look* at her," Asher challenged hotly, putting out his hand in Laila's direction. Laila sank in her chair. "How could a beautiful, talented, loving woman like Laila possibly *hurt* you? How could me living my own life and having my own career *hurt* you? You're hurting *yourselves*," he shouted, walking around the table with a long-legged, rapid stride. He reached for Laila's hand. She stood awkwardly. "And I'm so fucking sick of it," he declared. Laila's heart felt like it froze in her chest when she saw his expression: so cold. So hurt.

"Please don't contact me anymore," Asher said as they began to walk away.

"*Asher*," both his mother and Laila said plaintively at once. Their voices didn't seem to penetrate. Laila looked over her shoulder as Asher led her toward the door. Her stare briefly met Madeline's. For a fraction of a second, she thought she saw a plea in the older woman's eyes. But there was nothing Laila could do or say.

"I'll be out of the condo by this Wednesday. You can do whatever you want with it. I won't be coming back. Don't try to call.

It'll just lead to disappointment. For all of us," he said, before he pulled Laila alongside him out the door.

"You never even told them you won the Pulitzer Prize," she said twenty minutes later. She felt numb, despite the warm, brilliantly sunny day. Traffic was lighter than it had been earlier. Plus Asher was driving extra fast in his agitation. They flew down Lake Shore Drive, not far from Asher's condominium.

She saw him grimace and his hands tighten on the wheel. "They wouldn't have cared, Laila. Don't you get that? Just because your parents think the sun rises and sets on you doesn't mean mine do."

"They love you, Asher. I know they do."

"How can you *defend* them?" he asked in a burst of anger as he took the Fullerton exit. "Look at how they treated you! It was unforgivable."

"I wouldn't say that. It was wrong, yes. They were rude. They don't know how to act around someone different than them."

"How can you just let people walk all over you like that?"

She gasped at his harshness.

"You're always doing that, apologizing in some way for who you are. What you are. *Whom* you want," he continued bitterly. "You put up the curtain when you perform, like you need to dim the reality of you. You're always caving. You're always bending over backward to please everyone. Instead, you should be showing the world how wonderful you are, and telling anyone who doesn't like what they see to go fuck themselves."

Electric indignation sizzled through her.

"Like you tell your parents to fuck themselves constantly, because they don't approve of you? That's not how I do things, Asher."

He made a sarcastic "well, that's obvious" sound and gesture that mounted her fury and helplessness.

"What's *wrong* with you?" she demanded, angered, but also bewildered and hurt by his bitter outburst.

"I don't know," he said irritably, frowning furiously.

"Yes, you do. This is our past rising up to the surface again, isn't it? You say that you've forgiven me, but you haven't. You try to pretend that you're okay with who I am and how I deal with my family, but you're *not*," she shouted. "The truth is, you think I should focus solely on what I want for my career and my life, and screw what anyone else thinks. For you, the selfish way is the right way, and to hell with whoever gets in your way. You think I should be like *you*, don't you? You know what, Asher?"

He turned to her as he slowed at a stoplight. His face was rigid with anger—and possible disbelief at her uncharacteristic shouting.

"You've got a lot of nerve, calling your father an arrogant WASP because he only thinks about *his* goals and *his* values and *his* needs. You're just like him. No wonder you two can't get along."

She opened up her car door and snatched her purse.

"Laila, what the *hell*? Get in the damn car," Asher yelled, reaching for her forearm.

She shook him off. He stared at her in angry disbelief when she stepped out and turned to slam the door shut.

"I'll catch a cab," she told him through the partially opened window. She turned and marched through two lanes of stopped cars to the curb and grassy verge.

Chapter Twenty-seven

Asher didn't call her that afternoon, nor did she call him. He didn't come to her performance that night. She knew that for certain, because she swallowed her pride and asked Rafe if he'd seen him in the audience. Rafe's answer had been no, but Laila had already known the truth. She'd learned that there was some nameless thing inside her that always alerted her to his presence, even when the curtain separated them. If he was there, her performance was different.

Because when he was there, she sang to him alone.

She was miserable at his absence. It would have been bad enough, under any circumstances, fighting with him. But she was agonizingly aware that the hours they had together were precious, because they were so few.

She couldn't eat much that Saturday. Tahi grew concerned about her when Laila didn't leave the condo. Knowing how she'd been spending every moment with Asher recently, Tahi immediately guessed that they'd fought or broken up. But Laila was too caught up in a sense of fatalistic fear to take solace from opening up to Tahi.

"Are we still leaving for Detroit in the morning?" Tahi asked her hesitantly that night when Laila joined her in the kitchen after her show. Laila felt bad for the people who had paid good money for her show. Her heart just hadn't been in her performance. Afterward, she'd taken the L home. But when she'd stepped past that white column in the underground, there'd been no Asher.

"I don't see any reason why we shouldn't," Laila told her cousin listlessly as she took down a glass for tea.

She noticed Tahi start to speak, and then stop herself. "What, Tahi?"

"You say that like if there had been a good reason, you would have. Isn't this disagreement you and Asher had good reason? It's just a few family dinners, Laila. You'll have a thousand more of them in the future. Why don't you stay back, and patch things up with Asher before he leaves for London? Say you came down with something. I'll back up your story."

The familiar trapped, panicked feeling she associated with that summer in Crescent Bay suddenly overwhelmed her. *Would* there be thousands of family gatherings in her future? She suddenly pictured it, a series of imagined dinners in Detroit taking place over the years. As time wore on, each of her cousins—even the younger ones—would be joined by a fiancé or spouse at their side. Yet no one special would ever sit beside Laila. Not in that familiar place, they wouldn't. Because that place would no longer be her home, she realized.

Because one thing was achingly absent from the picture: Asher.

A feeling of doubt and dread building in her, she mumbled an excuse to Tahi and fled the kitchen.

She tried to call Asher when she entered her bedroom. The

sinking feeling in the pit of her stomach swelled when it almost immediately went over to voicemail. He'd turned off his phone.

"Hi. It's me," she said. "Look, I know you're mad. So am I, still. A little anyway. But I don't want it to go on. We need to talk. I'll be in Detroit tomorrow. I wasn't sure if you remembered," she mumbled, feeling a bit stupid, because *of course* he'd remember. They'd fought about it. For him, it was one of the examples of how she existed in two different worlds, never committing fully to one. She swiped irritably at a fallen tear on her cheek. "Anyway, I just wanted you to know where I was. I hope we can talk when I get back Monday morning." She hesitated.

"I miss you. So much." More tears spilled down her face. She hung up the phone with a trembling hand, afraid she would say more, terrified she'd humiliate herself by begging him on hands and knees not to shut her out of his life.

Asher hunched over the bar at the Galway Arms, staring down blankly at his half-full glass of Scotch. The alcohol wasn't doing much to still the whirlwind of his thoughts.

"You need to talk to her. In person," Jimmy Rothschild said from the seat next to him. Asher glanced aside at his friend. Jimmy was dressed casually, for once, it being the weekend. Weekend or not, Jimmy had been in the office working when Asher called and asked if he'd have a drink with him. He'd spilled the whole story about Laila. Jimmy had been surprised, and then fascinated, to discover that Laila Barek, that shy, beautiful girl from Crescent Bay, was the magnetic stage performer known as the Veiled Siren. He didn't seem too surprised to find out that they had resumed their love affair.

"She's at her folks' house up in Detroit, celebrating the engagement of a cousin. That's the one place I can't go."

"That really bugs you, doesn't it?" Jimmy observed.

"Shouldn't it? I feel like I'm a leper in that part of her life."

He noticed Jimmy's furrowed brow. "That's a pretty strong way of stating it."

Asher shrugged in an "I'm just saying it like it is" gesture.

"But what do you mean you *can't* go to Detroit and try to see her?" Jimmy persisted.

Asher scowled. "Don't you remember what happened in Crescent Bay? I don't think I'd be making things better for Laila and me by crashing a family gathering."

"So her parents wouldn't like you being there."

"Or her aunts and uncles or fist-happy male cousins," Asher muttered, taking a sip of whiskey.

"You were pretty fist-happy yourself, if I recall things correctly from that night," Jimmy reminded him wryly. "What about Laila?"

Asher shrugged. "Like I said, I don't think she'd appreciate me making a stir."

"So you definitely are operating under the impression that things are just the same as they were eight years ago?" Asher glanced over at his friend. Jimmy's expression was that of a seasoned prosecutor teasing out a complicated truth, Asher realized.

"No, things aren't exactly the same. Of course not," Asher said.

"Then what's different?"

"Laila is older, for one. She makes a good living. She owns her own place. She's not dependent on her parents anymore."

"She's not like most women you date, where the idea of a parent's disapproval rarely, if ever, comes up."

"She's not like *anyone* I've ever dated."

"Yeah. That's obvious." Asher glanced over at him. "Even back then, in Crescent Bay, it was crystal clear you were nuts about her. It was like witnessing some kind of rare natural phenomenon occurring, like an erupting volcano or something," Jimmy said, smiling slightly as he took a sip of his drink. He set his glass down on the bar. "So what are you going to do?" Jimmy asked. "Are you really going to just fly off to London and leave her behind?"

"I don't have much of a choice, if that's what she wants."

"And you know for certain that's what she'd choose?"

"Well, no . . . but given everything else, I have no reason to believe—"

"You just said she wasn't the same person as she was back then. Why don't you just *ask* her what she wants to do in regard to the two of you?"

"She's pissed off at me at the moment. Is that a good time to talk about our future?"

"It's the only time," Jimmy said, shrugging. "You're leaving in four days. Do you want to know what I think?"

"I'm not so sure," Asher said darkly. But of course he did want to hear the unvarnished truth. That was why he'd called Jimmy in the first place.

"I think you're scared to bring up the topic with her because you're afraid she'll do what she did eight years ago. I saw how much her walking away hurt you then. I think you're scared of being rejected all over again." Asher didn't deny or confirm it. It seemed to him Jimmy knew the truth, anyway.

"But just imagine how Laila must be feeling. It sounds to me like she's as crazy about you as she ever was. You two are in love. She knows that there would be conflict with her family, if you two decided to be together on a permanent basis. Maybe most importantly, she knows you're leaving in four days. She must be scared to death about being separated again."

"She doesn't press me about it," Asher said gruffly. "If she was that worried, wouldn't she bring it up?"

"*You're* not bringing it up. Maybe she thinks she's following your preference. She probably feels guilty about hurting you back then. Maybe she doesn't feel she has the right to ask questions and make demands."

He considered that for a moment.

"That *does* kind of sound like Laila," he said slowly, frowning.

"Just go and talk to her, Ash."

Something clicked inside him.

Jimmy was right. That old fear of rejection—of loss—was making him behave in ways he normally wouldn't. It was making him hesitate, when normally, he would have jumped full-out.

But now wasn't the time for caution.

"Yeah. Maybe you're right." He stood abruptly and threw some cash on the bar. "I've got to get going. Thanks, man. It really helped."

"Good. Hey, Ash," he called when Asher turned to walk away. Asher turned back. "Don't forget to invite me to your wedding."

Asher gave a half grin and a wave. He wished like hell he could be as optimistic as his friend. As things stood, maybe there weren't as many barriers between Laila and him as there had been eight years ago.

But there were enough to make this whole situation a damn steep risk.

On Monday morning, Laila came up behind her cousin Driss where he stood in the kitchen surrounded by various gabbing family members. She tugged on his elbow gently, praying her aunt Nadine wouldn't notice Laila stealing away her son for a moment. Driss was a captain in the Navy, six feet two inches tall, with a build that had helped him make the Michigan All-State football team as an offensive lineman back in high school. But he was comically helpless when it came to his tiny mother's demands, and Nadine was being uncommonly clingy with him during this brief visit. Nadine was orchestrating the breakfast preparation though, so there was a good chance they could get a few moments of privacy. When Driss turned and saw her silent plea for silence, he followed her down the hall into the empty sitting room. As planned, Tahi was already there, waiting for them.

"What are you two up to?" Driss asked, laughing.

"We need to talk to you," Laila said, shutting the door. "About something important."

Driss's amusement faded when he noticed their somber expressions.

"You've seen how emotional Aunt Nadine is, with you being here with Sara," Tahi began. "She starts crying every other minute, it seems like."

"She misses Zara," Laila said starkly. Driss started slightly at having his sister's name said out loud, but Laila was tired of beating around the bush. Zara was a person—a member of the family whom they all loved. She was sick of taking part in this ridiculous drama and constantly leaping over the topic of her. "We all miss her," she added, stepping toward her cousin.

"Of course we do," Driss said, recovering. "And of course I've noticed how emotional Mom is."

"Your upcoming wedding is making her miss Zara even more than usual," Laila stated.

A flicker of pain went across her cousin's face. "I know, but what can I do about it?"

"You've always been reasonable, Driss. More reasonable than most of the people in this family. You must realize this whole thing with Zara being labeled an outcast can't go on forever. She's your sister, for goodness' sake," Tahi said, frowning.

"Zara is the one who left."

"She left because she no longer felt welcome in her own home," Laila defended hotly. When she saw Driss's expression tighten at her outburst, she inhaled, trying to calm herself. "You honestly can't be okay with this . . . this *thing* we do, ignoring Zara's existence, treating her like an anathema, denouncing her like she's cursed. She's still your sister. She's still Aunt Nadine and Uncle Reda's daughter. *Isn't* she?"

The ensuing silence rang in her ears. For a few seconds, Laila's heart squeezed tight in anguish as she sensed the battle waging inside Driss to answer. Yes, she and Tahi had decided on the drive to Detroit to speak to Driss and enlist his help in doing something to address the Zara issue. Driss was the perfect person to get involved. He was the apple of his mother's eye, and he and Zara had always shared a close relationship. But Laila hadn't realized until that moment just how personally invested she was in healing this rift between Zara and the family. It was like part of her believed that if her family couldn't ever accept Zara, then she—Laila—was certainly doomed if she ever exposed her true feelings for Asher.

And in a flash, she realized the futility of her anguish. She would *never* be able to twist her family's emotions to meet her personal desires.

"I don't think I can do anything to change my parents' mind, if that's what you're getting at," Driss said. A feeling of profound sadness went through her, because she felt the truth of his words in the very core of her in that moment. "Besides, what difference does it make? Zara is gone. We don't even know where she is."

"We do," Tahi stated. She gave Laila an anxious glance. "Or at least we *have*, several times in the past, before she moved on to another job. We've been trying to track her whereabouts over the years. We think she's still in Detroit, or at least she was as of recently." Tahi went on to explain all the details to Driss about their attempts to contact Zara. Laila didn't speak, sensing Driss's doubts about their proposed plan to bring Zara back into the fold . . . feeling her own sense of loss and sadness growing.

"So . . . can we depend on you to help us try to right things with Zara and the family?" Tahi asked breathlessly after several minutes.

"I can't change my parents' mind," Driss said. He noticed Tahi's disappointment. "But I *can* do one thing," Driss added quickly. He gave Laila a glance. "I can try to join in the hunt and help you find her."

"You will?" Laila asked, her heart thawing a little.

Driss nodded. "She's my sister, and I miss her. I'm not the whole family, but I'm one more person on your side. That's something, isn't it?"

Laila glanced over at Tahi, who was watching her with shining eyes. Her chest ached. Tahi had always stood by her. She'd always been her family, not just in name, but in deed. She walked over to Tahi and grabbed her hand before turning to Driss.

"It's more than just something, Driss. It's huge. And maybe it's all we can hope for," she said, her voice hoarse with emotion. She squeezed Tahi's hand. "One family member at a time."

Her large extended family gathered on the front porch of *Ami* Reda's house. It was a sunny, cool autumn day. They'd just finished a huge breakfast. Reda and her Uncle Taha would be driving Driss and Sara to the airport.

The good-byes had been going on for a good forty-five minutes now. So far, Sara and Driss had only progressed about twenty feet, from the foyer to the front steps. Driss's mother seemed incapable of releasing her son. Driss's gaze met Laila's over his mother's shoulder as Nadine gave him yet another tearful hug. They shared a glance of understanding and compassion.

"We'd better get going," *Ami* Reda said for the tenth time. "If there's traffic, these two will miss their flight."

Driss and Sara finally broke away from the many outstretched arms and kisses. Laila's dad, Tahi, Laila and Driss's little sister, Sophia, trailed Sara and Driss down the staircase to the sidewalk. Even the next-door neighbors—the Kantari family—were on their front porch, waving and calling out good wishes to the couple.

"Have a safe trip. We'll talk soon about wedding plans," Laila promised Sara, whom she'd ended up liking very much. They all gave Sara one last hug. Reda, Taha, Sara and Driss finally made it to the car. Laila and Tahi shared an exhausted smile when they drove off, and turned to walk back up to the porch. She was glad Driss and Sara were so happy together—seeing her whole family rejoicing over the couple.

But it had left her sad, heartsore and very lonely, as well. It was like she was there with her family as a shadow rather than flesh . . .

. . . like she no longer belonged.

She noticed that her father hadn't turned and started back to the house with them. He stood alone on the sidewalk.

"Baba? What is it?" Laila asked, walking back toward him. She noticed his sober expression and narrowed gaze.

"That car that just parked in front of our house a minute ago," her dad mused thoughtfully. Laila turned to look at where he stared. Her parents' house was only two residences down from her uncle Reda's. "There's someone waiting inside," her dad continued. "And the car has Illinois plates."

Laila immediately recognized Asher's rental car parked in the street at the curb. Her father calmly started to walk down the sidewalk toward the car.

Adrenaline poured through her, making her veins sting. She began to follow him. She glanced back nervously but saw that everyone else was filing back into Reda and Nadine's house. No one seemed to have noticed Laila and her father walking away.

As they approached the car, Asher opened the door and got out. He wore a pair of jeans, boots, an ivory button-down shirt and a rugged brown jacket. Despite her anxiety at seeing him standing on the curb in the neighborhood where she'd grown up, her heart jumped at the vision of him. He stood there, waiting for them to approach patiently, his vivid, clear eyes trained on her, his expression somber.

When Laila's dad got about fifteen feet away, he abruptly paused on the sidewalk.

"You," he simply said. Laila noticed his expression of recognition and surprise. Laila inhaled shakily for courage and took her father's hand. She urged him toward Asher.

"I'm sorry," Asher said quietly to Laila. He looked worried, and very sincere. "I didn't mean to interrupt your family gathering. I was going to wait until I could get your attention for a private word."

"You mean you were waiting to pounce on her when she was alone?" Baba interrupted.

"Stop it," Laila implored her father. She inhaled slowly. "Baba, this is Asher Gaites. Asher, meet my father, Anass Barek. I don't think you two were ever really formally introduced."

Asher stepped onto the verge, holding out his hand. "It's an honor to meet you, sir."

Her father didn't accept his hand, though. He looked very confused. His obvious vulnerability pained Laila. Especially because this time, she knew she couldn't do anything to make it better.

"What's going on?" her dad asked Laila.

"Asher and I haven't been in contact since that summer in Crescent Bay, Baba. But he returned to Chicago recently, and we ran into each other. We've been seeing each other," she explained quietly.

Her father's gaze transferred to Asher. Asher slowly lowered his outstretched hand.

"I think you'd better go, young man," her dad said.

"I came to see Laila," Asher said politely but firmly, holding her father's stare. "It's important."

"I love him, Baba."

Both men looked at her. She felt as if she'd just punched her father, but she forced herself to continue. "I've never stopped loving him. You said I was too young to know better back then, but you were wrong. Since Asher and I have been together in Chicago, my heart has been so full," she said, touching her chest lightly, beseeching him to understand. "I've never been so happy and alive as I am when I'm with him. He is my other half, Baba. I don't feel whole without him. Can you please try to be happy for me?"

"I don't understand what's happening," her father said, his brow creasing. "Why haven't you mentioned any of this to us before?"

"Because I knew it would make you and Mamma unhappy."

"You knew it would make your mother and me unhappy because you know it's *wrong*," her father said.

"No, Baba," she said, reaching to take his hand. He looked at her, startled by her touch. She saw bewilderment and hurt in his dark eyes. "Asher and I are *not* wrong. We're so *right*. He's the most wonderful man. I wish you would get to know him—"

"No," her father said, releasing her hand and deliberately placing it away from him. "I don't accept any of this. I don't understand to whom I speak. Where is my daughter? You know how much it's going to hurt your mother, and yet you insist on seeing him? *Ma'anashi Farhan*, Laila."

She flinched in pain. Her father—whom she adored and loved—had just told her how unhappy he was with what was happening, but it was the expression on his face that hurt her more than anything. He looked so sad, like he was losing the most important thing in the world to him.

"I'm going with Asher now, Baba. We need to talk, that's all. There's no need for you to get so—"

"No," her father interrupted sternly. He pointed at Asher. "I told you once, years ago, that I'd allow you to go and talk with this man one last time. *Never* again."

A shudder of emotion went through her when she saw the coldness in her father's usually warm, shining eyes. Asher stepped forward and put his arm around her waist. He'd obviously noticed the effect of her father's words on her. Baba looked down to where Asher touched her, anger and dawning helplessness stiffening his face.

"If you go with him now, Laila, then don't come back," her father said.

Icy shivers poured across her arms. She couldn't believe this was happening.

That it *had* to happen.

And yet it felt so strangely inevitable, too. Because as much as she loved the man standing in front of her, his hurt eyes filling her vision, it was Asher who was her future. Her family.

"I know I'm making you unhappy. I'm sorry I disappoint you, Baba. More sorry than I can say. I hope in the future that can change. I want to continue to have a relationship with you and Mamma and my family. It won't be *me* who prevents that. But I'm going to have to try to live without your acceptance for now, if you won't accept Asher. If you won't accept *us*."

Her father didn't reply, and she could tell by his expression and tight mouth he wouldn't utter another word.

"Please tell Mamma I'll call and speak to her, if she'll speak to me. Would you please ask Tahi to bring my things back to Chicago with her?"

Saying it all scraped at her throat, but she couldn't escape this truth. Her father didn't respond. It was like he'd turned deaf to her voice. She took Asher's hand in hers and urged him toward the parked car.

They rode in silence all the way until they reached the interstate. Even though neither of them spoke, they clasped hands tightly across the console. Laila came out of her trance of dazed misery when she realized Asher had taken I-96 west instead of I-94, which was how they normally would have traveled to Chicago.

"Why are we going this way?" she asked him.

He glanced over at her, his gaze running over her face. Abruptly, he pulled off onto the shoulder of the road. He shoved the gear into park and reached for her. They hugged tightly across the console. At his touch, she convulsed with emotion. He kissed the side of her head and neck passionately.

"You're so brave. I'm so sorry you had to go through that," he muttered thickly as he kissed her repeatedly. "I'm so sorry, period. I'm sorry about what I said the other day. The last thing you are is spineless. You're thoughtful and kind, and you care about the people in your life so much. You show strength and restraint every minute of your life. You were right. I'm the one who is single-minded and selfish."

"You're not, Asher. I was so wrong to say that too. I know how hard you try to love your parents. I had no right to criticize you. *I'm* not the one who had taken the brunt of a lifetime of disapproval from them. I realize you must feel like you have to stand up to them or be bulldozed into submission. You don't handle them like I would, but that doesn't mean you're wrong." She turned her face, seeking him blindly. Their lips brushed together, and then clung. "Please forgive me," she whispered fervently a moment later.

"There's nothing to forgive. I love you for who you are. I get that we're different. I get that we're not always going to agree on the right way to handle family."

A spasm of emotion tightened her face at the mention of family. He cupped her cheek, his thumb caressing her gently.

"It was so courageous of you, baby. Saying what you did. Doing what you did. I know you must have been dying inside. I know how much you adore your father. I'm so sorry. I wish like hell we could be together without hurting anyone."

She swallowed back the surge of emotion. "I wish that too. But it's not the hand we were dealt, is it?"

He pressed his forehead to hers and shook it slowly. After a moment, she realized he'd pulled back several inches and was studying her closely.

"What?" she whispered.

"Did you really mean those things that you said to your father?" he asked her gruffly. "That I was your other half? And that you weren't willing to give me up again?"

She reached, digging her fingers into his thick, soft hair.

"I meant it with every fiber of my being."

He closed his eyes briefly.

"Thank God," he muttered fervently, before his mouth covered hers.

Chapter Twenty-eight

Two hours later they pulled into the idyllic, sleepy little town. Her eyes burned as they drove down Main Street slowly.

"Crescent Bay," she murmured in wonder. She spied the ice cream parlor where she'd been standing when Asher crossed the street eight years ago. She recalled how everything in her vision had gone blurry and out of focus, save him.

I never stood a chance in this thing. The second he walked into my life, I was ruined for anyone else.

"When is the last time you were here?" Asher asked.

"The summer I met you. We never came back after that. My parents were upset with me, but it was Zara leaving that really seemed to sour everyone on the idea of vacationing here again. Too many memories."

Asher squeezed her hand as he turned onto Silver Dune Drive. "Not all of them bad, I hope."

She shivered as she looked out at the white dunes and glistening blue lake. She recalled sitting on one of those dunes with Asher in the moonlight, feeling so overwhelmed and mortified by her need for him.

"No," she whispered, squeezing his hand back. "Some of those memories are the best of my life."

The feeling of poignant nostalgia stayed with her after Asher had parked the car and they made their way down to the beach, hand in hand. The trail to the secret lake was choked with weeds, but they were able to make it out. Part of her was shocked that Asher had driven them here, and that now they hiked toward their special spot. But another part of her felt like something was unwinding in just the way it should, like she walked on a path that was destined. They were meant to be at this place at this moment, as though this were the one location where all the confusion and hurt and uncertainty faded.

They were safe here. Protected, somehow.

"I don't think there's been another guardian for the secret lake since we left," she said wistfully.

"It doesn't look like it, does it?" Asher said as he moved aside some encroaching stalks of weeds so that she could pass. The path was so overgrown, Laila wondered if the little rocky beach might have altered in their absence. But when they finally cleared the woods and stepped onto the beach, she gasped in wonder.

"It looks exactly the same," she murmured. She turned to study Asher's profile. He pointed at the lake.

"That's where I first saw you," he said. He glanced over at her, his eyes alight at the memory. "I'd never seen anything so beautiful in my life. I think the same thing, every time I look at you."

Tears stung her eyes. She went into his arms, squeezing his waist tightly. "I thought the same thing about you, once I got over my shock. I couldn't stop thinking about you. What they say is true, isn't it? That love can hit like a thunderbolt sometimes."

He ran his fingers through her hair. "And you're as helpless as a baby when it does." She tilted her head back to see him and he kissed her gently.

"Come sit over here, on the big rock," he said.

"Okay," she agreed, a little taken aback by his solemnness.

He took both of her hands and urged her to sit on the rock. He stood before her, his handsome face cast in shadow.

"Do you remember when we made love here once, and the condom broke?" he asked her. She blinked and laughed, surprised by his question.

"Yeah. We were worried I'd be pregnant," she recalled.

"I never told you, but part of me wished you were."

The water soughed gently against the beach in the silence that followed.

"I hoped for it too, once. Briefly," she admitted. "I felt guilty about wishing it, but I did anyway. It would have forced our hand."

"We would have had no choice but to stay together, given those circumstances. We would have had to be honest about being together. We would have been forced to accept the consequences."

She nodded, holding her breath as she looked up at him. She'd never seen him so serious.

"The thing is. . . I thought it again, the other day when we made love without protection. Part of me *wanted* to make a baby with you."

"You did?" she asked in dawning amazement.

He nodded. "And I've been thinking about that a lot. Because I couldn't figure out why I was fantasizing about it so much, why I was becoming fixated on the idea. And I realized it was the same reason I felt it back here, in Crescent Bay years ago." He squeezed her hands. "I wanted you to get pregnant. Yes, because there's some kind of caveman in me that wants to see you growing big with our baby. I want to see that tangible evidence that we're one . . . that we're a family."

"Asher," she whispered feelingly. He reached up and cradled her jaw in his hand. A pressure swelled in her chest at the love she saw in his eyes at that moment.

"But part of me wanted it too because it would mean no going back. A baby would mean no one or nothing could keep us apart. But what I realized this weekend is that a baby isn't the point. I mean—it would be great, don't get me wrong. It'll be unbelievable if we're lucky enough to ever have that happen to us," he assured her. "I just mean that I realized we don't need an external pressure like that, forcing our hand. What's required is that we accept how we feel about each other, and what it means. What's needed is for us to commit to each other, no matter what. I know there are obstacles. But why do I need an excuse, like you being pregnant, to be with you? I love you more than anything, and I want to spend my life with you. That should be more than reason enough for me to at least ask you this."

She watched, her breath burning in her lungs, as he reached into his breast pocket. She saw the ring box. He opened it. She stared in numb disbelief at the stunningly simple and elegant diamond ring.

"When I saw you that first time standing naked in this lake, it was like I'd stumbled onto something sacred . . . onto a whole different world I hadn't known existed," he said. "We used to call this place our world. It was the only place where we could exist together, and no one could pull us apart. It was our secret. But now I want our world to be everywhere. As long as we're together, I'll exist in this sacred place, whether we're in Chicago or London or Casablanca, for all I care. So . . . will you make that place with me, Laila? Will you marry me? Will you be my family?"

She stared up at him, entirely in awe at the vision of the afternoon sun glowing behind him and his shadowed, solemn face as he extended the ring . . . as he risked his heart. Was it possible for a human being to feel this much love and not burst into a million pieces at the strength of it? She recalled looking at him once, years ago, and sensing his focus, the sheer force of him. Yes. With him, they could create a whole new world. With Asher, anything was possible, no matter what the obstacles.

"Yes. I'll be your wife. I'll be your family," she pledged.

He smiled. He took the ring out of the box and slipped it on her finger. The single, large, round diamond dazzled in the sunlight. Joy swelled in her, fracturing fear and uncertainty. There wasn't room for them, at that moment. Not in this sacred place. She smiled so widely that tears rained down her cheeks. He lifted her from her sitting position and pulled her against him.

"Then you've just made me the happiest man in existence, bar none," he said, before he pressed his mouth to hers.

They lay together with their limbs entwined later that night, spent from lovemaking. Asher listened to the sound of his rapid heartbeat slow to a steady throb in his ears. He ran his hand down the length of Laila's spine, absorbing her delicate shiver.

"Where would you like to live?" he asked her quietly.

She turned her head on the pillow, meeting his stare. "Wherever you are," she whispered.

He smiled and brushed back a strand of her dark hair from her cheek. It was almost ludicrous, how much he loved her. "Los Angeles? I could get a job there. It would be a good place for you to build your career."

She pursed her lips as if in thought and shook her head.

"No?" he murmured. "Do you want to stay here in Chicago?"

Again, she shook her head. His smile widened. She clearly had something in mind.

"Where, then? Detroit?"

Her soft hair tickled him as she shook her head again. "No," she replied hoarsely. "That would be too hard on our marriage, especially at the beginning. I think we should go someplace new. Some place fresh to make our own little world."

"Such as?"

"Well . . . I *would* fantasize now and then that you'd ask me to go to London with you."

His stroking fingers paused. "You want to go to London?"

"If you do."

"You're not worried about short-circuiting your career with a move like that?"

"London has a very vibrant entertainment industry," she reasoned.

"You're right. It does. And you're so talented, I know you can make a success of things there. Anywhere. But what about your recording contract?"

"I'll fly to Los Angeles and do the recording," she said. "It'll only be a few weeks. Maybe we can fly back and forth and see each other a few times. I know it'll be hard, but—"

"No. It's doable," he said, coming up onto his elbow. "Okay. London. Let's do it," he said gamely after considering for a moment.

"Do you think we're being foolish and impulsive and idealistic?" she asked him, grinning.

"Definitely," he replied, wrapping her hand in his. He kissed her knuckle and the ring she wore. "It feels great, doesn't it?"

She nodded in agreement. He leaned down and kissed her small, Mona Lisa smile.

"Now we just have to decide where to get married," he said. "And when."

"I vote for tomorrow."

She blinked in surprise when she saw he was serious. "*Tomor-*

row," she repeated, coming up on her elbow. "How is that possible?"

"We'll fly to Vegas," he said, as if the answer was obvious.

"*Vegas*," she breathed out. He saw her brow furrow and knew she was trying to imagine it. She gave him a helpless glance.

"Oh, Asher, I *can't*. I'm sorry."

He stiffened. His stomach had felt like it dropped a few inches. "You can't marry me?"

"Of course I'll marry you," she exclaimed. "But *Vegas* . . ." She noticed his confused expression. "You've never attended a Moroccan wedding, have you?"

He shook his head.

"That whole thing that I attended this weekend in Detroit, my cousin Driss and his fiancée's visit? That's the beginning of a Moroccan wedding tradition. It starts a whole year before the couple gets married. So much tradition and special food and ritual goes into the whole thing."

"So . . . you're saying you want to have a Moroccan wedding?"

"Oh no. That would take too much time, and I think we should get married as soon as possible. Besides, it's not as if my parents would be willing to give us a traditional wedding."

He reached and caressed her cheek, somehow sensing her sadness even though she kept it carefully hidden. She grabbed his hand and smiled.

"If you agree we should get married as soon as possible, what's the problem with Vegas?"

"*Vegas*," she said, cringing slightly. She gave him an apologetic glance and kissed his palm. "It's so the opposite of what I imagined my wedding would be for my whole life. I don't even think my parents would consider that a viable marriage. And no," she said, interrupting when she saw him open his mouth. "What they think doesn't matter, in this instance. But what *I* think does. And

I can't help it. It's part of my upbringing. The idea of getting married in Vegas seems so . . . *unofficial*, somehow."

"What do you suggest, then?"

"Well. . . we could get married here in Chicago by a judge."

He smiled and smoothed his fingers through her hair. "That would satisfy your sense of officialdom?"

"Yeah, it would. And to be honest, I think it would my mom and dad's too, even if they didn't like it. The law of the land is binding enough, in the Barek mind."

He grinned. "I'll call in the morning about applying for a marriage certificate."

"I have to get a ticket to London too. And break the news to Rafe, of course. He's not going to take that well." She suddenly looked worried. "What am I going to tell Tahi about the condo? We share the mortgage. *Oh* . . . and what if the waiting period to get married is too long?" She sat up abruptly in bed, pulling the sheet up around her breasts. Asher sat up with her. She glanced over in surprise when he laughed.

"How can you *laugh* at a moment like this?" she asked, grinning despite her anxiety.

He put his arms around her and gave her a smacking kiss on the mouth. "Because. We can handle whatever comes up. Come on, Laila. Those things are nothing compared to what we've been through to get to this point in our life."

She smiled slowly. "You're right."

"I know I am." He ticked off with his fingers. "If the waiting period for marriage is longer than we have before I'm supposed to fly to London, I'll ask my boss for a few extra days before I have to report in London. I have money. We'll keep paying Tahi for the mortgage until she decides what she wants to do."

"I have savings, Asher. I don't need your—"

"It's our money," he interrupted before she could finish. "It doesn't matter what bank account it comes from. But we're not going to leave Tahi hanging. Besides, a condo in the city is a good investment. I'm not worried about it. My point is, all of those things are details, *not* obstacles. As long as you promise to marry me, nothing can stop us."

"Well, I definitely promise," she said, her lips curving.

"Then it's *going* to happen," he said, leaning down and capturing her alluring smile with his lips.

Chapter Twenty-nine

They were married on Tuesday. Maybe most people would think it was a less-than-ideal wedding. But in Laila's eyes, it was perfect.

It was a crystal clear, brilliant fall afternoon. Laila felt like her heart was a helium balloon in her chest as they exchanged their vows and she looked into Asher's eyes, spying their future in the depths. She saw that familiar glint of determination too. He was a force of nature. He always had been. It might have taken them eight years. But they'd gotten here. And it was where they belonged.

Tahi was there in the courtroom with them, along with Rudy and Jimmy. Laila was so thankful to share the sacred moment with at least a small sampling of family and friends. She and Asher had decided to tell their parents everything once they were in London. It wasn't going to be an easy phone call for either of them to make. There was no point in making it beforehand, no rationalization for dimming their moment.

HEADLINE
ETERNAL

"We deserve to make it special," Laila had told Asher the day before when they'd made their decision about their parents. "I want it to just be about us. Our happiness at beginning a life together."

Did that mean she wasn't aware, in some distant part of her mind, that her actions would have consequences for those she loved? That Asher's parents too would be hurt by their decision? No. She went into this with eyes open. She knew that their decision to marry would leave some broken hearts in its wake.

But she also knew that she was meant to be with Asher. There was still a future ahead of them, one in which they could try to come to terms with family as best they could. It would be hard.

But she wasn't going to give up on anyone they loved.

Right now was for them, though. Today was *their* day.

Laila felt that truth with every fiber of her being as the five of them left the Circuit Court of Cook County building that afternoon. She carried the beautiful bouquet Asher had given her earlier. With her other hand, she grasped Asher's hand tightly. They walked into the sunny plaza. Tahi wanted to take pictures of them out by a fountain.

A horde of pigeons took flight in front of them. Asher turned toward her, pulling her against him. He kissed her warmly.

"*Perfect* picture," Tahi called enthusiastically several feet behind them, making their kiss part into pressing smiles.

"I remember thinking once, years ago, that you were going to change my life forever," Laila whispered softly.

"I wish I hadn't brought so much difficulty and strain. I just want to make you happy."

Her smile widened. "If you made me any happier than I am at this moment, I think I'd be flying away with all those birds."

"I will give you the wedding of your dreams someday," he said.

She shook her head, smiling. She went up on her tiptoes and

kissed him again. "This may not be the wedding I dreamed of when I was sixteen years old. But marrying you is the *best* dream I could begin to conjure up in my mind at this moment. For the rest of my life. You're my family now, Asher Gaites."

"And you're my whole world," he said.

He firmed his hold on her hand. They took the next step into their future together.